B

CW01637992

QUARRY GIRL

A compelling saga of love, loss and self-discovery

TANIA CROSSE

Originally published as
A Dream Rides By

JOFFE BOOKS

Revised edition 2020
Joffe Books, London
www.joffebooks.com

First published in Great Britain as
A Dream Rides By 2009

© Tania Crosse

This book is a work of fiction. Names, characters, businesses, organisations, places and events are either the product of the author's imagination or are used fictitiously. Any resemblance to actual persons, living or dead, events or locales is entirely coincidental. The spelling used is British English except where fidelity to the author's rendering of accent or dialect supersedes this. The right of Tania Crosse to be identified as author of this work has been asserted by her in accordance with the Copyright, Designs and Patents Act 1988.

Join our mailing list and become one of 1,000s of readers enjoying free Kindle crime thriller, detective, mystery, and romance books and new releases. Receive your first bargain book this month!

We love to hear from our readers! Please email any feedback you have to: feedback@joffebooks.com

ISBN 978-1-78931-499-1

For the Uxbridge Folk
And as always for my dear husband who helped me catch my dreams

ACKNOWLEDGEMENTS

Once again, I must thank my good friend, Paul Rendell, Dartmoor guide and historian, and editor of *The Dartmoor News*, for all his input and loans from his private library. In particular, my deep gratitude goes to the late Dr Marshall Barr, retired physician and co-founder of the Berkshire Medical Heritage Centre, for his help with the medical matters in the story. And finally I must thank the late Nick Luff, railway historian, who filled me in on details concerning the Princetown Railway.

AUTHOR'S NOTES

The Princetown Steam Railway ran from August 1883 to March 1956, covering one of the most spectacular routes in Britain. Now, the disused line provides a glorious route for walkers over one of the most dramatic areas of Dartmoor.

I have given the six real-life characters marooned on the train in the 1891 blizzard their proper names, but imagined their personalities from newspaper reports of the time. Likewise, Farmer Hilson and his wife, Stationmaster Higman and William Duke, proprietor of the quarry at Merrivale. I do not believe I have done them any injustice, but my story is not meant to convey an accurate account of these characters.

The abandoned quarry at Foggintor is a magnificent if eerie sight, and the foundations of the cottages where Ling and my other characters lived are clearly visible. The entire site can be extremely dangerous, so please take the greatest care if visiting as you do so at your own risk.

PART ONE

CHAPTER ONE

'Oh, Fanny! Now look what you've done!'

Ling Southcott sighed in exasperation. She and her mother had spent all morning washing the laundry they took in from The Saracen's Head, the isolated coaching inn three miles away, slap in the middle of Dartmoor. It was August and heating the required gallons of water on the range in the downstairs room of the one-up, one-down workman's cottage had made their red faces stream with sweat. It was a case of running back and forth to empty the pans into the wash-tubs outside, adding the soapflakes and the dirty linen, and plunging the wooden dolly up and down in a pall of steam. The snowy material was then rolled through the mangle and rinsed in fresh water, ready to be put through the mangle yet again. And now, as they pegged the washing on the lines that were strung across what was known as Big Tip, Fanny had dropped a pillowcase on the ground and was staring out across the moor.

Ling bit her tongue. It was hard to be angry with Fanny. As well as being partially deaf, she wasn't quite 'all there', as their mother would say with a patient shake of her head.

It was such a pity. A gentle, pretty child she was, like an angel. Everyone who lived at the quarrymen's hamlet of Foggintor, high up on the lonely, windswept wastes of western Dartmoor, knew and loved her, and made allowances for her affliction. Everyone except Harry Spence who was the bane of everyone's life. Ling still had the remnants of a bruise on her eye from a recent scrap with him when she had felt the need to protect her vulnerable little sister from his lewd mockery. And now her heart softened as she looked from the soiled pillowcase to the slip of a thing standing motionless beside her.

'What is it, Fanny?' she asked as Fanny silently raised her thin arm and pointed. It was the kind of action she often performed in her muted world, her fascination drawn by a butterfly, a wheatear fluttering from stone to stone, or a buzzard circling overhead. But there was something in her expression that made Ling follow the direction of her sister's gaze.

Her own eyes almost bolted from her head. Big Tip was literally that, a colossal mound of waste granite from the quarry accumulated over decades. The top of the dump extended outwards on the same level as the cottage gardens, and from the washing lines there was an uninterrupted view across the barren moorland. Ling's deep hazel eyes focused on something moving slowly around the base of King Tor, puffing little clouds of smoke as it chugged up the steady incline towards the far end of the Foggintor quarry settlement.

The very first steam train on the new Princetown railway!

Ling's heart gave a bound of excitement. Over the past two years, they had watched the track being constructed across the moor to the terminal at the prison settlement two miles away at Princetown. She had read that at the bottom end, the line swung westward to join the existing Great Western Railway at Horrabridge, connecting passengers to the main line and the entire national network. Oh, what a difference it was going to make to their restricted lives!

Ling beamed across at Fanny, her face illuminated with that spark of mischief which frequently heralded some mad escapade. 'Look! A train!' she called to anyone who might be listening, and grasping Fanny's hand, ran with her towards the quadrangle of little cottages.

'Mother! It's the train!' she yelled gleefully as they scudded past the long narrow gardens that radiated from the outer side of the square. In the gardens grew row upon row of essential vegetables to supplement the men's meagre wages. Ling saw her mother look up in amazement as she bailed out the water from the washtubs with an old enamel jug. But Ling didn't wait for any reply and instead raced with Fanny to the end of the gardens and skidded around the corner.

It seemed that they weren't the only ones to have spotted the train, even though it was well camouflaged against the green and brown of the moor and was really only distinguishable by grey-white smoke coming from the steam-engine chimney. The news had spread in moments. It was shortly after mid-day on Saturday and as the men and boys who worked in the massive amphitheatres of Foggintor quarry knocked off for their well-earned half-day, they joined Ling and Fanny as they made their way towards the post and wire fencing that separated the railway track from the surrounding moor.

'We'd better wait for your mother,' Arthur Southcott told his daughters as he found them in the gathering crowd and Ling turned impatiently to watch her mother pant up behind them.

'Well, I never did!' Mary exclaimed as she reached them. 'All the delays over the past weeks, and now the thing arrives totally unannounced! We could've missed it!'

'Best hurry, then!' Arthur called to his family, and they ran along the wide path, laughing and joking and making a grand commotion as they joined the other men and their wives and children all anxious to see the first great iron horse to conquer the rugged heights of Dartmoor.

'Well, this'll be a day to remember! August 11, 1883! Summat to tell our grandchildren one day, eh, Arthur, don't you think?'

Ling looked up at the beaming face of her father's best friend, Ambrose Tippet, but she was damned if she was going to stand at the back of the crowd to witness this historic moment!

'Get out of the way, Barney Mayhew, you great lummox! Let the little ones see!' she said as she gathered up the smaller children and ushered them to the front.

The healthy, glowing face of the young lad split with a grin. 'Not till you gie us a kiss, Miss Southcott,' he teased.

Ling gave a light giggle and planted a hearty kiss on his cheek. A chorus of jaunty ribaldry bantered about them, for everyone knew that Barney and Ling were walking out. Besides, this was a moment of deep joy and expectation, and everyone was in convivial mood.

Barney obediently stood back and Ling felt his dark eyes, full of admiration, upon her. The children, Barney's two younger brothers among them, all stood in an orderly line under her direction. She was proud to have their respect as their school assistant. She loved her work and tried to make afternoon school — when she was in charge — everyone's favourite time, singing and playing learning games with her pupils. Her heart would swell as out of the corner of her eye, she caught Mr Norrish, the schoolteacher, looking on approvingly while he supervised the little tykes who had been naughty in the morning and so had to repeat their formal lessons instead.

'I'm really proud of you, you know,' Mr Norrish had said, taking her aside when she had shortly been expecting to leave the schoolroom behind for ever. 'Always stood out from the rest, you have. And I've really enjoyed those extra history and geography lessons I've given you after school each day. You've taught both your parents to read and write, and you've even cultivated your speech. So how would you like to become my assistant? You know how Mrs Warrington is so keen on schooling for the little ones? Well, she's willing to pay you four shillings a week.'

That had been nearly three years ago, but the vivid memory flashed like a beacon across Ling's brain. It was no time for such thoughts now, though, as she eagerly watched the smoke-snorting engine labouring along the track. She knew it would not be stopping since there was no station here, just a siding where it was planned that goods trains would call three days a week to transport the stone. Any passengers from Foggintor would be obliged to walk into Princetown before they could ride in one of the carriages that were trundling towards them now. The clattering engine was looming larger and larger, gathering speed as the track became less steep, the wheels turning faster, clickety-clack, on the metal rails. On spying the festive throng, the driver blew the whistle three times, and the gigantic train thundered past with a whooshing roar, making the ground tremble beneath the spectators' feet. Some threw their caps in the air, others waved with abandon to the dignitaries on board, children squealed with delight or screamed in terror. And then it was gone, wending its way, quite straight now after its tortuous climb, to the end of its journey.

Ling stood mesmerised. It was magnificent, a thing of noise and power, and in some strange way, of beauty. Being so close to the majestic dragon and standing on ground level, its size was overwhelming. Her eye had caught the fascinating motion of the coupling rods that drove the wheels, the incandescent blaze in the open firebox as the fireman shovelled in more coal. And this wondrous sight was to be part of their daily lives from now on. People were cheering all about her, children tugging at her skirt and calling, 'Miss! Miss!' But she was staring rapturously after the train. Somehow that brief moment had opened up her heart. She loved Dartmoor, its wild uplands, its calm, wooded valleys with bubbling brooks and rivers, and she had never thought beyond her life at Foggintor, despite all she had studied in Mr Norrish's books. But the railway had suddenly made the outside world seem *accessible*, and it had plunged her into a dreamlike reverie.

It was Fanny's hand on her arm that snapped her back to reality. The younger girl's face was flushed with elation, though she said nothing, her brain, as so often happened, unable to find the words she needed to express her emotions.

Ling grinned down at her. 'Wasn't that marvellous?' she cried.

Fanny nodded, her fair curls bobbing around her head. Ling drew in a quivering breath, but before she could release it, Barney pulled her against him. He was as excited as all the apprentices were, for young men would always be inspired by a gleaming machine of such strength and magnitude, but he was the only one among them to have a sweetheart, and this public show of affection was a way of boasting about it. Ling knew that some of the adults would frown upon his action, but she allowed him to hold her for a moment, her mind lost elsewhere.

The crowd was slowly dispersing with much elbowing among the apprentices, and Ling pulled a disparaging grimace at them as she disengaged herself from Barney's arm. The eldest of them, a quiet lad called Sam, gave her a sympathetic wink, and she took Fanny's hand as they all walked back towards the hamlet, her mind already returning to the laundry. But as she went to turn down between the square of cottages and the short row of similar dwellings opposite, she glanced back once more in the direction of the railway line.

CHAPTER TWO

'The celebrations are going to be on Wednesday,' Arthur announced, 'and Mr Warren's said we can have the day off!'

'Oo, hear that, Fanny?' Ling grabbed her sister's hands and bounced up and down with bursting anticipation. 'What fun we're going to have! They've had bunting up in Princetown for the last two weeks, just waiting for the word! There's going to be a big party with fireworks and everything, isn't there?'

'There certainly is!' her father grinned back. ''Twill be worth the waiting for! Apparently after all the delays, the Board of Trade suddenly decided on Friday evening to certify the train for public use. It were all so sudden, the two committees in Princetown had no time to put all their festivity plans into action, so they've decided on Wednesday instead.'

'Oh, I can't wait! I don't think I've ever seen fireworks, have I? It'll be marvellous, Fanny! And there's going to be sports and a band, to say nothing of the train itself and all the special people in their fine clothes! Oh, Mother, what a treat it'll be!'

Ling let go of Fanny's hands and danced her mother round the tiny room instead. Arthur watched, amusement curving his mouth upwards at the corners. There might be dignitaries in splendid attire travelling on the train, but not one of them would possibly be able to match the picture of passion and vivacity that was his elder daughter. With his comely wife and Fanny like a fairy, no man could ever be more proud of his family than Arthur Southcott was!

* * *

When Ling came round the corner on Wednesday morning, Barney was lounging against a boulder waiting for her, whistling to himself with his hands thrust into his pockets in what he evidently considered a manly fashion. Ling smiled to herself, her eyes shining as they took in his best suit and well brushed hair, all to impress her, she knew. Just as he had struggled, albeit with little success, to improve his literacy to show her how much she meant to him. Not that there was any need. At nearly eighteen and with his apprenticeship nearly over, he was the only man for her. Only Sam Tippet came anywhere near him for looks. A nice lad was Sam, but so quiet and reserved, he could never touch her heart as Barney did.

'Morning, Barney!'

'You looks proper lovely,' he greeted her.

'Why, thank you, Barney. I'm really looking forward to the day, aren't you? Where are the others?'

'They've gone on ahead.'

'Oh.' Ling's face fell, and she glanced over her shoulder as her family came up behind her.

'You two'd better catch 'em up, then,' Arthur winked. 'You young folk should be together on a day such as this.'

Ling drew in an expectant breath and her eyes met Barney's. 'Come on, then!' she goaded him, and taking his hand in one of hers, she picked up the hem of her skirt — showing more than a little ankle — and began to run. Barney was jolted forward, his cap flying from his head so that he had to break away to retrieve it. As he returned to Ling, hand outstretched in sure anticipation of holding hers again, she dodged neatly out of his reach, and laughing merrily, launched herself along the track in a froth of petticoat and flying feet. When he finally caught her, they danced about each other, panting and gasping, before hurrying on again and disappearing from view.

Mary Southcott was smiling at their backs, but then her face clouded with doubt. 'Are you sure 'tis a good idea, they two going off together?'

'To join their friends? What harm can she come to? Besides, she's a good head on her shoulders. And, Mary, she be growing up. There comes a time when you has to accept that. Now, then, let's hurry along, or we'll be missing half the fun!'

* * *

By the time they caught up with the group of jocund youngsters, Barney was sweating uncomfortably, his dark hair stuck to his forehead, even though it wasn't a particularly warm day, the sky being grey and overcast. Ling, though, still looked as fresh as a daisy, even if her face shone with exhilaration and her hat was somewhat awry on her head. Barney's chest swelled with contentment as he contemplated her. She looked quite stunning, her tall, willowy figure clad in its serviceable Sunday best and her mane of springing copper curls already escaped from beneath her straw hat. There was no other maid to match Ling in either looks or personality, and she was his. Barney Mayhew's. And the sooner he got a ring on her finger, the better.

'You two have bin a long time getting yere! Stopped off behind a boulder for a few minutes, eh, did we? 'Tis all it takes, I've yeard tell!'

Ling's eyes narrowed in disgust. Her altercation with Harry Spence two weeks ago was still fresh in her mind. No one liked the uncouth youth who was unfortunately part of everyone's daily company, and for two pins Ling would have liked to knee him again where it hurt most. But there were other ways to skin a cat!

'Little boys shouldn't joke about something they know nothing about!' she scorned and so saying, she sprang forward with a gleeful cry. Before he had a chance to stop her, she pulled Harry's cap down over his eyes. Blinded for an instant as he struggled to remove it, she spun him round, disorientating him further. He stumbled onto his knees, and when he finally released himself from the blindfold, he was met by a chorus of hooting laughter.

'Well done, Ling!' Sam Tippet chortled. ''Twill keep 'en quiet for a bit.'

'Met your match, eh, Harry?' someone else jeered cheerfully, and Barney's eyes flashed. It was all very well everyone congratulating Ling which, of course, filled him with pride, but just so long as they didn't start coveting *her* into the bargain! But Ling took his hand, her head thrown back in glorious triumph as she skipped along beside him. The incident, in her mind, was already forgotten as she at last felt she had got even with Harry Spence.

Her eyes crinkled at the corners as she smiled at Barney and he held her hand even more tightly. He was looking forward immensely to the day ahead — a *whole day* and the evening, too, with fireworks and a dance. Then they would walk home in the dark of the August evening. What could be more romantic? Perhaps he would even get a more passionate kiss than her usual peck on the cheek!

The views across the moor as they followed alongside the new railway seemed to Ling even more breath-taking than ever, the particular quality of the light that day lending a dramatic blue tinge to the spectacular landscape. It was always changing, Dartmoor, as if it were alive, and that was what Ling loved about it. Green and welcoming in the sunshine with banks of vibrant yellow gorse and purple heather, sprinkled white with winter snow, lashed with driving rain from a granite sky, or enveloped in swirling, mysterious fog that could descend in minutes even in the middle of summer. But today the weather was still and set, with the sort of cloud that might produce a brief shower. Ling crossed her fingers that it would remain dry as they hurried a little now as no one wanted to miss the arrival of the train.

The moorland peace was interrupted by the cacophony of voices raised in good humour, and the general clamour muffled the rhythmical drumming of the horse's hooves until it was almost upon the larking youngsters. Ling's attention was drawn to the animal as it overtook them, leaving a safe, wide berth. It was unusual to witness anyone riding at breakneck speed on the moor and this horse was so striking, white but with a few small grey rings on its rump and a grey mane and tail. Ling hardly noticed the rider but her eyes sparkled in appreciation of the beautiful steed.

Barney saw the wonderment on her face and scowled. 'Bloody idjit,' he barked irritably. 'Could've knocked someone over.'

'Hardly,' Ling blinked at him. 'He was keeping well away.'

'Huh! Racing the train, more like!'

'Talking of which, look, everyone!' Ling shouted as she turned round. 'Look! The train! It's coming!'

Sure enough, in the distance behind them, a trail of grey smoke was all that distinguished the locomotive from the camouflaging background of the moor. A moment's hush fell over the awestruck faces, broken almost instantly by excited whoops of joy.

'Come on! Come on! We won't get there in time!'

Dozens of feet broke into a run. Older people or those with small children would have to content themselves with watching as the train passed by. But the youngsters' strong legs bore them forward at a good pace until they rushed into the already crowded station as so many people wanted to be on the platform to witness the train's arrival.

Barney muscled his way through, hauling Ling along behind him with an inescapable grip on her wrist. He wanted to prove himself the man of the group, and that he could care for Ling better than anyone else. Besides, he had spied the distinctive dapple-grey horse tethered outside the station, and his nose had wrinkled with disdain as he had pushed past the well-dressed rider he had instantly recognised. Ling had not seemed to have noticed the stranger, and Barney was determined it should remain that way. So he shouldered himself forward much to the annoyance of those who had deliberately arrived in plenty of time. Ling cast apologetic glances in every direction as it wasn't her fault she was being propelled to the front of the crowd. But she had to admit to a thrill of elation at the uninterrupted view down the single track and way beyond the signal box.

And there she was, the gleaming green engine pulling two resplendent coaches. No more than a wisp of smoke was wafting from her chimney as she sauntered along the flat. The driver had closed the regulator so that the train would coast into the station, and he pulled the whistle-cord three times in salutation. A resounding cheer rose from the waiting crowd, adults clapped and children jumped up and down. Passengers in the crowded carriages waved their handkerchiefs out of the windows, including the elegant Mrs Warrington. Ling had heard that the respected and generous lady was a major shareholder in the Princetown Railway Company, even though the Great Western Railway was, in fact, to run the line and held the controlling interest in it.

The whole spectacle was a sight to behold, and Ling felt bound in her own world. The engine, massive now as it rolled into the station, was almost magical, like some mythical, fiery dragon. Ling stared, captivated, as it drew nearer, almost unaware of the milling throng about her which, unwittingly, was surging forward. Harry Spence, who had taken advantage of Barney's elbowing his way to the front, had followed in his wake. Jostled by the crowd, he saw it all as one huge joke and dug Barney in the ribs, throwing him off-balance. Barney staggered sideways against the tall, slender girl beside him, knocking her off her feet.

It all happened so quickly, Ling didn't have the chance to scream as she tumbled over the edge of the platform. She felt herself falling through the air, and then she knew she had landed, quite winded, onto something hard. The wooden sleepers of the track. A tearing pain raked her ankle, but though she knew it was there, the agony did not register in her brain. Her body was so stunned that all she could do was stare in appalled, frozen horror as the gigantic, monstrous train trundled relentlessly towards her, its colossal wheels and mighty engine towering above her. She could even feel the sizzling heat as it bore down towards her, but every last muscle was locked in paralysis. The last she saw before she passed out was Barney's petrified gaze from the platform as his terror-struck eyes bolted from his ashen face.

CHAPTER THREE

She was floating on a cloud, lulled, protected. Seeing nothing, feeling nothing. No fear. Voices, sounds, reached her from somewhere far, far away. Someone screamed. A woman, she thought.

'Whoa!' she caught the stationmaster's cry above the throaty rumble of the mighty engine as it coasted into the station. 'There be someone fallen on the line!'

Oh, yes, that was *her*, wasn't it? But it didn't matter. It didn't mean anything. She was swaying gently in a different world. A different universe.

The shriek of metal scraping on metal as the engine driver wrenched on the brake lever in his battle to bring the tons of heavy steel and ironwork to a screeching halt. Clank, lurch, hissing of steam. The weight and power that would crush a human form like a twig. Would it take her? She would have to wait and see. But it wouldn't. It was unreal. None of this was happening. She had the vague sensation of being moved, dragged. Smell the heat, the coal fire, the hot engine oil.

'Well done, sir!' The voice was nearer this time. 'Can I have some help here?'

She was moving again, flying, feeling discomfort now. Oh, it was better before, so she let herself sink beneath the waves of oblivion where it was peaceful and safe.

* * *

She could hear voices again, one of them familiar and comforting.

'Let me in! I be her best friend! We'm from the quarries. Us was yere together.'

'Yes, I saw,' the other voice cut in tersely. ''Twas you pushed her onto the line.'

'No! Well, yes, but 'tweren't my fault. I were pushed from behind and—'

Ah, Barney. She would be all right now. She could come back. She struggled to focus her mind, claw her way back to reality.

'Barney.'

That was her own voice, wasn't it? Yet it sounded so weak and feeble. Her muscles still refused to work and she couldn't open her eyes. And then she felt Barney crush her against him, safe and warm.

'No!' another voice she didn't recognise, a young man's this time, commanded. 'Lie her down on the floor and raise her legs.'

'Who the hell d'you think—'

'I'm a doctor. Now do as I say.'

Oh, no. Please don't argue. I feel sick as it is. The black curtain enshrouding her vision began to lift and as she moaned softly, her eyelids flickered open. The first thing she saw was Barney, an expression like thunder on his face, and then her gaze wandered about the strange room. She was lying on the floor of what must be the ladies' waiting room. A vile wave of fear washed through her as she remembered falling beneath the huge, terrifying monster of the train.

'What . . . what happened?' she whispered hoarsely.

'You was pushed off the platform,' she was told by an older man, who she guessed by his uniform must be the stationmaster. She saw him throw a disparaging glance in Barney's direction. 'Accidental, like,' he added tightly. 'But then this young gentleman saved you. A doctor, he be,' he concluded with a deferential bob of his head.

It was only then that Ling noticed, kneeling down next to her, the rider of the striking dapple horse that had streaked past them at such speed. He had taken her wrist and now he looked up and smiled.

'Your pulse is settling nicely now so you should start to feel better.'

'Yes, I am,' she answered, surprised how quickly the queasiness had passed.

'Good. Now I want you to keep your head still and follow my finger with your eyes.'

She obeyed meekly but she would much rather have continued studying his face which was very handsome in a quiet, steadfast sort of way.

'Excellent,' he pronounced, smiling again, and behind him, the stationmaster cleared his throat.

'Can you manage now, sir? I really should be getting back to my duties. Though I'm not sure I should be leaving this young girl alone with you two gentlemen.'

'I am a man of the professional class,' the young doctor assured him, 'so I believe I am to be trusted. But is there anyone we can fetch for the young lady?'

'Oh, Barney, find my parents, would you?' Ling asked, beginning to feel like her normal self. But as she lifted her eyes to Barney's, she caught the stranger's gaze on her before he quickly turned away in embarrassment. Then she saw Barney give an ill-tempered frown as he followed the stationmaster out of the waiting room, allowing the door to slam closed behind him.

'Do you have any pain anywhere?'

Ling was glad to allow her attention to be drawn back to the handsome stranger. 'My ankle's throbbing. I think I twisted it as I fell.'

'I'll take a look, if you'll permit me. But first I should like to feel over your head and you must tell me if it hurts anywhere. I believe you only fainted, but we should make sure you didn't hit your head. No, just lie still,' he instructed as she went to sit up.

He proceeded to remove her hat which had only stayed attached because of the long pin Mary had fixed through it that morning. Then he brushed the hair back from each of her ears in turn, appearing to check them for Ling didn't know what, before carefully moving his hands over her skull. Ling kept still, her head clearer now and the strange situation beginning to dawn on her. Here she was, alone with this most polite but nonetheless unknown person, who she was now allowing to remove her boot and sock. And yet somehow she felt perfectly at ease with him.

'You seem . . . very young for a doctor,' she faltered.

He raised a bashful eyebrow at her. 'I'm not,' he admitted somewhat sheepishly. 'At least, not yet. I'm a medical *student.* I've been assisting Dr Greenwood in Tavistock for the past year. But next month, I'm off to London. To Guy's. To become fully qualified. It'll take years, mind. Now, can you push against my hand?'

The examination was uncomfortable, but he was very gentle, his long fingers cool on her puffed ankle. He seemed unhurried and thorough, his lips softly pursed in concentration, and Ling felt disappointed when the door burst open and Barney marched back in with Arthur, Mary and Fanny on his heels.

'Ling!' her mother cried, flinging herself on her knees and wrapping her elder daughter in her arms.

'No need to cry, Mother! I'm proper clever now.'

Nevertheless, Mary's shoulders shook convulsively, and it was Arthur who held out his hand. 'We can't believe what happened,' he said gravely. 'I must be thanking you, sir, from the bottom of my heart.'

'You was that brave, sir, jumping down in front of the train like that!' Mary added her gratitude as her husband vigorously shook the fellow's hand.

'Is that what you did?' Ling suddenly remembered what the stationmaster had said about the young stranger having saved her and she sat up abruptly, her eyes wide and aware of a shiver of pleasure slithering down her spine.

'This young gentleman risked his own life to save yourn, and if he hadn't, 'tis certain 'twould have been a wake and not a celebration we'd be having now! And as for you!' Arthur spun round, his normally gentle demeanour flung to the four winds. 'As her friend and a young man at that, I expect you to take care on my daughter, not push her under a bloody train!'

Barney had been standing, grinding his teeth in black resentment at the praise being heaped upon the stranger, but now Ling noticed the colour flaming into his face. She knew that her father, usually such a mild man, must have been furious to have used such language. She saw Barney take a step backwards, but then brace his shoulders as youthful indignation flared within him.

She had to go to his rescue. 'Oh, it wasn't Barney's fault! The crowd was jostling and—'

'Hmm!' Arthur's forehead pleated fiercely. 'Well, I suggest you make yersel scarce for today, boy. We'll take care on our daughter ourselves.'

Barney lifted his chin, and Ling saw his eyes move beneath their swooping brows. He must have understood her father's anger as he obediently backed out of the room though with a churlish scowl on his face. Through the open door came the sound of the Tavistock Volunteer Band striking up the first rousing march with which it was to lead the procession of flag-waving children towards the centre of Princetown, cheered on by the gathered crowds who were not only celebrating the arrival of the new railway but the salvation of the young girl who had fallen into its path.

Barney clenched his jaw and went to join them.

CHAPTER FOUR

'I don't think it's broken, just badly sprained.'

The young gentleman examining Ling's ankle glanced up and his mouth widened into a smile, accentuating the strong line of his jaw and revealing evenly set teeth. Ling felt a thrill of excitement. He was so quiet and unassuming, as if putting his own life in danger to rescue others was something he did every day. He was obviously well educated — which was attractive to Ling in itself — and although far above her in social rank, he put on no airs and graces. His eyes smiled warmly at her, a deep blue with a hint of green in them, and his fair hair fell in a roguish wave over his broad forehead. It was his hair more than anything that Ling recognised, for the horseman on the moor had been bareheaded, unusual in anyone, let alone someone wealthy enough to be riding a horse! So perhaps he possessed some secret determination in his character that was not immediately apparent. All the more intriguing!

'Are you sure, Mr . . . er . . . Dr . . . ?' Arthur questioned him. 'I mean no offence, but you seem mighty young . . .'

'Franfield, sir. Elliott Franfield. And you're right. I'm not a doctor yet, just a medical student. But I have dealt with many a twisted ankle. Under supervision, of course, but it is a common injury and I'm positive it isn't broken. But it should be strapped up and rested as much as possible.'

Ling was happily impressed. But just then, a loud knock rapped on the door and Ling looked up to see Mrs Warrington sweep into the waiting room like a whirlwind. The stunningly beautiful lady hurried across to Ling, her expressive face melting with relief.

'Ling, my dear! When I heard it was you! And you must be the young man . . .'

It seemed to Ling that the spacious room was suddenly filled with the woman's presence, but that was Rose Warrington for you! Her violet-blue eyes darted from one face to the other, and then she squatted down on her heels by Ling's side in the most unladylike fashion.

'Oh, my dear child, I hope you're not hurt!'

'Just twisted my ankle,' Ling answered easily. 'Mr Franfield's learning to be a doctor and he assures me it isn't broken.'

'Oh, what a relief!' Ling saw Mrs Warrington glance at her bare foot still resting in Elliott Franfield's hand. 'Well, it certainly doesn't look like when my husband broke his ankle. Black and blue it was, and that swollen! My dearest, would you take a look?' she called over her shoulder to the tall, lean gentleman lingering hesitantly in the doorway. 'You must have been terrified, poor lamb!' Mrs Warrington sympathised, turning back to Ling, and a moment later, Mr Warrington and Elliott were exchanging words over Ling's foot, asking her when it hurt as they carefully moved it this way and that.

Ling herself was somewhat bewildered as she was being engaged in two conversations at once, but she felt compelled to answer Rose Warrington first. 'Not really. It all happened too quickly. I remember falling, and then the train coming. I must have fainted because I don't remember anything else. The next I knew, I was in here and . . . and Mr Franfield was taking care of me.' She turned her eyes back to the two men discussing her ankle, aware of the rush of colour into her cheeks as she looked at the younger of them and hoping no one else had noticed.

'I saw plenty of twisted ankles in the army,' Mr Warrington nodded, 'and I agree with Mr Franfield that it just needs strapping. I'll see if the stationmaster has a medical box.'

He went outside, and Ling was almost disappointed when Elliott lowered her heel onto the floor again.

'Oh, I'm so sorry, I should have introduced myself. Rose Warrington,' the good lady at once went on, and holding out her gloved hand to the bemused Mr Franfield, she shook his heartily. 'We live at Fencott Place, the other side of Princetown. Perhaps you know it?'

'I'm afraid I don't have that pleasure. I live in Tavistock and don't usually venture so far onto the moor. And I'm afraid any spare time is spent with my head in a medical textbook. But I thought I would grant myself a day's leave and witness the magnificent sight of the railway arriving here in Princetown. And am I glad that I did!' he concluded, turning his steady gaze on Ling once more so that she shivered with delight.

'Arthur Southcott.' Her father introduced himself, touching his forelock. 'Quarryman at Foggintor. This is my wife, and our daughters, Ling, of course, and Fanny.'

'Fanny, dear, how are you today?' Ling realised that Mrs Warrington had raised her voice a little for Fanny's benefit and then Fanny dipped a silent curtsey in return. 'Ling is assistant at Foggintor school of which I suppose you might say I am patron,' Rose went on to explain to the young gentleman. 'Which is how we know each other.'

'Ah, I see.' Elliott smiled again. 'Well, it's my pleasure to meet you all. And I'm so glad I was able to be of some assistance.'

'Assistance? Good heavens, you saved my life!'

Ling was overjoyed at the opportunity of both thanking the affable young man and showing her admiration. She was feeling herself again now and when he blushed with embarrassment, her heart soared. She loved Barney, of course, but Mr Franfield was brave, kind, gentle, to say nothing of his good looks, intelligent and — ah, there was the rub — educated and from a class she could never aspire to. He was the stuff of dreams — so she might as well enjoy his company while she could!

'I assume you're on your own, Mr Franfield?' she enquired, hoping her eagerness was not too apparent. 'So, would you care to join us for the day? It would be much more fun for you than being on your own.'

Out of the corner of her eye, she saw the horror on her father's face at her forwardness. Elliott Franfield appeared equally astonished, his eyebrows lifted into his forehead, but almost immediately he broke into a boyish grin.

'Why, thank you very much. I should be honoured.'

Ling's chest swelled with happiness. She might nearly have been killed less than half an hour ago, but it seemed unreal, already a half-forgotten dream. And without it, she would never have met the horseman who had drawn her attention earlier on. Her ankle throbbed, but it wasn't *so* bad, and it was worth it to have Mr Franfield attend to it!

Seth Warrington returned with the bandages from the stationmaster's medical box, and holding Ling's ankle while the student doctor strapped it most expertly, nodded approvingly at Elliott's handiwork. A reserved man was Mr Warrington, somewhat of a mystery, and there were some strange rumours as to his background. Ling had heard it said he was leading a campaign for prison reform and in particular something to do with an appeal system. It was also rumoured that he had once been a cavalry officer. Ling decided she quite liked him, and if Mrs Warrington was so devoted to him, that was good enough!

'There,' Elliott announced. 'How does that feel?'

'Yes, better, thank you,' she answered truthfully.

'Not too tight? Can you wriggle your toes? If they start feeling cold or you get pins and needles, you must say.'

'No, it feels fine. So may I suggest we catch up with everyone? I don't want you all missing the fun because of me.'

'And as shareholders in the line, we must get back to the official party,' Rose declared.

Her husband nodded. 'Let's just see if this young lady can walk, shall we?'

Ling's cheeks burned with pride as, with a fine gentleman on either side, she was lifted onto her feet. She tentatively put her weight on her injured ankle, but winced as the pain shot up her leg, taking her by surprise as the strapping had made it feel so much more comfortable.

'I'll tell you what,' Elliott suggested. 'I have my horse outside. Have you ever ridden?'

Ling's jaw dropped open. She couldn't believe all this was happening. 'We have heavy horses at the quarry for pulling the carts, but no one ever rides them,' she explained in reply.

'Well, there's a first time for everything,' Elliott grinned. 'Now lean on me while I get you outside.'

He put one arm about her waist, strongly supporting her so that she was partly leaning against him. Her whole body sizzled at the sensation, but Elliott seemed oblivious to the way her heart was beating like a drum. Outside, a short, heavy shower had evidently interrupted the proceedings. The band had ceased playing and the children from Princetown School had sung their short repertoire. Now the crowds of merrymakers were wending their way towards the sports field. Ling hopped on Elliott's arm to where his beautiful horse was tethered and the mare whickered softly as her master approached.

'Better introduce yourself to her first,' Elliott said as the animal nuzzled his shoulder.

'She's lovely!' Ling crooned, stroking the soft, velvety nose. 'What's her name?'

'Ghost. I've had her a year, and I've never had a moment's temper from her.'

'She's certainly a fine specimen.' Ling noticed Seth Warrington run an expert hand down the creature's legs. Even Fanny was prompted to hold up her hand and giggled when Ghost licked her fingers with her rough tongue.

'Always hold your hand flat, like so,' Elliott demonstrated. 'That way you won't get nipped by mistake.'

But Fanny's face became shuttered at being addressed by the stranger, and as Seth and Rose hurried away, Ling's attention was distracted as Elliott lifted her onto Ghost's back. She relished his hands on her small waist, surprised by the strength of his lean arms. It felt so peculiar sitting aloft on the mare's back and she was frightened she might slide off at any moment! She clung on tightly to what Elliott had called the pommel, and every few strides as he led Ghost forward, he looked up to make sure she was safe. And each time he did so, she bristled with excitement.

As they joined in the mass exodus towards the sports field, the sun decided to show its face for the first time that day. Ling was hailed by so many, neighbours from Foggintor and strangers enquiring as to her health since just about everyone had heard of the near tragedy. It was kind of them, but she would much rather be left alone to engage in private conversation with Mr Franfield!

Ling's family had already found a space alongside the marked lines. Mary had brought two rugs, and Ling quivered with quiet expectancy as Elliott lifted her down from Ghost, his hands tightly about her waist once more, and set her upon one of the rugs while Arthur and Mary sat on the other. Ling could scarcely believe that once Elliott had disappeared for ten minutes to find stabling for Ghost at one of the nearby inns, he returned to sit beside her. She noticed Barney and her own group of friends further along on the opposite side of the running track. She caught Barney glaring across, his face clamped in disgruntled lines, but she pretended she hadn't seen him. This was an afternoon of a lifetime, and her young mind told her to make the most of every second!

'Are you sure you're comfortable, Miss Southcott?' Elliott asked.

'Why, yes thank you. But I really must insist that you call me Ling.'

'It's a most unusual name,' he commented, and Ling's heart beat a little faster at what appeared to be genuine interest.

'Oh, it isn't my proper name,' she explained. 'My real name's Heather, but ling is the kind of heather that grows most commonly on the moor. Father always said I reminded him of it, small but strong-willed. I'm always getting into scrapes, you see,' she confided with a grimace. 'Of course, I've grown quite tall now, but the name stuck. So that's why I've come to be known as Ling rather than Heather. Silly, really.'

'On the contrary, I think it's rather lovely.' Elliott's clear blue eyes were directed straight at hers, making the breath quicken in her throat. 'Your father said he's a quarryman, and Mrs Warrington mentioned that you're a school assistant?'

He lent an enquiring tone to his voice, unconsciously tipping his head a little as he spoke, making Ling feel even more confident. 'That's right. Mr Norrish — he's the schoolmaster — he taught me. I loved school so much that he gave me extra lessons and now I've been his assistant for three years. It's ideal, and it means I don't have to go into service. I'd hate that!' She snatched in her breath, her lips closing in a soft knot, and lowered her eyes. Oh, no! She'd ruined everything! 'Oh, I'm sorry,' she scarcely murmured. 'No doubt you have servants and expect them to know their place.'

Elliott seemed to stare right through her, but then his mouth spread in a teasing grin. 'Yes, we have servants. Two, anyway. And yes, my parents expect them to toe the line, my mother especially, but I think we treat them quite kindly.' He half turned away, so that he was looking at her askew with one eyebrow raised cheekily. 'But I think I can see that you'd find it hard to know your place. And I mean that as a compliment. You are quite forward for a young lady, but in the most charming way. And most level-headed. Most girls would have turned to jelly at the fright you've just had.'

'Oh, but I hardly had time to be afeared.' She glanced back at him, her eyes wide. It seemed she could be herself with Elliott Franfield, and he even *liked* her for it! 'The train, though, it's a wonderful sight, don't you think?' she went on, wanting to turn the conversation away from herself. 'It runs right past where we live. And it'll make such a difference to everyone's lives.'

'Yes, I imagine it will. It's really quite isolated up here. Especially if you don't have a horse to ride which I doubt many do.'

'Well, no. And that's why you caused such a stir yourself, racing the train like that.'

Elliott shook his head with a soft laugh that endeared him to her even further. 'Oh, I wasn't actually racing. I just wanted to be at the station in time. To witness the historic moment. I hadn't intended to stay on for the celebrations, not knowing anyone here. But,' and Ling noticed a slight hesitation, perhaps of awkwardness, 'now I've met you, it's different.'

For a long, exquisite moment, the world about her seemed to fall away and a delicious warmth seeped through Ling's veins as she gazed at the suddenly serious face of the handsome young gentleman. Never in a million years would she have imagined herself sitting on a rug and chatting so freely to someone from a class so far above her own. She wanted to wrap the sensation in a little box and store it in her heart for ever.

'Oh, they're off!' she cried as a general cheer drew her attention to the starting line.

She saw Elliott's face light with amusement. 'Oh, just look at them!' he chuckled, and Ling leaned forward to watch a higgledy-piggledy line of toddlers being chivvied along by their parents. Races for older children followed, spectators shouting encouragement and applauding as the competitors reached the finishing line. When one of Ling's pupils was involved, she did the same, joining with abandon the high spirits all around them.

'I can see why you love your work. You're very fond of your children, aren't you?'

Ling nodded, appreciating the way he called them *her* children. 'Yes, I am. I have the odd rascal but I see that as a challenge. And you?' she dared to ask. 'You look as if you're enjoying watching them, too.'

'Oh, I love children. I think you and I share something there. You with your pupils, and me with my patients. Or rather, Dr Greenwood's patients at the moment, but my own when I'm qualified. As a physician, you must *feel* for the people in your care. Some doctors like to consider themselves tin gods, and others are so engrossed in the workings of the human body that they forget there's a real person inside. But I think patients must recover more quickly if they feel you're really involved in their welfare. Dr Greenwood, now. You can see at once how much he genuinely cares. And not just for his wealthier patients. He still stands in as Medical Officer at the workhouse occasionally, and he's just the same there. That's the sort of doctor I want to be.'

Their eyes met fleetingly, a common bond seeming to spin its web about them. But just then, the crowd exploded into raucous hilarity as the first adult competition began, a donkey race, when one man had to carry another on his back to a half-way point where they had to change over. Ling was aware of Elliott's diversion beside her, and somehow it pleased her no end. Other races followed, adult wheelbarrow and steeplechases, and Barney threw a proud glance in Ling's direction, deliberately swelling his chest as he won every race he competed in. Ling waved back heartily, then curbed her congratulations as she felt her father's eyes on her.

'Father's not too happy with Barney,' she whispered, and suddenly her face sparked with mischief. 'Why don't you join in? I'm sure you'd win!'

Elliott recoiled slightly. 'Well, I don't know,' he muttered. 'Do you think they'd let me? Not being local, I mean?'

'Oh, I'm sure it would be all right. Let me give you this,' she said, giving him her clean handkerchief. 'It can be my favour, and you can be my knight. Like in days of old,' she grinned.

'In that case, how can I refuse, milady?'

He rose to his feet, bowing deeply, and making Ling giggle. He removed his coat, hurrying away jauntily and was lost in the crowd. A few minutes later, Ling was sitting forward as the line of young men flew down the track. She held her breath as Barney and Elliott out-streaked the rest of the field, running neck and neck as they charged across the finishing line. The crowd burst into deafening ovation, and Ling was bouncing up and down as she clapped with gusto.

It was then that she caught the fury stamped on Barney's features, even though it was being announced that the race had ended in a dead heat. But she chose to ignore it as Elliott came towards her and flung himself down on the rug.

'Ooph!' he breathed out heavily. 'I haven't run like that since I was at school. It was quite exhilarating. Perhaps I should seek out a sports club when I go to London. It would help keep me fit and healthy.'

A shadow darkened Ling's heart. In a few weeks' time, Elliott would be going to the capital to study for years on end and she would never see him again. They had passed the day most pleasantly, but he belonged to a different world and no doubt his mind, unlike hers, was not wandering dreamily into a future that could never be.

She shook her head, throwing out the fantasy. She should not allow its impossibility to mar the rest of the day. The races were over, and Ling hobbled on Elliott's arm to the recreation room where the adult tea was being served — and where there was much interest in the amiable young gentleman who had saved Ling's life!

'And now I should take you home on Ghost, Miss Southcott,' Elliott announced when the tea was over, 'as I cannot imagine how else you can manage.'

Ling's heart dropped. She had been surprised how she herself had so naturally fallen in with his refined speech, but the day was nearly over and soon she would be bidding him farewell.

'Will you not stay for the fireworks?' she asked optimistically when her parents had gone in search of Fanny who had partaken of the free children's refreshments. 'There's to be a dance afterwards, though that will be of no use to me!' she joked mildly.

'Fireworks?'

'Yes. They say it'll light the whole sky, though I've never seen any myself afore.'

'Then I cannot prevent your enjoyment. But surely it must be dark to appreciate them fully?'

'Oh, it'll be dark in an hour or so if you don't mind waiting. But . . . I suppose your parents will be worrying.'

'Oh, no,' Elliott assured her. 'It infuriates my mother, but she knows I'm the most appalling time-keeper. It comes with my line of work, you see. If I'm out on a case with Dr Greenwood, well, it can take all night sometimes. No, I should like to watch the spectacle myself, and I'll take you home afterwards. If you don't mind waiting ten minutes, though, I'd like to check on Ghost.'

No. Ling did not mind waiting at all. Not if it meant the dream could last a few hours longer.

CHAPTER FIVE

Ling gasped in wonderment as the first rocket exploded into a rippling orb of silvery stars and then cascaded earthward in a breathtaking shower of glittering rain. The marvelling crowd stared up at the awesome sight, some shrieking their delight but most, like Ling, dumbfounded by the spectacular display. The dazzling pinpoints of colour slashed through the darkness, falling gently until their shimmering radiance faded and they died on the air like soft spirits of the night. The twinkling reflections spangled in Ling's eyes, and when she glanced up at Elliott, her face was alive with wide-eyed amazement. A magical end to a magical day, and she didn't want it to end.

While others had waited impatiently for darkness to fall, Ling had relished every minute. Elliott had told her about the London hospital where he would be training, and how he couldn't wait to begin his studies — unaware that he was twisting the knife in her side. His father was a wealthy merchant dealing in fine furniture, his business being in Plymouth although he preferred to live in Tavistock. Mrs Franfield had wanted Elliott to follow in his father's lucrative footsteps, and had been appalled when her son had announced his intention to become a physician instead. But

Mr Franfield had convinced his wife that it was a commendable profession, and she had finally relented.

Not that she would have stopped him, Elliott had grinned with the unassuming confidence Ling had already become familiar with, just as if, she mused, she had known him all her life rather than just a few hours. And now that short, bitter-sweet time was over. The last ember of the final firework had dissipated into the black velvet of the night, and the spectators were dispersing, some homeward while others were ambling towards the recreation room for the celebration dance.

'Come along, girls.' Arthur smiled at his daughters. "Tis time we was getting you home.'

'I'll fetch my horse, then, for Ling to ride.'

"Tis most kind of you, young man.'

'The pleasure's all mine. I've enjoyed myself immensely.'

Ling watched through a shroud of sadness as Elliott weaved his way through the crowd. Fanny was still bubbling with excitement over the fireworks, and Arthur, as a quarryman who had worked with explosives all his life, was musing as to how the gunpowder was turned to such artistic usage.

For once, the Dartmoor air was still and the smoke from the fireworks hung in a dense, acrid cloud. As Ling, seated on Ghost, and her family and Elliott followed down the side of the fenced railway track, the sounds of the continuing celebrations gradually died away. The nocturnal silence of the moor was broken only by the steady plodding of Ghost's hooves and the occasional haunting call of a distant owl or the bark of a hunting fox. The little troop found itself cloaked in the secret mystery of the lonely upland as if the legendary Dartmoor pixies really were lurking behind every exposed granite boulder they passed. And when a group of Devon cattle loomed out of the murk, Fanny let out a squeal of fear.

'She's very nervy, your sister,' Elliott observed hesitantly, keeping his voice low so as not to be overheard. 'And she's a little deaf if I'm not mistaken.'

'Yes,' Ling answered, daring to lean down a little as she was growing used to the feel of Ghost's movement beneath her. 'It was measles. And she's, well, a little slow, I suppose you might say.'

'I'm so sorry to hear that.' Elliott released a heart-felt sigh as he watched the back of the pretty child who was walking a few yards ahead of them between her parents. 'Some of these illnesses can have such devastating effects. Maybe one day they'll invent a vaccine against some of them, like we have for smallpox. I really admire the way some doctors work on cures for diseases, or just understanding what causes them in the first place. Often it's just hit and miss, so I'm full of admiration for their patience and tenacity. Not my cup of tea, I'm afraid. I prefer to work with patients rather than test tubes. It's going to be so frustrating, though, when there are so many people that you just can't help.'

Ling nodded in reply. Elliott's caring nature shone from him in every way, and Ling deeply appreciated his attitude towards her sister when people like Harry Spence still took pleasure from making fun of her.

'Fanny's learnt quite a lot at school, mind,' she told Elliott confidentially. 'And I give her extra help at home when she needs it.'

'I can see you're very close. And what about you? What aspirations do *you* have for the future?'

'Me? Oh, I hadn't really thought.' Ling felt herself blush at his interest. She didn't want to tell him the truth, that she supposed she would marry Barney and have his children and be a poor quarryman's wife for the rest of her days. So far, Elliott had no reason to think that she and Barney were walking out, and somehow she wanted to keep it that way, as if it would ruin the romanticism of the day if he knew. 'I really enjoy teaching,' she said instead. 'I think I'd just like to go on doing that.'

'Well, it's good to know what you want to do with your life. Like me and my course.'

'Yes, I suppose it is,' Ling muttered almost to herself. The reminder that their relationship, such as it was, was drawing to a close, filled her with dismay as they left the railway track and turned towards the hamlet at Foggintor. A glimmer of light flickered from the upstairs window of the manager's house, shedding a supernatural dimness on their path and making the way a little easier to see.

'Until today I had no idea there was a village here,' Elliott admitted, his voice low in case there were people already abed. 'I saw the train coming round the bend and wondered about crossing the moor to get to it. And then I saw the track and found myself here. It's dreadfully isolated.'

'Yes, but we have each other. And the railway will be so good for us. It was really built for the quarries and the prison, but it'll be wonderful for passengers as well.'

There was no time for Elliott to comment as Arthur, Mary and Fanny were waiting by the pathway.

'Thank you so much for everything,' Arthur said, shaking Elliott's hand. 'I think Ling can manage now. 'Tis only a few yards.'

'No, no. I insist on taking her to your front door.'

Ling was gripped by a sudden panic. She didn't want Elliott to see their humble abode. He had treated her like an equal, but the tiny cottage was so cramped and lowly, it would accentuate horribly the differences between their backgrounds. Differences that could never be bridged, and she wanted to hug the dream, unspoilt, to her heart for ever.

'I can manage, honestly,' she protested.

'No. I really don't want you putting any weight on that ankle for several days. If you tripped again, I'd never forgive myself.'

He led Ghost forward, following between the two sets of cottages. Ling held her breath. This was it. Before she knew it, Elliott had lifted her down from the saddle and was carrying her up the garden path, past Arthur's immaculate rows of vegetables and through the yard where earlier that day, she and her mother, with Fanny's dubious assistance, had sweated over another consignment of laundry. Thank goodness there was no sign of it now. She didn't mind Elliott believing that her father's skills provided them with a decent life. But she didn't want him knowing that, despite what she herself earned as the school assistant, her mother had to take in washing so that they could maintain a reasonable standard of living.

Elliott's eyes swept about the small, Spartan room, not judging it, but looking for somewhere to deposit his burden. There was no such thing as an armchair, only a rustic settle and four kitchen chairs around the table, one of which Arthur pulled out for him. Ling felt the shame burn in her cheeks, relieved that at least the straw palliasse she slept on was stored out of sight during the day.

'Well, I'd better be off,' Elliott announced, and Ling's heart groaned. 'Keep off your foot for some days, and keep it elevated as much as possible.'

'Yes, I will,' she promised, though inside she was aching. 'And you take care on the way home.'

'I'll follow the track along to the main road, so I'll be all right. I won't get lost and with any luck, there might even be some moonlight.'

'Well, thank you, Elliott,' she almost choked as she used his name for the first — and last — time. 'For everything. And especially for saving my life.'

'Don't mention it. Good-bye, then, Ling. And I hope your ankle recovers soon.'

And he was lost from her view as her parents wished him well and showed him out of the door.

'What an extraordinary day!' Arthur declared. 'Now, up to bed with you, Fanny. 'Tis very late.'

And before too long, Ling was snuggled up on her mattress on the floor. She couldn't sleep, turning the day's events over in her mind. The massive engine came back to her then, huge and horrific and ready to crush her in its hungry jowls. Her heart raced with crippling terror at what had so very nearly happened. And then the handsome face of her saviour swam into her weary mind and tears of regret trickled down her cheeks.

* * *

Barney Mayhew cavorted around the dance floor with all the elegance of a prize bull. He was broad of shoulder and strong, and you couldn't have it all ways. He was proud of his physique, of the hard nature of his work at the quarry. And you wouldn't catch him dandying up and down the room as he was convinced that milksop would have done if he'd been there and not gone off to fetch his white charger to take Ling home on, just like some bloody knight in shining armour! Oh, yes, Barney had seen them as he had waited in the queue at the doors to the recreation room, and resentment had seethed within him. It wasn't Ling's fault, of course. It was her father's, dismissing him from the room like that. Not that he could blame him, he supposed. He liked and respected Arthur Southcott. He had been happy to pass on his skills, a better, steadier worker than his own father.

No. It was that bloody foppish rake who had ruined everything! A second later and it would have been Barney down there on the railway track, dragging Ling clear of the train. Wasn't he furious at himself, at his own inability to move a muscle, so shocked had he been? He had felt sickened to the pit of his stomach, and the vision of the roaring, hissing monster about to crush his darling . . . He couldn't help his own natural reaction, the vicious trembling that had paralysed him.

A lump the size of an apple swelled in his throat. Dear God, he loved Ling so much, and when all was said and done, he should be thanking the young gentleman, whoever he was, from the bottom of his heart for saving his beloved girl. He hadn't realised he had stopped still, the swirling dancers spinning past him unnoticed, as he imagined the horror of his life without Ling, of a gravestone, perhaps cut by his own hand, with her name . . .

But if only the knave who had saved her in his place had not been so young and good-looking and a *bloody doctor*! Well, he couldn't be a *proper* doctor, even Barney could work that one out as he only looked a few years older than himself. But, damn him, he had clearly impressed the Southcotts and Ling, too, by the starry-eyed way she was looking at him. Barney had been so looking forward to spending the festive day with her and to the romantic atmosphere he was sure the evening would create. And when he thought about it, everything had been ruined by that idiot, Harry Spence. Oh, Barney could cheerfully murder him!

CHAPTER SIX

'You'm not still angered with us, are you?'

'Pardon?'

Ling blinked her thoughtful eyes. It was Saturday morning two and a half weeks after the grand celebrations to mark the opening of the railway, and Ling was thinking of the young gentleman who had saved her life and whom she had not clapped eyes on again since he had ridden off into the darkness.

The weather had been glorious for the past week and Ling had sat outside with her leg elevated, unable to assist her mother with the laundry. She had devoured the newspapers and had been shocked to read about the eruption of Krakatoa and its dreadful consequences. But that was on the other side of the world, and her young mind kept drifting back to the realms of fantasy, daydreaming of how life might be as a doctor's wife.

Even now as she was trying out her ankle, she could see Elliott's concerned face. It seemed to obliterate everything about her, from the men calling to each other to the clanking of hammer on anvil in the nearby smithy where Jake Stevens and his boy would be sharpening drill-bits and chisels and mending links in the huge chains that were used on the cranes. So that when Barney had hailed her, his voice had sliced through her reverie and brought her, reluctantly, from another world. She sighed with a helpless sense of futility, folding the dream away as she dragged herself back to the present.

'I said, I hope you'm not still angered,' Barney repeated. ''Twasn't my fault, you knows. 'Twas Harry Spence, larking about like the soft idjit he is. Pushed us, he did, and—'

'Of course I don't blame you, silly.'

'Really? You'm certain? I mean, you've bin proper distant—'

'Have I?' She felt her cheeks flame crimson as she prayed he wouldn't guess at her innermost thoughts. Ridiculous, the aspirations that kept wandering into her head. 'Oh, I'm sorry, Barney. I don't mean to be. It was just all such a shock—'

'Barney? Oh, there you are! Skiving as usual. Come on, lad, work's not over yet. I needs your help with that there bench we blasted earlier. Oh, good day, you. How's that foot?'

'Much better, thank you, Mr Mayhew.' Ling nodded at Barney's father and out of the corner of her eye, she saw Barney pull a mocking face, for if anyone ever shirked his duties, it was Mr Mayhew himself!

'Good to hear it,' the man grumbled, not sounding the least pleased. 'Come on then, Barney. Work to be done.'

As Barney turned to follow him, Ling heard the heavy rumbling of the train as it passed the quarries on its winding descent towards Horrabridge. The sound sent a strange shudder down her spine. Her adventurous heart was yearning to take a ride in one of the splendid carriages, and yet her desire was tempered with the memory that the railway had very nearly taken her life.

'Tell the time by that there train,' Barney grinned. 'Pity 'tis not arter us finishes for the arternoon, mind. Us could've gone into Tavistock to look at that there new swimming baths. Mind you, 'tis a daft idea if you ask me. What does us want to larn to swim for?'

He ran after his father and Ling shook her head with a smile. The idea of the town's swimming pool, opened exactly a week ago, appealed to her sense of fun. Perhaps she could take Fanny one day when her ankle was better. She had read in the newspaper that it only cost tuppence and you could hire bathing suits. It would be lovely to splash about in the water and learn to swim, and perhaps she might meet Elliott in the town . . .

But then there was the train fare, and Ling's heart sank. They lived comfortably but there was never a penny to spare, and none of them wanted to take in lodgers as Widow Rodgers next door had to. She and her two young daughters slept in the bedroom while their two stonemason lodgers slept downstairs on a mattress. Ling knew her father would never submit to such invasion of his privacy.

Ling tossed her head. She must stop these pipe dreams, these ideas above her station. It was just because of a few hours spent in Elliott Franfield's company, one chance meeting. She was nothing more than a quarryman's daughter, and one day, would be a quarryman's wife. Barney's wife.

As Mr Mayhew had said, they had been blasting that morning. It was the quarryman's work to drill deep holes into the granite's natural faults by hammering in a boring rod to the required depth. It took days of tedious, gruelling labour to drill one hole, three or four men working as a team. Then men with the required skill — and Arthur Southcott was one of them — would carefully charge the holes with gunpowder, using just sufficient explosive to move the block away from the quarry surface. The detached block of stone, or bench as it was called, would then be lowered by crane onto a waiting truck, and this was what Barney was needed for now.

Arthur had been a quarryman at Foggintor all his life, and so Ling had observed the workings in the quarry — naturally at a safe distance — since she was a child. It could be hot, dusty toil on a day such as this, especially when they had been blasting. Today, though, Ling knew the dust would have settled by now after the earlier explosion and the area declared safe. And so she hobbled to the quarry floor to watch.

Barney and his father were preparing to lower the stone bench. The gigantic quarry was for ever changing as stone was removed, but the overwhelming impression remained the same. The towering rock faces gave the appearance of having been deliberately hewn into monumental squares, when in fact it was Mother Nature who had provided the cracks in this densest of stone that were so useful to the humans who harvested it. The granite was cut away in colossal steps so that the workmen could get from the soaring height of the quarry to its floor, or vice versa, by a series of ladders propped against the vertical surfaces and resting on wide ridges. The sight of it always reminded Ling of the wooden building bricks she used in school to teach the youngest children to count, multiply and divide. Except that these massive bricks could be fatal since the ladders were never fixed and the idea of safety ropes was scorned by the men. They were proud of their skills and would not have used any security aids even if they had existed. Indeed, there was Ling's father shinning up the rock face like an ant!

She watched as he joined his friend and fellow-labourer, Ambrose Tippet, and his son, the quiet and gentle Sam who, like Barney, had almost completed his apprenticeship. Sam held the boring rod, giving it a quarter turn between each blow of the sledgehammers that were being administered alternately by his own father and Arthur. It always seemed to Ling perilous in the extreme to be holding the rod. The massive hammers only needed to slip or miss their mark, and she could envisage some horrific accident. But Ling had learnt to trust their skill. Indeed, Arthur was considered the most senior among the experienced powder monkeys, the name given to those who dealt with the explosives. He was intelligent, and had quickly latched on to the reading and writing Ling had taught him, always eager to know what she was studying in the books Mr Norrish lent her. Born in different circumstances, she could have imagined him as a successful businessman, or whatever a man of class and education could achieve.

Oh, what *was* the matter with her? Ever since she had met Elliott Franfield, she had felt ill at ease with her own world. But . . . it was stupid. And selfish. Barney worked hard. Prided himself on his strength and the skill he had acquired. He was dependable, his joking reserved for his leisure hours. And Ling *loved* him.

Now he was perched on one of the giant steps in the side of the quarry. Several metal hooks called dogs had been driven into the sides of the granite bench and were attached to chains suspended from the crane. Barney and his father were carefully watching the stone and using hand signals to direct the crane operator. From where she was sitting, Ling could just make out the bench beginning to lift.

Quite what happened, she didn't see, but Barney was suddenly thrown sideways. For one sickening moment, Ling's heart stood still. Her face drained of its colour as in that split second, Barney managed to twist himself away from the sheer drop and instead fell against the rock face behind him, his cry echoing about the quarry walls. Ling found herself scudding across the quarry floor, heedless of her ankle as she neatly dodged the tramway rails and scattered stones. By the time she reached the base of the rock face on which Barney and Mr Mayhew had been working, other labourers, her father among them, were scrambling up or down the patchwork of ladders to reach them.

'He's all right!' someone shouted, and a murmur of relief rippled through the quarrymen who had congregated by Ling's side.

They began moving away, leaving her trembling on the spot. Barney was all right. Well, perhaps he was, but it had only been his own quick reaction that had prevented him from being flung to certain death. Oh, dear God, it had been *that* close, and her insides clenched into a tight knot at what might have been. She just couldn't bear the thought of what her life without Barney would be, his sense of fun that matched her own, his smiling face flushed with pride that she was *his* girl. Oh, how could she ever have let her heart wander elsewhere, to something that would never be?

And actually, she realised with horror, Barney wasn't all right at all. Her spirit plummeted as she could see now that his father was helping him to climb slowly down the long wooden ladders. His left arm was cradled across his chest so that he only had one hand to hold on with which was why he was moving so cautiously. Every second seemed an eternity as Ling hovered by the bottom ladder so that she was there, ready to comfort and care for the boy she loved the instant his feet came to rest on solid ground.

His young, usually boisterous face was grey and stiff, his brow dotted with pearls of cold sweat. Ling knew by his silence that he was in agony as he would normally shrug off quite a severe knock with a manful laugh. In the warmth of the late summer sunshine, the men had been working with their sleeves rolled up above their elbows and Ling had to stifle her horrified cry as her gaze rested on Barney's forearm. It was already livid and badly misshapen, and a sharp edge was trying to protrude up through the skin. It didn't need an expert to know that the bone was broken.

'Send for the doctor,' Mr Mayhew growled.

'I'll go.' And within seconds, Sam had dashed across to the quarry entrance and disappeared.

It flashed across Ling's brain that a physician could mean Elliott Franfield, and she angrily pushed the thought aside. A few minutes ago, her conscience had made a promise that she would forget the young medical student for ever, and here she was, already thinking about him when poor Barney, *her* Barney, was in physical torment. The doctor in question would be the prison surgeon who also treated, when required, the local population. The jail was so much nearer than Tavistock and anyway, Ling had no idea where Elliott lived. Besides which, this was clearly no simple break and would need the skills of an experienced doctor.

Ashamed of herself, Ling put her arm about Barney's shoulders. She could feel he was shivering from pain and shock, and the smile he tried to offer her ended in a grimace.

'W-what happened?' she mumbled, though what did it really matter *how* her dear Barney had been injured?

''Twould seem one of the dogs slipped out,' Arthur answered as he came towards them, having stopped to investigate the cause of the accident. 'With the strain already on the chains, it must've swung out with some force and hit the poor lad afore he knew it.'

Ling caught the accusing look her father cast at Mr Mayhew. As the experienced quarryman in charge of an apprentice — even if Barney was his own son and had less than a year to go before he was qualified — it was his responsibility to ensure the dogs were all properly hammered into the stone before it was lifted. But then, it wouldn't be the first time that Arthur had complained that Barney's father wasn't as thorough as he should be.

'We'd best get you home, lad,' Arthur said with firm compassion, taking command since Mr Mayhew seemed too aghast to organise what was needed. 'Then Ambrose and I'll fetch that bench down. We won't mind working on a while, and the cutters'll want it ready for Monday morning.'

Barney glanced up, his features strained and rigid as he nodded briefly. As Ling well knew, they were all of them, quarrymen and masons alike, paid on the end product. If there was a delay caused by an accident, everyone would understand, but if anyone could make up the lost time, they would do so.

'Take your time, son,' Mr Mayhew said as he and Arthur helped Barney across the uneven floor of the quarry. Ling's heart ached with frustration as, for the moment, there was nothing she could do to help. She had heard of people losing their limbs because of broken bones, or fractures as she remembered Elliott had called them as they had chatted on that enchanted afternoon. A break could interfere with the nerves or blood supply, he had explained, or if an operation was needed, there was always the danger of a potentially lethal infection. Ling's hands were tightened into balls at her sides. This was all her fault. Her retribution for letting her attentions wander, if only fleetingly, elsewhere. Please, God, forgive me, she prayed silently, and don't take Barney away.

* * *

To Ling's utter relief, the surgeon was able to put Barney to sleep, reset the two broken bones since both had been damaged, and encase the arm in a plaster of Paris cast without recourse to surgery. Afterwards, Ling was allowed to sit by Barney's bedside, holding his other hand and crooning softly to him. His eyes flickered open, he gave what seemed to her a wan but contented smile, and then drifted asleep again.

Ling dropped her head into her hands. Thank God he was all right.

CHAPTER SEVEN

'Get yersel out from under my feet, Barney Mayhew!'

Barney was only too happy to oblige. He had been struggling with a book Ling had given him to read while he couldn't work, and he was glad of any excuse to abandon it. The sight of his sister wielding a broomstick was all he needed. Since their mother had died many years ago, Eleanor had taken charge of all things domestic, wearing the crown over both their father and Barney himself, and yet despite her always seeming to be rushed off her feet, chaos reigned perpetually. Apart from his passionate love for Ling, Barney was also looking forward to living in her parents' orderly household — as he imagined they would for the first few years of their marriage until they could afford somewhere of their own.

He smiled indulgently under Eleanor's challenging gaze. Reading was all very well when the school day was over and Ling was free to sit at his side, his senses stimulated by the curve of her jaw line and her pretty, laughing eyes. But on his own, the words seemed to dance up and down on the page and he was grateful to Eleanor for driving him outside.

The pleasant early September morning seemed to ease his frustration. Now that the excruciating pain in his arm had completely gone, he longed to be back at work, where his skill and physical strength gave him a feeling of usefulness and pride. But it would be another five weeks or so before he could return to the quarry. What could he possibly do to while away the time, starting with today? Well, he supposed he had two good legs, so he could at least go for a walk. It wasn't very productive, but with only one arm, he couldn't exactly dig over the vegetable plot!

His legs took him to the tiny chapel at the corner of the square of cottages. During the day, the small building doubled as the school and inside, either Mr Norrish or Ling would be teaching the motley band of scholars. He could hear them now, chanting their times tables.

A smile played on his lips at the thought that only the stone walls separated him from his beloved. He breathed in deeply as if he could smell the intoxicating scent of her. At least his accident seemed to have brought them closer again. She had doted on him, and he had supped on each sweet moment, the stranger who had interrupted their relationship seemingly fled from her memory. Barney only had to get back to work and complete his apprenticeship, saving every penny he could. Maybe even next year, he might have enough money to marry her, and everything would be settled.

The idea lifted his spirits, as he walked along the track past Yellowmeade Farm, stepping on the stone slabs or setts from the branch of the original horse-drawn tramway that had preceded the new steam railway. Yellowmeade was farmed by a former quarryman. Like the local miners, all quarry workers and masons grew much of their own food in their gardens, and with livestock all around, it was perhaps an easy step to farming, at least on a small scale. Possibly, one day, Barney would retire to a cosy farmstead, and he and Ling would see out their lives in blissful peace.

As he reached the row of humble dwellings known as Red Cottages — renamed as such when their porous walls had been clad in corrugated iron and painted with red lead to keep out the damp — Barney's pleasant reverie was fragmented into dust. His attention was drawn by the sound of hooves, and when he saw the distinctive dapple grey horse coming towards him, disdain seethed in his breast.

'Good morning!' Elliott brought the mare to a halt and swinging his leg over the hairy neck, alighted on the uneven track. 'Barney, isn't it? Remember me? I've come to see Ling. Miss Southcott. Is her ankle better? Oh!' His animated, gabbling words came to an abrupt end as he took in the sling tied about Barney's neck. 'Oh, dear me, what happened to you?'

Oh, yes! I remember you all too well! Barney growled in his head, but he forced a casual smile to his lips as he shrugged at the young man who was, in his eyes, his rival. 'An accident at the quarry. Bad break, the prison surgeon said. Us always uses *him*, you see.'

The last comment was meant to intimate that the Medical Officer at the jail was far superior to any fancy physician from Tavistock, and certainly better than Elliott Franfield. But it totally missed its mark.

'Oh, you poor fellow.' The concern in Elliott's voice was so genuine that Barney's mouth twitched with remorse. 'Did he have to reset it? I wish I'd been there. To observe, I mean, not because you were hurt. How does it feel now?'

'Oh, 'tis proper fine,' Barney answered, slightly taken aback at Elliott's genial attitude. 'Just a nuisance not being able to work.'

'Yes, I can appreciate that. I wish you well, anyway.' And the expression on his face altered to one of eager anticipation as he continued, 'Do you know where Miss Southcott is? I wanted to visit her before, but I've been so busy and I didn't want to appear too forward. I trust her ankle is mended? What a day that was!'

His obvious expectation prickled Barney's skin. He thought the stranger had gone from their lives, and now here he was, as bold as brass, come to see Ling and full of the joys of spring! Well, Barney wasn't having it!

'She bain't yere,' he said affably, since the blackguard mustn't suspect he was lying. 'But I'll tell her you called to see her.'

Barney felt the swell of satisfaction as Elliott's face fell. 'Oh,' he murmured flatly. 'Oh, well, perhaps you wouldn't mind giving her this for me. I wrote it just in case she wasn't here. Just a short letter with my address in London. She can write to me there. That's, well, if she wants to. Would you mind?'

A surge of anger blackened Barney's heart as he took the envelope from Elliott's hand. 'No, of course not. When does you go? To London, I means?'

'Friday.'

'Ah,' Barney nodded. 'Must be getting excited like?'

'Well, yes.' Elliott raised his eyebrows with a wistful sigh. 'I shall miss all this, though.' He turned to gesture vaguely about him. 'I don't get that much time to come up on the moor, but I do love it. I love Tavistock, too, as a small country town. London's not really for me, but I'll get the best training there.'

'Well, good luck with it,' Barney drawled. And good riddance, too, he thought to himself.

'Thank you very much. You will give the note to Ling? And tell her I'm sorry I missed her.'

'Will do,' Barney promised.

Elliott seemed reluctant to leave and his eyes swept sadly about him before he swung himself back into the saddle. 'Thank you, Barney. Take care of that arm, now.'

Barney nodded, and watched as Elliott turned Ghost about and set off at a trot. Barney stood stock still, allowing the scowl to come to his face now. Did the bugger really expect him to . . . ? But then, Elliott Franfield clearly had no idea that he and Ling were walking out. So, Barney's brain deduced, that must mean Ling hadn't told him.

And why not?

Barney crunched the letter in his fist in a jealous rage. Was Ling so dissatisfied with their relationship that she had encouraged the handsome, intelligent, courageous stranger? Or had the devil deliberately tried to woo and impress her? Oh, he must protect her from Elliott Franfield, yes, that was it! The stranger could not *love* Ling as he did. He hardly knew her. She would be a mere dalliance to him, and Ling would be deeply hurt. But . . . what if Ling really did have feelings for him?

No! Barney couldn't let it happen! He and Ling were made for each other. She was the reason for his waking up each morning, why he wanted to outshine all the other apprentices so that he could make a good home for her and their children when the time came.

He forgot all about his walk and stood, grinding the toe of his boot into the ground. Damn Elliott Franfield! And continuing to swear under his breath, he stomped back home.

'You'm back then?' Eleanor grunted. 'Range 'as gone out. Couldn't manage fer relight it, could yer?'

Barney pursed his lips as he set about the task, scrunching a few precious sheets of old newspaper — which had hardly been read, of course — into balls, and carefully arranging sticks of kindling on top. He managed to hold the matchbox in the exposed fingers of his left hand while he struck the match against it, and once the firewood had taken, he broke off pieces of dried peat turf to add to the growing flames. Well, at least he still had *some* use!

And then the thought slithered into his brain, bringing him out in a sweat. The letter. He had promised. And morally, he supposed, he had no right. But his love for Ling was too strong.

His heart hammered against his ribs as he glanced over his shoulder. Eleanor had gone outside to the vegetable plot. So no one would ever know. Elliott Franfield was off to London, and Ling would soon be forgotten. It was better this way.

Barney's fingers shook as he threw the letter into the firebox. He watched it scorch at the edges, curl, and then flare up with a blue flame. And then it was gone for ever. Barney heard Eleanor trudge back inside and he quickly used the poker to scatter the grey paper ash into the turf so that not a shred of evidence remained.

CHAPTER EIGHT

'You sure you won't come?'

Ling's lips were pursed as she frowned at Barney. He had seemed in a strange mood recently, sometimes distant as if he were treading carefully about her, and at other times prickly and sullen. It was so unlike the fun-loving boy she knew and loved, and she put it down to the frustration his plastered arm was creating. He was a physical person, and must feel as if the rug had been whisked away from beneath his feet. He had her every sympathy, and she had fussed over him and showed him how very much she cared, even allowing him — for the first time — the excitement of placing the palm of his other hand over her breast. His fingers had been warm and tender, shaking slightly as her heart had beaten hard and fast beneath them. Her virgin flesh was confused and torn between fear and yearning and wanting to comfort Barney in some way that nobody else could.

Just now, however, he was being ungracious and surly, his eyebrows fiercely swooped. 'How can I possibly go swimming with this?' he barked, waving his left arm at her.

'Well, I don't mean for you to go swimming, silly,' she smiled, ignoring his churlishness. 'Besides, men and women can't bathe at the same time. You'd have to wander about the town while Fanny and I are at the baths, but I thought you'd jump at the chance to ride on the train. It'd be such an adventure!'

'For those as can afford it! We'm struggling to put meat on the table twice a week with me out of work, without gallivanting off on a daytrip to Tavistock!'

'Oh, I'm sorry, Barney. I should've thought. I'd pay for you, too, only I've just got enough to pay for Fanny and me, and she'd be so disappointed if I took you instead. You don't really mind if we go without you, do you? I'd much rather you'd have come, though.'

The hard lines about Barney's mouth softened as the expectancy in her shining eyes tugged at his better nature. 'No, of course not,' he relented. ''Tis just me being selfish. I wait all week for you to finish at school, and so tomorrow being Saturday—'

'I'll make it up to you, I promise.'

Her butterscotch eyes searched his deep brown ones as she tilted her head to bring her warm, moist lips against his. This was her Barney. His accident, and the idea of losing him, had made her realise how much she loved him. And instead of the usual fleeting peck, her mouth remained pressed to his, moving softly and delicately, awakening the budding passion in her young heart. She caught the surprised pleasure in Barney's expression and then closed her eyes as he returned her kiss. The tip of his tongue played on her lips, sending a shiver down her spine. When they finally drew apart, they stared at each other, breathless with exhilaration.

'Have a wonderful day tomorrow,' Barney gulped. 'Tell me all 'bout it when you gets back.'

'Yes, I will,' Ling nodded, her cheeks flushed and her heart in such turmoil that she all but fled home.

Barney sat back with an enormous inhalation of breath. That were unexpected! And delightful, too! What more proof did he need that she loved him? Perhaps there had been no need to destroy the letter from Elliott Franfield after all. Guilt tore at Barney's heart. It had been wrong of him, he knew, but he had to protect Ling. What if that scoundrel enticed her away with promises of a better life? The devil couldn't possibly love Ling as much as he did!

His forehead tightened into a scowl. Elliott Franfield was gone from their lives, hundreds of miles away in London. And would remain there for years while he trained, hopefully never to return. And if he did, by then Ling would have been Mrs Barney Mayhew for many moons, in a happy home with children at her feet.

Barney shook his head. He must put it behind him, forget the moment he had jealously committed the letter to flames. But somewhere inside him, his wounded conscience continued to fester.

* * *

'Come on, Ling! 'Twill go without us!'

The shrill words came at her through a muffling veil as she became aware of the hand tugging urgently on her sleeve. Her eyes were riveted on the spot where, little more than a month before, she had fallen into the path of the towering railway engine. The rekindled terror of those seconds before she blacked out moistened her skin with a clammy sweat. But Fanny's agitation beside her — Fanny, whose normal reactions were so slow and laboured, but who was now alight with excitement — dragged her back from the horrific memory and as they stepped up into the third-class carriage, she found herself caught up in eager expectation once more. They sat opposite each other and their eyes met merrily at the gentle jolt as the train began to move.

'We're off!' Ling cried, her eyes shining as she took in the sheer delight on Fanny's face.

As they bowled along, the familiar landscape seemed fresh and new from their elevated position. It felt as if they were flying even though the train was crawling cautiously on its steep descent. But for two young girls who had never travelled faster than their own two legs could carry them, they were racing along at the speed of light!

'Look, we're coming to Foggintor already!' Ling gasped.

Fanny pressed her nose against the glass for a better view. It had only taken minutes to reach the quarry settlement that they had left on foot an hour earlier to be sure of catching the train, and now here they were back again! Ling's eyebrows shot into her forehead for there, next to the railway line, stood a familiar figure. Barney, bless him, had walked up to catch a glimpse of her on her historic journey, and was vigorously waving his good arm at the train.

Ling leapt to her feet and struggling to pull down the window, waved back furiously so that Barney would spot her. He did. And as she was carried past him, his handsome face was smiling broadly. Then the carriage lurched and Ling fell back on the seat. Fanny hooted with laughter and Ling answered her with a jaunty giggle as she straightened her hat. Oh, what fun their excursion was turning out to be!

The countryside streaked past them. The track gradually coiled its way downhill across the moor before eventually stopping at the little station at Dousland. Then after the tunnel at Yelverton, they steamed through the gentler countryside and into Horrabridge Station and the end of the line for the Princetown Railway.

They did not have to wait very long for the connecting train since two railway companies shared the route from Plymouth to Tavistock and beyond. The first smoke-belching engine that pulled in against the platform was drawing several coaches, dwarfing the little moorland train and making Ling feel a little nervous as they climbed up into one of the carriages which was already quite full of passengers. Then the train juddered and steamed slowly out of the station, swaying gently as it gathered speed.

'Look at the view!' Ling cried as she pointed to the moor rising majestically in the distance.

'And 'tis like we'm flying!'

'We're crossing the Magpie and Walkham viaducts,' Ling explained, quite enthralled herself. Only minutes later, they were plunged into darkness while the train burrowed through a long tunnel and coasted into Whitchurch Station. They were off again, and before they knew it, the engine was drifting into Tavistock.

They stood, disorientated, on the platform. How Ling wished Barney had come with them, to enjoy the day and to protect them, as she knew he would. Oh, her dear, *dearest* Barney. But the passengers who had alighted were streaming towards the exit and Ling led Fanny after them. Her little sister was more animated than Ling had ever known her. Were the noise of the train and the hustle and bustle of the station on such a level that Fanny could hear it more clearly and so felt part of it, rather than being marooned in her usual muted world? At least she seemed to be enjoying herself to the full!

Ling handed in their tickets and followed the other passengers out of the station. The path descended alongside the gushing waters of the Tavy and Ling recognised the bridge from their annual trip to Tavistock for the Goose Fair each October, when they either walked the seven miles or hitched a lift with the carrier, both of which took hours. But now with the new railway up to Princetown, perhaps they might visit the town more frequently!

They reached the wide town square flanked on one side by the grandiose old church and on the other by the magnificent gothic-style town hall. Ling loved the moor, the sense of freedom and infinity it invoked, its stunning views of rugged crags and pretty valleys. But Tavistock bustled with activity and held such excitement for her. London, now that would have frightened her with its dark and dingy backstreets that covered acre upon acre, filth-ridden courts where the sun never entered, dens of crime, iniquity and disease, and which had swallowed up the youth and enthusiasm of Elliott Franfield. Ling shuddered involuntarily, and drove the horrible vision to the deepest recess of her mind. She was here, in Tavistock's lovely Bedford Square, the sun was shining, and she was happy.

It was a busy Saturday morning with people aiming for the shops. But Ling and Fanny's destination lay up a long, steep hill out of the centre. By the time they reached the summit, they were both quite out of breath, their faces pink and their hearts beating nervously, for here at last, under the shadow of the workhouse, they had arrived at the swimming baths!

They paid the entrance fee, tuppence for Ling and a penny for Fanny as she was under fourteen, and hired bathing costumes and towels. They were taken through by a girl little older than Ling, and they stopped, side by side, gazing in awestruck fascination.

The bath was a giant rectangle in the ground full of clean, inviting water, rippled only by the movements of the people submersed in it. Most were floundering in the shallow end under the hawk-like eye of a senior attendant. Only one lady was gliding effortlessly back and forth across the deep end, her limbs moving in a slow, unhurried rhythm. The water slapping against the sides echoed strangely within the enclosing walls, and there was an odd, acrid smell of dampness, not exactly musty, but something Ling could not put a name to.

The girl attendant smiled as she waited for them. 'First time?' she asked, and Ling nodded. Yes, it was the first time for so many things today!

Her excitement was tempered with not a little nervousness as they locked themselves in the little cubicle.

'Which way round does you think this goes?'

Ling frowned at the hired bathing suit Fanny was twisting this way and that. 'No, the other way, I think.' She turned her back to struggle into the strange attire and then glanced over her shoulder at Fanny. 'Oh, we do look funny!' she hooted. 'Like a cross between our underwear and a sailor's uniform! And with these mob-caps stuck on our heads!'

They collapsed into peals of laughter, but it didn't seem so amusing as they stepped outside feeling shy and embarrassed, and with grim resolve, Ling took Fanny's hand and walked over to the steps.

The coldness of the water took her breath away. She at once turned to Fanny, but the child was giggling as the water lapped against her chest. Ling's courage flooded back. As long as Fanny was happy, it was enough for her.

The sunshine was dazzling on the clear water in spangling diamonds. Ling would have loved to play, sending glittering arcs of spray over her sister as they did in the Dartmoor streams, but the stern eye of the senior attendant put paid to that! Ling met Fanny's sparkling gaze and tipped her head towards the other women and girls who were attempting the strokes with varying degrees of success.

'Come on, let's try.'

But the water immediately closed over Ling's head, gurgling in her ears. She stood up, spluttering and gasping for breath, as she searched for Fanny.

'I's all right!' she realised Fanny was coughing beside her, her little face streaming as she spat water from her mouth.

'Can I help?'

Ling looked up into the smiling face of the lady who had been swimming with ease in the deep end. 'Oh, yes, please, ma'am. We haven't the remotest idea.'

The stranger's smile broadened at the girl's politeness. 'Hold onto the side and I'll show you the leg action.'

They forgot the coldness of the water as they obeyed the lady's instruction. She was extremely patient and soon they could each swim two whole strokes before they sank.

'There. It's just practice now.' Their teacher winked and lowered her voice. 'Pity that dragon's on duty. With the other one, you can play. Build up your confidence in the water. You will come again, won't you? You've both done so well.'

'We'd like to, but we come from a long way and we can't afford it,' Ling somehow didn't feel ashamed to say. 'And usually we have to help our mother on Saturdays. This was just a special treat.'

'Oh, well, never mind. Perhaps you can save up during the winter, and I'll see you again in the spring. But I really must be going. My coachman will be waiting.'

Ling had to snap her jaw shut. This kind lady who had helped them, who had held them up in the water, must be, well, certainly wealthy and maybe even gentry!

'Oh,' Ling stammered. 'Oh, why, thank you so much, ma'am, for helping us. It was so good of you. We're really grateful.'

'Not at all. Physical exercise is so important. Get yourselves thoroughly dry. You don't want to catch a chill.'

Back in the cubicle, they vigorously rubbed each other dry. They felt bold and invigorated by their adventure, and they had learnt to swim! Well, almost! What a tale they would have to relate to their parents and their friends, and Ling couldn't wait to tell Barney all about it! They spent some time in the town, gazing in shop windows at beautiful objects they could never afford, but all too soon, it was time to make their way back to the station, for they must not miss the evening train back up to Princetown.

As they crossed the station foyer, Ling's attention was drawn by a finely dressed lady who was addressing the man in the ticket office in a high and imperious voice.

'Do make sure you reserve our seats in first class, my man, or you'll have me to answer to! I have no intention of standing all the way to London!'

'I assure you, Mrs Franfield, that all will be in order. I shall take care of it personally.'

Ling stopped dead in her tracks, her mouth instantly dry. She hardly thought of Elliott nowadays, and now here she was — face to face as the woman turned round — with his mother. She looked into Mrs Franfield's eyes, a totally different shape from Elliott's but coloured the same green-hued blue.

There was no time to consider as the memory of the exquisite, dreamlike hours she had spent with Elliott flashed across her mind. Her heart rose on the crest of some reckless hope, bearing her along on a tide of confusion which was stronger and greater than she was. She didn't flinch as she stood squarely in front of the startled woman. 'Please forgive me, ma'am,' she said boldly, though with a little dip of her knees, 'but are you Mrs Franfield? Elliott's mother?'

The expression on the elegant, sophisticated face turned from surprise to disapproval, and the woman nodded cautiously, her eyes cold. But Ling would not be daunted.

'I'm so pleased to make your acquaintance,' she smiled politely.

Mrs Franfield's head seemed to retract into her neck as she glanced at Ling with utter disdain, but Ling determinedly held her gaze, glad that her height allowed her to look down into the woman's face. She was as good a human being as anyone, and after a few moments her tenacity was rewarded with a questioning frown.

A kernel of hope took seed in Ling's breast. 'I'm Heather Southcott,' she announced confidently. 'I met your son at the opening of the Princetown Railway. Perhaps he mentioned me? I had a . . . a little accident, and he took care of me.'

Her words had trailed off under the woman's frozen stare. 'I'm sorry, child,' Elliott's mother spoke at last. 'I vaguely remember my son going to witness the event, but only because he did not have the courtesy to return in time for dinner. We were entertaining distinguished guests and I had specifically requested his presence. And Elliott's always helping people, so I'm afraid you are merely one of many.'

One of many. The phrase echoed in Ling's skull. But surely not! If that was so, Elliott would hardly have spent the entire day and evening with her! And it was not every day you rescued someone from beneath the wheels of a steam-engine! Elliott himself must remember, even if his mother did not — or *would* not — recall the event.

'Nevertheless, I'm surprised he did not mention it,' she continued stubbornly, ignoring the irritation on the woman's face. 'And I should be pleased to know how he is progressing in London. I am a schoolteacher, you see.' Well, she had to make an impression in *some* way, didn't she? 'So I should be eager to have some first-hand knowledge of the capital to relate to my pupils. Perhaps you would be kind enough to tell Elliott that I should be delighted to receive some correspondence from him? Anything addressed to the school at Foggintor will reach me.'

'All right, child.' Mrs Franfield forced a smile to her frosty lips. 'I shall be travelling to London next week to ensure my son's lodgings are satisfactory, and I shall make a point of passing on your message. Now, if you would excuse me . . .'

'Thank you so much, Mrs Franfield! And I'm so sorry to have kept you.'

Constance Franfield dipped her head as she swept out of the station. She had no intention of speaking to Elliott about the brazen little trollop, but she had had to say something to get rid of her! Persistent monkey! It was bad enough Elliott wanting to become a doctor in the first place. It was only her husband who had managed to persuade her that it was a respectable profession. That if they agreed to his training in London, he would hopefully remain in the capital and become physician to people of class and influence. She certainly didn't want him fraternising with the likes of that hussy who had publicly accosted her at the station!

Whatever next?

CHAPTER NINE

It seemed that Christmas Day was upon them before they knew it, and Ling stepped outside her parents' cottage on Barney's arm. It was a beautiful frosty morning, the sun twinkling on the icy crystals that encrusted the grass crunching beneath their feet as they walked the few yards to the little chapel-cum-school. Ling glanced up at Barney and felt the peace settle in her breast as he returned her smile.

Everyone was cramming into the small building that rang with yuletide greetings, and then Mr Warren, the manager of the quarry but who was also the chapel preacher, raised his arms to silence the congregation who swiftly obeyed, giving him their full attention. The service was relatively short, punctuated by voices uplifted in song as carols were rendered with happy gusto, and the sermon was as bright and optimistic as the sunshine outside.

There was a queue to leave, people pausing to shake Mr Warren's hand and wishing each other a merry Christmas. When Ling finally emerged into the stingingly cold air, she saw that Seth and Rose Warrington were there, handing an apple and an orange to each child, and pressing what Ling assumed to be a coin into every adult's hand. Ling smiled to herself. It was typical of the lovely Mrs Warrington, and though there might have been those who would refuse her charity, her overwhelming charm prevented it. She had not been born to riches, and simply wanted to share her present wealth with people less fortunate than herself.

'Ah, Ling! Merry Christmas, my dear! We have something special for you.' And she handed Ling a small package.

'Why, thank you, Mrs Warrington! And Mr Warrington.'

'I hope you like it,' he said quietly. 'Rose chose it especially for you.'

'It's very good of you both.'

'Well, you deserve it. And it gives my wife such pleasure to help others. We're off to the powder mills next.'

Ling nodded appreciatively, and then had to move along as the rest of the congregation spilled from the chapel. She couldn't wait to open her present which felt suspiciously like a book, and as soon as they were back inside the cottage, she carefully unwrapped it. An anthology of poetry!

'Very nice, dear,' her mother nodded, 'but could you see to the vegetables? And Fanny, set the table, please.'

Ling raised her eyebrows, catching her sigh in mid-breath. Never mind. She could have a good read later. After all, the book was hers for ever, the first she had ever owned. Oh, Mr and Mrs Warrington, thank you so much!

When dinner was over — goose adorned with vegetables from Arthur's garden, followed by a small plum pudding — and the dishes had been washed and stowed away, it was time to exchange the gifts their shallow pockets permitted. Barney had eaten with them, and Ling noticed him lower his eyes to the tiny parcel in his hands that was wrapped in brown paper and tied with string.

'I'm sorry tidd'n much,' he said sheepishly. 'But we'm only just catching up from when I couldn't work cuz of my arm.'

'Well, at least it healed properly and that's the most important thing.' Her mouth moved into a soft, compassionate smile and Barney wondered why he had been so worried. But then, it wasn't the only thing he was ashamed about.

That little secret still niggled at the back of his mind. He wanted to make it up to Ling, and the ribbon he had bought for her hair hardly came near the mark.

'Oh, it's beautiful, Barney, and such a lovely colour! Thank you so much!' She reached up, placing a kiss on his cheek, and he felt himself flush. 'And can I read a poem to you all, now?' she asked excitedly.

'Of course,' Arthur answered, sitting himself down like a dignitary at some official event so that the rest of the family followed suit.

Ling chose a short verse by someone called Keats — whoever he was, her audience thought. She read it with such feeling, the words so beautiful and evocative that they brought a lump to her own throat so that she struggled to finish her moving rendition. She glanced at the bemused faces watching her, Fanny's eyes wide as if her sister had been speaking in some foreign tongue, and Barney frowning quizzically.

'Very good, I'm sure,' Mary smiled indulgently at her daughter. 'Now, what games shall we play?'

It was only Arthur who sat for some moments, slowly moving his head up and down in appreciation as the words settled in his brain. Yes. This elder child of his was special. He had known it the minute she had come into the world.

'I'd best be getting home,' Barney announced reluctantly when the day was finally over. 'Thank you so much for such a lovely day, Mrs Southcott, Mr Southcott.'

'You'm welcome, lad.'

Barney rammed his cap on his head and grasped his coat, Ling following him to the door. She shivered on the threshold as the cold night air caught in her lungs. The frosty stillness was almost tangible, and she glanced up at the bright full moon that scattered a silvery dust over the frozen earth.

'Good night, Ling.'

Barney's voice was husky as he brought his lips softly against hers in a lingering kiss that tumbled down her spine. Her eyes rested on his face as he drew away, and then he was waving at her as he hurried down the path.

Back inside, Fanny had gone up to bed and Arthur and Mary followed shortly afterwards. Ling sat for a while, contemplating the glowing embers in the range whose door she had opened to allow its warmth to reach into the room. She languidly picked up the little tome of verse and by the flickering light of the last red festive candle, feasted on two more poems, the inspiring, spiritual images lifting her soul to sublime heights.

She sat back with a rueful sigh. There was something more out there, something great and elusive she had the passion but not the means to attain. It had been a pleasant Christmas Day, another year of her life ticked off the list.

It would have been nice if she had received a card from Elliott Franfield. He knew where to send one, but he had chosen not to. He had probably never even thought of her, and never would.

CHAPTER TEN

'Well, since you ask, Barney lad, I won't answer you with a lie.' Mr Warren frowned at the apprentice over the top of his spectacles since he had not expected a question in his role of preacher. 'Provided they have their parents' consent, a lad can marry at fourteen and a cheel at twelve, although she cannot have physical relations until she is thirteen. That is the law. However,' and here he abruptly got to his feet, his fingers taking a tight hold on his coat lapels as if to emphasise his disapproval, 'there are those who exploit the law for their own despicable purposes, while people like Mr and Mrs Warrington are campaigning to have the Age of Consent raised to sixteen. In the meantime, all decent, God-fearing preachers try to discourage marriage under that age. If, as I assume, your intentions are to be made known to Arthur Southcott regarding his elder daughter, I should advise you to wait until her birthday, even if it is not legally necessary.'

Barney had been listening intently and now he nodded wisely. 'Thank you, Mr Warren, sir. 'Tis good advice.'

'Mr Southcott may not give his consent, of course. Or he may want you to wait until you have completed your apprenticeship and can afford to rent one of the empty cottages.'

'Well, I'm hoping us can live wi' Ling's parents for a while, until I'm established.' And seeing the misgiving that clouded Mr Warren's face, Barney went on earnestly, 'I'll really work hard for her, I love her that much.'

'I'm sure you will. But remember, love doesn't put food on your plate.'

'No, I realise that, Mr Warren.'

'Well, think on what I've said, lad.'

'I will. And thank you again for your help.'

Mr Warren resumed his seat, his lips pursed against his joined forefingers. A good fellow was Barney Mayhew, and it was clear he was passionately in love with Ling Southcott. And who could wonder at it? A lovely girl she was. And Barney was solid and reliable. But would that be enough for *her*?

The preacher sat back in his chair with a sigh. Only time would tell.

* * *

'Good afternoon, children.'

'Good arternoon, Miss Southcott.'

With a flurry of release, the band of children including Fanny escaped out into the May sunshine. Ling watched them leave, shaking her head with a half-amused, half-exasperated smile. A quiet excitement was brewing inside her as not only was it the first truly warm day that year, but she also had another reason to celebrate.

'Off you go, then, Ling. You go and enjoy your birthday. I'll finish up here.'

'Thank you, Mr Norrish.' And as she failed to suppress the skip in her step, the straw hat she had clamped on her bouncing curls sprang off again. She retrieved it from the floor but could not be bothered to try fixing it to her head a second time, and so danced outside, dangling the headgear by its ribbons. She was surprised to see Mrs Warrington's smart pony and governess cart there as the generous lady hadn't come to the school which was the usual object of her visits.

Ling hurried home and to her amazement, there was Rose sitting on the rustic settle, as elegant as ever in a sensible yet splendid day-dress and fashionable matching hat. And yet the poor woman looked ghastly.

'Oh, dear, is anything the matter?' Ling burst out.

Both Mary Southcott and Rose Warrington turned their surprised faces on her. Ling's mother glanced from her visitor to her daughter and back again, clearly not sure if she should speak before her distinguished guest did, but Rose's lips stretched in a warm smile.

'No, my dear. I simply came to wish you a happy birthday.'

Ling's forehead puckered. 'Well, thank you, Mrs Warrington. But you look dreadful, if you don't mind my saying so.'

'Ah.' There was a sparkle in Rose's violet-blue eyes as she spoke and her pale cheeks coloured. 'There's a good reason for that. But it's happy news. After all this time, all these years, I'm . . .' She drew in her lips, hunching her shoulders as if entering into some great conspiracy as she whispered, 'I'm with child.'

'Oh, how wonderful!' Ling shrieked with glee, and ignoring the restraint she should have shown given their differing stations in life, she hugged Rose tightly. 'You must be delighted!'

'We certainly are, even if I am feeling somewhat queasy.' Rose's face lengthened in a mock grimace, but then she took Ling's hands earnestly. 'Do sit down, Ling, as this has brought about something that concerns you. In fact, I've been thinking about it for some time, and this has given me a good excuse.'

Ling blinked at her, tipping her head to one side, and saw her mother nod.

'You sit down here, cheel,' Mary said quietly, getting up from the chair she had pulled out from the table, 'and I'll make some tea.'

Ling obediently sat down, perching on the edge as Rose's words had sparked some flame inside her. Her heart had begun to trip nervously and her hazel eyes had opened wide as she concentrated on Rose's face.

'Well, as I said,' Rose began afresh, 'I've been thinking about it for some time. I've never had a lady's maid and companion. But now, with the child on the way, it would be an ideal opportunity to engage such a person. Someone who could help to look after the baby as well when the time comes. And I can't think of anyone I'd like better than yourself.'

Ling's jaw fell open in amazement. She was stunned, and a hundred thoughts chased each other round in her brain until she could make no sense of any of them.

'Oh . . . er . . . But I know so little about children.'

'You teach them every day,' Rose reasoned.

'Children, not babies. I'd be no use as a nanny.'

'Oh, Florrie will be our nanny, just as she was mine. You can learn from her. Only she's not as young as she was, so she'll need help. But as much as anything, I'd like you to keep me company when Seth's away. He often has to go to London on business. I usually go with him, but I won't be able to once the baby's born. And I have to oversee the horses. You know we breed them, only in a small way, mind. So an extra pair of hands would really come in useful. Oh, do say yes, Ling!'

Ling shook her head as the enormity of the proposition swamped her, but a bud of joy was unfolding in her heart. To live at Fencott Place, be part of the stunning Mrs Warrington's daily round, and yet not be far from her family, why, such a dream had never conjured itself in her mind.

'What about the school?' she asked as she returned to her senses. 'I can't let Mr Norrish or the children down.'

'All taken care of. I spoke to Mr Norrish last week. You know his daughter was walking out with one of the Civil Guards at the prison? Well, he's been posted elsewhere, and so she'd like to take your place, to keep her mind off things so to speak.'

Rose paused, her eyes boring into Ling's with crystal brilliance. Ling sucked in her lips as if to contain the exhilaration that bubbled up within her.

'Oh, Mother, what do you think? Could you manage without me? The laundry and everything? And what about Fanny?'

'You can visit your family every week,' Rose was telling her, 'and I'll give you a good wage as well as providing your keep.'

'Oh!' Ling burst into a rapturous smile. 'You seem to have thought of everything!' she laughed aloud now. 'And what will Father say?'

'I'm certain he'll agree,' her mother replied, her own face aglow with pride for this wonderful daughter of hers. Arthur had always said there was something special about her, something that Mrs Warrington also recognised, and now a new world was opening up to her because of it.

* * *

Barney had washed, scrubbing his fingernails until they were as clean as a dandy's, and his face stung from the vicious assault he had made on it with soap and water. He donned a clean shirt and his Sunday suit, and then, smoothing his thick hair and pulling his better cap down over it, strode towards Ling's home, his chest swelled with the jubilant anticipation of asking for her hand. They probably wouldn't marry for another few years, but at least they would be *promised*, and that was all he asked.

The chatter of happy voices reached him through the open door as he came up the garden path. He would hopefully find the opportunity to take Ling's father aside to ask his permission, which he would surely grant at once. And then later, he would suggest that he and Ling take a romantic stroll in the balmy spring evening, and he would pop the question as they watched the gilded sun sinking over the moor.

'Barney!'

Ling waltzed outside to greet him, her face radiant and her eyes almost translucent with joy. Barney had never seen her look so beautiful, and his heart lurched.

'Happy Birthday, my darling,' he mumbled so breathlessly that she didn't even hear him.

'See, Barney, Mrs Warrington's here!' Ling grinned exuberantly as they went inside.

'Barney, son.' Arthur, still in his working clothes, nodded gravely, making Barney feel uneasy.

'Mrs Warrington.' Barney bowed his head cautiously. The woman had always expressed a fondness for Ling but why was she in the Southcott's home?

'Ling has some news, Barney,' Arthur announced, and from the expression in his merry eyes, the boy knew that, whatever it was, it pleased Ling's father immensely. 'But I expect she'd like to tell you herself.'

Barney took in Ling's elated face, and his heart began to beat faster. His own jubilation was instinctively dampened, and his mouth suddenly felt dry. He knew what Ling was going to say before she even opened her mouth.

'Mrs Warrington has asked me to go and work for her. As her companion!' she cried triumphantly, since Rose had sworn her and Mary to secrecy regarding the baby.

Barney was poleaxed. Ling. *His* Ling. His girl, his *wife*, to be spirited away from him, and they all looked so bloody *delighted* about it! The room seemed to spin, and he had to take a staggering step sideways to keep his balance.

'Congratulations.' He was amazed to recognise that the flat voice that spoke was his own. It was all he could do to stay standing as Ling hopped across to him, her face alight and exultant. 'Happy birthday.' The strange voice spoke again and his hand held out the tiny package containing his present to her.

Ling drew in a gasp as she opened the little brooch, and a spark twinkled in the blackness of Barney's soul.

'Oh, thank you, Barney! It's lovely! I shall wear it always!'

She reached up to plant a kiss on his cheek, and then she was away, the brooch he was paying off at a hard-earned penny a week for the next two months pinned to the bodice of her dress, but forgotten as she chatted merrily to her family.

'Now I really must go,' Rose declared at length, 'or Seth will be starting to worry.'

There were farewells and thanks all round, and Ling felt it right and proper that she should accompany her new employer to where the pony and trap was waiting. Barney had been slowly returning to his senses, and now he shot out of the door after them. He'd bloody well assert himself in whatever way he could, and tell that jumped-up woman that she couldn't just come breezing in, destroying people's lives like that!

The pony and trap, however, was already disappearing along the track and Barney's face was set in a mutinous scowl as he came up behind Ling as she waved to Rose's back.

'Isn't it wonderful?' Ling turned to face him, her eyes gleaming, and his heart ripped. It must have shown, for her eyebrows dipped questioningly. 'What's the matter, Barney?'

'I were going to ask you to marry me,' he blurted out at once, his voice tight. 'This evening. On your birthday. I'd been planning it for months, and now—'

'Oh, Barney.' Her words were soft and her eyes stared into his with infinite compassion as she cupped his cheek in her hand. 'Of course I'll marry you. In a few years' time. But this is a unique opportunity. Surely you don't begrudge it me? I'll only be a few miles away, and we'll see each other often. And I will marry you,' she repeated, her brow knitted earnestly. 'One day, I promise.'

Her eyes were gentle, appealing, wide with honesty. Oh, yes, she meant it *now*, Barney knew that. But he remembered how it had been when she had met that Elliott Franfield last summer. It had taken her weeks, months, to settle down after that one day in more elevated company. So God knew what she'd be like after *years* living with Mr and Mrs High and Mighty Warrington!

CHAPTER ELEVEN

Ling paused by the wide gateway and attempted to calm the anticipation that frothed inside her. She had passed Fencott Place so many times on walks across the lonely moor, never dreaming that the grand building would one day become her home. She had never even stepped inside the manager's house at the quarry, and now she was to live in what to her seemed like a palace.

It might have appeared incongruous to find such a fine house so isolated on the moor, but Ling knew that it had been built at the very end of the previous century by one of several affluent gentlemen who had shared the famous Sir Thomas Tyrwhitt's dream of improving the land and cultivating that part of the moor. Fencott Place had even outshone Sir Thomas's Tor Royal, but when the entire project had collapsed and Sir Thomas had nevertheless kept up Tor Royal, all the other pioneers, including the owner of Fencott Place, had sold their holdings to men who knew that rearing sheep and cattle was the best use of the high moor. The properties and the acreage that came with them were leasehold but with extremely long leases, and Fencott Place was by far the most magnificent of them all. And now Mr and

Mrs Warrington bred horses on their enclosed fields that had originally been earmarked for cultivation.

The long walk on the warm June afternoon had allowed Ling time to meditate quietly on the new direction her life was taking. And now, as she walked steadfastly up the drive, her feet crunching on the gravel, she was bursting with expectation.

She rang the bell and waited under the pillared portico. It seemed only seconds before the right-hand side of the double door was opened and a neatly-dressed girl, several years her senior, smiled at her in welcome.

'You'm Miss Southcott, bain't you? I's Daisy. Parlour maid. Kitchen maid. Well, anything maid, really. Us just all pitches in together. 'Tis how Mistress Rose and Mr Seth likes it. And you wouldn't find many masters and mistresses wanting to be called like that, neither. Oh, what must you think of me, keeping you on the doorstep, like? Come on in, and I'll tell the mistress you'm yere.'

Ling stepped inside the spacious hall, waiting while the older girl bustled off through an adjoining door, and Ling was glad of the few moments alone to swallow down her excitement at being inside this lovely, substantial house. The hall alone was three times the size of her parents' humble cottage and was two storeys high. Light flooded in through tall casement windows and an ornate staircase swept up to a galleried landing.

The door Daisy had entered was opened again, and a flurry of leaping fur and claws clicking on the polished floorboards preceded the rustle of swishing hems as Rose hurried forward to greet Ling like a long-lost cousin. There seemed to be dogs everywhere, almost knocking Ling over as they bounced around her knees and their rough tongues sought out her hands.

'Dogs, *down*!' Rose ordered, trying to dampen the huge grin on her face. 'They won't hurt you, but sometimes they're too friendly for words. Now then.' She paused for breath, and Ling noticed her cheeks were flushed with pleasure. 'I'll show you the room I've chosen for you. Next door but one to ours. And then I'll show you over the whole house so that you won't get lost.'

Her lavender eyes were dancing as she drew Ling towards the staircase and Ling felt herself whisked up into the whirlwind that her employer created wherever she went. Rose Warrington's contented effervescence was certainly overwhelming!

'You seem a deal brighter, Mrs Warrington, if I may say so,' Ling ventured.

'That's because I'm feeling so much better,' Rose declared as they climbed the stairs. 'The sickness is passing, and Dr Ratcliffe reckons I must be a good three months gone. So the baby should be here about the end of November. Oh, Ling, I just can't wait! And it'll be wonderful to have you here as my friend and companion!'

Ling smiled back. Rose's joy was infectious, driving away the thorn that pricked Ling's heart at the mention of the doctor even if it wasn't the physician Elliott Franfield had studied under. But Ling's fond memory of that afternoon almost a year ago now was gradually fading. Elliott had never called to see if she had recovered from the terrible incident that could so easily have taken both their lives. He had never even responded to the message she had sent to him through his mother. Ah, well. She still had dear Barney, his brooch pinned at her neck every day. And she had this new and exciting adventure to occupy the few years until she felt the time was right for them to marry.

Rose showed her the entire building, and Ling marvelled at everything her eyes feasted upon. Nothing was too fancy or ornate, but the whole place oozed with good taste. Every room was light and airy, and yet none was so large as to feel cold and unwelcoming. To Ling, it was perfect. And most fascinating of all was a flushing lavatory on each floor — the upstairs ones being new, Rose had said — with the most prettily adorned china pans! Certainly a massive step up from the draughty wooden huts that housed the earth-closets on Big Tip!

'Help yourself to any books you'd like to read,' Rose was saying now as she flapped her hand at the bursting shelves in the study. 'No need to ask. And now, come into the kitchen and I'll introduce you to the staff.'

Ling nodded, too dumbfounded to do anything more than smile in amazement. As they approached a door at the rear of the impressive hallway, her senses were assailed by the most unusual, tantalising aroma that at once set her mouth watering. Her nose must have wrinkled as she sniffed the air and Rose chuckled.

'We're having curried mutton as our main course for dinner tonight,' she explained.

Ling frowned. 'Having . . . Pardon, what did you say, Mrs Warrington?'

'Rose, please. Or Mistress Rose if you must. Curried mutton. It's like a stew with lots of different spices. Seth introduced us to it. He was out in India for four years with the cavalry, you see. Cook wasn't keen at first, but Seth won her over and now we all like it. But we can cook something plain for you if you prefer.'

'Oh, no!' And as Rose opened the kitchen door, Ling's nostrils received the full blast of the intriguing smell. 'I can't wait to try it!'

Indeed, she could feel her stomach rumbling as she was greeted by a smiling Cook, another maid by the name of Patsy who seemed as shy as Daisy was talkative, and the homely, grey-haired Florrie Bennett. Ling would have been happy to talk to these friendly, easy-going servants, but Rose whisked her outside. A terrace ran along the back of the house opening onto a splendid garden, but Rose led Ling through a stable yard and out to some walled fields beyond.

'Seth!' she called. 'Seth!'

Ling looked across to where the tall, slender man waved back to them from a couple of fields away. She was about to protest that there was really no need for the master to come over all that way, but just then a colossal black horse thundered across to them and skidded to a halt. Ling's heart leapt into her throat since the beast was so huge and powerful, and she was relieved it was on the opposite side of the wall. But then it pushed its elegant head over the stake and wire fence that topped the stone walling, nuzzling into Rose's shoulder.

'Now, Gospel, this is Ling and you must always be nice to her,' Rose was telling the fearsome animal just as if it was a human being. 'You mustn't be afraid of him, Ling. Now he's seen you with me, he'll recognise you as a friend. Stroke him and let him smell your hand.'

Ling had not expected to come, quite literally, face to face with the fearsome monster on whose back she had so often witnessed Rose charging across the moor. Nevertheless, with Rose beside her, she did as she was instructed. The giant's coat was beautifully warm and soft, glistening in the sunlight, and admiration started to take the place of Ling's fear.

'He's seventeen now, but he's still as lively as ever. All he needs is a little love and understanding, don't you, my darling?' Rose pressed her cheek against the horse's, kissing his nose, and Ling could only smile as she watched them.

'Thinks more of that blessed nag than she does me!'

As he joined them, Seth Warrington's face was lit with a teasing smile and his eyes twinkled mischievously as his arm went about his wife's waist. 'Welcome to Fencott Place,' he said amiably. 'I trust Rose has been taking care of you?'

'Oh, absolutely, sir,' Ling assured him.

'Well, perhaps you'll allow me to show you the horses while madam here goes for her rest. Now, no arguing, Rose! This little one is very precious to us, and if the doctor recommends you put your feet up every afternoon, then that's precisely what you will do!'

Rose pulled a feigned grimace. 'Yes, sir,' she scowled, but then threw up her head with a tinkling laugh before dancing away towards the house. Ling noticed Seth watch her go, his eyes soft with love for his wife and their unborn child. It was so touching that Ling shivered with delight. Oh, she was going to be so happy living here!

'Tansy was our first brood mare.' Seth's voice interrupted her thoughts. 'The bright chestnut. She's an old lady now, but she always was as docile as a lamb. We've bred three foals from her, but she's getting on a bit to have any more. That's the last one over there. Good price he'll fetch with such a mild temperament.'

Ling had begun to relax as she listened to Seth chatting about the horses. She found herself increasingly at ease with the softly spoken, equable master of Fencott Place and he soon gave her a good overall picture of the Warringtons' stud farm.

'I must go back to the house now,' he announced at length. 'I have a pile of paperwork to deal with. I expect Rose has told you the horses are only a small part of our business. Our main interests are in the worldwide investments she inherited. Of course, we have an excellent broker who advises us but I'm going up to London tomorrow for a few days to meet with him, so I need to look at everything first. Come back to the house with me, and I'll introduce you to the groom and the stable lad on the way.'

'Thank you, sir.'

She saw his eyes dart across at her, a little amused, she thought. Seth Warrington was a reserved man, but once you got to know him, he was extremely amicable. The servants clearly loved and respected him as much as they did their impulsive mistress. Seth accompanied Ling into the kitchen — something which would have been out of the question in most grand households! He even checked on the curried mutton simmering on the massive range, and politely asked Patsy if she wouldn't mind bringing a tray of coffee into the study for him.

'Would you like a drink, my dear?' Cook asked Ling when the master had sauntered out of the room. 'What about a nice cold glass of lemonade? I saw you had a few bits and pieces to unpack, so you could take it up to your room if you likes. And when you've done, come down and we'll all have a nice cup of tea together. Florrie'll be awake again then,' she winked, nodding at the elderly woman dozing in the rocking-chair.

Ling simply could not believe her good fortune. Her room was spacious with large casement windows facing south. A plush, square carpet covered most of the gleaming floorboards, there was a marble-topped washstand, a chest of drawers and matching wardrobe, and the bed was so comfortable, lying on it was like floating on a cloud. Ling unpacked her few possessions and then returned to the kitchen where the women were enjoying their afternoon tea before the busy activity of preparing the evening meal. Ling felt so perfectly at home, and then her mistress reappeared after her nap, and the house burst into life again.

'Now then, Ling, we'll take a stroll together,' Rose announced, 'and afterwards you will help me change for dinner. I'm sure that's what companions do, though I've not had one before! You will eat in the dining room with us, of course. Oh, yes!' she grinned as Ling went to protest. 'Florrie always eats with us, and you shall, too!'

And indeed, she did, feeling a little awkward at being served by the two maids she had been chatting with in the kitchen. But there was no standing on ceremony and the atmosphere was perfectly relaxed and natural. Ling felt no embarrassment as Rose explained to her the daunting array of cutlery she was expected to use. The curried mutton was delicious, even if she did have to cool her mouth with several glasses of Cook's lemonade!

'What a pity Seth has to go to London tomorrow,' Rose declared. 'But that's just when I shall be grateful for the extra company.'

'I've got an audience with the Home Secretary,' Seth explained somewhat grimly, and Ling looked up in astonishment. That sounded proper grand, but Seth appeared more exasperated than anything. 'I've been trying to speak with him for years. You know I'm campaigning for an appeal system for convicts? At the moment, once a felon is convicted, that's it. Unless you have someone of remarkable power and influence who can work miracles for you.' He broke off, exchanging wary glances with his wife as if they shared some hidden secret. 'I mean, if someone's guilty of a crime, that's fair enough. They should be punished. But I bet you there's more than one poor devil in there,' and here he paused to wave his fork in the direction of the nearby prison, 'who's innocent and could prove it if given half the chance.'

Ling's curiosity was aroused by the bitter tone in his voice, but just then Cook came in, proudly carrying a sumptuous dessert of meringue layered with cream and fresh strawberries. Ling was sure she had never consumed such a meal, nor been treated so well. Everything felt so right, and she would serve this household with unfailing love and loyalty!

CHAPTER TWELVE

'They're coming! Adam and Becky are coming!'

Ling flicked round her head at Rose's shriek of delight as she read the telegram. It was six weeks since Ling had come to Fencott Place and her life had changed dramatically. Seth had been away twice and without Ling's company, Rose would not have known what to do with herself. They took long, healthy walks across the moor, exercise that Dr Ratcliffe approved of wholeheartedly. On several occasions they had taken the train from Princetown changing at the new station atYelverton for Plymouth where Ling had her first experience of the sea.

Then there were preparations for the baby, a layette to be sewn while Florrie knitted the umpteen blankets, shawls and bonnets that would keep the little one warm through the winter. And, of course, there was Rose's expanding figure to be clothed.

On a more challenging front, national and international matters were topics of conversation at the meal table. Seth taught Ling about stocks and shares, and she helped entertain prospective buyers for the horses. Together with Rose she listened intently to Seth's frustrations over his campaign. In the event, his long-awaited session with the Home Secretary had been restricted to a useless five minutes. He was, however, gathering support, meeting with likeminded, influential people in London, but it was a slow process. There was a daily pile of correspondence from supporters nationwide, and it was Ling's job to open and sort the letters. And now she was to meet Adam and Rebecca Bradley, who she understood were equally as intellectual. Rose had told her that Captain Bradley was a man of both wealth and principle, and while he supported Seth's campaign, they were both also involved in the fight to raise the Age of Consent to sixteen.

'Oh, there's such a lot to do!' Rose cried joyfully. 'We must set to work at once!'

The already bustling household exploded into a frenzy of activity, everyone scurrying about preparing bedrooms, Florrie and Cook busy planning menus, and Rose overseeing the entire operation which was conducted like a military campaign! The Bradley family was travelling by train and would be met at Princetown Station by the Warrington's carriage. On the morning of their arrival, Rose could hardly contain herself and the house erupted in happy chaos. Rebecca Bradley was a pretty, petite woman, Ling considered, several years older than Rose but equally as brimming in vitality. Her husband was perhaps in his mid to late forties, tall and distinguished but with a warm smile that soon set Ling at ease.

Rose asked her to pour the tea that Daisy had carried in on a huge silver tray, and then Ling perched on the edge of her chair, watching to see whose cup needed refilling. Her gaze clashed awkwardly with the dark, almost coal-black eyes of Toby, the eldest of the Bradley children, and they both looked away at once. Although Ling was Rose's companion, she was still a servant, while Toby Bradley's family would *employ* servants, and she must show the young man nothing but deference. He was a handsome lad, but her loyalty to Barney would not allow her to find any other male attractive.

'Oh, look at you two fidgeting away!' Mrs Bradley turned her attention on her younger children who sat like peas in a pod but for a small age difference. 'You're dying to see the horses, aren't you, my lovelies? Why don't all you young people go outside? 'Tis all right, isn't it, Seth?'

'Of course. You wouldn't mind taking them, would you, Ling?'

Ling's mouth dried as she was gripped with a sudden timidity. Young Master Bradley looked no older than herself, but perhaps that was precisely why she felt nervous. She was still trying to find a polite answer when his younger brother and sister shot past her in an eager furore, nearly knocking her over as they rushed towards the open French doors to the garden.

'Slow down!' the captain called after them in vain reprimand as the offenders disappeared from sight. 'Horse mad!' he despaired, though Ling noticed that his mouth was curved in an affectionate smile. 'At least, Charlotte is, and whatever she does, James follows. Keep an eye on them, will you, Toby?'

The adults resumed their animated conversation, unaware of the two adolescents hesitating by the doorway. Ling caught her breath as Toby stood back. Oh, dear. Did he want her to go first? Was that correct? After a moment's reflection, she decided the best thing would be to say a polite thank you and step over the threshold. Well, that seemed to work, thank the Lord. The boy shot her a coy smile, and they found themselves walking towards the stable yard, the two younger children having run on ahead.

Ling waited. But Toby Bradley said nothing. Ling's lips twitched. As a servant and a female at that, surely she should not speak until spoken to, but really, this silence was quite absurd!

'I take it you do not share your brother and sister's passion for horses, Master Bradley?' she ventured.

To her immense relief, he replied with a natural shrug of his shoulders. 'Not exactly. Give me a ship any day.'

She caught the flash of enthusiasm in his voice and felt encouraged. 'It must be in your blood,' she said with a half-smile.

'Oh, no. Father's, well, he's my *step*father. Didn't you know? My real father died before I was born.'

Ling felt her cheeks colour. 'I'm sorry,' she mumbled. 'No one told me.'

But Toby merely raised his dark eyebrows in a good-natured arch. 'No need to be sorry. I couldn't have had a better father. Perhaps it's because I admire him so much, but I've never wanted anything else than to go to sea.'

They had come into the stable yard just in time to see Charlotte and James racing off towards the fields where they knew the horses would be. They evidently knew the way!

'You wouldn't think we had horses at home!' Toby observed. 'Not so many as here, of course. Do you ride, Miss . . . ? What did Uncle Seth say your name is? I apologise, but I didn't catch it.'

Ling's eyes stretched wide. To have this young *gentleman* apologising to *her*! 'Ling,' she told him with a suppressed grin.

'Oh, I say, what's that? It sounds, I don't know, oriental.'

'Not at all!' she laughed easily now. 'Ling's a kind of heather. That's my real name, you see. Heather.'

'Oh, I see! How lovely! Shall we?'

Ling fell into step beside him. She felt more relaxed now in the young man's company. 'So, I imagine you must have sailed with your father quite often?' she prompted him.

'Not that often, actually. He doesn't sail much nowadays. He has too many other business matters to attend to. A pity, though. His seamanship is second to none. Even Uncle Misha still looks up to him, and he's Father's chief master.'

'Misha? Now you're the one with exotic sounding relatives!'

Toby grinned broadly. 'Oh, Uncle Misha really is! I mean, not exotic, but he *is* Russian. I've sailed with him more than I have with Father. On the *Emily*. You see, Father says I must know how to handle a sailing ship first. He's taught me a great deal of the theory and all about navigation. I'm to finish my general education, and then I'm to sail with Uncle Misha for two years. And after that, Father says I can go to naval training college. It's steamships I want to sail, mind. Father owns one, but he refuses to captain it himself. It's sailing he loves.'

Toby's eyes were gleaming and Ling was so pleased she had dared to break the ice. The groom took charge of Charlotte and James, and so Ling and Toby felt able to talk freely as they lounged against the gate to the field where Gospel was kicking up his heels and gambolling in circles more like a spring lamb than the ageing gentleman that he was.

'Still showing off to Tansy!' Ling chuckled. 'I've been here nearly two months and I've already learnt so much about horses. I knew virtually nothing before.'

'And has Uncle Seth told you about his time in India? Fascinating! I'd love to travel. Would you, Ling, if you don't mind me calling you that?'

'Well, I'd never really thought about it. I imagined I should always live on the moor and only ever travel as far as Tavistock once a year for the Goose Fair. But now the railway's come to Princetown, I've been there several times. And Mistress Rose has taken me to Plymouth once or twice on the train, which I'd never expected before. But it must be interesting to travel. I imagine you've been all over the world.'

'Not at all. I've only ever been on short trips. France mainly. And Spain once or twice. I've not been through the Straits of Gibraltar yet. But when I'm fully qualified to master Father's steamship,' he said proudly, 'I shall sail to the West Indies for him, to buy rum and sugar and bananas.'

Ling gave a light-hearted laugh. It appeared that Toby had it all worked out! As well as his shipping line, Captain Bradley owned a wine and spirits merchants, his family's original business, and he was already grooming his elder son in knowledge of the trade. And then there was the huge estate in Herefordshire that he had inherited. Toby oozed devotion as he told Ling about his stepfather and also his mother whom he adored. The family had just come from spending a week at the river port of Morwellham the other side of Tavistock and where Rebecca's father was still Harbour Master. Toby was so interesting that Ling could hardly believe it when Daisy was sent out to fetch them since dinner would be served in an hour and Ling, of course, was required to assist Rose to change.

'Ling, my dear,' Rose almost sang as Ling unhooked the back of her day-dress. 'We're all going to spend a few days at our friends, the Pencarrows, over near Peter Tavy. Richard can't leave the farm, you see, so we always go to them. You'd love Beth, but I thought perhaps you'd like to take the opportunity to go home for a day or two? I know Beth would be delighted to have you, and I'd love to take you with us, but that would be selfish of me. I'm certain you'd rather spend the time with your family. And then there's your young man. There'll be times when the baby comes when I can't spare you, so you ought to make the most of it now.'

Ling stared into her mistress's radiant face. Mistress Rose was being kind and thoughtful, but Ling was astounded and confused by her own reaction. She relished her weekly visits home when she would sit and chat with her mother while Fanny would sidle up to her, thumb plugged in her mouth. When Arthur finished his work at six o'clock, or at noon if it happened to be Saturday, Ling would relate the serious aspects of life at Fencott Place, business matters and the various campaigns the Warringtons were involved in, or Seth's stories of India. Mary and Fanny would listen with mesmerised devotion, hardly understanding a word, while Arthur nodded in comprehension, the only one among them to ask intelligent questions.

And then there was dear Barney. Ling cherished every moment with him, every tender kiss, every strong and protective embrace in his muscled arms. He had just completed his apprenticeship and was beginning to put money aside for the day they would marry. He planned on renting one of the empty cottages, he said, and making her a good quarryman's home, and Ling had no doubt that he would.

But . . . go home for a few *days*? Sleep on the thin straw mattress on the kitchen floor again? It wasn't that she had come to look down on her own kind. They were good, God-fearing people and she loved them with every beat of her steadfast heart. But they had no thought beyond the roof over their heads and the food on their plates. It wasn't their fault. It was what they were conditioned to. Only her father could see beyond the quarry. Not even Barney could understand that there were principles to fight for beyond their own lives. When she thought of the Warringtons and the Bradleys, working tirelessly to help others, of Toby and his desire to see the world, there was no comparison.

She had to stifle her gasp of shame. Yes. She would go home for those few days. It would be wrong of her not to.

But the truth of it was that she didn't want to, and the realisation was crucifying.

CHAPTER THIRTEEN

'And how's my lovely godson, then?'

Rebecca Bradley swept into the nursery and Ling glanced up, her eyes like warm toffee as she played with nine-month-old Henry Warrington. Although a little angel, Hal, as he was known, was into every mischief imaginable. The Bradley family had been due at any minute, and Ling had carried him upstairs to the nursery until the inevitable chaos caused by the visitors' arrival had subsided.

Ling's favourite occupation in the Warrington's employment was caring for baby Hal. She had been working at Fencott Place for well over a year, more as one of the family than a servant. Since the day he had been born, Hal had been the core of his parents' lives, but they also had a business and investments to take care of, and to give Florrie a break, Ling was often left in charge of the little chap. She had been encouraging him to build a tower with some little wooden bricks as they sat opposite each other, cross-legged, on the rug. The boy's face burst into a proud grin when he eventually succeeded in balancing one brick upon another, and clapped his chubby hands in glee.

'Oh, clever boy!' Ling whooped with delight as she heard the noisy advent of the guests down in the hallway.

This would be the fourth occasion on which the Bradleys had come to stay, and each time she and Toby had strengthened their friendship. So that now she looked forward to being in his company with as much eagerness as Seth and Rose anticipated being with Adam and Rebecca.

'Mrs Bradley! How lovely to see you!'

She leapt to her feet and bobbed a curtsy. Rebecca Bradley gave her a vivacious smile and bent to scoop Hal into her arms. He was such a happy soul, surrounded by nothing but love, and opened his mouth in a wide grin, revealing tiny front teeth in his otherwise toothless gums.

'Ling, my dear! You're looking well. And look at *you*, little man! 'Tis so big you've grown since we saw you last!'

Ling had no need to conceal the smile on her lips. She had come to love her employers and their friends as she loved her own family. Later, when Hal had been put down for his afternoon nap with Florrie dozing in the chair beside his cot, Ling was free to join the two families in the drawing room and found herself sitting beside Toby. Her hands were clasped loosely in her lap as she watched Charlotte and James lolling on the floor with the dogs so that she almost jumped when she heard Toby clear his throat.

'Ling, I wonder if you'd mind . . .' he faltered. 'I'd like to talk to you about something.'

Ling stole an inquisitive glance at Toby's dark, earnest eyes. He had grown taller and broader of shoulder in the year they had known each other, and though possessed of a wiry, narrow frame, he was altogether a more mature figure. Ling nodded at him and having politely excused themselves from the adults, Toby offered her his arm and they stepped out onto the terrace. Her fingers rested uneasily in the crook of his elbow. What on earth did he have to say to her that was of such importance? When he finally spoke, his voice was low and solemn.

'Ling, I believe I am in love,' he told her gravely. 'No. I *know* I am.'

Ling almost stopped in her tracks. They had become good friends, but surely she wasn't worthy of such a solemn confidence? Unless . . . Oh, dear Lord, surely he didn't mean *her*?

'Only I don't know how to tell her. It's Chantal, you see. Chantal Pencarrow. You know we've just come from there. You've never met her, but she's . . . Oh, she's so full of life. And she still has this enchanting French accent. Her mother was French, you see, but she died when Chantal was a baby. She lived in France until she was six and then Uncle Richard brought her back to the family home at Peter Tavy. And then Uncle Richard married Auntie Beth, so Chantal has two half-brothers and two half-sisters now.' Toby paused, and when he turned to gaze into Ling's face, she saw his eyes twinkling with stars. 'Chantal's just so beautiful,' he went on, his voice trembling. 'The problem is I become tongue-tied when I'm with her. She's three years older than me, you see, so I'm afraid she'll just look upon me as a silly child. I'm not, though. I've known her for years, and you know, I think I've always loved her.'

Ling's head swam, the paving slabs seeming to waver beneath her feet. What *had* she expected? Toby had never been anything other than a good friend. She was way beneath him, so why for one precious, thrilling moment had she thought he was going to confess that he was in love with *her*? She was overwhelmingly relieved that he hadn't, of course! She was engaged to Barney! But wouldn't her life have changed for ever if she had been free and Toby *had* been in love with her?

'Is there no one else?' she considered sombrely. 'For her, I mean?'

'I believe not.'

'Then . . .' She lifted her eyes to his face, a natural smile on her lips. 'Just be yourself. I'm sure . . . When will you see her again?'

'I don't know. Not until Christmas, I don't suppose.'

'Then write to her. Tell her your feelings for her have grown to more than just affection, and is there any way she might feel the same? Leastways, that's how *I'd* like to hear it.'

'Oh, thank you, Ling! You think she might like me, then?'

'Of course! How could anyone not?'

'Really?' Toby's face was so astonished that Ling couldn't help but chuckle and she watched his expression change to one of relief. 'I feel so much better now. Let's go back inside. And by the way, I've not mentioned my feelings to anyone else. So you won't tell anyone, will you? Not until I know how Chantal feels?'

Ling smiled reassuringly. No. She wouldn't tell a soul. Why should she when it would bring the secret embarrassment of their conversation back to haunt her? She wouldn't have wanted Toby to be in love with her, so how could she possibly have thought he might have been? But it had been the same with Elliott Franfield, hadn't it? They were both so friendly in her company, treating her as an equal. But the truth of it was that she came from a different class.

'Did you see the paper this morning, Adam?' Seth was saying as they reached the drawing room again. 'You know how William Stead purchased that thirteen-year-old girl to show just how easy it is to procure young girls for prostitution?'

Ling caught the wary glance Captain Bradley threw at his younger children at the unmentionable word. They were, though, too young to understand even if they hadn't been so engrossed in playing with the dogs that all conversation was going over their heads. Adam seemed satisfied as he replied, 'He published the results of his investigation in his paper, the *Pall Mall Gazette*, didn't he?'

'And for his trouble, he and five others have been charged with kidnapping a minor and have been committed for trial at the Old Bailey. Oh, it makes my blood boil! The poor man's trying to do some good, to open Parliament's eyes to the appalling situation, and ends up in prison himself.'

Seth Warrington smashed his fist into the arm of the chair and the dull thud brought Ling from her reverie. Normally, she would have been all ears to hear news of the campaign. But just now, she was lost in her own thoughts and wondering about Chantal Pencarrow.

* * *

'No, you stay and enjoy yourself.' Rose nodded vigorously at Ling's surprised face. 'We have to get back to Hal. Poor Florrie will be worn out looking after him all afternoon. But you deserve some time off.'

'And your friends — and one young man in particular, I believe — will be coming along after they finish work, so we insist you stay on. In fact,' Seth added, pressing several coins into Ling's hand, 'that will help you have a really good evening.'

'Why, thank you, sir! I won't be late back and I'm sure Barney will walk me home.'

'Enjoy yourself, then!'

Ling watched, bursting with happiness, as her master and mistress wended their way through the crowds. It was Princetown's annual September fair, and people had come from all the outlying farms. The occasion differed from the August cattle fair, being more of a general celebration. Seth was always on the lookout for good breeding stock in the horse sale, and so Ling had provided company for Rose as they wandered among the booths and stalls and other entertainments. While many farmers, agricultural labourers and off-duty prison warders were able to come to the fair during the day, others such as miners and quarrymen could not join the festivities until later. The revelries therefore extended throughout the evening, when the public houses expected to have one of the best night's business of the year.

Ling found her mother and sister laughing at the Punch and Judy Show, and was proud to be able to treat them to some supper from the money her master had given her. The setting sun was hidden behind a gathering layer of cloud when Mary decided it was time to take Fanny home, and Ling perched on a boulder not far from the station so that she could meet Barney as he walked into Princetown with their friends from Foggintor.

She sat motionless, a smile on her lips as she recalled amusing moments of the day and caught the distant sounds of merriment from the village. She gazed out over the moor, her heart lulled in contentment. She worked for generous, progressive-thinking people, yet her family were nearby and they all lived in one of the most breathtaking, spectacular places on earth: Dartmoor. She had Barney who loved her and who in a few years' time, she would marry. And if she never got to see any of the places she had learned about, that Toby, Mister Seth and the captain had spoken of, well, she couldn't complain.

Way across the moor, the last train of the day was chugging towards Princetown with a fine wisp of smoke trailing from the engine chimney. It looked so tiny from here, like a toy, and yet she knew better than most how monstrously huge it was at close quarters. On a foggy day, the engine would loom out of the ether like some megalithic dragon spitting sparks and flames from the firebox in the cab as it rumbled past and dissipated into thin air again. And yet what pleasure, what freedom, it had brought to the people of the area despite the irony of its chief purpose being to serve the prison. The new station at Yelverton allowed passengers to change onto the main line long before Horrabridge making the journey to Plymouth even quicker. It was to Tavistock, though, that Ling travelled most, taking Fanny to the swimming baths most weeks during the summer on her day off. They frequently met Mrs Penrith there, the lady who had helped them on their very first visit, and they had become good friends.

'Boo!'

Ling started so violently that she slipped from the boulder and onto her feet. She spun on her heel to glare into Barney's grin to the derision of their friends grouped behind him, especially Harry Spence who was almost splitting his sides.

'Oh, very funny!' Ling snapped with a withering glance aimed particularly at Harry.

'Oh, come on, Ling!' Barney's handsome face stretched. 'Where be your sense of humour gone?'

He nudged her playfully in the ribs, his head tipped pleadingly to one side, and Ling felt the irritation slide away.

She could never be cross with Barney for more than a minute, especially when he smiled at her with that warmth in his eyes that was reserved for her alone. After all, he wasn't to know he had intruded into her wistful reverie. And perhaps it was just as well. The sooner she came down to earth and accepted that her destiny lay with Barney, the better.

Her face burst into a broad grin and before Barney knew it, she had pulled his cap down over his eyes and skipped away. A madcap game of cat and mouse ensued, everyone joining in as they made their noisy way into the village. The Prince of Wales was their destination, females being accepted on fair days, and someone struck up a tune on a fiddle. Tables were cleared away to make room, and Ling found herself being whisked around to the lively jigs and reels that were being played. They skipped beneath an archway of arms or made wheels of eight, faces bright and flushed with exertion. Ling was swept up in a whirlpool of exhilaration as merry faces and the vibrant colours of neckties and hair ribbons flashed across her vision.

She was quite out of breath as she gazed into Barney's jubilant face and they broke off for ten minutes to recover. Barney bought her a third glass of still, sharp cider to quench her thirst, and soon they were romping about to the music once more. The blood rushed around her head as she spun in circles, her senses reeling away as Barney's strong hand guided her through the jovial crowd. Another drink, then, the room swimming about her in twirling disarray until she nearly tripped over her own unsteady feet.

'Oh, dear, I'm worn out!' she giggled up at Barney's animated grin.

'And I think 'tis time I walked you home. Some of us has work in the morning. *Proper* work!' he teased.

'Are you suggesting it isn't proper work I do?' she challenged him as he led her out into the balmy darkness of the night.

'No, of course not. But tidd'n the same as quarrying. Oh, Ling.' He stopped, swinging her round towards him.

'When will you leave that place and come to be my wife? I've money enough now.'

Ling held her breath, fighting to concentrate her thoughts. 'No, Barney. Not yet. I'm only seventeen. There's plenty of time. And I enjoy my work so much. But let's not spoil such a lovely evening. I've had such a wonderful time!'

The scowl on Barney's face slackened, and his arm went about her waist as they walked through the centre of Princetown and then took the track out towards Fencott Place. Ling was sure the ground was swaying beneath her feet, and clung onto Barney to stop herself staggering. She felt strange, unbelievably happy as if nothing else mattered, not even the tiny doubt that niggled at the back of her mind.

They left the village behind, and the moor rolled away into the darkness before them. They could not see the ground and when Barney caught his foot in a pothole and measured his length on the hard-packed earth, Ling toppled over with him and they landed in a helpless, mirthful pile. Their faces were so close, and suddenly their laughter faded. Barney's lips brushed lightly against hers, sending that strange, delightful tension down to her stomach. They had kissed many times before, deeply, the soft, moist contact setting every nerve of her being on edge, and Barney had often gently fondled her breast through her clothes, sparking shockwaves down her spine.

But this was different.

Her head whirled dizzily, her hold on reality dropping away as she felt his fingers fumbling with the buttons of her dress. She didn't stop him. His hand was warm and comforting as it slipped beneath her underwear, stroking her naked flesh for the first time.

She held her breath, powerless against this drowning force that erupted inside her as Barney carried her to the seclusion of a gully a little way from the track. He settled her onto the springing heather, his caresses drawing her into some deep chasm. She wanted him to stop, and yet she yearned for him to go on, to take her on this exciting journey.

And when he drew up her skirt, finding the soft, sweet core of her and slipping himself inside, she gasped with the sudden pain and the frenzied desire that tumbled in its wake. She felt Barney's body convulse against hers, and then he pulled away, leaving a tearing fire inside her. She stared at him in the darkness, stunned, aching, confused. And when he gathered her in his arms, she wept against him.

'You'm mine now, my darling,' he whispered lovingly into her hair. And the joy of it trembled in his voice.

CHAPTER FOURTEEN

Seth Warrington's voice was vibrant with triumph as he breezed into the nursery, waving a newspaper in his hand. 'It's going through!' he crowed euphorically. 'The *Criminal Law Amendment Act*! Raising the Age of Consent to sixteen!'

'Oh, my dearest, that's wonderful news!'

Rose turned her vivid smile on her beloved husband. She was sitting with little Hal on her lap, showing him a brightly coloured picture book. The child was attempting to turn the pages himself, his face in a deep study, but the moment he saw his father, his mouth widened in a grin that could melt the coldest heart.

As she folded a pile of freshly laundered napkins, Ling observed the domestic scene as if through a glass screen. She felt truncated from the world, trapped in her own shameful misery. The appalling realisation had slowly crept up on her with the stealth of a cat, and she would have to face up to it soon. The hope that she was mistaken had long ago died. And a glittering tear trickled unheeded down each of her pale cheeks.

The broad smile slipped from Rose's face. 'Ling, my dear, whatever's the matter?'

Her words were so soft that they pricked even more acutely into Ling's heart. She turned her head away, trying to hide her anguish, but her shoulders shook with uncontrolled sobs. Rose quickly stood up and passing Hal into Seth's arms, crossed the room to enfold Ling in her embrace. It was no good fighting back, and the disgrace washed through her in a damning torrent.

'I'm so sorry,' she wept, dragging the sounds from her throat. 'I've let you down. And when you've been so kind, and now . . . Oh, Mistress Rose, I'm . . . I'm pregnant.'

She heard Rose's little intake of breath. Oh, God, what would happen next? They would have to throw her out at once, before she brought ignominy on the household. Dismissed as a whore and a slut.

'Are you sure, dear?' Rose said calmly.

Ling nodded. 'It was . . . the night of the Princetown fair,' she gulped. 'Three months ago. It only happened once, I swear.'

'And I assume it was your young man?'

Ling lifted her head, Rose's tenderness giving her courage. 'Yes. We didn't mean it to happen. It was just that . . . I think we'd both had too much to drink and—'

'Well, child, you're not the first, and you'll not be the last,' she heard her master's voice from the other side of the room. 'And it isn't the end of the world.'

'Seth's right.' Rose bobbed her head vigorously. 'You love each other, don't you? And you're unofficially promised?'

Ling blinked at her, hardly able to believe Rose's composure. Yes. She loved Barney. Of course, she did, or she would never have let it happen. It was just that lately she had thought that perhaps there might be more for her in life than being a poor quarryman's wife for the rest of her days. Oh, how naıve had she been!

'Then you just need to get married as soon as possible. And you can stay on working here for a while yet—'

'Oh, no, I couldn't possibly! People would talk!'

'And when did Rose ever care about what other people think? And look on the bright side. You'll have a bundle of your own like this little tyke to lavish your affections on!'

Seth was chuckling as Hal decided it would be fun to pull at his father's neatly tied stock, and Ling couldn't help but give a watery smile as the fear emptied out of her.

'I shall miss you, mind,' Rose was saying.

Ling averted her eyes. Not as much as she would miss *Rose* — to say nothing of the dreams that had once filled her head.

* * *

Ling broke the news to Barney in a shamefaced rush when she met him after the morning shift. It was a cold, damp, miserable day, and seeing Ling unexpectedly waiting for him had gladdened his heart. But now he all but staggered under the shock. Anyone observing them would have seen them talking earnestly and then Barney crushed Ling to him, lifting her chin to kiss her lightly on the lips. They exchanged a few more words and she shook her head. The few yards to the cottages were quickly covered. Ling hesitated before marching decisively towards her parents' home, while Barney turned for his own humble abode.

'Ling!' Fanny squeaked with glee at seeing her sister.

'Us wasn't expecting you today, cheel! Come and sit down and warm yersel arter that long walk. You must be frozed!'

Ling sat down on the settle next to the range, gratefully holding her hands out to the welcome heat. But it wasn't just the bitter weather that was making her shiver.

'Father'll be back in a minute,' Mary told her as she added a place to the dinner table. ''Tis a nice hot stew and dumplings. Lucky there's plenty in the pot.'

'Thank you, Mother,' Ling murmured absently, biting her lip. For how was she going to tell them?

'Good day, sweetheart! I saw you at the quarry just now, talking to Barney. Couldn't wait for your old father, eh?' Arthur teased as he strode in with a jocular grin. Ling bowed her head as he dropped a kiss on her forehead, and Arthur frowned. 'There's nort wrong, is there, cheel?'

Sweat stung down Ling's spine. Would her parents, loving as they were but staunch Methodists, be as understanding as the Warringtons had been? A savage remorse tore her apart, but at least she and Barney would be happily married before the child was born. There was only one way to do this. She drew herself to her full height, shoulders squared and her chin lifted. 'I'm going to have Barney's child,' she announced bravely. 'We're to be married within the month, or just as soon as the banns can be read. I assume you'll give your consent, Father?'

She was sure the cottage had never been so silent. She saw her mother's hand cover her mouth, while her father blinked at her, a slow swoop and lift of his eyelids. It was Fanny who sidled forward, suddenly shy of this big sister who was the idol of her young life.

'You'm going to have a babby?' she asked curiously, since how these things happened was a mystery to her. 'Can I help look arter it?'

The rapture on Fanny's angelic face melted the ice in Ling's breast, and she caught the smile that crept onto her mother's face.

'Well, at least you'm doing it in the right order, if only just.' Mary embraced her daughter as if welcoming her back into the bosom of her family where, in her opinion, Ling belonged! 'And I'm to be a granmer! Fancy that!'

It was only Arthur who said nothing as they sat down to eat. Ling hardly touched the bowl that her mother put in front of her while Mary and Fanny chatted merrily. What sort of wedding celebration would they have? Would they rent one of the empty cottages now Barney was a fully fledged quarryman? Arthur barely spoke, eating his dinner in pensive silence. As soon as he cleared his dish, he rose to his feet and shrugged back into his old working coat.

'You'm going back to work already?'

'We've just finished drilling the last hole and I want to get the powder in and ready for blasting this arternoon.'

His voice was low and tight as he made for the back door. He hadn't spoken a word to Ling, cutting into her wretchedness as she watched him leave the cottage. She was so proud of her father, not only second in command to the quarry foreman, but also the most experienced and respected 'powder monkey' of all three quarries in the vicinity. Poorly educated, Ling knew he had reached this position by his natural intelligence and determination. There was a special bond between them, one which Ling was not prepared to sacrifice and she shot out of the door after him.

'Father,' she begged miserably. 'I'm so sorry. Please, forgive me. And . . . and you will give your consent, won't you?'

He stopped in his tracks, his back to her for several tense, shattering seconds before he slowly turned round. 'Of course,' he mumbled. 'I've no objections to Barney. But . . .' He paused, his eyes boring into hers. ''Tis not what I wanted for you, cheel. The wife of a quarryman, struggling to make ends meet. I'd hoped that working for the Warringtons, you might have made yersel a better life, found a young man of a higher status. Like that young doctor fellow, remember? Look at you! So clever and beautiful. And now this. 'Tis not what you deserve.'

Ling lowered her eyes, unable to hold his gaze. 'Perhaps it *is*,' she muttered. 'It was my own fault.'

'Well, 'tis too late now. I'll speak to Barney later. And you should go inside. You'll freeze to dead without a coat. And make certain you leave in plenty of time to get back to Fencott Place afore 'tis dark. Assuming they've not thrown you out.'

'No. Not at all. In fact, I'm welcome to stay on as long as I can.'

'Good people, the Warringtons. Now you look arter my grandchild.' And with that, he spun on his heel and strode off towards the quarry.

Ling rubbed her crossed arms on opposite shoulders. Yes, it was bitingly raw and her teeth were chattering. She hurried back inside, and Mary pressed a cup of weak, black tea into her hands. They talked about where she and Barney would live and what they would do for furniture.

Second-hand probably, but perhaps Arthur and Barney could cobble together a table and a couple of chairs using odd bits of wood. Ling inwardly sighed. Yes, her father was right. The struggle had already begun.

She was pulling on her coat ready to leave when the explosion silenced their conversation and their eyes met, wide with dread as the sound rolled away like a distant thunder-clap. It was far too soon. The other workers were still at lunch and there had been no blowing of whistles to clear the area before the fuses were lit.

They stood, frozen like three statues hewn out of ice. A numbing fear spread through Ling's limbs. She . . . must . . . run. But her legs were like lead, immovable. And then she broke free, hurling herself outside like some mad, demented creature and streaked across to the quarry entrance, screaming out to her father as her eyes swooped over the towering rock faces before her.

They caught her up then, the men who knew from experience that something was horribly, unutterably wrong. It was Ambrose Tippet, her father's closest friend, who grasped her arm. He had been working with Arthur on the drill holes all week and knew exactly where he would be.

Ambrose's eyes flashed into Ling's wild, bloodless face. 'Keep her here,' he growled at his son, and scudding across the quarry floor, began to shin expertly up the series of ladders.

Ling watched as if in some horrendous nightmare. And then as reality clawed at her throat, she struggled to escape from Sam's tight hold. The young man was tall and strong, pinning her arms to her sides, but when she sank her teeth deep into his hand, he yelped in pain, releasing his grip so that she plunged forward, stumbling blindly in Ambrose's wake. She could hear Sam hot on her heels as she climbed the ladders like a mountain goat. This was all her fault. Her father had been distracted by her news, not concentrating on his perilous work. And now . . .

She came to the broad ledge, and there was Ambrose kneeling on the exposed rock. He glanced up at her, his face a taut, ghastly mask. She saw then. And as the appalling cry scraped from her lungs, shock seared through her like a burning flame and she shuffled forward and sank onto her knees.

She wasn't sure what she saw first, the raw, scorched, mutilated flesh that until a few moments ago had been strong, dextrous hands, or the shattered wooden swopstick that he would have been using to tamp down the powder in the drill hole. The blast that had thrown Arthur onto his back had driven the stick up through his stomach to . . . to God knew where. His savage, stricken eyes stared at Ling out of his blackened face and he coughed convulsively. A scarlet fountain sprayed from his mouth, smothering his cry of agony, and the horror closed about Ling's chest in a crushing vice.

'Father,' she mouthed, for her voice had no sound. She wanted to take his hand but . . .

'Heather,' he gurgled, the crimson bubbling from his lips. 'Do . . . what's best for *you*. You deserve more than . . .'

He spluttered, choking and gasping. A final breath wheezed frantically into his chest, and as his head sagged back onto Ambrose's arm, Ling watched the life flow out of him. Ambrose's work-worn fingers reached to where Arthur's pulse should have beaten beneath his jaw. And he shook his head.

The unearthly howl that rasped from Ling's lungs reverberated inside the quarry and spiralled upwards, echoing across the moor in a deep, sepulchral lament. Her senses fell away, and it was only Barney's strong arms as he joined them on the ledge that stopped her from dissolving onto the cold, hard granite. There were others about them now, shocked and horrified. And they would decide how best to lower the body to the quarry floor.

Ling glanced down. Her mother was shrieking hysterically, while beside her, Fanny stood like a silent effigy.

Oh, dear God. What had she done? The answer roared back in her ears.

CHAPTER FIFTEEN

They buried him in the traditional quarryman's way.

Mr Warren held a short Methodist gathering in the cramped chapel-cum-school where Arthur had worshipped and Ling had both learnt and taught for so long. It was just for the family and their closest friends, and Mary had agreed to Ling's inviting Mr and Mrs Warrington since Arthur would have liked that, she had sobbed. Only Ling knew how much he would have done.

And then the procession had begun. The bowler hats and black waistcoats, contrasting starkly with the white trousers and gloves, had appeared as if by magic from every male's closet. In time-honoured fashion, every worker and mason from the local quarries assembled in a double column. The coffin was solemnly borne along on the shoulders of the six quarrymen at the rear. At intervals, their six comrades leading the procession would stand back, allowing the mourners to pass between them. When the sad burden finally reached them, they would step forward again to relieve the bearers, and thus each man in his turn was able to perform his sombre duty to the deceased. Hence Arthur Southcott made his final journey alongside the railway to Princetown and the good Christian burial that awaited him at St Michaels's and All Saints.

Mary stumbled along behind the procession supported by Ambrose and his wife, while Sam took kind and gentle care of Fanny who seemed totally bewildered by everything that was happening. Behind them, Ling walked on blindly, not knowing how her feet placed themselves one in front of the other. She had not slept for the three days and nights since Arthur's death, tortured by her sorrow and guilt. Everyone knew how Arthur had died. Only she knew why. Every time she closed her eyes, his blackened face swam before her, his agony and his love for her in his dying moments driving the arrow deeper into her heart.

''Twill do the babby no good if you doesn't get some rest,' Barney had told her anxiously.

Dear Barney. Good and steady, a pillar of strength. She couldn't tell him that he was part of the reason why Arthur had died because it wasn't really true. Her father had lost his concentration for that fatal split second, not noticed whatever it was, a small flint or stray fragment of metal that had slipped into the drill hole and caused the spark as he rammed down the swopstick. He had not noticed because he was thinking about *her*, not Barney. And now he was dead, and it was all her fault. As for the baby, she scarcely cared. If it weren't for the life that was growing inside her, her father would still be alive.

The two miles or so into Princetown seemed to take for ever with the coffin being periodically passed to a new set of shoulders. A train was puffing down from the station, but when the driver saw the funeral cortege, he brought the engine to a respectful halt. So he might, Ling thought bitterly. Without the railway, she would never have met Elliott Franfield, and without that chance encounter, neither she nor her father would ever have considered there could be more to her future than being a poor quarryman's wife. Yes. That was how the dream had started. And this was how it had ended.

No more stupid, selfish aspirations. She must face up to her responsibilities. She had her mother and sister to care for. And soon she would have a husband and a child as well. Look after my grandchild, Arthur had said as he went back to work, a fit and healthy man barely in his forties. She saw his face again as his coffin was lowered into the ground. Smiling at her. Heard his voice. *Look after my grandchild.*

Yes, Father. I know where my duty lies now. I won't let you down this time. I promise.

* * *

She and Barney were married between Christmas and New Year. There were no celebrations. How could there be when the marriage took place in the church where her father's funeral service had been held just a few weeks before? When her father was no longer there to give her away to her new husband? As her employer on the day of Arthur's death, Seth had been asked to take over the role. Rose was there, too, seated by Ling's mother and showing her respect for the unfortunate situation. After the ceremony, everyone was standing awkwardly outside in the churchyard, not quite sure what to do in view of the circumstances, and Ling felt grateful when Seth took command by firmly shaking Barney's hand.

'And may I be permitted to kiss the bride?'

It was the first and only moment when Ling glimpsed at what a bride should really feel on her wedding day. She raised her head to receive Seth's fleeting peck on her cheek, and somehow had the most overwhelming desire to burst into tears.

'And I mustn't forget our wedding present to you.' Seth's light, sensitive voice drove away the damning sensation as he placed an envelope in her hands.

'Never be afraid to come to us if you need to,' Rose added sincerely, and then Mr and Mrs Warrington, no longer Ling's employers, walked down to their waiting carriage and headed home to Fencott Place. The clip-clop of the horses' hooves and the rumble of the wheels grew fainter as the future Ling's life might have held crumbled into dust.

She shivered, and Barney put his arm around her, his shoulders straightened with pride. 'Come along, Mrs Mayhew!' he grinned encouragingly.

Ling forced a smile to her lips as she gazed into her husband's exultant face. Barney had got what he wanted. Not that he would ever have wished for it to have happened in this way. And overnight he had become the breadwinner for not only himself and his new wife, but her mother and sister as well. It wasn't going to be easy, but Barney had never baulked at the sudden, huge responsibility, and Ling blessed him for it.

They turned for home. No one would follow them for five or ten minutes, allowing the newlyweds a little privacy. Ling linked her arm through Barney's and shivered as she kept as close to him as she could.

'That wind's bitter.'

Barney nodded. 'I'm glad I weren't working out in it this arternoon. And the quicker us walks, the warmer we'll be and the sooner we'll be home.'

They hardly spoke, saving their breath to hurry along as fast as they could. But at least it wasn't raining so they were thankful for small mercies. It wasn't unusual for a couple to wed without celebration, since very few could afford to provide such a luxury. So they went straight to the lowly abode where they were to spend their future life together.

'Open it then,' Barney urged as Ling put the envelope Seth had given her on the rustic wooden table.

Ling's mouth firmed to a thin line. The only wedding present she wanted was to have her father back, and no one could give her that. But it was kind of Seth and Rose, especially after all their generosity in the past, and so she carefully opened the envelope.

'Twenty-five pounds,' she mumbled.

'What!' Barney's eyes almost stood out on stalks as he snatched the money from her. 'Half a year's pay, give or take! We could've had some sort o' do arter all!'

The taste of bitterness galvanised Ling's tongue into action. 'Not with my father not cold in his grave, we couldn't!' she snapped, whisking the notes out of Barney's hand. 'And we'll need all this. In case you hadn't noticed, we've four mouths to feed.'

'But what about Fanny?' Barney asked hesitantly. 'She be old enough to go into service now.'

'*Service!*' Ling's eyes glinted like fire. 'I'll not see her in service! Besides, no one would take her on. I know as well as anyone that she's somewhat lacking in wit. And even if they did, she might be, well, taken advantage of. I know it's illegal now below the age of sixteen, thanks to the efforts of people like Mr Warrington, but —'

'Oh, Ling, I didn't mean to upset you!' Barney's forehead folded with remorse. 'I were only thinking of possibilities. Us'll manage, just see if we doesn't. And us'll only use this if us really has to. But we'd better hide it somewheres safe.'

Ling nodded, and then found herself in her husband's embrace, his strong arms soothing her tumbled emotions. She felt all at odds with herself, but at least she knew she could rely on Barney's steadfast strength. She pulled away and began to set the table for tea, burying herself in the practical task and trying to seal her mind to her grief.

'Your father were proud o' you today,' Mary smiled that evening as she took herself upstairs to bed, since Barney was to share Ling's mattress downstairs. They could hardly throw her mother out of the marital bed and expect her to sleep on the floor instead. And of course, Fanny had her small bed upstairs as well, so the cramped kitchen-cum-living-room offered the only solution.

Barney dragged the mattress from its daytime home behind the settle while Ling took the bedding from the cupboard where she stored it each morning. If it had not been for the gale blowing straight in under the two outside doors, it might have been quite cosy, so Barney got down on his hands and knees and stuffed some old newspaper tightly into the gaps. Then he came towards his wife, his eyes flaming with ardour.

'Now then, Mrs Mayhew,' he murmured thickly.

He opened the door to the range firebox and the golden heat flooded into the room. Ling watched as he stripped off his clothes, his stocky build strong and dependable and yet firm of waist. Not the perfect athlete, but familiar and comforting. Her Barney, who had loved her ever since she could remember. Her stomach cramped tightly, not with the excitement of that balmy September evening when her mind had been hazed with alcohol, but with apprehension and regret. This, the act of love between herself and Barney, was what had killed her father. She took no pleasure from it, though Barney's inexperienced body was gentle enough as he satisfied his need. He cuddled her afterwards for a few minutes, but soon he was asleep and breathing deep and heavily.

Ling lay with her eyes refusing to shut, memories of the day, her wedding day, wandering unbidden into her mind. Seth and Rose, how kind they had been. Oh, how she longed to be back at Fencott Place. Fanny, pretty as a picture, and her mother's smile. But what was it she had said? Your father was proud of you today? Should it not have been *would have been* proud? Ling sighed with dejection. Proud? Of what she had done? No. She was ashamed. And she was going to have to live with it for the rest of her days.

* * *

Ling stared at the table her mother had just set for dinner. Since the day her husband had died, Mary had shuffled aimlessly about the cottage like an old woman, unable to perform the merest task and barely uttering a word. This was the first time she had lifted a finger in the home of which she had once been so proud. It was as if her misery had blanked out the person that was Mary Southcott and now she was reaching the other side of her personal hell. Or was she? Ling gulped down her horror as she realised her mother had set five places.

'Mother,' she croaked from her dry throat, 'you've laid for one too many.'

'No, cheel. 'Tis right. You and Barney, Fanny, and me and Arthur.'

Ling felt the ice trickle down her spine. Oh, dear God. Her mother . . . She must find the right words. She took Mary gently by the arm.

'You know,' she faltered, her voice quivering, 'Father's . . . he's not coming back.'

But Mary's face lit up with a serene smile. 'He'll be in later. He just wanted to get that drill hole finished.'

Ling held her breath, pinching her bottom lip between her forefinger and thumb as her heart sickened. 'You just sit down there, nice and warm,' she said tenderly, directing her mother to the settle beside the range. 'Fanny, make some tea, would you?'

But the girl tugged on Ling's sleeve. 'Does she think Father's still alive?' she whispered, her eyes wide with confusion.

Ling studied her sister's appalled expression. She had hardly absorbed the shock of it herself, and now here was Fanny coping with the horrible truth. 'Yes, I think she does,' she answered gravely. 'And I think, for now at least, we must leave her be. It's just her way of being sad. Do you understand, Fanny? Just be nice to her, eh?'

The younger girl frowned, and Ling felt her own heart sigh. What should she do for the best? It had been hard enough explaining to Fanny that their father was gone, but her simple mind had accepted that he had simply gone to heaven. But if Mary was so lost in despair that she was beginning — Ling hardly dared to think it — to lose her mind, Ling wondered how she could cope? She prayed it was just one moment of aberration.

* * *

It wasn't. Over the next few weeks, it seemed that her mother was slowly sinking into a comfortable world of her own, a soothing universe where Arthur still lived and breathed and all was well. Ling couldn't bear to destroy it for her. Surely it was better to leave her mother rocked in a cradle of consolation than to spear her with the brutal truth?

'I'm just going out to meet your father,' Mary announced one miserable evening when rain was lashing against the front of the cottage.

'Oh, no!' Ling chided softly. 'Father wouldn't want you going out in this. No sense in both of you getting soaked.'

She cringed at the pretence on her tongue, and putting her arm about Mary's shoulders, led her back to the rustic settle, something she seemed to be doing several times a day of late.

'Now you get on with knitting this blanket for the baby,' she smiled, placing the long needles and ball of wool in her mother's hands. 'Father'll be back soon.'

She caught the frown on Fanny's face as her sister quizzed her from across the table. Fanny, who had always venerated her elder sibling, was beginning to question her judgement. And perhaps she was right. But what could she do but follow her own instincts? She just prayed that time would heal, and perhaps the arrival of the infant would bring her mother back to reality.

The weeks dragged by. Ling was nearly six months gone now, her swelling stomach inhibiting her movements as she slaved over the laundry tubs. She couldn't let her mother out of her sight, as Mary was forever wandering off 'to meet Arthur'. Ling would lie awake at night, increasingly uncomfortable on the lumpy mattress on the floor. Beside her, Barney was lost in a deep slumber after his hard day's toil at the quarry. She couldn't fault him as a husband, working long hours for extra money. There was demand enough for granite at the moment, but who knew what the future held? Despite the untouched nest-egg, Barney never asked for a few pennies to go for a pint with his mates. Never complained that he was providing not only for his wife, but for her mother and sister as well, and Ling loved him for it. When he made love to her, she allowed him to gently satisfy his lust. It meant nothing to her, the passion swept away. Her joyful love for life had slowly seeped into oblivion, leaving an empty shell, and she only had herself to blame.

'You don't mind if I have a little lie down on your bed, do you, Mother?' she asked wearily one evening when Fanny was already asleep upstairs. 'My back's aching proper badly.'

Mary glanced up meekly from clicking her knitting needles. 'Of course not, cheel. You go on up.'

'You all right?' Barney frowned, and his gaze rested anxiously on the dark smudges beneath his wife's eyes. 'You shouldn't be doing all that washing. I thinks you should stop. Perhaps 'tis time to dip into that money.'

Ling's eyes flashed at him, but the fiery light in them faded almost at once. 'Perhaps,' she mumbled, and plodded up the creaking wooden staircase.

A wild, glacial north-easterly was driving across the open moor and whistling beneath the roof slates. Ling was relieved to take the weight off her feet, but her back was hurting miserably and she'd felt a dull ache in her lower abdomen all afternoon. Barney was right. But at the back of her mind she knew that working intolerably hard was her way of punishing herself for her father's death. But perhaps it was time to put her guilt aside and concentrate on the precious life that would make its appearance in three months' time.

Oh, when would the spring come? It had seemed an interminably long, hard winter with, Ling had read in the paper, soup kitchens opening in Tavistock to feed the growing numbers of unemployed as farmers faced lean times and virtually all the mines that had once peppered the area had closed. She supposed they were lucky that Barney was still working, that they were permitted to harvest peat from the moor for fuel, and that they could supplement their frugal diet with vegetables from the garden and eggs from their hens. But making ends meet was a constant, wearing struggle.

Ling tossed and turned, but she was too cold to settle. The cosy warmth downstairs suddenly seemed overwhelmingly appealing, and perhaps if she put a cushion behind her back she would be much more comfortable.

She stopped dead halfway down the stairs. 'Where's Mother?' she demanded stiffly.

Barney looked up, his eyebrows arched in surprise. 'Went to use the privy.'

'How long ago?'

Even in the dim light from the tallow candles on the table, Ling saw the colour drain from Barney's face. 'I-I'm not certain,' he faltered, his eyes widening. 'I were concentrating on this yere book you gave us.'

They both bolted to the door, grasping their coats as they went, and then struggled across to the little wooden sheds on Big Tip. The biting, arctic gale threatened to have them over, tearing at their clothes and whipping loose strands of Ling's hair about her face. She hardly noticed. All she wanted was to find her mother but she was nowhere to be seen and the row of closets was empty.

Ling's desperate moan was drowned by the howling squall. She turned a full circle, peering out into the pitch darkness and buffeted by the powerful gusts that swept unchecked across the moor. It was only Barney's strong arm about her that stopped her from being blown over.

'Perhaps she called into Widow Rodgers!' he yelled in her ear.

Clinging onto Barney, Ling staggered back towards the cottages, her eyes searching the inky obscurity that enveloped them. But Mary wasn't at her neighbour's. They tried all the other cottages to no avail, a crippling panic gripping Ling's belly more cruelly with every passing second. She chose to ignore it. All that mattered just now was her mother.

People were emerging from their cottages, wrapped up against the bitter, angry wind that swooped around them, for everyone knew how the loss of her husband had turned Mary Southcott's mind. Hurricane lamps swung precariously in the vicious, icy blasts, and strong bodies were bent against the driving force of the storm. All the menfolk, Ambrose, Sam, even Harry Spence who was never known to help anyone but himself, and Mr Warren the manager, were braving the weather to join in the search.

''Tis no place for you out in this,' Barney had stated fiercely, but Ling straightened her back, her mouth set in that mutinous way Barney knew all too well. 'All right,' he conceded through tight lips. 'But you stay next to me.'

She did. They searched along the base of Big Tip in case Mary had lost her way and fallen over the edge, scrambling over the piles of discarded granite by the wavering light from each lamp. When they rounded the far end to comb the other side, they were exposed to the full fury of the gale. It began to rain then, icy shards that drove into their faces like tiny arrows, running down the back of their necks and drenching them to the skin. Not a man gave up as they slipped and slithered over the rocks. Ling clambered on all fours, cursing the sodden hem of her skirt. Her dripping hair was a tangle about her head, lashing into her eyes as she desperately searched the tip of waste rock.

'We'm going to try the quarry!' Ambrose hollered as the rescue party huddled in the shelter of the barn at Eva's Farm. 'She might've gone to look for Arthur there!'

They set off again, battling against the ferocious tempest, most of the men clambering up and around the quarry rim. Down inside the amphitheatre, though, it was eerily calm while the wind raged and roared overhead. Ling stumbled over the treacherous ground, tearing at any stray rock with her bare hands in case her mother might be hidden behind it.

'Listen to me, Ling! She bain't yere!'

It took some moments for her crazed brain to accept Barney's words, and she became aware for the first time of her own exhaustion, the penetrating cold and damp that had frozen her to the marrow and the ache that racked every inch of her body. The men were congregating back at the quarry entrance, and she allowed Barney to half carry her there, since the last vestige of her strength had suddenly drained away.

'We'll start searching the moor.' Mr Warren was issuing instructions as he took charge. 'We'll go towards Princetown, spread out in a line.' He turned towards Ling, his face lurid in the lamplight. 'If we don't find her soon, we'll have to leave it until daybreak.'

A whimper of protest lodged in Ling's throat. But she knew he was right. The men would be dead with fatigue, their loyalty to one of their own pushed beyond endurance.

'And you *must* go home!' Barney insisted, raising his voice. 'If Fanny wakes up, she'll wonder what the hell be going on!'

Fanny! In her frantic anguish, she hadn't thought of Fanny, fast asleep — at least she hoped she still was — in the upstairs room. 'Yes, of course! You go on now!'

She watched the search party go, the maddened wind abating a little now but the darkness so intense the light from the hurricane lamps was soon no more than pinpricks in a coal black void. Ling turned away, groping along the path back to the cottages since it was almost as if her eyes had been put out.

The little room seemed uncannily quiet. She stoked up the range, stripped off her sodden clothes and dressed in some dry ones, ready to go out again at dawn. Weariness clawed at her, but she could not relax, her muscles so tense that every inch of her hurt and each spasm that clenched her stomach was indistinguishable from the rest of her torment. She waited, every minute a tortured eternity. She wanted to crawl away, to hide in some safe and secret hole and wake to find it had all been a horrific nightmare.

There was just a faint glimmer of light in the sky when Barney came in, his shoulders drooping. Ling had drifted into some agonised, twilight sleep, and came to with a start, the memory of the night ripping into her mind.

Barney came towards her, lines of fatigue deep in his young face. 'We found her,' his tired voice grated.

Ling gasped, the relief not quite registering in her brain, but Barney's eyes dropped as he took her hands, and she knew before he spoke. 'She were alive when we found her. Just,' he whispered. 'But you knows how 'twas freezing cold out there. We men, we kept on the move, but she . . . Us tried to revive her but . . . by the time we carried her back, she were gone.'

Ling froze. She was stunned. This wasn't real. It was what she had feared, what she had dreaded, but now it had come, she felt indifferent. Too drained. She stood for a moment like a block of stone, motionless and scarcely breathing. And then the pain that cramped her protruding stomach made her bend double and she lifted her head to stare wide-eyed with shock at her husband.

PART TWO

CHAPTER SIXTEEN

Good Lord! What on earth was that?

Ling jerked in the bed and her ears at once latched on to a low, menacing grumble that rolled, deep-throated, across the moor, echoing lingeringly until it died away with reluctance. Thunder. Ling relaxed with a heavy sigh. She might have known. The still air had been sultry and oppressive throughout the previous day. She had been working in the vegetable garden to help Barney who was obliged to nurture the vegetables in his father's plot as well, seeing as Mr Mayhew senior was as lax in that as in all his other responsibilities. But better that than have her father-in-law give up the rental of his own cottage and move in with Ling and Barney and Fanny, bringing Eleanor and the boys with them! There were plenty of families who lived like sardines in a tin, but Ling felt her parents would turn in their graves if Barney's lackadaisical family ever took over their ordered abode!

Another rumbling peal of thunder crackled ominously across the night, drawing Ling back from her wandering thoughts. The July evening had been so warm and uncomfortable, it had taken her some time to get to sleep. When she had finally drifted off, it had been into a fitful doze and only needed the distant summer storm to disturb her again.

She tried to go back to sleep, but as so often happened if she woke in the small hours, her mind was troubled by her enduring grief over her stillborn child. During the four years since those tragic events, the highlight of her life had been her summertime visits with Fanny to the swimming baths. They had strengthened their friendship with Mrs Penrith, sometimes returning with her to her beautiful house set in magnificent grounds up on Mount Tavy. Mrs Penrith was a rich widow with, sadly, no family of her own. While Ling appreciated the woman's intelligent company — just as she did her occasional visits to Fencott Place where two little girls had added to Seth and Rose's happiness — Fanny lapped up the hot chocolate and other delicacies Mrs Penrith provided. Ling wasn't sure being spoilt was good for Fanny. She had blossomed, becoming almost *too* confident of late, Ling sometimes considered, since her sister still seemed young and naive to her, and had recently taken to disappearing on her own to God knew where. But Ling's protection was tiring. Fanny was almost seventeen, and Ling couldn't keep an eye on her for ever.

She turned over, trying to ignore the vociferous weather that was obviously some way off, but her mind refused to shut down. She had just closed the little school for the summer. Mr Norrish and his family had moved on and Ling had taken over as school mistress, her salary meaning they were relatively well-off, a fact that hadn't escaped the eagle-eyed notice of Barney's family. Fanny kept house, but generally speaking, she was becoming a liability. Though Ling loved her devotedly, she was at her wits' end to know what to do about her. Beautiful, a wisp of a thing like some spirit of the air, she remained slow-witted and vulnerable. It was like having a young child to look out for.

A child. Ah! Ling knotted her lips in rebellion. Wanting to lash out at, well, God knew what. Three times she had appeared to have fallen pregnant since she had lost that first infant. And on each occasion, she had gone through an agonising miscarriage at about thirteen weeks. So that now, whenever her monthly was due, she mentally held her breath. Would she become pregnant once more, only to have her hopes dashed yet again three months later? She almost prayed that her period would arrive on time so that she wouldn't have to repeat the dreadful torment. Besides, if she had a child, she would have to give up her teaching post, and they would be hard pushed to survive on Barney's income alone. She would be forced to return to taking in washing, committed to a life of drudgery. Oh, how different it might have been if she had remained in the Warringtons' employment. And who did she have to blame but herself?

She pressed her hot cheek into the pillow. Oh, she must get some sleep! Although there would be no more school until September, there was much to do during the summer months, pickling and preserving their own produce, or picking wild whortleberries to make into pies and jams, with any left over being sold in Tavistock market. There was peat turf to be cut on the allotted ties towards King Tor, turned and dried, and stored in the 'backs' for winter. Heavy, men's work, but Ling would help where she could. And trapping the multitudes of rabbits that inhabited Big Tip, as they were permitted to do, was far more pleasant in the summer. Rabbit stew was constantly on the menu, and the skins could be sold to Mr Perkins who came once a fortnight to collect them.

And they were lucky that there had been plenty of work at the quarries over the last few years. Pethicks, the owners, were also the main contractors for the London and South Western Railway who had been constructing an alternative track to the one they had shared with the GWR, taking a completely different route between Tavistock and Plymouth. This had required amazing feats of engineering, including a massive viaduct over the northern part of Tavistock. Wherever possible, Pethicks had naturally used their own granite mainly from Swell Tor Quarry which was but ten minutes' walk from Foggintor, so Barney had been in full employment. But the work was completed now and the new line open, and who knew what the future might hold, especially with concrete gradually ousting granite in the building industry?

Another violent crash, this time so much nearer, snapped Ling from her reverie. Barney mumbled his displeasure, and then as a blinding flash scorched through the curtains onto his closed eyelids, followed a second later by the explosion of a thunderclap that rocked the sturdy cottage on its foundations, he sat bolt upright. Almost at once, another bolt of lightning ripped across the sky and the air was torn asunder by a deafening roar that burst in their eardrums and rattled the glass in the open windows.

'Bloody hell,' Barney muttered, leaping from the bed and standing naked by the window as he had discarded his nightshirt earlier because of the heat. The sky lit up like a beacon once again, and for an instant, Ling saw the silhouette of his body, tall but stockier now with his twenty-five years, thirteen of which had known nothing but hard, physical toil. It was strong and dependable, giving her a sense of security, but there was something lacking, she knew, in what she felt. She repaid his support and his love with her own loyalty and affection, giving him the comfort of her own body. But it was a duty not a passion, and she was always relieved when it was over.

'Ling!' Fanny stood in the doorway like a little ghost in her white nightgown and Ling threw back the covers to invite her sister into bed. Fanny dived in beside her, in her panic clearly oblivious to Barney's naked form by the window. Ling saw him reach at once for his underdrawers and trousers which lay on the floor where he had left them, but he need not have worried. Fanny was terrified of storms at the best of times, and this one was phenomenal. It raged over the moor like some demented fury, ferocious and angry, until the rain began to fall, in huge, heavy splashes at first, then gathering force until it plummeted from above in torrential, unstoppable sheets. Ling had to run to fetch a bucket from downstairs as water began to drip through the ceiling, and Barney cursed, something he did more often now, as it meant he would have to search out the leak and repair it. The storm itself was over, leaving the rain which came down in stair-rods.

When dawn finally broke, the sky was slate-grey with dark clouds that still seemed intent upon drowning the world in an apocalyptic deluge. Ling joined her husband by the window, and her heart flipped over as she saw the reason for his grim expression. The summer vegetables had been flattened, and the seedlings of sprouts and cabbage and other winter produce they had planted washed away. The entire crop, and all their hard work, was ruined.

Ling stared over Barney's shoulder on the verge of tears. But then she heard a horrified cry and realised that Widow Rodgers was leaning out of her upstairs window next door, moaning in utter hopelessness as her garden had suffered the same fate. The poor woman had struggled for years, her only income since her husband's death in a quarry accident being from the laundry she took in and her two weekday lodgers. Her elder daughter was now in service and sent home a few coins each week, but the widow's own produce was essential. And now it was gone.

'Don't you worry, Mrs Rodgers,' Ling called out, hoping her voice sounded more cheerful than she felt. 'We'll help you put it back together.'

'Thank you, Ling dear,' the woman sniffed back. 'But I doesn't know as us can.'

In truth, neither did Ling. But if something went wrong, you just had to get on and put it right as best you could, even if it meant your hopes and dreams fell by the wayside. Life had taught Ling that. There was no point, though, doing anything until the rain stopped. They had breakfast and Barney left for work early. He knew it would be all hands to the pumps since the quarries would be flooded and would need to be emptied before work could begin. And as they were only paid by what they produced, rectifying the situation was paramount.

It was well into the morning before the rain eased off. Ling had discovered that it had got into the shed and the chicken feed they had stocked up on recently was so wet it would have to be discarded for fear of developing dangerous mould. And their prize laying hen had drowned. Ling's sole relief was that the pig they were rearing jointly with Mrs Rodgers appeared to be wallowing in the sea of mud that was its pen.

Everyone pulled together. With the men and their apprentice sons at the quarries, the women and younger children were left to clear up the unholy mess the storm had wreaked. Ling and Fanny helped Mrs Rodgers first, rescuing anything that might be salvaged. Exposed root vegetables were re-buried in the swampy earth, and it was prayed swelling onions would not rot in the ground. Stronger seedlings which weren't totally ruined were replanted, though how much hope there was of their surviving, Ling wasn't sure.

By lunch time, Mrs Rodgers's patch had been returned to some semblance of normality, though it was now only half full. Ling's back ached wretchedly. She had been squelching up to her ankles in the mire of well-manured earth that seeped inside her boots, the hem of her skirt was plastered in mud to her knees, and her hands were encrusted with filth. When he returned for the mid-day meal, Barney was dismayed at the sorry state he discovered the women-folk in. But it was the same at every one of the cottages, and Mr Warren, the manager, had apparently offered money to any of the men who would help put his pretty ornamental garden, of which he was so proud, back together that evening.

'Just as well,' Barney grumbled, his mouth full of the cheese and stale bread Mrs Rodgers had offered as a thank you. 'Taken us all morning to pump out the quarry so there's been no work done yet. I'll put in a couple of hours at Mr Warren's precious garden tonight.' And with that, he was gone.

Ling sighed and looked down at her fingers. She had managed to wash off the worst of the mud before she ate, but her nails were still black and probably would remain so for days. The stench of mud had stuck in her nostrils, making her feel sick and she had gagged on every morsel she had forced down her throat. She really didn't feel she could face tackling their own garden, but there was really no alternative.

Her back hurt so much that she winced each time she bent, and her clothes were so dirty and stained, she might just as well kneel in the mud and glutinous muck that stuck to her skin. She sent Fanny inside to wash the vegetables that might be edible. At least that was something Fanny could do unsupervised, and Ling could get on with the miserable task without having to look over her shoulder all the time at Fanny's less than competent efforts in the garden. Ling worked mechanically, deciding on which scrap of vegetation might yet again flourish, and which was beyond saving. She ran the back of her hand across her moist forehead leaving a streak of dirt on her skin. A cup of tea and ten minutes' break would set her up again, and she got to her feet, stretching her back and staggering up to the cottage.

'Fanny, shall we . . . ?'

She broke off as she peered around the open door, not wanting to tread mud inside. The cleaned vegetables sat neatly in bowls on the table, but Fanny was nowhere to be seen.

'Damn you, Fanny Southcott!' Ling mumbled under her breath as she unlaced her boots, pulled off her woollen stockings that were just as filthy, and padded inside in her bare feet. She made her own tea, crashing the kettle onto the hotplate of the range which also required some attention, and sat down at last to sip the hot, soothing liquid while the weariness pulsed down her legs. But there was work to be done, work that must be finished that day as no uprooted plant would survive longer than that. So she went back out to the quagmire, her heart heavier than ever.

She toiled on, her shoulders, every muscle, screaming in protest, only kept going by the camaraderie of her equally distressed neighbours as they called to each other over the stone walls that separated the gardens. But even when she had finished, would it have been worthwhile? She had seen Eleanor earlier that day. The girl had shrugged at the decimated garden her father carelessly tended with Barney's help. She might 'have a go at it' later, she had said unenthusiastically, making Ling's blood boil for she knew her sister-in-law had her eye on the two full wages coming into her brother's household. She and Barney worked so hard, as a result sometimes snapping at each other in exhaustion, and she didn't see why that lazy baggage should take advantage of their back-breaking industry!

'Where the hell have you been?'

Her disgruntled mind was just in the mood for a fight when Fanny arrived at the gate. She felt so betrayed at Fanny's disappearing off without a word that for the first few seconds, she didn't notice that her sister was soaked to the skin, her wet clothes clinging to her elfin frame and her blouse so transparent against her breasts that had it not been for her dripping hair hanging down over them, she would have been quite indecent!

Ling's mouth dropped open in appalled astonishment and she was struggling to take in the fact that the drowned rat before her was actually Fanny, when another figure materialised behind her. A shiver tingled down Ling's spine as she recognised Harry Spence. She hadn't been surprised when a couple of years previously he had left Foggintor after some suspicion over some missing money. Although Barney had helped Mr Warren with the investigation, nothing had ever been proved, and Harry had found employment at the nearby quarry at Merrivale, lodging at one of the local farms. He was said to be doing well for himself. But Ling distrusted him, and when Fanny looked up at him and her face took on a gentle pink glow, Ling felt the ice run through her veins.

'I went down to look at the river,' Fanny bubbled, breathless with excitement and seemingly oblivious to the drenched and revealing state of her apparel. 'You should see it, Ling! The Walkham's burst its banks. I were standing on the bridge and it shook and gave way. I were washed into the water. 'Tweren't like at the baths. I tried to swim but it were all foaming and tossing me about! If 'tweren't for Harry dashing in and saving me, I reckon as I'd have drowned!'

She glanced adoringly at her saviour again, and though Ling could see Harry's clothes were indeed soaked up to his chest, she didn't like the quiet smirk that had crept onto his lips.

'What were you doing by the river?' Ling interrogated him sourly. 'You should have been at work at the quarry.'

'Garden wall were washed away at the back o' the inn and some of us had gone to help. Then I sees Fanny on the bridge and he suddenly collapses. Couldn't leave her to drown now, could I?' He turned to wink at Fanny and then Ling's stomach executed a somersault as he looked back at her with the sly smile of a fox.

'Well, thank you for saving my sister, Mr Spence,' she said tartly, deliberately being formal to distance him from them. 'I suggest you get home now and put on some dry clothes. Come along, Fanny, you must do the same.' And she almost dragged the girl up the path and into the cottage, slamming the door in Harry Spence's face.

'They say Ward Bridge were partly destroyed and all!' Fanny gabbled on as she allowed Ling to strip off her clothes. 'Bridges be broke all over the place, Peter Tavy, Harford, old wooden clams completely washed away. And half of Tavistock be under water, a man on a horse said. He were from the *Gazette*,' she announced proudly. 'Said he'd put it in the paper about Harry rescuing me.'

Ling sucked in her cheeks. Half of Tavistock submerged meant homes, businesses, lives destroyed. But Ling felt sick to the stomach for another reason. Harry Spence was the last person on earth she would have wished for as her gullible sister's saviour!

CHAPTER SEVENTEEN

Ling frowned at the clock as she stirred the stew once again. It was half past six, the evening was beginning to draw in and still there was no sign of Fanny. She had been there when Ling had come back after school was over. The kettle was on the go and Fanny had made her sister sit down with her feet up to drink the welcome cup of tea.

She had smiled gratefully at Fanny as she leant back on the settle and closed her eyes. The warm, crisp smell of fresh ironing soothed her nostrils as she slowly relaxed, only opening her eyes to sip at the scalding tea and then shut them again as she lowered the cup back onto its saucer. She heard Fanny go out, but assumed it was for one of many reasons, to use the privy, check for hens' eggs or take the vegetable peelings out to the pig. It wasn't until a little time had passed that Ling realised Fanny had performed one of her disappearing tricks.

Ling sighed in weary exasperation. She herself had always liked to roam the moor at that age, and Fanny *had* completed all her tasks for the day. The difference was that Ling had always told her parents when and where she was going, she invariably took Fanny with her for company and she had her head screwed on. Fanny, on the other hand, was so innocent and trusting, even though Ling had explained to her the dangers a young girl might face. Fanny had stared at her quite mystified, and Ling had repeated the lesson on numerous occasions, but she still wasn't convinced her younger sister understood her warnings.

She was probably worrying unnecessarily, she told herself as she folded the freshly ironed laundry, placing Fanny's underwear in the drawer. As she did so, her fingers touched something tucked away at the back. It wasn't curiosity that made her investigate, just concern that Fanny had put something in there by mistake which she would later be frantically searching for. But when Ling pulled out several items of jewellery, cheap, shiny things made of paste gems, but which would nevertheless enthral her sister, her chin dropped and she began to shake. For where had Fanny come by them?

She had everything spread out on the table when Fanny waltzed back in, her cheeks flushed. Ling saw her stop short for an instant when her eyes scanned the items, but then she gave that sweet, warm smile of hers, and Ling's head reeled in confusion.

'Mighty pretty, isn't they?' Fanny cooed. 'You can borrow them if you wants.'

Ling bit her lip, caught part way between anger and dismay, and her overwhelming desire to protect this impressionable child she loved so much. 'Where did you get them from?' she asked casually while her heart pounded in her chest. 'You didn't steal them?'

'What?' Fanny's eyes opened wide in horror. 'No! I wouldn't do a thing like that!'

Ling lifted her chin, her eyes hardening as they bore into Fanny's face. 'Then who gave them to you?'

The younger girl's mouth tightened into a pout and she shrugged. 'No one,' she muttered, but her eyes shifted evasively.

'It must have been someone, Fanny. And where have you been? It's starting to get dark.'

'Oh, there's no need to worry about me, I promise. I wouldn't stay out on the moor after dark. 'Tis too dangerous.'

Ling studied her earnest expression for a moment. Perhaps she *was* being overprotective. But there was still the question of the presents. 'Who have you been with, then, Fanny?' she pressed her. 'You should always tell me where you're going, for safety's sake.'

Fanny's eyes at once deepened to a defiant indigo. 'I doesn't have to tell you anything!' she rounded on her sister with a vehemence so uncharacteristic that Ling gasped with shock. 'You'm not my guardian! You've not taken out any legal papers, have you?' she nodded triumphantly. And then Ling's heart ruptured as Fanny's eyes filled with tears and she cried out, 'You cas'n take Mother and Father's place, try as you may! They'm dead, and all that talk of waiting for us in heaven be proper rubbish! We'll never see them again, not ever!'

Ling's courage was ripped into tatters. All this time, Fanny's grief had been secretly fermenting, and Ling's guilt over her parents' deaths erupted inside her like a volcano. She opened her arms with desperate compassion and as Fanny stepped into them, she gently soothed her. Fanny must be seeing someone. Someone who had talked about legal matters for that wasn't something Fanny had thought up herself. Perhaps official guardianship was something Ling should discuss with Seth Warrington. He would know what to do about it. But for now, Fanny needed comforting, not chastising.

'You just be careful, whoever it is,' she muttered into Fanny's ear. She just prayed it wasn't going to lead to trouble.

* * *

'We'm playing euchre tonight, so I need some money,' Barney announced after their meal.

Ling had replaced Fanny's little treasures in the drawer. She needed to think deeply before she told Barney about it. Although she refused to say who her admirer was, Fanny had promised not to wander off on her own again. She would keep near Foggintor, she had stated adamantly, and seemed so content with this compromise that Ling decided with relief it must be someone at the quarry. And since there was no young man there who she would disapprove of as a brother-in-law if it went that far, Ling felt reassured. She was still uneasy, though, and ready to bark at Barney's request.

'Euchre? Again?' she snapped tersely. 'You never used to play for money. And I hope you're not asking me for cash! All mine's gone on housekeeping, so *I* should be asking *you* for some!'

Barney's mouth twisted with embarrassment. 'Father didn't have the money for the rent this week,' he announced sheepishly. 'Their vegetables are running out cuz o' the storm and—'

'Then Eleanor should've got off her backside and replanted like the rest of us did! She may be your sister, but she's a lazy, good-for-nothing slut!'

'Don't call her that,' Barney growled back. 'Besides, Ed's boots had been mended so often they was falling apart and his feet has grown so—'

'And your father's quite capable of earning as much as you! And he'd have a sight more money if he didn't drink and gamble so much, and you're rapidly going the same way!'

Their eyes locked across the room, Ling's jaw set stubbornly while Barney ran his tongue over his top lip.

'They'm still my family, Ling,' he said quietly. 'And we does have that money. I works hard for you, Ling, you knows that. You can relax with a book of an evening, but you knows I cas'n. Doesn't I deserve a game of euchre and a glass of beer with my friends after a hard day's work?'

Ling lowered her eyes. He was right, of course. She hated to argue and Barney knew nothing of the earlier event that had upset her.

'I'm sorry,' she mumbled faintly.

'And I'm sorry you cas'n have a babby,' he whispered back, bending to kiss her tenderly on the lips. 'I knows 'tis at the root of it all. But we'll keep trying, eh? I'll make you happy, Ling, I promise. I loves you so much, I'll do anything, you knows that.'

Ling had to avert her gaze. Yes, she knew he would. But she didn't feel she could ever be truly happy again.

* * *

'Fanny!'

Ling leaped to her feet with a surge of anger as she prepared to give her sister the length of her tongue. Fanny had kept to her word for the past month or so, but today was Saturday. Ling had gone into Tavistock to catch the very last session at the swimming baths before it closed for the winter. Fanny had stayed at home, declaring it was too cold, and being the end of October, she was probably right. Ling almost had the pool to herself, and even the stalwart Mrs Penrith wasn't there. Ling was so quick, she had time to visit the public library and borrow another book.

When she arrived home, Fanny was missing. The girl had eaten lunch with Barney after he had finished work, but he hadn't seen her since. She wouldn't have gone far, though, he said cheerily. But then he didn't know about the little hoard of presents. Ling had kept it to herself since Fanny had been behaving but as time ticked by, she was becoming increasingly worried.

When Fanny appeared in the doorway, the tirade of approbation died on Ling's lips. Fanny resembled a little waif, her shoulders drooping and her blue eyes, far too large for her pinched, heart-shaped face, red-rimmed with tears. Clearly something was horribly wrong, and deep compassion drove the anger from Ling's breast.

'What on earth's the matter?'

She felt herself trembling as she stepped forward. Fanny was in a pitiable state, strands of hair that had come loose from the single plait down her back wild and unkempt about her face. Ling swallowed hard. Oh, no! Surely to God Fanny hadn't been . . . ? Oh, it didn't bear thinking about!

'You've not been attacked?' she blurted out in horror.

Fanny at once reared away, her face taking on a shuttered look. 'Oh, no. Nort like that.'

She pushed past Ling and sat down decisively on the settle. Ling watched her, eyebrows knitted. The worst hadn't happened, but something else had and she felt sick with fear.

Fanny looked up again, this time with her chin tilted defiantly. 'I were only doing the same as you,' she said boldly. 'Only unlike Barney, he won't marry me. I only wanted a home of my own. 'Tis not such a bad thing to want, is it?'

Ling rocked on her feet and staggered forward blindly, somehow finding a chair to sink onto before she collapsed with shock. Fanny was pregnant. Her sweet, innocent little sister was pregnant. Was she sure? Fanny's monthlies weren't monthly at all they were so few and far between, more irregular even than Ling's own erratic cycle. But when Ling thought about it, the only rags to have been boiled up to remove the stains the entire summer had been her own. And she had noticed that Fanny had been putting on a little weight, growing more curvaceous, but Ling had put it down to maturity. Then she thought of the times Fanny had looked pasty first thing in the morning, though that had passed now. Good Lord! She must be, what, four months gone by now. Oh, the stupid little cow! But then Ling bent under the cruel weight of her own shame. She had been guilty of the very same sin, and Fanny had merely followed her example. Only Fanny was too ignorant, too simple, to recognise the difference in their situations. She and Barney had been betrothed. In love. But then she supposed Fanny had believed herself to be in love, and her seducer in love with her. It was clearly far from the truth!

'What's going on? I saw Fanny come back running like the devil hissel' were arter her.'

Ling's eyes swivelled round to meet the anxiety on Barney's face. She wanted to run into the comfort of his arms, but it wouldn't change anything. What had happened couldn't be undone.

'Fanny's having a baby,' she murmured flatly since she couldn't think of any other way to say it.

She saw the blood drain from Barney's weather-browned cheeks. 'What!'

'We shouldn't be cross with her,' Ling said defensively. 'She was copying what we did. She thought . . . you thought he loved you, didn't you, Fanny?' she prompted as Fanny's wide, innocent eyes were moving from one to the other of them as if she was nothing to do with what they were discussing. 'Only he didn't,' Ling concluded briefly. 'And now he won't marry her.'

'Oh, he won't, won't he? We'll soon see about that! So who was it, Fanny? Who be the father?'

Fanny was visibly cowed beneath Barney's threatening attitude, and Ling caught his arm. 'Don't frighten her, Barney. She's frightened enough already.'

But Barney shrugged off Ling's hand. 'Who was it, Fanny?' he repeated.

'He said I weren't to tell,' Fanny sniffled as her tears began afresh. 'He said 'twas our little secret.'

'I bet he bloody did!' Barney cried in a fit of rage. 'Well, there be only one person round yere I knows who be cowardly and devious enough to take advantage of Fanny being so . . . naive, and that be Harry Spence! 'Twas him, weren't it, Fanny?'

But Fanny merely buried her face in her hands.

'Leave her be, Barney. We mustn't blame her.'

'I doesn't! That bloody bastard would've led her on, the filthy varmint! But I'll damned well make sure he pays for it, the low-down scum!' And with that, he spun on his heel and thundered out of the door.

The silence in his wake was heavy and oppressive. Ling felt weak at the knees, the situation raking up all the guilt and pain her own unplanned pregnancy had caused. At least Fanny hadn't been responsible for the tragic deaths of their parents! Ling knelt down in front of Fanny and took her hands.

'Don't worry, little maid. It isn't so bad. We'll sort something out.'

Fanny lifted her tearstained face. 'I'm sorry, Ling. I really believed him. And I didn't like doing . . . you knows. 'Tweren't nice and it hurt. But he said 'twould show I loved 'en. And other than that, he were always so kind to me and he gave me all those pretty things.'

Ling's heart ached as she closed her arms about her sister. How could anyone be so callous as to trick a child like Fanny? She had never liked Harry Spence, for like Barney, she was convinced he was the culprit. He'd always been mean and untrustworthy. It was because of his stupidity that she had nearly been crushed beneath the railway engine. He knew it and yet had always resented Barney telling the truth about it. And it was Barney who had aroused the suspicions about that stolen money. Ling had decided long ago that Harry was jealous of Barney. Was this his twisted way of getting back at him?

When Barney returned, he flung himself onto a chair, resting his elbows on his knees and rubbing his hands over his face before looking up darkly.

'He denies it, of course,' he sighed dejectedly. 'Had the gall to grin at me and say what should I expect with someone as dim-witted as Fanny? I laid him flat cuz o' that, and he still denied it. Says he hasn't seen Fanny since the day of the flood.'

'I hardly think that's true. But I reckon it had already happened by then. I don't suppose she went to look at the river at all. She went to see him. I've no doubt it was brave of him to save her from the water, but it would have suited him, too. Made him a hero in her eyes, and she'll not betray him.'

A resentful grunt escaped Barney's throat. He stood up again and as she was arranging the table, he turned Fanny round to face him, his hands on her shoulders. 'Listen, Fanny. I'm not cross with you. But if you says who the father is, it may be possible to at least get him to take some responsibility for the child.'

Fanny stared up at him, her eyes watery pools. 'I cas'n,' she answered honestly. 'He said he'd kill me.'

Ling watched Barney close his eyes. "'Tis all the answer I needed,' he mumbled.

Ling came up behind him and rested her cheek on his shoulder. 'I wouldn't want Fanny married to a man like that, anyway. Would you? We can take care of her, can't we, and the child? We can't have one of our own, so maybe we should see this as a blessing.'

Barney turned round and encircled her in his strong arms. 'If 'twill make you happy,' he smiled with such ineffable love that she began to cry.

CHAPTER EIGHTEEN

Ling's eyelids flickered open. She had come home for their frugal lunch and had nodded off on the settle by the warmth of the range. She had been dreaming she was walking along some beautiful foreign shore, her bare feet sinking in golden, sun-drenched sand and lapped by gentle, lazy waves. She felt soothed and relaxed, and the reality of the Spartan room and the angry wind that was beginning to tear at the little cottage struck her like a sledgehammer. She was unaware of the wistful sigh that whined from her lungs. She would never visit such exotic climes. That in itself did not bother her. But if she showed Barney photographs of such places in the books she borrowed from the library, describing how she envisaged the images in colour, the sun beating on her shoulders and the smell of the sea and hot sand, he would look at her as if she were crazed. He would shrug, kiss the top of her head, and announce that he was off to play euchre with his mates, taking another shilling from their now sadly depleted nest egg.

She sagged against the back of the settle, wanting to hold on to the comforting dream a little longer. Yet as she observed Fanny through half-shut eyes, it was already slipping away. From behind, her sister was as tiny and ethereal as ever, so that when she turned round to reveal her jutting stomach, it was still quite a shock. Once they had given up on trying to drag the father's identity from her, Fanny had appeared to blossom. In her childlike world, she seemed ignorant of the stigma her illegitimate baby would cause. Here at Foggintor she was one of the fold, nearly everyone feeling protective towards the simple creature they had known since she was a child herself and who had been duped by some callous blackguard.

Ling's lips moved into a bitter line. While Fanny was bearing a child she could well do without, Ling would never know the joys of motherhood herself, and her hopes had withered away, dragging her spirit with it. She would lavish all her love on Fanny's child, but it wouldn't be the same. Somehow she was beginning not to care anymore. Everything was falling apart. Even Barney spent most of his spare time with his male companions nowadays. He worked hard on the orders that came to the quarry, but since the completion of the second Tavistock railway, there was only call for smaller items. Gone were the days when the Dartmoor Quarries had supplied stone for far away London and such structures as Nelson's Column or the Houses of Parliament. Trade trickled on, the quarrymen only just managing to earn an honest crust. Ling couldn't begrudge Barney time relaxing with his friends. He never came home drunk as some husbands did, but she could see their savings rapidly dwindling, not helped by Barney's constantly having to help his father pay his rent. But they were surviving while others in the county starved, so she should be thankful for that. And if her dreams and aspirations had been shattered, she had accepted that years ago.

As Barney came in through the door, a vicious blast of air licked hungrily at whatever it could and tossed the curtains in the air. Barney quickly shut the door, but even then the wind whistled beneath it, and Ling met Barney's gaze as he warmed his hands by the range.

'Food be on the table, Barney,' Fanny smiled proudly. 'And then would you mind if I takes a little rest on your bed?'

'Course not. You goes on up,' Barney mumbled as he sat down at the table. 'That old wind be getting up. Strange when February were so calm and mild. But 'twould seem this month's plunged us back into winter.'

Ling's lips twitched. It was invariably windy up on the exposed ridge where the cottages were situated, and she had other matters on her mind. 'I'm worried about Fanny,' she said, her words low though Fanny was unlikely to hear from upstairs. 'I reckon she's near her time, and she's so big and with her being so small-framed. And, well, I don't think she'll stand the pain. I know what it's like.' She lowered her eyes, her voice petering into a thin trail. 'I've been there myself. But never with a full-term child,' she went on more strongly now. 'And I'm worried it's too big for her. We could end up losing her as well as the baby.'

Barney finished chewing and swallowed, washing down the morsel of food with a swig of lukewarm tea. 'So you wants her to have a doctor for the birth.'

'I think she should see one *now*, before it comes. Being out here, if it comes at night—'

''Twill cost some,' Barney considered.

'I know. But we still have some of that money left.'

Barney looked up sharply. 'But 'tis all we has. I works as hard as I can, you knows that, but trade could easily fall right off and we could have nort coming in for weeks. Us'd be relying on that money to survive.'

'And there'd be a lot more of it left if you weren't for ever paying the rent for that good-for-nothing father of yourn and wasting money on gambling!'

'I doesn't spend that much!' Barney snapped defensively. 'And 'tis my family we're talking about yere!'

'And Fanny's my sister, and it's her *life* that could be at risk! And if it weren't for *my* connections with Mistress Rose, we wouldn't have had that money in the first place!' She shook her head agonisingly as she failed to hold back the words that had been sticking to her tongue for years. 'Much as I love you, Barney, I sometimes wish to God I'd never had to leave the Warringtons and marry you. My life could have been so different and my parents might still have been alive!'

Barney stared at her aghast. His jaw dropped open and then snapped shut again in retaliation. 'Well if you thinks so highly of the great Warringtons, why doesn't you go to them for help now?'

Ling glared at him, fists clenched at her sides. 'I couldn't possibly ask them after all they've done for me in the past! And have you no pride, Barney Mayhew? That money's *mine*, and if I want to spend it on my sister's health, then I will. Besides, if we go to the prison physician, it won't cost as much as getting one from Tavistock.'

'There bain't one at present, at the prison, I means. Medical assistant but no proper doctor as I've yeard tell.'

'Oh.' Ling felt the anger deflate inside her and a niggling concern took its place, her thoughts now occupied with how to *find* a physician, never mind how to pay for one. Perhaps she would have to enlist Rose's help after all.

'Let's not argue, Ling,' Barney begged, taking her hand. 'I's certain there must be an answer. In fact, now don't be angered with me, but, well, what about the workhouse?'

'The workhouse!'

'Why not? 'Tis not like it used to be. There be a special wing for having babbies for girls like Fanny. She don't have no money of her own. And Walkhampton Parish be part of the union, so she qualifies. She'd be well cared for, and if she goes there now, afore the babby comes, 'twould solve the problem of fetching a doctor out yere. Could take hours, and as you say, it could be too late.'

Ling frowned. She didn't like the idea of leaving Fanny all alone in the bleak edifice at the top of Bannawell Street, but everything else Barney had said was undeniably true. 'So how do I get her into the workhouse?' she asked unsurely.

Barney sniffed and shook his head. 'I's not rightly sure. Back along, you had to apply to the Board of Guardians, but that were when 'twas for the able-bodied, I thinks they used to call it, and you had to prove you was destitute and couldn't find work. But nowadays, I believes 'tis mainly for orphans and the old and infirm. And girls like Fanny. A letter from Mr Warren, being our preacher, might help, mind. But I reckon if you takes Fanny there and just leaves her on the doorstep, they'll take her in. Anyways, I must get back to work while I can. 'Tis getting that windy, we might have to stop. Cas'n use the cranes in a gale.'

He pulled on his coat and went back outside, a ferocious gust of air wrenching the door handle from his grip and all but taking the door off its hinges. Ling hardly noticed as she chewed on her fingernail. Barney was right. And though it tore at her heart to do so, she would put the plan into action that very day.

Afternoon school was due to start shortly, so she would have to catch Mr Warren before he, too, went back to work. The quarry manager looked surprised, but he quickly wrote a note, recommending Fanny's case to the workhouse before leaving for the quarry, holding his bowler hat on his head to stop it blowing away. Ling hurried back to the schoolroom, ringing the bell loudly so that children scuttled forth from the cottages, glad to huddle together in the small building. But the wind was moaning menacingly about the solid stone walls and every pair of eyes glanced upwards as a slate was lifted and slithered noisily down the roof to smash on the ground below. No one could concentrate, let alone Ling herself who could only think of Fanny and the daunting prospect of leaving her at the workhouse door.

They hadn't long been back in the classroom before Ling clapped her hands. 'I think you'd best all go home with this weather,' she announced to the delighted children. 'Class dismissed.'

The room emptied in a noisy clatter. Ling would have liked a few silent moments alone to reflect on what she was about to do, but the angry weather put paid to that. So with a determined sigh, she shut up the schoolroom and hastened back home. Fanny was sipping a cup of tea, and Ling's heart clenched at what she felt was a betrayal of her sister's trust.

'Fanny, get your coat, dear. We're going into Tavistock.'

Fanny's blue eyes opened wide. 'Tavistock?'

'Yes. We're going on an adventure,' Ling smiled back, cringing at the falsehood. 'We'll get the afternoon train.' She was about to add that there would be just enough time to do their business and catch the last train back up to Princetown, but she bit her tongue, for though *she* would be travelling home, Fanny wouldn't. And while the heavily pregnant girl went in search of the worn coat that bulged open across her stomach, Ling wrote a message for Barney to meet her at the station as she didn't relish the prospect of walking back across the moor alone in what promised to be a wild night. At least her husband's literacy skills were up to reading the brief note, she mused ruefully as she placed it in a prominent position on the table.

Fanny stood before her, expectancy lighting her small face, and Ling all but changed her mind as she tied Fanny's scarf over her battered felt hat. Fanny remained still, like a child gazing up at its mother. A lump swelled in Ling's throat and she forced it down as she prepared herself for the journey.

Outside, the force of the north-easterly nearly had them off their feet as it funnelled down the narrow path between the two stone walls. Fanny giggled aloud, but Ling set her jaw grimly. She wasn't sure she should be doing this, but it was now or never. Another week, another few days even, might be too late.

They struggled past the quarries to the railway line, Fanny's cheeks glowing at what she considered to be tremendous fun while Ling forced a smile to her lips. Then they turned into the wind and it took their breath away. They instinctively leaned forward into this powerful, living being that wanted to play with them like a wilful child tossing about its toys.

Fanny was still laughing, the burden of the unborn infant seemingly not hindering her enjoyment of what she saw as a game. But Ling's eye was on the low, ominous sky, its slate grey clouds tainted with jaundiced sworls that raced furiously overhead. The wind was gaining even more strength, tearing at their clothes as they made slow progress towards the station.

Snow began then, falling as tiny pinpricks that swirled about in agitated flurries but thankfully dissolved on the ground. Ling frowned. Perhaps this wasn't such a good idea after all, but she needed to have Fanny safely in the workhouse as soon as possible. If only she had spoken to Barney earlier. She agreed with him that the Institution was the best solution, but it had never entered her head before. She silently cursed herself, for she knew that at the back of her mind, she had been putting off the conversation, and as a result she now found herself struggling across the moor in a gale with her little sister, close to her time, beside her.

Fanny had become quiet. Fighting against the ferocious wind that moaned uncannily across the open wilderness had soon lost its appeal. Should they turn back? But they were halfway there now, and while the snowflakes were melting on the earth, it made sense to press on.

Ten minutes later, Ling wasn't so sure. The snow was coming down more heavily, spiralling in twisting whirlwinds and settling on the rough grass beside the path. A sudden blast threw Ling sideways and she put out her hands to break her fall. And as she went down, she saw Fanny thump down hard on her bottom.

Pain seared through Ling's wrist, but her thoughts instantly turned back to Fanny, fear churning in the pit of her belly. To her relief, Fanny appeared none the worse, though she glared at Ling as if the storm was all her fault.

'I wants to go home,' she shouted, pouting fiercely and raising her voice to make herself heard above the screaming wind.

Ling shifted herself on the ground. She didn't want Fanny to realise that she herself was worried. 'But we're nearly there, and then we'll be on the train and down in Tavistock before you know it,' she cried, forcing an enthusiastic grin.

'And look how pretty the snow is on the moor. Come along now, Fanny, for *my* sake.'

Fanny reluctantly hauled herself to her feet but staggered backwards as she was caught by another forceful gust. Ling gritted her teeth. Whatever happened, it would surely be better to reach the safety of the station than to tramp back across the moor. The buildings of the yard would have been in sight had the snow not been descending even more thickly, filling the air with feather-light, powdery flakes that were nonetheless driving into their faces like icy needles. It was becoming a nightmare as they stumbled onwards against what was now a raging storm. Ling's wrist was aching mercilessly but she hardly noticed it, so great was her anxiety to reach shelter. The snow was blinding, and she heard rather than saw the huge engine rumble its deafening way past them as it clattered along the home run to the station, and yet its thunderous roar was muffled by the shriek of the gale.

'Come on, Fanny! We must hurry or we'll miss the train!'

They tried to walk faster but it was impossible as the battle drained their strength. The snow was an inch deep on the path now and Ling could feel tears of desperation pricking her eyes. And when the train rattled past them again on its descent, she could have wept. But no matter. The most important thing in her head was to get Fanny into the ladies' waiting room, and then she could think what to do next.

The relief was overwhelming when, ten minutes later, they found Mr Higman, the stationmaster, in his tiny office, huddled by the equally tiny stove. The man was astounded when he glanced up at the tap on his window and he took in the two bedraggled figures, hats awry and so covered in white that they were scarcely recognisable.

'Good Lord! 'Tis Ling and young Fanny if I'm not mistaken. You've missed the train, I'm afeared, if 'tis what you was arter. Now you goes straight along to the waiting room and I'll be there in a minute.'

Those last few steps along the platform where the scornful wind was already driving the powdery snow into little drifts seemed interminable. Ling turned the brass handle of the waiting-room door, forgetting her damaged wrist in her desperation to escape the storm. The heavy door was at once wrenched from her hold, swinging back with a crash, and the agony shot up her arm again like fire. The pain transfixed her for a moment so that it was Fanny who sprang inside first. Ling stumbled across the threshold after her, and between them they managed to heave the door closed.

For several seconds, they simply stood and stared at each other. The deafening roar of the wind was slightly muffled, but still it licked, outraged, around the walls of the small building, seeking a way in at its prey. How safe were they even now? Ling pressed her apprehension to the back of her mind. It wouldn't do to let Fanny see she was still worried. But at that moment, the door flew open again and Mr Higman hurriedly stepped inside.

'What you two doing out in this weather, then? ' he asked, poking the small fire in the grate. 'Been slates coming off roofs and sheets o' corrugated iron thrown about like feathers. Wouldn't surprise me if trees and telegraph poles doesn't come down. 'Tis proper dangerous to be abroad, so it took us right by surprise to see you.'

'I'd never have set out if I'd realised,' Ling told him. 'We'd planned on going into Tavistock and being back on the last train,' she faltered, not mentioning in front of Fanny that she would have been returning alone. 'But now we've missed the train, I don't know what to do.'

Mr Higman rubbed his chin thoughtfully. 'Well, seems to me you'm stuck in this yere waiting room. Unless you takes the mail train. Goes at six thirty-five, but I's sure you knows that. There'll be one carriage. Get down off the moor, and you'll be safely out of the storm.'

Ling glanced across at Fanny. Would that be best for her? If they went into Tavistock, it would be too late to apply officially, but perhaps armed with the letter from Mr Warren and on such a night as this, the workhouse wouldn't leave a heavily pregnant young girl on the doorstep. Ling wouldn't be able to get back, of course, but perhaps she could seek refuge with Mrs Penrith. She was sure the good lady would understand.

She drew Mr Higman aside. 'A return ticket for me, then,' she whispered, pressing the coins into his hand. 'And a single for Fanny. I'm taking her to the workhouse infirmary to have the baby, only I haven't told her yet.'

'Ah,' the older man nodded. 'I understand. I won't let on, I promise.' And with that, he battled back outside.

The door slammed shut behind him, taken by the wind, and uneasiness churned in Ling's belly again. Fanny had settled herself on the bench next to the fire, and Ling sat down beside her with a nervous smile. Fanny didn't appear to have fathomed that once they arrived in Tavistock, they would be stranded, and Ling prayed it wouldn't dawn on her. The storm still raged fiendishly about them, showing no sign of abating. The wind wailed around the building, making the windowpanes rattle in their wooden frames, and Ling was convinced the canopy over the platform would be lifted clean away. The howl of the gale was punctuated with ominous crashes as God alone knew what was happening outside. Ling sat rigid, her eyes riveted on the snow that was blowing in under the door.

She suddenly realised that the sound her ears had begun to concentrate on was not the storm trying desperately to get inside, but a person! She sprang up — her throbbing wrist reminding her to use her other hand this time — and helped whoever it was to open the door. She was met by the back of a short, plump woman struggling courageously to close down her umbrella that had turned completely inside out and was suddenly whipped from her grasp and taken off into the darkness. The woman let out a cry and stamped her foot in anger, but realising there was nothing she could do, bustled her way inside.

'That were my best umbrella,' she grumbled. 'Only brought it cuz I were visiting my sister, and now 'tis gone. Well, I never did see such a night as this. But the train's running, so perhaps we should be grateful for small mercies.'

Ling instantly felt encouraged by the lively little woman's company. She saw her sharp eyes take in Fanny's obvious condition, but she read no disapprobation in them, and soon they fell into an animated conversation on the atrocious weather. The worst the woman had ever seen in her entire life, she declared triumphantly. She introduced herself as Mary Huggins, and then proceeded to chat away nineteen to the dozen so that the time passed more quickly and it didn't seem long before the deep rumble of the engine, vying to be heard above the storm, announced the arrival of the final train to Yelverton.

They ventured out into a different world. It was fully dark, and yet the whiteness of the snow that had been falling thick and fast all the while lent a strange luminosity to the murky night. The snow was still coming down in powder rather than flakes, illuminated eerily in the glow from the station lamps, and chasing round in mindless swirls and eddies. Here the platform was merely dusted in white specks, while there a white mountain had piled up against the wall. Under the canopy sheltered Mr Higman and a handful of other passengers courageous — or foolhardy — enough to brave the storm. They resembled human snowmen so peppered were they with thick white dust, and the blizzard was driving so fiercely beyond the end of the platform that the air was nothing but a white curtain.

'I know you's only got third class tickets,' Mr Higman shouted in Ling's ear, 'but I wants you in second class with these other folk. Don't want you in a compartment on your own in this weather. If anyone asks, you just say Stationmaster Higman said so.'

Ling nodded her thanks and waited, snow lashing painfully into her face, while a middle-aged couple and then Mrs Huggins clambered up into the train. Ling and Fanny joined them inside while the wind whistled about the carriage, seeking out every nook and cranny and bringing a deposit of white powder with it. Edward Worth, the mail-boy, was there to accompany the five mailbags, and the remainder of the party was made up of three young men, one of whom by his uniform was an army private, probably to do with the prison, Ling assumed. Another was dressed like a gentleman, although with the collar of his snow-encrusted coat turned up against the wind and his hat rammed down low on his head, his face was all but obscured.

'Good luck!' Mr Higman called. 'And God speed!' he added anxiously, although no one heard since his voice was carried away by the storm.

'Oh, my word, I be that glad to get on this yere train,' Mrs Huggins declared, and young Edward announced proudly that it was his duty to stay with his mailbags no matter what. His face was flushed with excitement at the adventure the blizzard was presenting, and when the train jerked and began to inch forward, Ling at last began to feel safe.

A low conversation developed, all about the dreadful weather and how the blizzard was so much worse even than the heavy snow of ten years previously. There hadn't been any wind then, Mrs Huggins recalled, not like now when she had found it hard to locate the station, the snow was blinding her so. Ling was sitting by the window and indeed could see nothing but driving shafts of white. To her amazement, the powder was seeping in at the top of the closed windows and around the doors, and when she looked up, it was even blustering in through the air-vents.

'Oh, my!' Mrs Huggins exclaimed, and withdrawing her handkerchief, crammed it into the crack at the top of the window. Her action precipitated a flurry of activity as everyone followed suit, stuffing paper or anything else they could find into the tiny, one would have thought impenetrable, gaps.

The train slowed and stopped. Ling met Fanny's gaze and her pulse began to race. Oh, dear Lord! Surely they hadn't become stuck? But an instant later, they began to creep forward again.

Ling peered out of the window. She could just about see that the engine was dragging them through a drift at least five feet deep. The engine was gaining speed again, and Ling released a sigh of relief, but they had a long way to go yet, across exposed moorland. Despite their efforts, the snow was still determined to force its way into the carriage. Already a white layer was scattered across the floor and settling on the passengers' laps and shoulders. The older man even opened his umbrella and gave it to his wife, but it was to little avail as the fine particles merely blew in underneath.

The train was moving along steadily now, although slower than normal, and Ling would be glad when they chugged into Yelverton Station and perhaps escaped the worst of the blizzard on the moor. But suddenly, without warning, the train lurched to a standstill. The passengers were jolted forward and Ling was flung onto the floor, putting out her hands to protect herself. It was all so quick she wasn't sure what happened. But the next thing she knew, she was lying in a crumpled heap and her wrist which had been throbbing from her earlier fall now burned in agony.

An uncanny silence sang in her ears, followed by groans and low cries of 'Are you all right?' and the sound of people moving slowly. Ling heard a voice, strange and yet oddly familiar as if it came from the deepest recess of her mind, ask with concern, 'Are you all right, Fanny?'

Somehow Ling felt comforted by the voice and a wave of peace washed over her as Fanny answered in the affirmative. It was only then that Ling became fully aware of the acute pain that scorched through her wrist. She cried out, cradling it to her chest, and then she felt a strong arm about her shoulders, raising her up, and that soothing voice spoke calmly and confidently once again.

'It's all right, Ling. I'll take care of you. I really *am* a doctor this time.'

CHAPTER NINETEEN

For a few seconds, Ling was totally stunned. And then a quiet excitement began to ferment deep down inside her, making her feel like a young girl, the same girl who had been rescued from beneath the crushing wheels of a steam-engine by a valiant knight on a white charger.

She pulled herself up short, ashamed. That was years ago. She was a married woman now, with responsibilities on her shoulders. Tangled emotions ripped through her, tearing away that moment of pure joy as Elliott's strong arms carefully raised her from her undignified position on the floor.

'Fanny, are you sure you're all right?' she asked at once, for surely Fanny was far more important than she was just now. To her relief, Elliott was already taking care of the situation.

'No pain anywhere, Fanny?' his clear, calm voice enquired as he squatted down in front of Fanny so that she could hear his words. Good Lord, he remembered Fanny's problems after all that time!

'No.' Fanny shook her head and then grinned. 'Oo, the babby just kicked,' she said coyly.

'There you are, then. The little one will be fine. Nicely cushioned in its bag of fluid as nature intended. Unlike your wrist.'

'And everyone else?' Ling asked.

In the dim glow from the carriage lamp, she saw Elliott colour slightly. In his anxiety over *her*, he had forgotten the others who had been subjected to the same violent jolt.

'My wife's a little shaken,' the middle-aged man replied, 'but 'tis all.'

'And 'twill take more than that to hurt Mary Huggins,' the plump, friendly woman announced cheerily.

'There, you see.' The corners of Elliott's mouth curved upwards as he looked straight at Ling, and her heart at once began to race. She realised now he was the gentleman who had been sitting in the far corner, hidden by the turned-up collar of his coat and the hat which must have been knocked off in the commotion since it was no longer on his head. Even so, Ling wondered if she would have recognised him. Gone were the boyish good looks. His face was slightly haggard as if he had much to worry him, but it remained a strong, handsome face which would instil confidence in his patients.

'We've not moved yet.'

'Driver's trying, mind.'

The concerned voices as the great wheels indeed squealed on the metal track drew Ling from her dazed state. The engine driver was evidently attempting to coax the train forward but it wouldn't budge, and even when he put it into reverse, it shunted but an inch or two as the wheels ground uselessly on the snow-bound rails.

'Seems we'm stuck fast.'

'Saints preserve us!'

'Well, let's not get too worried yet,' Elliott said sensibly. 'I suggest you all see if you can find anything else to stop the snow blowing in while I see to this young lady's wrist.'

There was a general mumble of agreement and everyone searched in their pockets for anything that might be of use, leaving Elliott to sit beside Ling and take her hand gently but firmly in his, cautiously flexing it this way and that.

'I slipped over on the way to the station,' she told him, her flesh tingling at his touch. 'Or at least, we were both blown over by a gust of wind. I'm worried about Fanny.'

'Hmm.' Elliott glanced briefly at Fanny as she concentrated on stuffing her handkerchief into the air vent above her head. 'I'll keep an eye on her. She looks as if she's near her time.'

'She is. I was taking her to the workhouse infirmary.'

Elliott raised an eyebrow, and Ling was grateful that he didn't press her as the gravity of their situation began to grip her chest in an iron hold. What if the baby decided to come now? Oh, it didn't bear thinking about!

'Well, if I have to deliver her baby on the train, it'll be a sight cleaner than many of the places I've delivered babies before. Now, can you make a fist for me? Good. And now squeeze my hand as tightly as you can. There. Just a sprain,' he nodded at her, looking up with that half smile once more. 'I seem to be making a habit of telling you that, don't I, Miss Southcott? I'll just strap it up for you to make it more comfortable.'

'Mrs Mayhew now.' The words were blurted out in a rush as if she must put a stop at once to the longing, the regret that had seized her.

'Ah.' Elliott's tone was flat as he reached up to take his medical bag from the luggage rack, but it seemed for just an instant that he shot her a wistful glance. Or was she imagining it as her pulse tripped and began to beat even faster?

'Barney,' she went on, for her own sake rather than his. To drive away the guilt. She should *not* feel like this!

'Oh, yes, I remember. You married him. Well, congratulations! When was that?'

'Five years ago.'

'Really? Now just hold your hand like that for me. That's right. And did his broken arm mend well? It was nasty as I remember.'

'Yes, it did. But how did you know about it?'

'Well, I met him. At the quarry. I came to see you before I left for London. To give you my address so that you could write to me. Barney said you weren't there so he was going to pass it on to you. Don't you remember? I'd have liked it if you had written, but I can understand why you didn't. Miles away, and I *was* there seven years. There, that's done. It should feel better now.'

Ling stiffened with shock. Had Barney deceived her all those years ago? Had he been that jealous? Suspicion and dismay heaved in her breast as all the frustrations she had thought to have buried long ago vaulted to the surface again.

She was thankfully distracted by the older man suddenly springing to his feet. He at once pulled down the window and the wind roared into the compartment, driving a hail of white snowflakes over the travellers.

'Need any help?' the man's voice boomed to whoever was outside. There was evidently a reply, and then the window was heaved shut, the storm battering against the glass again.

'Sorry 'bout that. That were the guard. Appears the engine's stuck in a drift right up to the chimney. He and the driver and the fireman are trying to dig us out, but sounds like a hopeless task to me.'

An apprehensive murmur circulated among the passengers and Ling saw Fanny's face blanch. She had heard the man's Stentorian announcement well enough. Ling squeezed her hand and smiled. She was pretty anxious herself, but somehow Elliott's presence had given her confidence.

'Looks like we'll be here for some time,' declared the man with the loud voice. 'So we might as well introduce ourselves. I'm Sergeant Watts.'

Ah, that explained his manner, Ling thought to herself, and then saw the young lad in military uniform instantly stand to attention. 'Private Hancock, Sergeant,' he saluted briskly.

Elliott caught Ling's eye as he snapped shut his medical bag, and winked surreptitiously at her. He still had that reserved sense of humour, and Ling's heart sung because that special link she had felt between them during those long-ago celebrations seemed to have survived.

'At ease, Private,' Sergeant Watts commanded, and the soldier immediately relaxed again. But at the same time, the eyes of the youngest passenger shone with admiration.

'Edward Worth, mail-boy, in charge of the mailbags,' he repeated proudly from earlier on the journey. ''Tis my duty to accompany them all the way!'

'And I's Palk, sir. Samuel Palk, porter in the Goods Department on the GWR.'

Mrs Huggins had no need to introduce herself again but jauntily did so anyway. Elliott held out his hand and Sergeant Watts took great delight in pumping it up and down. There followed a general shaking of hands as if Elliott had led the way to this ritual which seemed to bond these strangers together. A hubbub of conversation broke out among them. But their words went unheard by Ling's tormented mind. All she could think of was that she could have remained in contact with Elliott all those years, and who knew how different her life might have been?

'I expect he just forgot,' she muttered, for that was what she wanted to believe. 'Barney. Your note. I would have written.'

She blinked at Elliott, waiting for his reaction. He seemed pleasantly surprised and his mouth stretched into a smile. 'I'd have liked that,' he answered quite naturally.

'And I'd have liked to have heard about London. And your work.' And a great deal more besides, she thought to herself.

'Oh, most of London is overcrowded and very dirty. I spent all my time studying or working at the hospital. Or treating people in their filthy slums. I relished every minute of my training and learned from some of the finest surgeons in the country. But I can't tell you how relieved I am to be back in Tavistock again.'

Ling nodded politely, since this must seem nothing more than a friendly conversation. But some overwhelming force drove her to ask the next question, something so powerful she could not fight against it. 'And I imagine you must have brought a wife with you? What does she think of our part of the world after London?' Her thoughts were spinning in a tortured dance. She wanted desperately for Elliott to be married, to be out of reach of her own fantasies which she had thought to have died long ago. Please God . . .

'A wife? Good heavens, I hardly had time to eat and sleep, let alone go courting! And I've been so busy since I've been back that socialising remains a luxury. Much to my mother's chagrin. She would have me introduced to every eligible young lady in town if -'

The remainder of his sentence was drowned as the guard reported back. Useless. He would strike out for Dousland Station. The driver and fireman would remain in the cab. The words seemed far away, in another universe that existed entirely separately from Ling's anguished mind. Elliott's mother. The haughty, imperious woman had obviously considered her beneath her son. Or was she maligning Mrs Franfield? Perhaps she had merely forgotten to pass on the message, just as Barney might have omitted to give her Elliott's note. The sword of fate twisted painfully somewhere below Ling's ribs. Coincidence or betrayal on both counts? But what did it matter? It was all too late. She was a married woman. And anyway, she knew so little about Elliott. Oh, it must just be the tension of being marooned on the train and not knowing what was in store for them.

'We looks like gingerbread men with icing sugar sprinkled on top!' Mrs Huggins was saying brightly since the snow was still managing to blow in through every packed crevice.

'Oh, don't talk about food, missis. I'm starving.'

'Try to think of summat else then. How's about a song?'

She proceeded to lead them all in some traditional tunes which for a while took their minds off the blizzard which continued to rage about them with no sign of abating. But the merriment gradually faded as the vicious gale drove relentlessly against the windows and shook the carriage like a plaything. Outside it was pitch black beyond the snow piling up against the glass panes. It was like being wrapped inside a chrysalis with no earthly idea of how they might ever emerge.

Within the hour, the guard was back, declaring that in the dark with the wind and the lashing snow, he would never have reached Dousland Station alive so there was certainly no chance of being rescued that night. Mrs Watts moaned pitifully and her husband patted her hand. Fanny's eyes were wide as she glanced towards Ling for reassurance, and in her turn, Ling swivelled her gaze to Elliott.

'Well, don't panic, ladies,' he said with quiet confidence. 'The heating pipes might have gone cold, but there's enough of us to keep sufficiently warm, and the lamp has enough paraffin to see us through the night if we turn it down low.'

'I's not worried. 'Tis quite an adventure as I sees it,' Edward Worth chirped perkily. 'Wouldn't mind joining the army one day. What does you think, Sergeant Watts?'

'Well, young fellow -'

The sergeant's reply was masked by other conversations starting afresh among the stranded passengers. While others chatted on, Ling was trapped in her own thoughts. After all these years when Elliott had faded into the shadow of her memory, she was now about to spend the night with him, albeit in the company of others. Her nerves were taut, her elation sadly tempered by stinging remorse. She was married to Barney. Whom she loved.

'You'd already recognised me, hadn't you?' her lips whispered, formulating the question her mind was trying desperately to deny. 'So why didn't you say anything?'

She was staring at her hands and her neatly bound wrist, head bowed over her lap, so she did not notice the awkwardness on Elliott's face.

'I thought it best,' he answered, his voice equally hushed. 'I assumed you hadn't wanted to keep in touch. Sometimes it's better not to reawaken the past.'

His words were faltering as if he, too, regretted the lack of communication between them. It was all Ling needed and she turned to him with a rueful smile. 'What a pity Barney lost your address. You know . . .' Should she go on? Might he guess the true depth of her feelings, the regret that even now was almost choking her?

'I thought of you so often,' she wrenched the tortured admission from her throat. 'We seemed to have so much in common. You know, I went to work for Mr and Mrs Warrington. You remember them?'

'I do indeed. But surely you weren't in service?'

She cast a coy smile at him. 'Not exactly. I was there as Mistress Rose's companion, and then to help when baby Hal was born. It was the happiest time of my life. I learned so much from them. Mister Seth had been in the army out in India and he used to tell me all about it. And he was involved in the campaign to raise the Age of Consent. You must remember that. And he's for ever lobbying everyone in Parliament about appeal rights for convicts. He says so often it's poverty that brings men to crime, and they pay dearly for it.'

Her heart had soared at being able to discuss such matters again, grave though they were, but she was brought up short by the frown that creased Elliott's forehead. 'You can say that again,' he murmured. 'I've just come from the prison. They've no MO at present, so I've been standing in. I've just had to oversee a flogging, and I tell you, it's the most barbaric thing I've ever witnessed. I know it isn't administered lightly nowadays, but surely they can devise less sadistic methods of punishment?'

Ling shuddered at the sickening image. This was 1891, and shouldn't there be an answer to so many injustices? 'I don't suppose the world will ever be perfect,' she replied sombrely, and no one knew the truth of it more than she did.

Elliott nodded in agreement and then they fell into an easy silence. The blizzard continued to rampage wildly across the moor, gnashing its teeth at the ensnared little train as if it would swallow it whole, piling up the snow so that the engine and its one carriage were obliterated in the ivory blanket that smothered the landscape. Those inside shared the few provisions they had, a few biscuits and a bar of chocolate.

They grew tired as the night wore on, but hunger and thirst gnawed at every stomach and cold kept them from sleep.

Midnight came and went. Used to harsh conditions, the sergeant and Private Hancock finally succumbed to exhaustion, the older man snoring rhythmically and his wife, finding comfort with her head on his familiar chest, at last dozing fitfully. Ling closed her eyes, her head tipped back against the seat as she tried to block the howling gale from her ears. Would Barney be worried about her, or would he trust her to take care of Fanny and herself? And what had happened to the paper with Elliott's address on it? Her last thought as she shivered into a broken and disturbed slumber was of Elliott, now silent and still beside her.

CHAPTER TWENTY

Ling slipped reluctantly into wakefulness. The hours of night had been passed in a somnolent haze, always conscious of the cold and the screaming wind. Ling realised with a jolt that her head was resting on Elliott's shoulder. She went to pull away, but then it dawned on her that she would never again have the excuse to lean against him. She would savour the moment for ever, the one gleam of happiness in the dark sterility her life had become.

She dared to open one eye a fraction and in the faint glimmer from the lamp, she studied Elliott's firm jawline, shadowed with overnight stubble, and she could just see the long brown lashes of one eye fanned out on his high cheekbone. His looks were not as striking as Barney's had once been, but he was nonetheless a handsome man whose face portrayed a reserved inner strength. The kind of face one would trust implicitly.

Oh, why was she instinctively comparing him with Barney? She loved Barney. Didn't she? He was good and dependable, had never failed in his duty to care for her mother before she died and, of course, for Fanny. There was tension between them at times, but only because of the demands old Mr Mayhew unfairly put upon his son and,

Ling's heart admitted with a wrenching sigh, her inability to produce a child. Would that blessing have clinched their contentment? Perhaps. But Ling knew deep inside that she had always needed more to her life than being a quarryman's wife. It was something her father had recognised, not a desire for wealth or an easy life, for she was not afraid of hard work and making do, but a desire for the riches of the mind. The happiest time of her life had been when she worked for the Warringtons because she had *learnt* so much.

And then there had been Toby Bradley. He was engaged to Chantal Pencarrow now. Ling had never met the Pencarrow family over at their farm near Peter Tavy, and because of his naval training, Toby was rarely able to accompany his parents on their visits to Fencott Place. But whenever Ling did see him, they were like old friends, because they communicated on a different plain. The same plain that had attracted her to Elliott all those years ago, and which had instantly attracted her to him again. And that was the difference. With Barney, life had been fun, easy-going, relaxed and steady. But the fun was long gone, and she was pledged to Barney for life.

Elliott began to stir and Ling quickly drew away. She felt Elliott slowly stretching beside her, heard him stifle a yawn. He turned to her, blinking the sleep from his eyes, and seeing her awake, smiled softly at her. And her heart turned over again.

'Did you get some sleep?' he whispered.

She nodded. 'I wonder what the time is. It's still dark.'

Elliott took out his pocket watch and tilted it into the dim glow of the still burning lantern. 'Half past five. And hark at that wind still,' he added, raising his eyes to the roof of the train. 'It hasn't let up all night.'

Ling glanced about the compartment. There were dark patches on the floor where some of the snow had melted, while in other places, little white drifts had been heaped up inches deep.

Ling shivered. 'I'm so cold,' she muttered under her breath, 'and stiff as a poker.'

Elliott breathed in through his teeth. 'Yes, so am I. When everyone wakes up, we must do some exercises to get the blood circulating. That'll warm us up, and once it's light, we'll see what can be done to get us out of here. But look,' he invited her a little hesitantly, raising his arm. 'If you don't think it inappropriate, snuggle up to me. It'll help keep us both warm.'

Ling's eyebrows arched. No, she didn't think it inappropriate at all! She was so cold, she was beyond caring, and it wasn't just body heat that began to ease the cramps of cold as she leaned against Elliott and he put his arm around her, drawing her close. A beacon of warmth began to glow inside her. And for that short while before their companions started to stir, she was going to cast her conscience aside and relish every moment.

'I'm worried about Fanny,' she voiced her thoughts a little later. 'Will she be all right?'

'She needs some fluids. We all do, but Fanny especially. Let's keep our fingers crossed she doesn't go into labour. Has she seen a physician at all?'

'No.' Shame made Ling drop her voice even lower. 'We don't have a lot of money. I'm the schoolmistress now—'

'Really? Well, congratulations. You deserve it.'

'Only because Mr Norrish left. They don't really like married women as teachers, but they couldn't get anyone else. And because I'm a woman, they pay me less. And there hasn't been so much work at the quarry lately. We manage, but there's little to spare. And the father of Fanny's child has abandoned her. We don't even know who it is, though we have our suspicions. And Fanny herself won't say.'

'Poor girl might not even realise how she became pregnant. Plenty don't.'

'Oh, I think she does. Strung her along until he got what he wanted and then dropped her like a stone.'

'Typical.' Elliott gave a bitter shake of his head. 'I've seen it often enough. I'm the MO at the workhouse as well, you see. Usually falls to the most junior physician in the town. All good experience, mind. So I could well end up delivering Fanny's baby anyway.'

'She'll be in good hands, then.'

Ling felt herself blush, and was glad Elliott couldn't see her face. But she had obviously embarrassed him as she heard him mumble, 'I'd like to think so.' An awkward silence followed, and Ling was thankful when he spoke again. 'And what do your parents think of all this?'

Ling's heart sank like a lead weight. 'They both died some years ago,' she told him.

'Good Lord, I'm sorry.' Elliott's sympathetic tone was genuine. 'But they were still young.'

'My father . . . had an accident,' she faltered at the dreadful memory. 'And my mother was so aggrieved she lost her mind. She kept wandering, and one night, we lost her. She died of exposure out on the moor. A little like us.'

'Oh, I somehow think we'll survive.'

Elliott's voice was warm and encouraging, but just then, the other passengers started to wake up with groans of discomfort, and Ling swiftly pulled away. Beside her, Fanny wriggled and fidgeted, heaving herself forward.

'I need the privy summat desprit,' she whispered in Ling's ear.

Ling bit her lip. So did she, and she knew from her own experience of pregnancy that Fanny must be bursting. But Elliott must have heard as he was already opening the carriage door. Driving snow whipped into the compartment again, and Elliott disappeared into the darkness. He was back in a matter of minutes, though, and knocking on the door.

'Blowing a blizzard still, I'm afraid,' he called as Sergeant Watts opened the door and took possession of the bucket Elliott had purloined from the fireman. 'Gentlemen, we must give the ladies some privacy. Be careful as you get down.'

The female companions were left alone to complete their ablutions, Mrs Huggins taking the lead by announcing she didn't have anything different from any other woman and that if Fanny didn't use the bucket first, she would. Mrs

Watts took more persuading, but at last they were all more comfortable. It was just as well, for the moment they had finished and the men clambered back inside, the wick in the lamp dried out and the flame flickered and died.

'Seven o'clock,' Elliott spoke into the shadows. 'As soon as it's light enough, the fireman and guard are setting out for Dousland Station, but the blizzard's still raging. Do any of you gentlemen want to risk going with them? It certainly isn't wise for any of the ladies to go, and I think I'd better stay. In case I'm needed,' he added under his breath.

Everyone seemed to agree that it was more sensible to stay put. Outside the wind still pounded the falling snow against the windows, and visibility was reduced to a matter of yards, despite full daylight. And when the engine driver later announced that he, too, was to strike out for Dousland, the trapped passengers felt their end was nigh.

'Now don't worry, my dear,' Sergeant Watts declared, turning to his wife whose face was grey with fear. 'I've faced worse than this. One time out in Zululand . . .' he began.

The story kept them diverted for half an hour since the sergeant was an imaginative narrator, and Ling was quite sorry when it seemed there was no more to tell and the continuing gale was once more all that assailed their ears. Every so often, Elliott insisted his fellow travellers carry out some exercises, but space was severely restricted and hearts became heavier as time dragged on. Minutes ticked by, and hours seemed like days while outside the snow continued to drive across the already obliterated landscape in blinding sheets. Stomachs were painful with hunger and, more seriously, nine throats were parched.

In a courageous effort, Elliott braved the weather to gather a fistful of fresh snow. It refused to melt, and when it finally did, there was but a spoonful for Fanny to suck from his palm — since her need was the most urgent — and Elliott's hand was blue and rigid with cold. That stroke of ingenuity having failed, they all tried to ignore their thirst, so when, around three o'clock in the afternoon, a commotion outside led them to haul two intrepid railway packers from Dousland Station up into the cramped compartment, there was jubilation on every elated face.

'The guard and fireman told us you was stranded yere!' one of the rescuers declared cheerfully. 'Mercy they got through! Took us two and an 'alf hour to get yere, an' we losed our way several times.'

'Cas'n see the railway track,' the other fellow chipped in. 'Cas'n hardly see the train, neither! 'Tis just like a heap o' white. Got some vi'tals for you, mind. Tidd'n much, but 'twill keep you going.'

'Oh, good man!' Elliott led a chorus of gratitude. 'Plenty to drink, I hope. It's what we need most.'

'Bottle o' watered down brandy were all we could find. And the missis made you up some bread and butter and some cake we had left over.'

Ling caught the misgiving that Elliott tried to disguise for the men had done their best, and the sergeant took charge, dividing the rations equally.

'Here, Fanny.'

Ling passed her small piece of cake to her sister at the precise instant Elliott did the same. She met his gaze and saw that reserved smile play on his lips. But in his eyes, she read something deep and affectionate, and she reared away from it.

'Well, us two must be getting back,' one of the packers announced, 'if us wants to arrive afore 'tis dark. Any o' you wants to come along? 'Twill be tough going, mind.'

Samuel Palk and the private exchanged glances but the meagre rations had done little to revive their strength and they all resigned themselves to another night stranded on the moor.

'Oh, I don't know if I can do this!' Mrs Watts whimpered.

'Of course you can, dearie,' Mrs Huggins insisted. 'See, those good men retrieved the guard's lamp for us, and us've still got that brandy. And I's sure someone'll have us out of here come the morning.'

Ling saw the faint lift of Elliott's eyebrows. He was worried, she could tell, and mainly about Fanny since he kept studying her keenly. Fanny herself, though, seemed quite relaxed. She appeared to have the sole attention of the lively Mrs Huggins, and though she must be as cold and uncomfortable as the rest of them, she was at least being admirably entertained.

Darkness closed in once more. Ling shuddered as she huddled between Fanny and Elliott, praying that the baby wouldn't decide to put in an appearance during the night. She had complete faith in Elliott but the crowded conditions in the carriage were hardly suitable for childbirth. Ling knew. And for the umpteenth time in her life bit down hard on her lip. If only she hadn't lost all her babies. Then, perhaps, her soul might not be ensnared in a tangled web as she looked at Elliott and experienced a painful longing she had no right to feel.

By eight o'clock, the last drop of the heavily watered-down brandy had trickled down Fanny's throat, and the second night marooned on the train began. They huddled together for warmth, hungry, thirsty, tired and aching. It was a nightmare. And yet Ling was happy to endure it. For she could spend it, guilt free, with Elliott, and let the future take its course.

CHAPTER TWENTY-ONE

'Good Lord, it's stopped!'

Ling felt Elliott sit up abruptly, drawing her from the exhausted sleep she had finally succumbed to in the early hours. After the ceaseless scream of the blizzard rampaging about the train for thirty-six hours, the silence rang in their ears. Sunlight was already gleaming through the encrusted windows, melting the snowflakes so that they were running down the panes in tiny rivulets. Elliott leaned across and, rubbing the condensation from the inside of the glass, peered through to the outside world.

As their fellow inmates came to life, a whoop of joy echoed from every pair of lips. The horrors of the two nights entrapped on the train were forgotten, and Elliott heaved the door open against the snowdrift that had piled up against it. The driven snow was light and powdery, falling away easily, and pushing the door wide, they stared out over an unfamiliar, ivory landscape that bore no resemblance to the moor they knew. The very shape of the rolling hills and high, craggy tors was unrecognisable, totally obliterated by the thick, pearly blanket, deep everywhere but heaped up in tall mounds in the oddest places, and hewn by the wind into strange and wondrous sculptures.

The instinct to escape the confines of the compartment was overwhelming, and Elliott jumped down, only to be swallowed in snow up to his armpits. He turned back to the train, laughing boyishly. He held up his arms, inviting Ling to climb down beside him, and a thrill of excitement darted through her as he held her around the waist. She stood at his side, drawing in the fresh, early morning air sharp with the tang of frost. Their own breath wreathed about them in a cloud, and for a moment, they were transfixed with wonderment. Despite the rigours of the previous two nights, their hearts were lifted by the beauty the blizzard had left in its wake. The rising, opalescent sun was bathing the virgin snow in gilded ripples, glittering with twinkling spangles of light as if millions of tiny diamonds had been scattered across a swathe of white velvet.

Voices behind them broke the magical spell as their male companions clambered down to join them, while Fanny and the two women looked out from the open doorway. The sight was so awe-inspiring that everyone was dumbstruck. Even those who after a few moments of stunned contemplation attempted to flounder through the fluffy, white mounds did so without uttering a sound. Although dawn had only just broken, the sun was dazzling on the snow, and the passengers, overjoyed at their release, blinked and squinted into the world of freedom.

It was Fanny who spotted him first. Bone-weary as her companions, she could not find the words to cry out. Instead, she noiselessly raised her hand and pointed, and it was only Ling who saw her as she turned back to grin at her sister.

'Fanny?' she frowned, pushing her way back through the snow. 'What is it?'

'Man,' was all Fanny could muster.

A dart of horror shuddered through Ling's body. Could it be the engine driver, for no one knew what had become of him? Had the poor man been so disorientated by the blizzard that he had walked round in circles and perished alone out on the moor yet within yards of the train? Ling made her way back to Elliott, her heart pounding, and whispered in his ear. His concerned eyes met hers and then, without a word to the others who were now finding their tongues and congratulating themselves on their survival, he began to force a path through the snow in the direction Ling had indicated.

Ling watched him go, a horrible sinking feeling in her belly. And then she heard Elliott's voice raised in delight and the amazed calls of another human being. Ling stumbled forward in the channel Elliott had created through the drift, astonished then as the level of snow suddenly dropped to no more than a few inches. And there, a mere two hundred yards from the train, a farmer was busy extricating some sheep from another deep drift and had now stopped to greet with pure astonishment the stranger approaching him across the white wilderness. Rescue was at hand! And Ling's fears that Fanny might go into labour on the train dissolved as Elliott and the farmer came towards her.

'Farmer Hilson,' he introduced himself. 'Proper mazed, I be! Had no idea you was yere! Cas'n see the train under that there heap o' snow, and us only yards away!'

'Not surprising with that blizzard!'

'What a night!'

'Two nights!'

'What! You'm been stuck in that there train since Monday?'

'And we've three other ladies on board.'

'Well, 'tis lucky my farm be not too far away. You must all come home to me. Accounted for all the sheep, I has, though I reckon there'll be plenty of others farmers who cas'n. So let's get they other womenfolk off the train.'

He led the way back to the carriage. Ling's legs were unsteady, and a grateful wave of pleasure rushed through her as Elliott took her arm. Did he know how she felt? Her admiration for his intelligence and worldliness rekindled, and now strengthened with the desires and yearnings of adulthood? Did he feel the same, or would he be horrified to know how she was drawn, nay confused, by his masculinity when she was married to another man? But what did it matter? It was too late. She had been betrayed long ago and this interlude would soon, *must* soon, be forgotten.

'Careful now, miss,' Sergeant Watts warned, but with the help of the men, Fanny climbed down safely from the carriage. It was only when they turned back to assist Mrs Watts that Fanny suddenly hunched her shoulders over her jutting abdomen and released a squeal of pain.

Ling's heart contracted. 'Elliott!' she breathed as Fanny turned her wide, cornflower blue eyes on her.

Elliott was instantly at her side. 'Now there, Fanny,' he said so calmly that Ling at once felt the salve soothing her apprehension. 'Lean on me and breathe slowly and deeply. Like this. Breathe with me.'

Fanny seemed instantly relaxed, and Ling felt that terrible pang of emptiness. If only she'd had Elliott to deliver her first stillborn child. If only she'd had *some* medical help, but there had been no time to fetch a doctor, the prison surgeon only arriving when it was all over. At least Barney had been right in wanting to get Fanny somewhere where care was available, even if it was within the austere and loveless walls of the workhouse. But if only . . .

'There. It's easing off now,' Elliott announced as his palm rested on Fanny's stomach. 'That's your first contraction. It means your baby's on the way. So the sooner we get to this farmhouse the better.'

They made a motley band, lurching through the deep snow. Tired, numb with cold, almost beyond hunger Sergeant Watts was virtually carrying his wife who had collapsed from exhaustion, and Private Hancock came to his assistance. Samuel Palk managed to chivvy along Mrs Huggins who had become oddly quiet, and young Edward Worth was moaning loudly about dereliction of duty at having to abandon his mailbags.

Fanny struggled on, supported on one side by Elliott and on the other by Ling, who refused to leave her sister's side despite Farmer Hilson's offer to take her place. Oh, thank God Elliott was there! And the last Ling saw as they turned their backs on the train was the adjoining compartment which had not had its cracks and crevices stuffed with handkerchiefs and paper. It was so strange, uncanny, for the seats were almost indistinguishable from the floor, encased in a solid block of white which clung in strange and wonderful shapes to the wire-mesh of the luggage racks. And Ling realised with a shudder of horror just how close to death they had come.

* * *

'Ling!'

Elliott's urgent whisper roused her from an almost unconscious sleep. To his wife's astonishment, Farmer Hilson had waved the exhausted passengers into the massive kitchen. After a hearty breakfast with endless mugs of steaming tea, the party had quickly recovered from its ordeal. Following a brief rest, the gentlemen and tough Mrs Huggins set out on foot, the latter declaring that a little snow never hurt anyone and that she was looking forward to walking through the magical land into which the moor had been transformed. Only Mrs Watts remained so frail that the kindly farmer's wife had put her to bed in one of the upstairs rooms, Sergeant Watts staying at the farmhouse to take care of her.

Though her labour was only in its early stages, Fanny's contractions were growing more frequent, and Mr and Mrs Hilson had given up their own bedroom, it being the largest in the house. Elliott examined Fanny with such swift dexterity that her embarrassment was over almost before it began, and then to Ling's relief she dropped instantly into the sleep of the dead.

Ling had sunk slowly into the depths of an old but comfortable armchair, and at long last, she was able to succumb to her exhaustion. Her stomach was fluttering nervously, holding her in a remorseless grip until her restless mind could take no more and she slipped into an abyss so deep that there was nothing but black, thoughtless stillness. So when Elliott roused her, her wandering eyes focused on his face in total bewilderment for some seconds before everything fell into place.

'What's the matter?' she demanded, cringing that in her anxiety her tone sounded quite rude and blunt, when Elliott, *dear* Elliott, had been caring for her sister while she slept on. For several hours, apparently, as it was already getting dark again.

Elliott put out a hand, resting it reassuringly on her arm, and for a few delicious seconds, that shaft of warmth overwhelmed her once more.

'Nothing to worry about,' Elliott was saying in a low voice. 'You know I said the baby's head wasn't properly engaged? I'd expected it to move down as labour progressed, but she's almost fully dilated and the baby's presenting with a shoulder. She's going to want to push soon, but she mustn't until I've moved the head into the correct position. So I want you to help her, talk to her, anything to stop her pushing. Just wish I had some nitrous oxide — laughing gas — to help her.'

Ling had been listening intently. She was ready to lavish all her frustrated love on the baby her sister was about to bring into the world, but what if the infant didn't survive or dear, sweet, vulnerable Fanny gave her own life in the process? The idea was unthinkable.

'Ling, listen to me.' Elliott's tone was touched with a sharp authority. 'It's by no means the first time I've done this. It really isn't a problem, but I do need you to help. She trusts you more than anyone in the world. And *you* need to trust *me*.'

Ling gazed back at him. Yes, she trusted Elliott implicitly. A moan drew her to the bed and she took Fanny's outstretched hand as another contraction clamped the girl's bulging abdomen. And then Elliott was there, issuing instructions as he gently manoeuvred the baby into a better position.

'All right now, Fanny. On the next one, you can push.'

She did. And though she screamed and gripped Ling's hand with excruciating force, Elliott was encouraging them with a progress report and within half an hour, a wriggling, squirming, miniature human being slithered into the world.

A little girl. Who cried healthily as the young doctor examined her gently and expertly. Then he wrapped her in the shawl Mrs Hilson had provided, and handed her to her astonished and overwhelmed mother while he got on with the business of delivering the afterbirth and stitching the neat little nick he had made to stop Fanny tearing as the head was delivered. Fanny scarcely noticed his attentions, her rapt eyes fixed on the minuscule form in her arms, its downy, blood-smeared hair stuck to its skull; button nose, pale wrinkled eyes and the tiny rosebud mouth that finally stretched in a toothless yawn and went on working even when the eyelids had closed in sleep. Ling watched, lost in wonderment, her cheeks wet with tears of joy — and grief that this was what she had been denied.

'What does I do with her now?' Fanny asked innocently, looking up at her beloved sister who always knew the answer.

Ling heard Elliott chuckle. 'Oh, she'll soon let you know! There. All finished for the time being. Now you get some sleep, Fanny. You'll be needed soon enough. Baby will need her first feed before too long.'

Fanny obediently relinquished her child into Ling's waiting arms. And when a few moments later, Elliott came up behind her, Ling was sobbing silently as she studied the sleeping infant, and she instinctively leaned against the man who had saved this little miracle and possibly its mother as well.

CHAPTER TWENTY-TWO

'Laura Heather May,' Ling whispered to the tiny girl who had finally fallen asleep in her arms. 'Aren't you beautiful?'

'She certainly is,' Elliott smiled over her shoulder. 'But do you think Fanny will be able to cope?'

'Oh, yes. Look how well she fed her just now. That's one thing about Fanny,' Ling told him as she settled little Laura into the drawer Mrs Hilson had produced as a makeshift cot. 'She does listen and do as she's told.'

'Which is probably how she got into trouble in the first place,' Elliott suggested not unkindly.

Ling breathed out on a sigh. 'Yes, probably. But you know, I'm glad she did. Just look at this lovely little mite. Oh, there'll be malicious tongues, but they'll get short shrift from me. And woe betide anyone who makes trouble for either of them!'

Her voice became harsh with determination, and Elliott chuckled in that soft, knowing way she found so attractive. She turned to face him, the flash of obstinacy melting from her heart. But then the lines on his face moved into an entirely different expression. 'I take it you have no children of your own?' he asked hesitantly.

The angry heartache Ling kept buried raised its ugly head and she sank down into the old armchair. And there was Elliott, his face creased with compassion, as she related to him everything that had happened since the day they had met at the opening of the Princetown railway. Everything apart from the one secret no one, especially Elliott himself, must ever know. That she had fallen in love with him eight years ago and, she realised now, had loved him ever since. Quite ridiculous, of course, since she hardly knew him, and yet here she was, opening up the very core of her soul to him.

'Life can be cruel,' Elliott murmured back, sinking on his haunches before her. 'But you cannot blame yourself for the death of your parents, either of them. Quarrying's a dangerous occupation. These things happen. And as for losing your child, the miscarriages, often it's nature's way if there's something not quite right with the pregnancy.'

'But . . . four times?' she choked.

Elliott's eyebrows arched with sympathy. 'Yes, I understand your concerns. But I'd say the stillbirth was unrelated to the miscarriages. Did you have a proper internal examination when things had settled down afterwards?'

Ling's flush of embarrassment subsided in an instant. It seemed so easy to talk to Elliott about these personal matters. 'No,' she answered steadily. 'We sent for the prison doctor when I had the stillbirth, but only at the time, not afterwards. He arrived too late anyway. And with the miscarriages, well, once it was over, there didn't seem much point. And to be honest, we couldn't really afford it.'

'Well, as we're friends — we are, aren't we? — I shouldn't really examine you, but I could arrange for Dr Greenwood to. But tell me, what's your monthly cycle like?'

Ling found herself answering without hesitation. 'Light and always late.'

'Well, it could well be that your body simply doesn't produce enough of the chemicals we believe are needed to sustain a pregnancy. Quite often, that can right itself. So,' he smiled in that encouraging way, 'my advice to you is to eat well and don't worry about it. And as soon as you think you might be pregnant again, see a doctor and get plenty of rest. Particularly around the three-month point. I had a patient in London with a similar history. In the end she took herself off to bed between the eleventh and fifteenth week, and that way ended up having three children in quick succession!'

Ling felt a little burst of joy. 'So, you think there's still hope?'

'I don't have a crystal ball, Ling, but if Dr Greenwood finds nothing wrong, then there's always a chance.'

Ling leaned back in the chair. A child of her own. Barney's child. Perhaps she could find contentment after all.

'Do you have any clothes for the baby?'

'Oh, yes. At home,' Ling replied, recovering from her daydream. 'I didn't bring them because I thought if we had them with us, they'd say at the workhouse that Fanny wasn't destitute and they wouldn't take her in.'

'Well, if everything's all right here in the morning, I thought I'd try to walk back to Princetown. See if my services as MO at the prison are required. And then if the telegraph wires aren't down, send a message to Dr Greenwood. And on the way back, I could call in to see your husband to let him know you're safe, and collect some of Laura's things then.'

Ling frowned. Perhaps it would be best if Barney didn't know that Elliott was back. After all, what *had* happened to that piece of paper?

'Oh, that's so kind of you, Elliott, but I'll go myself. I'd like to see Barney.'

'Of course. We can go together most of the way, though. Then I can make sure you're safe.'

'Yes, I'd like that.' But would it not make the pain even deeper, more unbearable? No matter. The desire to be in Elliott's company for as long as possible was a force against which she was powerless.

* * *

'Where the hell have you been?'

Ling stopped dead as she entered the cottage. She had been brought up short not so much by the state of the room as by the accusing scowl on Barney's face as he descended the stairs, a bucket full of snow in each hand. The blizzard had caused devastation to the buildings around the quarry. Roofs had collapsed and everywhere there were windows boarded up, slates missing and debris of all kinds scattered across the snow. The roofs of the stables and weighbridge house had completely disappeared and the masons' shed roof was a tangled and twisted wreck of corrugated iron some distance away. People were busy trying to repair the damage, but everyone had asked how she and Fanny were, relieved that they were safe. And yet here was Barney — her husband — apparently concerned only with his own problems.

'I'd have come yesterday,' she answered curtly. 'Only the wind was getting up again and I wasn't going to risk getting caught in another blizzard.'

It was perfectly true. Thursday morning had begun calm, but soon things were looking decidedly dubious once more and Ling and Elliott had decided against their planned expedition, since that was what the tramp across the snow-fields of the moor would be. And so they had finally set out together this morning, Friday.

Farmer Hilson had reported that convict work parties were clearing the drifts that blocked the Yelverton to Princetown road. But Elliott refused to let Ling brave the treacherous wastes to the quarries alone, and so had gone with her on the longer trek. Fortunately, it had not proved too hazardous and Ling would be able to return to the farm alone. They had parted by the Royal Oak sidings, and if anyone had asked Ling who the man was with her, she would answer quite truthfully that it was another passenger who had been marooned on the train.

'Well, I could've done with you yere,' Barney growled. 'Had to sort my father's place out, I has, as well as our own. Windows all blown in on that side o' the square and the house full o' snow inside. And *we* had a bloody great hole in the roof where the slates lifted off. Mended it, I has, but the loft's full o' snow and where 'tis melted, 'tis coming through the ceiling. So I be crawling round up there trying to empty it out afore it gets any worse. 'Tis a right mess up there an' my wife should've been yere instead o' gallivanting—'

'And I suppose you care nothing that Fanny and I were stranded on the train for thirty-six hours?' Ling couldn't stop herself retorting. 'And when we were rescued, we were half dead and then Fanny went into labour at the farm where we were taken in? Oh, no! All you're worried about is yourself!'

She watched, scarlet flaring into her cheeks, as Barney's mouth twisted in remorse. 'Well, how were I to know? I thought as you was safely down in Tavistock.'

'Didn't bother to ask, though, did you?' Her lips had clamped into a hard line as she pulled off her coat and rolled up the sleeves of her dress. Yes, Barney would be exhausted and she had no doubt that he would have been obliged to do everything to put his father's cottage back together. But Elliott had endured those two dreadful nights on the train, had seen Fanny through her labour when everyone else had been catching up on their sleep, and had been up and down with the new mother and child the following two nights as well. And there had been not a word of complaint from him, though he looked dead on his feet. The blizzard might have wreaked havoc everywhere, but it was no use moaning about it! There could well be others far worse off than they were!

'What did she have then?' Barney asked churlishly as he disappeared upstairs.

Ling glanced up at his footfall on the floor above just as a trickle of water began to drip through the crack between the floorboards. There was no lathe and plaster ceiling to spoil since the planks were simply laid across the beams that supported the upper storey. Ling quickly placed a bowl beneath it, and making sure Fanny's mattress was safely away from the dripping water, dashed up the stairs with the few old newspapers they possessed and an armful of thread-worn towels to soak up whatever she could.

'A girl,' she called at Barney's legs which were retreating into the loft above. Ling paused to survey the scene before she set to work. The plaster ceiling in the upstairs room was stained with greying patches that she knew would turn a dirty yellow when they finally dried. The air was rank with mustiness and everything — bedclothes, mattress, even their clothes — was damp and would have to be aired by the fire downstairs. Some, Widow Rodgers next door perhaps, might have wept, but Ling set to. It was no use crying over spilt milk. The most urgent task was clearly to remove the snow from the loft. So Ling ran downstairs to retrieve her largest saucepans.

'Use these while I empty the buckets,' she instructed, standing on the chair Barney was using to clamber up into the loft. He grunted as they made the exchange. The buckets were heavy and although Ling's wrist was still supported by the bandage, it was soon hurting so much she could no longer use it and so could only carry one bucket or saucepan at a time, running up and down the stairs until she was breathless.

'Since you ask,' she said scathingly as she heaved another bucket down from the loft, 'Fanny's fine.' And when Barney scarcely acknowledged her words, she threw caution to the wind. 'Could have been a difficult birth. But you were right. There's no proper doctor at the prison, but the locum from Tavistock happened to be on the train, and he delivered the baby.'

'Oh, yes?' Barney murmured disinterestedly as he disappeared into the gloom once again.

Ling felt the resentment rise in her gullet. Barney was concentrating on not putting his foot through the ceiling, but did he really *care* that much? She felt piqued at his lack of interest, driven by her bitterness to approach the next subject as if she was lashing out in retaliation. Or perhaps *because* she knew Barney was only half listening.

'I told him about my problems, the miscarriages and everything,' she went on, her pulse accelerating at her own truculence. 'He's arranging an examination for me.'

'Huh! And how much is he going to make out of that?' Barney grumbled as he poked his head through the hatch again.

'Not much,' Ling snapped back. 'How are you doing up there?'

'I've dug out as much as I can. The rest'll have to be left to dry out.'

'Well, I'll light the range so we can start airing bedclothes at least. Why did you let it go out in this weather?' she asked accusingly.

'No coal. Which you'd know if you'd been yere. Coal merchant's run out an' all, with no deliveries in this weather and everyone wanting it. Even the leat were blocked with snow so we had no water for two days.'

'Oh.' Ling bit her lip. Yes, she had been so engrossed in Fanny and the new baby that she supposed she hadn't considered just how widespread the disruption and suffering caused by the blizzard had been.

* * *

'Seems it covered the whole of the southwest,' Elliott told her as they sat in the Hilson's cosy sitting room that evening.'I managed to get a copy of the *Tavistock Gazette* in Princetown. There was a limited number delivered on horseback as there aren't any trains running yet. Printed on pink paper as they hadn't been able to have their usual delivery of white. But read it. There's something in there that'll make you smile.'

Ling took the paper and turned her attention to the headline, '*Terrific gale and heavy snowstorm in the West.*' Tavistock, it seemed, had been as buried in snow and battered by the hurricane as the moor. Had they reached it, walking in the town would have been perilous with slates being blown from roofs and chimneys collapsing in every street.

'Good Lord!' Ling sat bolt upright. 'It says here the chimney of the Workhouse Infirmary crashed through into the building. Thank God we never got there! It's a mercy no one was hurt!'

'People were hurt elsewhere, though, so I expect William and the other doctors have been quite busy. So I've escaped quite lightly.'

'Yes, I think we have. Trees down in their thousands, it says here. Mount Tavy was badly hit,' Ling gasped. 'Oh, I hope Mrs Penrith's all right.'

'Mrs Penrith?'

'Someone I know there. Lovely lady. And we weren't the only train that got stuck, though none for as long as we were. Oh, look! There's a really long report about what happened to us. They must have interviewed Private Hancock or Mr Palk, I reckon. Oh, and the Walkham Valley. It says Lady Bertha Mine is flooding because the leat that supplies the pumping machinery is blocked with snow. Barney said the leat at Foggintor was blocked so they were without water for two days. Oh, Elliott, I really don't see what I'm supposed to find amusing!'

Elliott shook his head. 'No. You're absolutely right. Some people caught out in the storm were lucky to survive and there's shortages of food and water, and fuel. It's going to take a long time to get the whole region back on its feet. But read on. You haven't got to the bit I meant yet.'

Ling frowned. She couldn't imagine Elliott feeling anything but sympathy for the thousands of people who must have been affected by the storm, so she turned her eyes back to the print. And then she, too, smiled. 'Mrs Huggins! Oh, they talked to her as well! "*Mrs Huggins stated that she felt no fear, as she had no doubt that when the weather had cleared she would find her way back to Tavistock.*" Oh, bless her! What a plucky lady she is!'

Elliott's face became serious as his eyes bore into hers. 'I must go back to Tavistock tomorrow, too. Walk if necessary. Fanny and Laura are doing well and Mrs Watts is quite recovered, but I'll be needed in Tavistock with all this.'

A knot froze solid in Ling's chest. This wonderful interlude was over. This interlude when Elliott had been able to relate to her his experiences in London, all his interesting and exciting tales; his company, close and intimate. It was all at an end. Her heart dragged with pain. Did Elliott know? Did he know how she yearned to be held in his arms? To have the ache of her life kissed away? He mustn't. He was good and kind, and that was all there must ever be between them.

CHAPTER TWENTY-THREE

'Oh, Fanny, she's beautiful.' Sam Tippet's face creased into an enraptured smile. Not that it was by any means the first time he had seen little Laura. Could it be that he was beginning to see Fanny as a woman rather than the child she had always been to him? Ling smiled to herself. Sam had found an excuse to visit Fanny every few days since they had returned from the Hilsons' hospitality three weeks ago, and Ling could not think of a more honest and trustworthy man to be her sister's suitor. And by the way Fanny was smiling at him now, well, who knew?

It would certainly be one weight off Ling's mind. She had received a note from Dr Greenwood asking her to attend at two o'clock this afternoon. Saturday, for Elliott knew she was teaching all week and there would be embarrassing questions if she closed the school for a day apparently just to go into Tavistock! There was a horrible churning deep down in the pit of her stomach. The examination wouldn't be pleasant, but Elliott had assured her that William Greenwood was one of the kindest and most understanding doctors he had ever met and a brilliant physician to boot.

But what would he discover? If he could find nothing obviously wrong, would she go on hoping, month after month, year after year, living continuously with bated breath? And what if he imparted to her the sad news that there was a definite reason why she could not bear a child? How would Barney react? He was a good husband but she knew that he kept inside his own disappointment and simply wasn't capable of offering her the comfort she craved.

Arthur had been quite right. Their simple life wasn't enough for Ling. She passed on her knowledge to her pupils, but when they left at twelve years old, how useful was that? A rudimentary grasp of reading, writing and reckoning, enough to get by in life, but few of them had any interest in the history, geography or even nature lessons she prepared for them. And why should they? Just like her, they were trapped.

Elliott. When she was with him, it was different. During those days at the farm, they had discussed all manner of subjects and seemed to share the same opinion on everything. Ling wondered if she might meet him at Dr Greenwood's house. It would be a joy to see him, but there again, that very joy would be wrong and would only add to the pain.

'I must get to work,' Sam declared. 'Barney'll be arter me seeing as he's already started! But perhaps I can come back this arternoon, Fanny, as 'tis half day?'

Fanny's angelic face lit up with a smile. 'Yes, I'd like that, Sam.'

Ling had to hide her pleasure at what she read in their expressions. 'And I must be off, too,' she announced, suddenly stiff with efficiency. 'I'm going to Fencott Place to see Mistress Rose before I catch the train. And I believe the Bradleys will be there and I haven't seen them since last summer. Now, you'll be all right, won't you, Fanny? Mrs Rodgers says you can fetch her if need be.'

She stepped out into a pleasant late April day. The mounds of drifted snow had finally melted, leaving the moor fresh and vibrant with the promise of spring. It had taken weeks of hard labour to unblock the water leats, to free up the roads and trains and have telegraphic communications fully operational again. The storm had affected the whole of

Devonshire and Cornwall, but walking into Princetown with the heady scent of spring gorse in her nostrils, it seemed to Ling that little had changed.

'Ling, how lovely to see you!' Rose came forward, grasping her hands. 'We're taking coffee. You got my letter, did you, so you know Adam and Rebecca are here?'

As usual, Rose spoke with such breathless ebullience that Ling had no chance to reply. The spacious hall was a tangled confusion of fur, tails wagging furiously and muted barks of joy at yet another visitor, and Rose laughingly pushed the dogs out of the way as she ushered Ling into the morning room.

'Ling!'

She was greeted all round by these good people who had taken her under their wing. The adults seemed unchanged, but Charlotte Bradley had grown into a young woman since Ling had seen her last and her brother James was not far behind. And then Ling spied Toby standing quietly by the window and felt a glow of pleasure.

'Toby!'

'Ling, what a delight!'

'I didn't expect you, too! How are you?'

Her face split in a grin. It really was like seeing an old friend. Within moments, the room had erupted in noisy conversation again and Ling found herself seated next to Toby.

'I heard you were caught on the train in the blizzard,' he said with genuine concern. 'It must have been appalling.'

Ling nodded wistfully. 'It wasn't much fun. But we survived, and others had it much worse. I expect you heard, lots of sailors drowned. Apparently the shore was littered with wrecks especially around Start Point. Driven onto the rocks and broken up like matchwood.'

'Yes, I know. I was there.'

His voice was low, suddenly trembling, and Ling held her breath. 'Oh, Toby,' she finally whispered, but Toby gave her that hesitant smile.

'It was the worst night of my life. But you know, I learnt so much. I was with Father, you see. And, do you know, he *sensed* the storm before it came? The barometer was doing strange things and so he took us right out into the Channel. It saved the ship. The wind threatened to drive us shoreward like everyone else, but Father's seamanship was superb. We couldn't see a thing because of the driving snow, but he steered us out of danger. He was a real hero that night but he was just angry that he couldn't do anything to save others.'

Ling saw the admiration glinting in Toby's eyes as he glanced across at Captain Bradley who was deep in conversation with Seth. Yes. She was with leaders of men here. People who could make a difference to the world and to those less fortunate than themselves. Oh, yes. These were the sort of people she liked to be with, people who were fighting for the common good. Ling's heart lurched, for in a different way, wasn't Elliott doing the same? Healing people and restoring them to health so that life was better?

'Yes, it was a dreadful few days,' Ling murmured. 'Let's hope we never see the likes of it again. But tell me, Toby, how are you yourself?'

'Oh, very well, thank you.' His naturally dark complexion deepened and he could not prevent the broad smile that broke over his face. 'Chantal and I are to be married next spring.'

'You've set the date at last! Oh, congratulations! You've waited a long time!'

'It was Father who wanted me to have reached a certain stage in my training. I'll still have a long way to go before I get my master's ticket, but I can at least claim to be an officer in the merchant navy.'

'And won't my big brother look dashing in uniform on his wedding day?' Charlotte Bradley grinned as she came over. 'Father has a uniform for his officers now on the Bradley Line. Maybe I'll find myself a husband among them one day!'

She laughed gaily, drawing the attention of the two older couples, and the lively chatter turned to a discussion of the wedding plans. The hour Ling had allowed herself for her visit passed in a trice and soon she was heading back to

Princetown Station, her spirits lifted. Only as she changed trains at Yelverton did her stomach begin to flutter again at the ordeal to come.

* * *

The examination was not nearly as traumatic as she had expected, Dr William Greenwood's sensitive manner swiftly overcoming her embarrassment. She could see at once why Elliott respected him so deeply. The news was that the experienced physician could discover no obvious reason for her failed pregnancies, and that he agreed with Elliott's theory that the chemicals believed to be produced during pregnancy were at fault.

'Unfortunately, we know so little about the subject,' he explained. 'In fact, there is so much we don't know about the human body that being a doctor must be one of the most frustrating occupations imaginable. I think Dr Franfield finds that hard to accept. But perhaps by the time he gets to my age, there will be more answers.'

Ling paid the surprisingly small fee — though Elliott had told her that Dr Greenwood charged according to his patients' means — and walked slowly back towards the town centre. People were shopping or calling in to the various establishments, carrying on their daily business while Ling was staring down the long, empty road of her future life. If only Dr Greenwood had found some small defect, something that could have been rectified, but now she was back where she had started. She had dear Barney, and she did still love him. But the sparkle had long gone from their childhood romance. Barney was no longer the carefree, joking lad she had loved. And she, well, just as the railway had in different ways opened her heart to new horizons, it had led to even greater frustrations. Perhaps, if she hadn't lost the child . . .

'Ling! Oh, I wondered if I might see you!'

She was in Duke Street now, so lost in her own dejection that she had literally bumped into Elliott as he emerged from the narrow passage that led through to the market house. The muscles in her chest contracted sharply. What she felt in his company was wrong. But to see his caring, smiling face when her heart was torn to shreds was too much, and she threw caution to the wind.

'Elliott!'

She let him shake her hand firmly while she watched the light shining in his green-blue eyes.

'How was it? Oh, dear me, what an insensitive question. Would you like . . . ?' He glanced around as if seeking inspiration. 'No, I insist. Let us take afternoon tea.'

Before she had time to decline, he had ushered her into a tearoom and they were sharing a pot of the hot, steaming beverage over a plate of freshly baked scones with homemade jam and clotted cream. Ling repeated what Dr Greenwood had said, and Elliott nodded positively.

'Well that's good news, then!'

Yes, Ling supposed it was. Elliott's very presence had rescued her from her own despondency. She smiled back, her mind lighter, and suddenly found herself ravenously hungry, as since breakfast, she had only eaten a biscuit with her coffee at Fencott Place. She bit lustily into a scone and then, in response to Elliott's enquiry, she updated him on Fanny and the baby's progress.

'And Sam Tippet, a friend who grew up with us,' she explained, 'is taking a great interest in them. And Fanny seems to be responding. It would be ideal. A lovely chap is Sam. He'd look after her.'

She nodded emphatically, and then tipped her head with a quizzical frown at the way Elliott was looking at her, his eyes dancing roguishly.

'What?' she all but giggled, his amusement infectious.

'I diagnose a grave case of cream on the nose, Heather Mayhew,' he announced in a serious tone as he battled to keep a straight face. 'I would recommend a creamectomy. Swab,' he commanded, slapping his serviette into his extended right palm. 'No anaesthetic necessary.' And then he leaned across the table and wiped the end of her nose. 'There. I declare the operation a complete success.'

She couldn't help but laugh aloud. How was it that Elliott made her feel like this? They had become so much better acquainted during those days at the farm, and yet she had always felt that she knew him so well, as if there was a special bond between them. He was smiling at her, his mouth stretched merrily revealing strong, even teeth. Oh, if only they hadn't lost contact, things might have been so different.

'Are you in any hurry? If you can spare half an hour, there's something I'd like to show you. I'm really quite excited about it, but it would be nice to share it with someone.'

Ling's eyes opened wide. She wasn't quite sure she should. But Elliott seemed so bubbling with anticipation, and besides, she was curious. Elliott paid the bill, and then they were walking down fashionable Plymouth Road, Ling's hand resting in Elliott's crooked elbow. She felt so proud, walking beside the handsome doctor dressed in his smart suit, and wishing . . . but she knew she mustn't.

'Where are we going?' she enquired instead, praying that Elliott couldn't read her thoughts.

'Don't be impatient,' he chuckled. 'We'll be there in a minute.'

They turned off right by the school and then left into Chapel Street, Elliott's stride lengthening. 'Nearly there!' he cried with a boyish grin. 'I live with my parents in Watts Road. Up there. In a very grand semi-detached villa in its own grounds.'

He said this nodding towards the steeply rising land to their right, a slightly deprecating expression on his face as if he didn't particularly care for the opulence of his family home. 'Well, not for much longer.' He stopped abruptly by a little house in one of the terraces overlooking the back gardens of the prosperous dwellings they had left behind in Plymouth Road. From his pocket, he withdrew a key and waved it proudly before Ling's nose. 'I'd just collected it from the Bedford Estate Office when I met you. This street belongs to the Duke, but His Grace was persuaded to allow me to buy this one as it's been untenanted for some time. I had to borrow the money from the bank, but I'll be paying it back over several years. My mother was fed up with patients calling for my services at any hour of the day or night, so she's glad to be rid of me. Though she does consider this a little beneath her dignity and says she will refuse to call on me here.'

Ling's eyes deepened to a warm, delighted cinnamon as she realised what Elliott was saying. 'So this is your new home?' she stammered.

'And you are my very first visitor!' Elliott declared, his face lit with exhilaration as he unlocked the front door. 'After you!'

She met his shining gaze, returning his elated smile before stepping over the threshold. Inside, the atmosphere smelt musty and once Elliott had shut the door, it was so dark that Ling could see very little until her eyes had adjusted from the spring sunshine outside.

'It'll need a fair amount of work before I can move in,' Elliott said with undaunted enthusiasm. 'But the building's sound. So, what do you think? Go on, wander round.'

Ling obediently opened the door to the front room. Even though the window was filthy, light flooded in and Ling found herself in a small parlour with an attractive cast iron fireplace. The walls were covered in dingy wallpaper, the woodwork was stained dark brown and a dubious looking rug was rucked up on the bare boards, but it seemed to Ling there was nothing that a good scrub couldn't put to rights. She felt like rolling up her sleeves there and then!

'It needs cleaning and disinfecting.' Elliott echoed her thoughts as he came up behind her. 'I'll paint it all nice and light. This room will be my surgery. William and I work in conjunction with each other, so I'll be working at his surgery sometimes, but I'll be working here mainly. The room behind, that'll be my main living room. Come and see.'

Ling followed him through to the back which was in an equally sorry state. But it was a good size with an adequate range and a long, narrow scullery at the back where an obviously brand-new pipe brought running water to a tap above a deep sink. Outside in the back yard were a wash house, a water closet and a coal house, and beyond them, the overgrown and neglected garden rose in steep terraces to a high retaining wall in the hill behind.

'You're going to be busy unless you can afford to hire someone to help.'

'Oh, I can't,' Elliott grimaced. 'But I'm not afraid of hard work. It just depends how much time I have. But come upstairs and see the bedrooms.'

He stood back, inviting Ling to precede him up the narrow staircase. Did Barney ever treat her like that? Indeed, no. It was only at Fencott Place that Seth and the gentlemen present had shown her respect as a lady, even when she had been employed by them. And now here was Elliott, the polite courtesy inbred in him coming so naturally to the fore. And how wonderful to live in this house — this house that Elliott had bought rather than rented — with its three separate bedrooms, running water and flushing lavatory. She could imagine herself helping patients, as Mrs Greenwood had done for her earlier, being *useful* to others, and perhaps acquiring some medical knowledge herself as Elliott's . . . as Elliott's wife.

Panic seized her by the throat and she swung round to see if Elliott was aware of her sudden trembling. But he was scanning the room with a critical eye, summing up what needed to be done.

'This one will be mine. Once it's decorated and furnished, of course. And has curtains at the window. I don't know how good I'll be at choosing soft furnishings, mind. Colours and so on. I-I don't suppose you'd like to help me?'

He cocked a hesitant, pleading eyebrow at her, and Ling's heart began to knock with such force that her vision blurred and she groped blindly for the doorway.

'Oh, I really must go or I'll miss my train,' she murmured almost pushing Elliott aside and flying down the stairs. She could hear Elliott scudding down behind her as she flung open the front door and gasped at the fresh air outside. And then she sprang across the tiny garden to the rickety gate.

'I'll come with you to the station,' Elliott called as he grasped his hat, one foot on the doorstep and his hand holding the latch.

'No, there's no need!' she shouted over her shoulder as she careered down the street. 'Good luck with it!' And she disappeared, leaving Elliott standing in a fog of bewilderment.

CHAPTER TWENTY-FOUR

'Don't forget I'm going to the swimming baths,' Ling reminded Barney. 'There's bread and cheese and ham for your lunch, and we can have the rest of the stew tonight.'

Barney turned towards her, his face in a dark scowl. 'You spend your life at they baths,' he complained. 'I thought as we had little enough money and you'm wasting it on all they train fares, to say nort o' the baths.'

'I spend no more than you do on gambling and drink!' Ling rounded on him. 'At least the exercise is good for me, and it is only during the summer.' *And it gets me away from you*, she felt like adding but managed to hold her tongue. That was unfair. She shouldn't blame Barney, and what he had said about their financial situation was true. Though they had enough money to survive, having Fanny and Laura to support was an added burden, and should demand drop and Barney find himself out of work, then where would they be? What little remained of the nest-egg that Seth and Rose had given them as a wedding present wouldn't last long if they had no other source of income!

And then there was baby Laura. Four months old now, and an absolute treasure. Fanny was a good little mother, one eye on her child now as she put away the washed breakfast dishes and laughing as Laura managed to guide her chubby foot to her mouth and suck her big toe. Laura was a gift to them all. Fanny had bloomed like a rose since the birth, and the infant had smoothed out the emptiness of Ling's own childlessness. And yet there were times when that very joy only served to wound her so deeply that she had to escape. The summer and the opening of the swimming baths for the season had given her the perfect excuse. And now that she had closed the school for the summer, she could go any day of the week, and she had chosen today because she knew Mrs Penrith would be there.

'Is it all right if Sam comes round arter dinner?' Fanny asked coyly.

A knowing, contented smile lifted Ling's mouth. 'Of course. Sam's always welcome.'

Fanny grinned back, a lovely hue blushing her cheeks, and Ling began to gather what she needed for the day. Within ten minutes, she was off, striding out in the fine July morning. The moor was beautiful, a luscious green interrupted with banks of heather and dotted with yellow gorse, all bathed in a clear, crystalline light. As the bustling noise of the quarries was left behind, the peace of the new day settled in Ling's heart. She would enjoy herself. Swim in the sparkling, sun-touched water and have lunch with Mrs Penrith. Window-shop, perhaps. She only hoped she didn't encounter Elliott.

She had not seen him since the afternoon she had abandoned him, slack-jawed, at the door of his new home back in April. Elliott had not tried to contact her. Had he read what was in her heart and been appalled by it? Or did he believe that their friendship was no more than a passing acquaintance that had drifted into oblivion? She sincerely hoped so. Guilt mauled her, yet it was nothing compared to the cruel torture of her denied love for Elliott. And yet that was how it must be for the remainder of her days.

But she should put her depression aside. It was a glorious day and she should relish it in a region where rain and mist as dense as soup were more likely even in high summer.

When she arrived there, Tavistock was a hive of activity, it being market day. Ling could hear the auctioneer's sing-song drone, interspersed with the lowing of cattle and the occasional bleat of a sheep coming from the animal market near the station. Bedford Square was clean and bright in the sunshine, but Ling crossed it, fearful that she might meet Elliott again. If she did, she would have to take a hold on herself. Smile. Ask politely if he had completed the refurbishment of his new home. Wish him well and walk on. Leaving part of her torn heart behind.

She reached the swimming baths at the top of the steep hill. The water was cold and took her breath away. Mrs Penrith appeared and Ling swam over to her, waiting while she climbed down the steps.

'Ling, my dear,' the older woman smiled apologetically. 'I'm so sorry I'm late. I just couldn't seem to motivate myself this morning.'

She spoke a little breathlessly and Ling tipped her head to one side, noticing the lines on her friend's face. She had always considered the sophisticated woman so handsome, but they had known each other eight years now, and she guessed that Mrs Penrith must be in her late fifties. The great blizzard had destroyed many of the lovely trees in the beautiful grounds of her house, which had saddened her terribly and, Ling realised with dismay, she was beginning to look her age.

'Well, never mind. You're here now. Shall we?'

A moment later, they were swimming side by side across the pool. Mrs Penrith seemed slower today, though, and several times Ling had to tread water while she caught up.

'I don't know, Ling, I don't seem to have any energy today,' she said at length. 'I think I'll change and then wait for you in my carriage. You will come to lunch, won't you? I've bought some new saplings and I'd like someone to help me decide where to plant them.'

Ling smiled back as she followed her companion up the steps. 'I should be honoured. But I don't mind coming now. I was here some time before you and I've had enough.'

'Well, if you're sure.'

Shortly afterwards, they were bowling along at a brisk pace across Abbey Bridge. Ling had travelled in the carriage on numerous occasions but she still found it a thrilling experience. Back at the house, Mrs Penrith ordered her maid to serve morning coffee out on the lawn as it was a little too early for lunch.

'I've only bought a few trees to start with,' she told Ling as she sipped from the bone china cup. 'I'll never see them fully grown, of course, but they will be my gift to posterity. To whoever owns this house after me.'

'I'm sure they'll look lovely, Mrs Penrith.'

'Oh, Ling, I believe we've known each other long enough. We are good friends, and I have watched you grow into a mature young woman. So I think it quite right that you should address me as Agnes from now on.'

Ling's mouth spread into a grin. Yes, she would like that. Mrs Penrith — Agnes — was like a friend and the mother she missed rolled into one. Except that Agnes was educated and sophisticated, nothing like Mary at all.

They walked around the grounds, the gardener moving the young trees, discussing their final shape and size and standing back to imagine the effect in twenty or thirty years' time. As they were coming back up the steeply sloping lawn, Agnes stopped dead. Ling heard a truncated intake of breath and a little cry seemed to stick in Agnes's throat as she suddenly squeezed Ling's arm in a grip of steel.

'Oh, my dear,' she barely croaked, releasing her hold and crossing her right hand tightly over her chest. Ling turned to her in horror as Agnes's face twisted in pain and she sank on her knees, toppling sideways onto the grass. With a hoarse cry of anguish, Ling dropped down beside her just in time to see Agnes's eyelids flutter in her grey, sweat-bedewed face before her body slackened and her head rolled onto her shoulder.

For a few dreadful seconds, Ling stared at her in disbelief, and then she was frantically calling her friend's name and shaking her, to no avail. She was aware of the gardener pounding up behind her and she screamed at him to fetch Mrs Penrith's doctor. And then, in one of the most appalling moments of her life, Ling was left alone with the unconscious woman.

Agnes Penrith's life could depend upon her.

What should she do? Loosen her clothing so that she could breathe more easily. But was she breathing? Ling tore at Agnes's dress which fortunately buttoned down the front. It came as no surprise that the slender figure was only lightly encased in stays which Ling's nimble fingers unhooked in seconds. Keep calm, don't panic. Oh, thank God! She could just hear the air passing in and out of the pale, open lips, but should she move her friend? Surely it was always easier to breathe sitting up? If only she *knew*! But surely it couldn't be wrong to raise Agnes's shoulders just a little?

'Oh, ma'am!'

Agnes's young maid had rushed across the lawn, her eyes horrified as she stared at her mistress, and Ling knew she had to take charge.

'Help me sit her up, just a fraction,' she said, amazed at her own calm voice and praying — oh, dear Lord — that it was the correct thing to do. The girl knelt down beside her and together they propped Agnes's limp form into a half sitting position so that she was leaning back against Ling's lap. And then Ling was swamped with relief as Agnes moaned softly and half opened her eyes.

'Oh, Mrs Penrith! Agnes!' Ling sighed, but for Agnes's sake, she must remain calm and strong. 'Now you just keep nice and still,' she said gently. 'We've sent for the doctor. He'll be here any minute.'

'Ah . . . yes . . . Dr Greenwood . . .'

The feeble words were lost in the sudden clatter of gravel scattering on the drive at the side of the house and Ling glanced over her shoulder almost faint with the comforting knowledge that help was at hand. And her heart vaulted painfully as she recognised the pretty dapple-grey horse and realised that the figure that had leapt from its back was none other than Elliott Franfield.

He hardly acknowledged her, his eyes meeting hers for only an instant.

'Mrs Penrith.' He spoke in that steady but efficient tone Ling had heard before, but now all she wanted was to get to her feet and run, hide away from the pain his presence was causing her. But she could not leave her friend and so she stayed put, quaking and the sweat oozing from her skin.

'Dr Greenwood was already on a call,' Elliott was explaining. 'I'm his colleague, Dr Franfield. Mrs Mayhew, can you tell me exactly what happened? Mrs Penrith, I don't want you to talk if possible. Just nod and lie still.'

Ling bit her lip. From Elliott's words, Agnes would doubtless have deduced that she and Elliott were already acquainted. She couldn't know *how* well, of course, since Ling had never mentioned Elliott to her, but she felt the shame burn hotly into her cheeks. Elliott, though, seemed unperturbed as he drew aside the unfastened front of Agnes's dress and listened to her heart through his stethoscope. Then he appeared to study the veins in her neck before placing his sensitive fingers beneath her jaw, his face set with concentration. He asked her questions to which she nodded periodically as he raised the hem of her skirt and examined her puffy ankles. He was so swift and unruffled, and not for the first time, Ling couldn't help admiring the calm confidence he seemed to create about him. But if only she didn't admire him so *much*!

'It all points to a brief heart attack, Mrs Penrith,' he said with a reassuring smile. 'But don't worry. It really isn't as frightening as it sounds. A few days' rest and a little daily medication will put you right. Now, if you would just open your mouth for me,' he instructed, carefully drawing a pipette of liquid from a bottle in his bag, 'I'm going to drop this tincture onto your tongue.'

As he did so, he shot Ling a grateful glance that said he appreciated the way she had handled the situation, a glance that under different circumstances, Ling might have basked in. But not now.

'There. Are you feeling better now?'

Elliott waited while Agnes, looking a lot less pasty, drew in a recuperating breath and released it slowly. 'Oh, yes, young man. I believe I am.'

'Well, if you feel up to being moved, I want you carried to your bed. You, there!' he called to the gardener and the coachman who had been hovering in great anxiety by the house. 'I need your help to carry your mistress inside.'

Ling waited while Elliott directed the transportation of her dear friend and then followed the party indoors. This wasn't the first time she had observed Elliott at work and it just made her feel — oh, she couldn't explain it — so right and natural to be by his side. It was more than a profession with him. It was a gift. The very gift of giving of oneself to help others, she supposed in the same way as she loved imparting her knowledge to her pupils, though there were precious few who really appreciated it. A gift that she shared with Elliott. And not with Barney who saw her work as nothing more than the means of a few extra shillings in the pot each week. And now she was here, with Elliott who treated her on his own intelligent level, and who was good and kind and thought only of others.

Her breast heaved in turmoil. Did Elliott realise the anguish in her heart, the shame that she should feel like this when she was a married woman and her dear friend was so ill?

'Would you be able to stay for a few days?' Elliott's level voice dragged her back to reality. 'I'd feel happier if she had someone with her with a sensible head on their shoulders. I'm sure she'll be all right now, but I'd rather *you* were here just in case.'

His arresting eyes were boring into her face. She didn't deserve this. His trust. When she was feeling something so different. It was unbearable.

* * *

Having just returned from sending a telegram to Barney, Ling sat down in Agnes's morning room, gratefully taking the tea Elliott poured her. 'How is Mrs Penrith now? I'm not sure I like her being upstairs alone—'

'I wanted her to get some sleep, but I'm just going to slip in and check on her, if you'll excuse me.'

Ling nodded, and for several minutes sat in the handsome room, silent but for the steady ticking of the clock. The rhythmical, ceaseless sound somehow set her stomach churning again. Goodness, the day had turned out differently from the one she had planned. Poor Agnes, seriously ill, and Ling herself thrown back with Elliott when she had been trying so valiantly to avoid him.

'Asleep,' Elliott assured her as he came back in. 'You really mustn't worry. But seeing as Mrs Penrith gave her permission earlier for me to discuss her health with you, I shall do so. I'm as sure as I can be that she'll make a full recovery. It seemed a relatively mild attack, and with daily medication, she should be able to lead a perfectly normal life. So, can we have a little smile, now?' he cajoled, trying to catch her eye.

Ling's mouth twitched. Yes, she was worried sick about Agnes, but she was so frightened that Elliott might guess at the confused havoc his very presence was wreaking on her.

'So, what caused it?' she stammered uncertainly. She wanted to know for Agnes's sake, of course she did. But also, oh dear God, she wanted to keep the conversation sensible, normal, so that Elliott wouldn't suspect the way her own heart was leaping about in her chest.

Elliott spread his hands. 'The heart can become tired over time,' he explained patiently. 'Why in some people and not others, we're not entirely sure. Our diet, perhaps, how active we are, heredity. Maybe one day we'll know more. But the heart is really a muscle, pumping the blood around our bodies. Sometimes it becomes overworked and needs to take a brief rest. This was just a warning for Mrs Penrith. A low dose of digitalis every day is bound to put it right. She might have to get used to taking life a little easier, mind. Being a widow, she might find that hard, though.'

Ling straightened her shoulders, grasping the opportunity of a practical discussion that might stop the breath fluttering in her throat. 'She has an advisor,' she volunteered. 'Her husband's business partner when he was alive. She still owns half the company. Engineering of some sort, I believe.'

'Well, at least she won't have any financial worries,' Elliott commented. 'Unlike many of our patients, poor devils. Most of us only charge them a nominal fee, but we make up for it from those that can afford it. Still seems wrong, though, taking money from people because they're sick. But as long as I have enough to survive, I'm happy. My mother isn't, mind. She considers we should charge professional fees to everyone and leave those who can't afford it to suffer.'

'Well, I think she should be proud of you!' Ling bristled, wondering at the indignation that made the hairs on the back of her neck stand on end, and praying that Elliott hadn't noticed the vehemence that had trembled in her voice.

Apparently he hadn't as he gave a wry smile. 'Oh, she is! When it suits her, that is. "My son, the physician." But she does nothing but complain that I can't afford a housekeeper. And if she knew that we doctors give our services free at the cottage hospital, she'd have a blue fit! But that's how it works, you see. Most of the physicians in the town devote a certain time for free. There's the matron to be paid, though, and various overheads, of course. But various companies about the town pay in, and there's other benefactors and church collections and so forth. So the patients themselves are charged very little. It seems to work quite well, and it's a good deal more pleasant than the workhouse.'

'Oh, I never realised. I'd heard of the Cottage Hospital, but I didn't know how it worked.'

'Trouble is, we could really do with expanding. Larger premises. Mind you, being in West Street, it's mighty convenient for me. Just a few minutes' walk away. I get enough exercise walking all over the town, running often if it's an emergency.'

'But you have Ghost. I was so pleased to see you still have her.'

'Yes. My mother wanted to sell her when I went to London, but I managed to persuade her otherwise. She's such a perfect mount. So calm and unruffled, and yet she can still go like the wind. William, Dr Greenwood, he rents the field behind his house and Ghost shares it with his horse. I was at William's today, so it was quicker to ride here than to walk.'

'And how is your house coming on?'

Elliott smiled ruefully. 'Not as quickly as I'd have wished. I have a decent consulting room and a clean bedroom to sleep in, but the rest of the place is still a shambles. And the garden! It's like a jungle this weather. I've had a go at it, but it grows up again so quickly. But why don't you come and see for yourself? It would be lovely to have a proper visitor. I don't hold a surgery on Thursdays, though I can still be called out.'

His eyes were shining with enthusiasm, his eyebrows arched in a way that Ling found hard to resist. Guilt tugged at her heart, but she turned her back on its gnawing teeth. Surely it could do no harm?

'Yes, I should like that,' she smiled back.

CHAPTER TWENTY-FIVE

Harry Spence sauntered towards the centre of Princetown. It was Saturday afternoon and he was on his way to an assignation with the pretty young barmaid from the Plume of Feathers. Last week they had ensconced themselves safely at the back of a straw-filled barn, and what a delight she had been! Her lust was even more insatiable than his own, tempting him, touching him, exposing herself to him. Not like the few occasions he had taken Fanny Southcott. He'd had the devil's own job, persuading her that he loved her, coaxing and flattering her. She'd been like a frightened mouse, lying there petrified, not moving an inch and refusing to remove a single item of clothing so that all he'd seen of her was a glimpse of her thin thighs as he'd lifted her skirt. It had been over in a matter of minutes, no fun at all. He had been well rid of her. Not like, well, he couldn't remember her name. But his mouth salivated at the thought of the pleasures to come.

It was as he ambled along past the shops in Caunters Row, eagerly anticipating the afternoon's activities, that he saw her. He stopped in his tracks. For there in front of him stood the said Fanny Southcott looking totally different. Still beautiful with that wispy, fairylike quality to her, but with an air of confidence that had never been there before. Her blond tresses were evidently scooped up in a knot beneath a nearly new, fashionable boater. Her high-necked blouse and the light bolero she wore over it both looked as if they had just come from the dressmaker, as did the serviceable but elegant skirt that fell from her tiny waist. She was leaning forward, cooing over the infant that lay in the perambulator she was pushing. Perambulator! And not just the homemade wooden box on wheels that most fathers knocked up in the back shed, but a proper affair with shining coachwork and a folding hood. It must have cost a fortune!

Harry had never been very bright, but he made up for it in cunning and he was quick enough when it came to money. He could smell it! And Fanny must have had a windfall of some sort to afford new clothes *and* a perambulator! Where had it come from? Harry didn't much care. All he knew was that he had never received a penny for risking his own life to save Fanny's in the swollen waters of the Walkham, and now his payment was due. Even if it meant marrying the girl, it didn't matter. She might lie like a block of ice in bed, but her purse would make up for it. And there would be nothing to stop him satisfying his desires elsewhere.

'Fanny! What a pleasure to see you!' He stepped forward, raising his hat politely. 'How are you?'

Fanny straightened up and the colour drained from her elfin face.

'My goodness, you're looking well!' Harry continued in as friendly a manner as he could muster. 'Shall we take tea in the tearooms? I should like so much to treat you. And is this my child?' he grinned, turning his attention now to Laura who gurgled happily up at the stranger. 'What did you have, a boy or a girl?'

Fanny's knuckles began to turn white as they gripped the handle of the perambulator. 'A g-girl,' she stuttered, and her heart thudded so hard she almost fainted as Harry plucked Laura into his arms and jiggled her up and down.

'Hello, my little love,' Harry crooned. 'You'm my daughter, and I'm going to make it up to you. Yes, that's right!' he nodded as Laura gave him her gummy smile. 'I'm your dada!'

'Oh, no, you're not!'

He hadn't seen Ling sweep out of the grocer's, dropping her basket and moving so swiftly that she had snatched Laura from his grasp before he knew what had happened. Anger shot through his veins and it was all he could do to stop himself attempting to wrest the brat from that bloody harridan's arms again! But he must contain his fury if he was to stand a chance of wheedling his way back into Fanny's affections.

'Ling, what a pleasant surprise!' he purred. 'I'd just invited your sister to take some refreshment in the tearooms. Won't you join us?'

'Over my dead body! And you can keep your hands off the baby!'

'Oh, come now! She is my daughter, after all.'

'Oh, no, she isn't.' Ling's voice was cold, like ice, her eyes sparking with rancour as she clutched Laura fiercely to her chest. 'Fanny's never named the father, not even to us. It could be anyone.'

'So your sister's a whore now, is she?' Harry sneered triumphantly, his patience beginning to fray.

'I'm sure you're not the only varmint low enough to trick an innocent young girl,' Ling spat back. 'But while I have no doubt that you're the king of such underhand treachery, don't fool yourself that you're the only such blackguard hereabouts! And there's no way you or anyone else can prove you're the father. And what would you want with the responsibility of someone else's child? Now get out of the way before I call the constable!'

Wrath suffused into Harry's face and his hands balled into fists at his sides, shaking as he fought to stop himself punching Ling Mayhew in the face. But he was sly enough to know when the force of the law could be brought against him. And the witch was right in one thing. He didn't want the by-blow, only the money it could bring with it. He would bide his time, wait for another opportunity to waylay its stupid and gullible mother. A time when her bloody sister wasn't there to protect her. And he'd find a way to get back at *her*, too!

And he scowled like some demon from hell as he watched them walk away, dressed smartly in Rose Warrington's cast-offs and pushing the perambulator the kind woman had lent them.

* * *

Ling briskly turned off Tavistock's Plymouth Road before she changed her mind. She had been to visit Agnes Penrith who, after two weeks of complete rest, was looking her old self. It was wonderful to see her recovered and the lively conversation helped to seal Ling's mind to the decision she would have to make when she arrived back in the town centre.

But she had already made it, hadn't she? Otherwise, she wouldn't have chosen a Thursday. Her heart was thumping nervously not only with guilt at what she was doing, but also with the excitement of seeing Elliott again. Excitement she must conceal for Elliott must never know what she felt for him, but which seemed to have given her a new reason for living.

She paused fleetingly by the front gate which she noted had been repaired so that it swung open easily when she pushed it as if the final barrier to her hesitation had been swept aside. She was visiting a friend, no more than that. A friend who just happened to be of the opposite sex. And taking a deep breath, she stepped up to the front door and rapped loudly with the knocker.

She waited. Observed with a smile the shining brass plate screwed into the wall. *Dr Elliott Franfield, M.D.* Some children were playing further along the otherwise quiet street. The sunshine warmed her back. And her spirits plummeted as after all her struggling with her conscience, she realised that no one was in.

She turned away, disappointed and empty. It was not to be and she would return to her frustrated, disconsolate life on the moor. She had clicked the gate-latch closed behind her and taken several steps along the road when she heard a door open and a male voice called out after her.

Ling spun on her heel. There was Elliott, his head poking out from the front door, his face pleated with anxiety and his entire body tensely poised. He was dressed in some old corduroy trousers held about his slim waist by a leather belt, and a striped, collarless shirt open at the neck and with the sleeves rolled up over his strong but slender forearms. His light hair fell waywardly over his forehead, and something tightened in the pit of Ling's belly.

'Ling!' His mouth spread into a welcoming smile. 'I was worried it might be an emergency. I was out doing battle with the back garden and wasn't sure I'd heard the front door or not. Oh, it's good to see you! Do come in! Take a look round and see what I've done. I'll just go through to the back and wash my hands.'

He left Ling alone in the hallway and all at once she felt peace and calm settle over her. The walls had been painted a brilliant white, banishing the gloomy atmosphere of her earlier visit. The floor gleamed, and a pair of small, nicely turned chairs stood one on either side of an equally small table, perfect for waiting patients in such a confined passage. The door to the front room was ajar and Ling couldn't resist walking inside. Elliott really had transformed it into a professional consulting room. The walls here were a soft, pale green with curtains of a slightly darker hue at the now sparkling windows. On the shining floorboards stood a large, beautifully carved desk and a matching chair. Against the wall behind was a massive bookcase crammed with well-thumbed volumes of, Ling assumed, medical treatises, and on the nearside of the desk, two chairs of equal quality for the patient and a companion. In one corner was an examination couch with a screen folded back against the wall, and the whole effect was finished off with several smart oil-lamps.

'So, what do you think?'

Ling glanced over her shoulder as Elliott appeared on the threshold, lounging languidly against the door frame.

'I'd say you've worked wonders! I love the colour of the walls. And the furniture's beautiful.'

'Ah, well, having a father who's built his empire on furniture and such-like does have its advantages,' Elliott said wryly. 'There's no way I could have afforded such lovely pieces myself.'

Ling nodded, running her finger along the edge of the desk, and then her eyes focused on the large print at the top of a small pile of pamphlets.

'What's this?' she asked innocently. '*The Law of Population*? What does that mean?'

'It's advice on contraception,' Elliott replied easily from the doorway. 'You know, preventing women conceiving a child. It's really hard sometimes to get information through to the poorer classes, and they're often the ones who need it most. They find it hard to discuss such matters even with a physician, so I lend them copies of this pamphlet. Those that can read. It's by Annie Besant. You might have heard of her. A fantastic woman! I met her once in London.'

Ling was grateful for the explanation. She'd never heard of, what did Elliott call it, contraception? And then she suddenly felt her heart fragment as the meaning of his words sank in. 'No. I've not heard of her,' she managed to answer his question, the old, familiar pain raking her throat. 'Life isn't always fair, is it?' she murmured distractedly. 'I suppose there must be those that have so many children, they don't want any more. And there's people like me who desperately want a child and can't have one.'

Her voice faded away in a thin trail and she stared down blindly at the desk. She heard Elliott come softly up behind her and she wanted so much to turn round and face him with a bright smile. But it was impossible, and she slowly sank beneath her own misery.

'I hate seeing you so unhappy, Ling.' Elliott's voice was low, tender with compassion, so close she could feel his breath fanning the back of her neck below her upswept hair. 'I just wish, as a physician, there was something I could do to help. And as a friend.'

Oh, dear God! She wanted to weep, to have Elliott take her in his arms so that she could sob against his shoulder, release her heart from the fetters that bound it. Let her tears wash clean the muddied depths of her soul. But she mustn't. And so she turned, a wistful smile curving the corners of her mouth.

'You know, I'm ashamed of it, but sometimes I feel glad I've not had Barney's child,' she found herself admitting in a hoarse whisper. 'It's a poor marriage if we need a child to bring us back together. I mean, I'm still fond of Barney, but . . . I sometimes wonder if I ever *really* loved him. We were only childhood sweethearts, and if it hadn't been for . . . If it weren't for that one, stupid mistake, I'm not sure we'd have ever been married. My parents would both have still been alive and I wouldn't have been trapped. It's my own fault, I know, but it's hardly a good reason to bring a child into the world.'

She had been staring sightlessly at the open neck of Elliott's shirt, unaware of the tears that meandered down her cheeks like silver pearls until Elliott delicately thumbed them away. She looked up then and her heart tripped. Those intense, green-blue eyes seemed to delve deep into her soul, holding, mesmerising her, his handsome, sensitive lips so close. And it just felt so right, so *meant*, when they brushed almost imperceptibly against hers. It was like some sweet unguent soothing her wounded soul, and her heart overflowed with peace.

He pulled away, leaving her breathless. Light-headed. 'Oh, may God forgive me,' he mumbled. And as Ling opened her eyes, he staggered backwards, his hand over his mouth and the blood drained from his face. 'Oh, God, Ling, I'm so sorry.'

They stared at each other across the few feet that separated them, Elliott's eyes wide with shock at his own actions while Ling's lips slowly dragged apart.

'Don't be,' she heard herself say, and she watched the horror on his face slacken as his forehead moved into a questioning frown. She stepped forward, her head bold and erect and her heart flying. Her eager mouth sought his again, tingling as they touched, feather-like at first, enticing, drawing her on, entangling her in some sublime force she had never known with Barney. She clung to him hungrily, knowing that this was passion far beyond anything she had experienced before.

Had Elliott taken her upstairs there and then, she would have been willing, but he suddenly drew back, running his hand through his hair and his expression confused and appalled.

'This is *wrong*, Ling,' he muttered, and shot out of the room, leaving her swooning where she stood. Elliott had kissed her, and if it was the only moment of true passion in her entire life, she would take the memory of it to her grave.

She followed him on unsteady legs into the back room where she found him spooning tea-leaves into a pot. 'W-we let ourselves get carried away,' he stammered, and Ling could see his hands were shaking.

'No. Not carried away.' Her voice was small, her words slow and carefully chosen. '*I* wasn't, anyway. I love you, Elliott. I think I always have. Ever since you rode past me on Ghost. Even before you rescued me from under the train.'

Elliott blinked at her, and his eyebrows shot up towards his hair. 'Do you really think so?' And then he suddenly laughed aloud. 'And when I saw this lanky young wench with a halo of chestnut hair, I really thought she'd taken me to heaven with her, and I've thought of no one else ever since! All those years in London, when I longed to receive a letter from you so that I could write back! If only . . .'

He stopped short, and the broad smile slid from both their faces. 'If only Barney had given me your note,' Ling finished for him.

They stared at each other for a full minute, their young hearts racing and ready to explode. Then Elliott sucked in his lower lip. 'We must think this through carefully, Ling. We must both decide what we really want.'

But in truth, they both already knew.

CHAPTER TWENTY-SIX

When Elliott opened the front door the following Thursday afternoon, he had his answer. No sooner had he closed the door behind her when Ling was wrapped in his embrace and the intense joy of being with him again galloped up and down her spine. He kissed her tenderly, ecstatically, without the deep force of the previous week, but just as passionate for that.

The kettle was already singing on the range in the back room, cups arranged on their saucers, and Ling felt the pulse that pounded at her temples ease with a touch of amusement. The English idiosyncrasy of the obligatory cup of tea was clearly deep rooted with Elliott. Perhaps he was as nervous as she was, but he was certainly a gentleman, and he pulled out a chair for her at the table. Then he picked up a pair of oven gloves and opening the oven door, removed a bun-tin with six sad-looking mounds of cake mixture in it.

His face fell. 'Oh, dear,' he mumbled. 'Aren't they supposed to expand or something?'

Ling gazed at him, her hesitation fleeing as she tried not to laugh at his crestfallen expression. 'They're not cooked yet, and I don't think the oven's hot enough. Put them on the top shelf, and maybe by the time we've made the tea, they'll be ready. They mightn't rise, though, now you've taken them out. And, well, to be honest, I've only just had lunch with Agnes,' she concluded.

'Yes. Of course you have.' His eyes met hers, suddenly dancing rakishly, and he threw up his head with that wonderful, soft laugh. 'Oh, dear, what an idiot! Trying to impress you with my non-existent culinary skills! I've never baked a cake in my life. Casseroles and stews are more my line.' He paused, his eyebrows raised quizzically. 'What *am* I doing, babbling on about my dietary arrangements when the loveliest woman in the world has come to visit me?'

It was Ling who was grinning now at his boyish expression. 'No!' she giggled, light-hearted now the initial tension had subsided. 'I want to know everything about you. What you were like as a little boy, for instance.'

'As a boy?' he asked in surprise as he proceeded to make the tea. 'Quite serious and well-behaved as I remember. It was as an adolescent that I began to rebel. I mean, not seriously. But I began to see *beyond* my mother's circle of friends. Tight-laced lot they were. Are. My father, now I've always got on rather better with him. He's more open-minded about people. But,' he said more sombrely as he poured the scalding liquid into the cups. 'What about you? What was your childhood like?'

Ling tipped her head sideways. 'Hard,' she replied thoughtfully. 'My father was a quarryman at Foggintor all his life. We always had the open moor to play on, and I've always loved living there. But, I don't know how to put it, you can feel trapped up there. Until the railway came. And I met you.'

She saw the muscles of his handsome face tighten, and lowered her eyes as doubt clouded her resolve once more. What *was* she doing here? Barney. But Barney had betrayed her all those years ago. Or had it merely slipped his mind? She supposed she would never know.

'Come and see what I've done in the garden.'

Elliott's voice was expressionless as if he, too, could make no sense of his conflicting emotions. Ling followed him outside, her legs unsteady. On the upper two terraces, Elliott had hacked the waist-high growth down to ground level, and the first flat surface beyond the yard had been worked to a perfect bed of finely raked earth.

'I'm going to sow grass seed,' he told her. 'At least then I'll have somewhere to sit out. When I have a spare moment,' he added with a grimace. 'And when it's not raining.'

He raised his eyes towards the dark sky as rain started to fall in large, heavy droplets and they both instinctively turned back into the house. As they went inside, the familiar churning gripped Ling's stomach. They had both been delaying the moment, both knowing what it was they truly wanted, but knowing it was unutterably wrong.

'You'd better take off your jacket. Hang it on the back of the chair to dry. I must say, you look very smart.'

'Mrs Warrington, you remember? She gave it to me. She's very generous.'

Ling arranged the tailored jacket so that it did not crease, and found herself facing Elliott across the small room. She saw the smouldering fire in his eyes, his face creased with the same pain of self-denial that was tearing her apart. The space between them suddenly disappeared and he was kissing her lips, soft as the touch of gossamer, her forehead, the tip of her nose, the fine line of her jaw. She felt his fingers fumbling with the buttons of her blouse and his hand slipped inside, gently cupping the swelling of her breast through her chemise. She could feel her heart pounding beneath his touch. Oh, Elliott! She loved him with a passion that confounded her own understanding, a passion against which she was powerless. Her own fingers entwined in his thick hair, her mouth seeking his again, her mind, her body, totally ready to give herself to him.

'Damn!'

So lost had she been in that state of frenzied euphoria that she had not heard the frantic knocking on the front door. But Elliott had, and he quickly smoothed down his hair as he rushed to the front door.

'Oh, Doctor, 'tis my little girl!' Ling heard the desperate voice as she buttoned up her blouse. 'She cas'n breathe!'

'Give her to me.'

Elliott's efficient tone drew Ling to the door. A short, thin woman clad in little better than rags was standing on the doorstep relinquishing a young child into Elliott's arms.

'Please save her!' the woman squealed as she tottered inside on the brink of collapse. 'I cas'n bear to lose her!'

The young mother's howl of despair wrenched at Ling's heart. She knew herself the agony of losing a child, even if her own had been a tiny, lifeless form when it had entered the world. She instinctively put her arm around the stranger as they followed Elliott into his consulting room. The little girl was already lying on the couch, her body writhing as she fought to draw breath and her pinched face turning blue.

'Has she swallowed a solid object? Or some sort of poison?' Elliott asked swiftly. 'Or has she been unwell? She feels really hot and her pulse is racing.'

'She came over sick yesterday,' the woman moaned. 'And she said this morning her throat were really bad.'

'Glands are hugely swollen,' Elliott muttered almost to himself. 'What's her name?'

'Maggie,' her mother sobbed. 'Oh, my little cheel . . .'

'Maggie, can you hear me? I'm Doctor Franfield. I need to look at your throat. Can you open your mouth for me? Ling, can you light that lamp and bring it over here?'

Ling caught her breath. There was something about Elliott's attitude that invaded her own being and she quickly and calmly obeyed Elliott's instructions, holding the lamp while he struggled to look into the restless child's mouth.

He glanced at her with a deep frown. 'Diphtheria. Get three masks out of the middle left-hand drawer of the desk and give one to the mother.'

Ling found herself moving as if she assisted Elliott every day. When she returned with the linen masks, he was withdrawing a needle from Maggie's arm and the girl was instantly relaxing.

'I'm going to make a hole in the windpipe and insert a tube so that she can breathe,' Elliott told Ling quietly. 'Get your own mask on first, then put mine on me, if you would. And then hold the lamp for me. You won't faint on me, will you? If you think you might, just don't look.'

She nodded, amazed at herself and ready to follow his advice. But it wasn't necessary. Within a matter of seconds, the incision in Maggie's neck was made, the tube inserted, and the horrendous wheezing in her throat ceased as she breathed more normally.

Elliott released a massive sigh. 'Right. It's got to be the workhouse infirmary. The cottage hospital doesn't take infectious cases. But we go *now*!' he commanded. 'Ling, can you bring my bag? Oh, and my keys. Make sure the house is locked. The medicines, you see.'

'Yes, of course.'

Elliott scooped Maggie in his arms and hurried out of the front door with the child's mother following, and Ling was left alone in the little house. The entire episode had taken less than five minutes, and she felt stunned, unreal. To think that only moments before, she had been about to go upstairs and make love to Elliott. Was fate trying to tell her something?

She donned her jacket and hat, secured all the doors and windows, and picked up Elliott's medical bag. He had not stopped to put on his coat and had gone out into the rain in his shirt sleeves. He would be wet through, so she rummaged through his wardrobe for a clean shirt, grasped his coat from the hall stand, and stepping outside, locked the front door behind her.

* * *

'Will she be all right?'

Ling sprang to her feet as Elliott walked into the cold and unwelcoming hall where she was waiting. She watched as he slumped down wearily on the hard wooden bench and exhaled heavily.

'I don't know. I've removed as much of the debris from the poor child's throat as I can, but heaven knows if it'll work. With careful nursing and God willing, she might recover. But even after five or six weeks when they seem over it, a patient can suddenly die. Terrible thing, diphtheria.' He shook his head in bitter frustration and turned to Ling, his solemn gaze meeting hers. 'I've been exposed to it quite often in London, so I've probably built up an immunity. But *you* haven't. It's highly unlikely that you'd catch it from such a short exposure, but promise me that if you feel at all unwell with even a hint of a sore throat, you'll send for William. Or the prison surgeon. They've got a new one now, thank God, so I don't have to act as locum anymore.'

Ling bit on her bottom lip. The incident with little Maggie had brought the gravity of Elliot's responsibilities home to her. Life and death decisions were part of his daily routine. And this hardly seemed an appropriate moment to start — oh, she could scarcely bring herself to think the word — an affair with him.

'Yes, I promise,' she answered gravely. 'But I must go now. Barney . . . will be wondering where I am.'

Elliott drew in a deep breath. 'Yes, I know,' he nodded. 'And I want to stay on here for the next few hours at least. I'm sorry, Ling.'

'Don't be.' The compassion on his face brought a soft smile to her lips. She loved him so much she felt her heart would break. She turned and made for the door. When she glanced back, Elliott was already marching briskly towards the wards.

CHAPTER TWENTY-SEVEN

'Ling!' Elliott gave a delighted grin. 'I didn't know if you'd come. So come in, come in!'

She stepped over the threshold, and all at once the qualms and misgivings that had been trundling round in her head were chased away by the sheer jubilation of being with him again. He lifted her hands to his lips, turning her palms upwards and softly brushing his mouth and tongue over the inside of each wrist in turn. The sensation that shot down her spine took her breath away.

'I-I had to know how little Maggie is,' she stammered, still taken aback at the effect his kisses had produced throughout her entire body.

'Holding her own, poor mite. But it's early days. We've put notices up in the town and in the *Gazette* for people to be vigilant, but there's been no more cases reported. Thank God it's the school holidays or it'd be spreading like wildfire. But as it is, I don't think we need worry.'

Elliott gave her that calm, reassuring smile, driving away the concern that had begun to grind in her heart. Into its place leapt the reason why she was there as the clear brilliance in Elliott's eyes seemed to deepen. He was still holding her hands as if he could not bear to let them go, but now he released one of them to gesture tentatively, hesitantly, towards the stairs. 'Shall we?' he barely croaked. 'If . . . if it's really what you want?'

Ling felt the lurch of her heart and she was sure it missed a beat. She swallowed and nodded, since her voice had suddenly become trapped in her throat. Elliott led her slowly and regally up the stairs and into the front bedroom. She gained a fleeting impression of the vast changes in the room, but she was blind to any detail as Elliott drew the curtains and stepped back across the room. She stood, still as a statue, as he removed her hat and then his fingers in her rebellious hair found the pins that secured it and it fell down around her shoulders in a foam of chestnut curls. He cupped her chin in one hand, tilting her mouth towards his and they met in a soft, moist, lingering kiss.

At last, he drew away and she opened her eyes as she was aware of him unfastening her jacket and the blouse beneath. His brow, though, was furrowed as he glanced at her face, seeking her consent and ready to stop if she so asked. She didn't. She knew it was wrong but she was lost in this heady passion, this desperate, overpowering yearning. She had never felt this way with Barney, not even on that inebriated evening all those years ago that had ruined all their lives. The mere shadow of remorse flickered across her mind, but was at once obliterated by the here and now, the need, the love that beat so furiously in her breast. Elliott slipped the jacket and blouse from her shoulders, and his fingers searched for the buttons at the waist of her skirt which an instant later joined her other garments on the floor. There was no going back.

'I'm glad to see you don't wear a corset,' Elliott muttered under his breath. 'So bad for the internal organs.'

The comment seemed so absurdly out of place and yet so typical of Elliott, ever the physician, that it made Ling chuckle. Or was it the perfect release as the tension drained away, leaving her body malleable and open to whatever Elliott wanted to do to her? He sat her on the edge of the bed and knelt at her feet, deftly removing her shoes and stockings, his eyes dark and smouldering as he lifted his hands to run them, soft and leisurely, down her arms. Her flesh tingled at his touch and she nearly swooned as in one swift movement, he whisked her chemise over her head, exposing her firm, naked breasts. She could feel herself quivering, the fire spiralling down to her loins, as Elliott stroked her shoulders, played his mouth over her neck, the well at her throat, tracing his tongue over the top of her breasts and sensitively drawing her nipple between his lips. Never, *never*, had Barney treated her like this, *loving* every inch of her. The sensation was intoxicating and she began to give herself entirely to its glory, dropping her head back as she moaned with desire.

The slight pressure of his hand on her shoulder had her lying back on the bed and his caresses stopped briefly while he took off his own clothing. Her eyes feasted avidly on his naked torso. He wasn't heavily muscled like Barney, rather his shoulders rippled with a hard, wiry strength, his waist retaining the slenderness of youth that Barney had long lost. He stood beside the bed, his own excitement well in evidence, allowing her to inspect him, his chin slightly raised as if he shared that bewildering mix of desire and embarrassment. And then he reached out, carefully untying the strings of her drawers and slid them down over her knees.

A shiver tumbled down Ling's spine and crept, strong and tantalising, into that secret place that was only hers and Barney's. And yet she yearned for it to be Elliott's, instinctively knowing by the way he had coaxed and enticed the rest of her body in a way Barney never bothered with, that he would bring that innermost part of her to some fever-pitch she had never known before. He lay down beside her, drawing her body against the hard length of his own, flesh against flesh, kissing her, the fragrance of fine lemon soap on his closely shaven jaw wafting into her nostrils as her hands sought his smooth, warm shoulders. She flinched as his fingers crept sensuously over her thighs and she saw his eyebrows tighten in a quizzing frown.

'Oh, God, what if I get pregnant!' she suddenly gasped in sickening terror. 'What if after all these years of trying with Barney—'

'You won't.' Elliott was smiling faintly, his eyes a deep aquamarine she could drown in. 'It would hardly be right for me to preach contraception to my patients and not use it myself. You do trust me, don't you, Ling?'

She blinked at him. Oh, yes, deep in her soul, she trusted him with all her heart. Trusted him and loved him. He encompassed her in his arms, comforting and reassuring her, soothing away the doubt. She whimpered softly as he began to lead her on once more, enticing her, exploring her body until it cried out with eager need, an urgent desire to reach some frenzied height of rapturous wonderment. He turned away from her for a few moments, and she wondered what he was doing. But then he was back, and when he slipped inside her, it wasn't the quick, painful thrusting that she was used to, but a slow, languid pulsing that sent exquisite ripples through her being until she suddenly exploded with an indescribable joy that flooded into every inch of her body. She gasped aloud, then realised that in that split second, Elliott had become rigid and then juddered against her. And they were clinging to each other, shocked, amazed, glorying in the natural intensity of their love. Was that what she should have felt each time she granted Barney his conjugal rights? And Elliott had not turned his back, leaving her in some cold shadow now that it was over. He was kissing her, holding her, and muttering endearments against her cheek.

'Do you know how I've longed for that, my darling? Oh, Jesus, if only you could be mine. *Really* mine.'

His voice vibrated with emotion and she stared deep into his anguished face. 'But I am, Elliott. I love you, and I wish so much . . . I never feel like that with Barney. He just . . . seeks his own pleasure. For me, it's just a duty. He never thinks that *I* might want to enjoy it, too. But I suppose you know how a woman really feels. You've had the experience—'

'Good Lord, no!' Elliott sat bolt upright in the bed. 'You don't think . . . ? I've studied female anatomy inside out, of course I have. But we don't study how a woman *feels*. And you may find this hard to believe, but until today . . . just now . . . I've never . . . Well, only some adolescent fumbling with the daughter of one of my mother's friends. My God, my mother would have killed me if she'd known!'

Ling was still in that sublime state of euphoric contentment and she sat up next to Elliott in astonishment, her hair falling forward over her breasts in a riot of cinnamon and gold. 'What! You mean this was your first time?'

'Oh, please don't laugh at me,' Elliott groaned. 'The first time *properly*, if you understand me.'

'I'm not laughing. I'm just surprised.'

'I know. Ridiculous, isn't it?' he murmured. 'Twenty-eight next month and never before . . . Most men have a tribe of children by my age. Or a string of bastards. I was mocked for not seeking female company but I didn't have *time* if I really wanted to study hard. And anyway, I had a teasing memory of a young girl who liked to jump under trains. And I just hoped with every week that passed that she'd write to me.'

'Oh, Elliott,' Ling breathed, resting her head against his shoulder. 'If only I had. If only I'd *known*. And then I wouldn't have to be sneaking away to see you.'

Elliott lifted her chin to gaze at her, his eyes ardent with desire again, and leaned forward to kiss her delicately on the lips before springing to his feet to pull on his underdrawers and trousers.

'Don't get cold. Put something round you, and I'll bring up a cup of tea.'

Ling laughed softly as she heard him pad downstairs. A cup of tea, what else? Oh, she felt so happy! At this very moment, she didn't care that she was an adulterous married woman. She loved Elliott. She was still fond of Barney, of course she was. But she recognised that she had never loved him with the force, the passion she felt for Elliott. Her father had been right.

She spied Elliott's dressing gown and slipped it around her naked form. The garment smelled of the same lemon fragrance she had noticed from Elliott's skin and she breathed it in deeply before wandering about the room. All was neat and tidy and very masculine. And then Ling saw the bookcase, not stuffed with medical tomes as downstairs in the consulting room, but overflowing with works of fiction and poetry, Browning, Keats, Wordsworth, Dickens, Elizabeth Gaskill, Hardy and even Mary Shelley's *Frankenstein*, every writer Ling could think of.

Elliott came back in with a tray. 'Help yourself. I know you love books. You can borrow anything you want.'

Ling stiffened. 'No. I don't think I'd better. Barney, you see.'

'Ah.' Elliott nodded knowingly as the dark cloud passed between them. Of course. They would have to be careful. 'That doesn't stop you looking at them now, though. Who's your favourite?'

'Oh, heavens, I don't know. I love Dickens, but Hardy's lighter to read.'

'Have you read his new one? *Tess of the D'Urbervilles*? Extraordinary, they say.'

'No, I haven't seen a copy of it yet.' She grinned at him across the room, ignoring the thought that Barney had never succeeded in reading a complete book in his life and dismissed poetry as silly rubbish. To know that Elliott appreciated good authors was simply another star among the myriad reasons why she felt so uplifted in his company. She withdrew a small volume of Shakespeare's sonnets, and climbing back onto the bed, opened it randomly and began to read aloud.

Elliott listened intently, nodding in appreciation. 'That was really good,' he commented when she had finished. 'It isn't easy to read Shakespeare aloud and get the sense of it properly, especially if you haven't seen it before. Unless you picked one out you already knew.'

'No, I didn't,' Ling answered, basking in pride. And then the old mischief that hadn't been there for years suddenly sparkled in her eyes. 'Now your turn!' she cried in glee.

Elliott puffed out his cheeks evasively. 'Well, no, I don't think so.'

'You don't get away with it that easily!' Ling chortled, and taking up the pillow behind her, began to pound him with it.

'Right!' Elliott grabbed the other pillow, fighting back as he roared with laughter. Ling leapt up with a squeal and he chased her around the room until they collapsed together back on the bed in a helpless, giggling muddle.

'Oh, dear, just look at my lovely tidy room!' Elliott sighed at length as their frolicking subsided.

'I'm sorry,' Ling spluttered with mock sympathy, her forefinger pressed over her lips to contain her next threatening guffaw. But in that instant, she caught sight of the clock on the mantelpiece and her joviality was at once extinguished. 'I'll have to go soon, Elliott.'

His face fell. 'Yes, I expect you will. But have your tea first, and I'll bring up some hot water. I expect you'd like to freshen up.'

Ling turned to him, cupping his cheek in her hand. 'Dear Elliott. You think of everything.'

His mouth moved into a rueful smile as he turned his head to kiss the palm of her hand. 'That's because I love you and I want you to come again. You will, won't you? I mean, we don't have to . . . We can just talk. Be friends.'

She lifted her eyes, a slow, upward sweep of her long, chestnut lashes. 'Of course I'll come,' she whispered through the sudden swelling in her throat.

CHAPTER TWENTY-EIGHT

'Where the devil have you been?'

'Oh, I'm sorry, Barney,' Ling pacified him as she removed the jacket that only hours earlier Elliott had peeled enticingly from her shoulders. 'I missed the train and had to wait for the next one.'

She wondered at the confidence in her voice, not even feeling a pang of remorse. But it was true. She *had* missed the train, except that she had done so deliberately so that she could spend a little longer with Elliott. She had sat by the window in the carriage on the second leg of the journey as the engine chugged up to Princetown. The savage beauty of the moor seemed heightened by the exhilaration that still beat in her breast. It wasn't just Elliott's sensitive, thoughtful caresses that had made the sexual act beautiful for her; it was everything about him. It wasn't until she began the long walk from Princetown back to Foggintor that she had thought of Barney and Fanny and baby Laura, and how she was deceiving them.

She tied on her apron to help Fanny prepare the evening meal. 'Have you had a good day?' she asked casually.

'Oh, yes.' Fanny blushed faintly. 'Sam and me took Laura to see the train go past at his midday break. 'Twas the first time she's been that close and she weren't the least bit afeared. And what about Mrs Penrith? Is she better?'

'Oh, yes, much. We went down to the town this afternoon and forgot the time, so you can judge how much better she is.'

The lie had come so easily, it astounded her. She had even swiftly calculated that Fanny had not been on the train down to Tavistock since Laura was born and was unlikely to do so for months. And by then, any details of Ling's visits would have been forgotten by Agnes Penrith in the unlikely event of the subject cropping up in their conversation.

Since Laura's birth and Sam's increasing interest, Fanny had not only matured but appeared to have discovered a deep and satisfying contentment. She might have arrived there via a tortuous route but Ling envied her. She had a beautiful baby daughter, a good man she was free to marry if and when Sam asked her, and she had no aspirations beyond a happy, homely life. Ling on the other hand . . .

Nature had denied her the joy of a child and she was married to, well, when all was said and done, the wrong man. A good man and true, oh, she knew that! But unsuitable. And now she was having to lie and deceive to snatch those few hours of blissful fulfilment, and the guilt and frustration were clawing at her until her conscience was ripped to shreds.

* * *

She watched as Elliott's eyes widened with a rapturous sparkle. 'Ling! I wasn't expecting you until this afternoon! If at all. Oh, come in!'

Ling stepped inside, closing the door behind her, and for several seconds, they contemplated each other in enchanted silence until Elliott took her in his arms and their lips met in a long, sensuous kiss.

'Well, it isn't a definite arrangement I have with Agnes,' Ling breathed when Elliott finally released her. 'I thought I'd spend the whole day with you instead.'

Elliott released a sigh of elation. 'Oh! Well!' he laughed. 'I was doing my cleaning, but what a wonderful excuse not to! The consulting room's finished, though, which is the most important. Oh, this is fantastic! A whole day together! What shall we do?'

His joyous, youthful smile had banished the knot of guilt that had persisted in Ling's chest throughout the journey, but now the niggling doubt slithered back into her mind like an evil serpent. 'Well, we can't go out, can we? People know you. And they'd be curious to know who I am.'

Elliott shrugged his eyebrows. 'Does that matter? I may be a doctor, but I *am* allowed to have friends. Even female ones.' He took her hands, lifting them to his lips and kissing them fervently. 'No one's to know that I love you.'

'But what if anyone sees me coming here so often?'

'Then I'll say you're my weekly housekeeper!' Elliott grinned with a flash of inspiration.

'Even more reason for us not to be seen out together. You'd hardly step out with your housekeeper.'

Elliott's mouth closed in a soft curve, his eyes reaching deep into hers. 'If you feel happier staying indoors, then of course we shall. And I won't object to spending the whole day in bed with you.'

Ling lowered her eyes as she felt the colour flush into her cheeks, and Elliott bent down, twisting his head to come into her line of vision. His gaze was mildly teasing, cajoling, and she couldn't help but smile at his boyish antics.

'Well, I'm not sure about *all* day—'

His mouth on hers silenced her words, the soft, moist contact at once spearing the exquisite, delicious tension to the hidden place between her thighs that began to pulse with the demand to be satisfied. Elliott suddenly swept her off her feet and carried her swiftly up the stairs. All hesitation was flung to the wind and she was laughing helplessly, kicking her legs in feigned resistance as Elliott struggled to turn the doorknob without putting her down.

'You don't make it easy for a chap, do you?' he grumbled, making her fight back even harder so that he staggered across the room and the pair of them fell onto the bed in a writhing, laughing tangle. Ling felt freed and she burst into enchanted, captivating life. Elliott's gleaming eyes narrowed, sending the thrill of expectation through Ling's veins as he slowly started to undress her, taking his time, turning her this way and that to give his full attention to every inch of her as it became exposed. Ling lay obediently, her normal reserve totally forsaking her. There was something so pure, so tender in the way Elliott was enticing her, drawing her body to the height of sensitivity, that she felt no shame as she finally lay naked on the bed. His eyes and his hands explored every intimate detail of her until she was on fire with desire and she tugged at his clothes, stripping them off until she was able to take the deep and unexpected pleasure of scrutinising him in return. The stroking, the kisses, the trailing of moist tongues across bare, throbbing flesh spiralled to a frenzy and the roaring joy that convulsed inside her was even more powerful than the last time Elliott had opened her senses to such passionate glory.

They lay side by side, panting, staring at the ceiling, each lost in some sensuous paradise, and then Ling curled up against Elliott's flank, her head on his shoulder and wondering with astonishment how he could light this desire in her. She could feel it rising again, and she propped herself up on her elbow, flaunting her rounded breasts and he was ready to take them in his hands.

They ate a frugal lunch of bread and cheese, talked of childhood memories, of their likes and dislikes, wanting to know each other's minds as well as their bodies. They discussed the world, history, geography, literature, the rights and wrongs of the human race, and finally they became lost once more to the fantasy that they were bound together in free, eternal love. Ling breathed Elliott into her soul, drew him into her body, wanting to brand the feel of him into her heart lest this heady euphoria be snatched from her for ever.

'Elliott, it's half past three.'

Elliott drew away, his eyes closing with regret. 'Oh, God, I wish you didn't have to go. I wish you could stay here forever.' His shoulders slumped as he broke off, and then he reared up his head like a savage lion. 'I wish to God Barney had given you my note so that now you'd be my wife and not his.' His eyes flashed at her, the anger in his expression astounding her. But then his face slackened and he smiled coyly. 'That is, if you'd have me.'

'Oh, Elliott, of course I would. I'd give anything, you know that.' Her voice trailed away, since there was nothing she *could* give. And then the clock loomed mockingly at her again. 'But I must get ready to go.'

'Yes.' Elliott sighed torturedly. 'But every minute I have to wait to see you again will be like an hour.'

'School starts again next week.' There. She had said it, blurted it out since the words had stung her lips.

There was a long silence, and when she dared to look up, Elliott's face was drained. 'B-but,' he stammered, staring at her helplessly. Hopelessly. Echoing the agony that tore at her own heart. And then his eyebrows dipped determinedly. 'We could meet. After school. All this,' and he gestured to the tumbled bed they were still lying on, 'is wonderful. But I can live without it. But I can't live without seeing the woman I love. Could you get the train down to Yelverton after school? There are several trains a day now, aren't there? We could meet for just half an hour. By the Rock on Roborough Down? And then you get the next train back up to Princetown.'

His brow folded into tight lines, and Ling's brain was turning cartwheels. It might be difficult, but it was possible.

'I'll try,' she nodded. 'But if I'm not there, it won't be because I don't want to be.' And slowly, reluctantly, she reached for her clothes.

* * *

'I hope that woman appreciates all your visits,' Barney pouted sullenly as he undressed himself that night. '*And* all the money you've spent on train fares.'

Ling felt her stomach turn over. She was going to have to lie again, and it went against all her beliefs. She needed to choose her words carefully. 'Agnes is a good friend, Barney,' she told him, glancing at him through the gloomy shadows the flickering candle cast across the bedroom.

She had already gone to bed, her thoughts wandering languidly over the bewitching hours she had spent with Elliott. She had heard Barney return from his nightly session with his workmates, and he climbed the staircase quietly, not wanting to disturb Fanny and the baby asleep downstairs. Ling turned over just as he opened the door, candlestick in his hand. She saw the whites of his eyes in the faint glimmer from the tiny flame, and he smiled at her.

Was it that old, familiar smile that tugged at her heart, that had meant the world to her as an adolescent girl? He was still a handsome man, but the pressures of life had driven the humour from his carefree spirit, and the loss of their own child had devastated him as deeply as it had Ling. Was it any wonder he had turned to the company of his comrades to escape the empty hearth of his own home? But he was still the same kind and gentle Barney who always treated her with love and respect, and she watched with renewed curiosity as he stripped off his clothes. But it was too late. Somehow the light had gone out. Oh, she wanted to love Barney, but her heart was simply elsewhere, down in the little house in Chapel Street. And the guilt was unbearable.

'Let's see if we can beget this child,' he whispered, his voice soft and loving as he climbed into bed beside her.

Ling's heart plummeted to her feet. Her body was satiated from her love-making with Elliott, and the last thing she wanted was Barney's attentions. But it was hardly his fault that she had spent all day in bed with her lover. Perhaps she should look upon this as her punishment.

Barney kissed her softly. She could smell the beer on his breath, just the one bottle a night, and who could blame him for that after the day's strenuous toil at the quarry? He lifted the hem of her nightdress and entered her, carefully but without preamble. Ling gritted her teeth. Her flesh was still a little tender from Elliott's thrilling attentions, but it wasn't as if Barney was inconsiderate. He simply didn't understand. Had she summoned the courage to tell him that she needed him to coax and entice her, he surely would have listened. But it was too late now. It was Elliott she loved in a way that would never be possible with Barney. Barney. Who was her husband. Forsaking him for no other for as long as they both should live. She had sworn it before God, and she had sinned while Barney had remained ever faithful, supporting her family, a good man and never abusive. And she had betrayed him.

Barney exhaled with a contented sigh. 'Perhaps that will be the one,' he whispered. He blew out the candle, kissed her forehead and then settled down to sleep.

Ling bit on her knuckles and stared into the empty void of the night.

* * *

'Elliott.'

She could see he was about to take her hands in greeting, a translucent smile reflecting in his green-blue eyes, and so she strode past him quite rudely. Ghost was leisurely cropping the grass while she waited patiently for her master, and raised her head slightly when he sprang after the young woman who hurried past him virtually without acknowledging his presence.

'Ling! For heaven's sake, what's the matter?'

Elliott's voice was choked as he chased after her. But Ling suddenly halted, her vision fixed on the distant heights of Dartmoor, knowing exactly where Foggintor — and her life — lay among the bracken and gorse. And then her shoulders drooped beneath the intolerable burden of what she had to do.

Elliott had stopped dead behind her, every taut nerve stretched to breaking point. In that appalling silence, he knew. Before she even spoke. His heart tore in agony, and yet he clung obstinately to the hope that he was mistaken. But when Ling turned to him, her face was ravaged with grief. He went to step towards her and encircle her in the comfort of his arms, but she put out her hand, fending him off in the most tortured moment of her life.

'I-I can't do this,' she told him in a forced whisper. 'I love you, Elliott, but I can't do this. It's wrong. And . . . your career. Everything you've worked so hard for—'

'You've never been my patient.' Elliott's face was white, a mask of tight muscles. 'It isn't as if I've abused my position as your doctor. Seduced you. So I can't be struck off for that.'

'Perhaps not. But if it was known you were seeing a married woman, it would destroy your career. People wouldn't want to be treated by you. This is an area of staunch Methodism, Elliott. You know that. People with strong beliefs. The other doctors would be obliged to ostracise you.'

Her voice had grown stronger as she spoke, the words coming from the sensible, logical side of her brain which for those few seconds had overtaken the quivering, crushed part of her that was slowly dying. She simply had to convince Elliott that the wondrous passion they had shared was over. No. Not over. For the love she felt for him would remain in her heart until the day she died.

She knew he would not take it easily and he fixed her with that penetrating gaze, his face alive and intense with pain. 'I don't give a damn about my career! What good is my life without the woman I love? I've dreamt about you for so long, and now to have found you, only to be taken away—'

'You'll find someone else. You're a good man, Elliott Franfield. Any woman would fall in love with you.'

She thought her own words would break her, and she reached out, cupping his jaw in her palm, but he pushed her away.

'I don't want another woman. I want *you*!' His eyes flashed at her, hard and unyielding. 'Yes, I can spend the years healing people. But I don't want to wake up one day when I'm an old man and realise my entire life has been wasted because *you* haven't been part of it!'

Torment twitched at his face and she bowed her head, twisting her hands in a mangled knot. 'I know,' she murmured wretchedly. 'I feel exactly the same—'

'Then come away with me.' His voice was suddenly so calm and level that she lifted her head. 'I'll say that I've decided to work in America. I'm a qualified doctor, for heaven's sake. I can set up practice wherever I want. We can start a new life. Travel, *be* as man and wife for the rest of our days. No one would ever know.'

Ling could see the excitement igniting in his eyes, and a wistful smile dragged at her lips. 'Dear Elliott.' Her voice was soft, lulled, as she peeped into the wonderful fantasy he had described. 'I really do believe you would do that. Give up everything here, just for me. But . . . *I* would know. And so would God.'

Elliott sucked a breath through his teeth. 'Does that matter?'

'Yes.' Her senses were reeling away and she fought not to sink beneath the dizziness that swamped her. 'And there's Fanny. She still needs me. And . . . and Barney.'

'Barney!' Elliott's expression was incredulous. 'It's because of him that we weren't together from the start! He betrayed us—'

'We don't know that. Not for sure.' Her voice was low, desperate, as she struggled to find the courage to persuade Elliott to believe what she herself was rebelling against. And yet she had to. 'And even if he deliberately kept your note from me, can you honestly blame him? We were all so young.' She met Elliott's gaze for a fleeting moment but she could not bear the anguish on his beloved face and turned away with a broken sigh. 'What's done is done,' she murmured.

'I can't do this to Barney. He *is* my husband. He doesn't deserve it.'

The silence was long and oppressive, heavy with the agony that wrapped its greedy tentacles about these two lost souls. Ling's feet were rooted to the spot as she drowned in her own misery, her heart numbing as the pain became too deep to endure. And then she felt Elliott touch her fingertips.

'Oh, my darling Ling.' His voice was barely a breath, like a soft mist. 'That's why I shall always love you. You're stronger than I am, you see. And I shall never *ever* stop loving you.'

She was in his arms for one brief, terrible, *final* moment, swaying as she was on the brink of fainting. Then he released her, smiling down at her as his eyes glistened with moisture. 'Go now,' he mouthed, since his voice refused to obey him, and his arms dropped hopelessly to his sides.

Ling turned, her feet dragging, her body moving in the direction of the station while her heart remained beside the man she loved. She mustn't look back. But she did. Elliott was watching her. Ghost nudged his shoulder, but he didn't notice. Ling wanted to rush back, but she mustn't. So she broke into a run, blinded, stumbling. And then she heard the rhythmical drumming of horse's hooves. She glanced over her shoulder. Elliott was galloping over the down towards Tavistock and out of her life. Just as he had entered it.

CHAPTER TWENTY-NINE

Ling picked her way along the crest of Big Tip. The sound of merry voices inside the cottage was soon muffled by the sighing wind that moaned across the moor and circled tauntingly about her head, whispering Elliott's name in her ear. It lifted shamelessly the hem of her skirt, tugged at the shawl she pulled more tightly about her shoulders and ran its mocking fingers through her hair since she was bare-headed having slipped surreptitiously from the front door. Christmas Day was drawing to a close, pewter grey clouds fringed with pearly lace scudding across a violet and amethyst sky as the light faded and the moors disappeared into mulberry shadows.

Happy Christmas, Elliott, my love.

The words echoed in her head, driving the pain deeper into her soul. She closed her eyes, trying to blank it out, but all she could see in her mind was a picture of Elliott. Was he in the little house in Chapel Street, perhaps all alone, or more likely at his parents' opulent villa higher up the hill in Watts Road? She could imagine him smartly dressed to please his mother, being polite to his parents' guests, and later excusing himself to visit a patient in one of the poorer areas of Tavistock, or even the workhouse as he was still the Medical Officer there.

There again, he might not be in the town at all. With the seed of adventure planted in his brain when she had ended their relationship back in September, he might have set out to America to start a new life. To forget her. She wished him well, but she would never forget *him*.

Oh, Elliott. She had no way of knowing what had become of him. He had not attempted to contact her, but of course there was no way he could without the risk of Barney discovering it. And she had deliberately not been to Tavistock since. She had written to Agnes explaining that now school had restarted, she had found herself so busy, and what with baby Laura beginning to shuffle about the floor on her bottom and soon to be in to everything, every second of the day was too precious to her. She missed Agnes's company, but they had continued to correspond by post and Ling fell on every letter she received from Agnes as if it was manna from heaven.

Ling found herself instead drawn back to Fencott Place where she was welcomed with open arms by Rose and Seth whenever she appeared. The house was still a noisy, disordered mêlée of dogs and children and Rose whisking through the rooms like a whirlwind. The house would be quiet now, though, for the family had decamped to Herefordshire to celebrate Christmas with Captain and Mrs Bradley on their estate. Chantal Pencarrow was travelling with them in order to be with Toby, one of the few chances they would have to be together before their marriage in the spring.

It seemed that weddings were in fashion. His face glowing with pride, Sam had officially announced over Christmas dinner that he and Fanny were to be wed. Ling and Barney had known since the previous evening when Sam had sought their permission to ask for Fanny's hand, and Fanny's eyes had glittered a lovely blue ever since. So the announcement had been a formality since everyone already knew. Ling was sure that, had baby Laura understood, she would have been filled with joy to know that the quiet, steady, gentle man who had featured so often in her life recently was to become her father — and take the place of the rogue who really was! Oh, how thrilled Arthur and Mary would have been to know their little girl was marrying the son of Arthur's best friend.

The vision in her head of Fanny walking down the aisle on Sam's arm drove away Ling's melancholy. She should get back to the festivities. Just because her own heart was breaking, she must not spoil Fanny's happiness. And she spun on her heel and marched brusquely back to the cottage.

* * *

'If anyone here present knows of any just cause or impediment why these two persons should not be joined in holy matrimony, you are to declare it, or else for ever hold your peace.'

Ling caught Fanny's eye, and grinned. Her sister was radiant, her cheeks blushed a pale rose beneath the gauzy white veil that billowed down over her golden curls from the mother-of-pearl comb that held it in place, all lent to her by the generous Rose Warrington. Fanny looked a picture, an ephemeral angel, as she turned back to gaze devotedly into Sam's pride-flushed face. Ling's heart turned over with contentment and she glanced down with a broad smile at little Laura who was resting, placid as ever, on Ling's hip in time-honoured fashion. Oh, what a joyous day! Even the February weather had remained quiet as a lamb, the cloudless sky providing a bright, sunny afternoon for the service in Princetown's church.

'She cas'n marry 'en! The babby's mine! She should be marrying me!'

The coarse bellow echoed inside the vast roof vaulting of the church like an explosion. The entire congregation gasped in unison as an appalled silence rained down like shards of glass. Shocked murmurs, then, as angry footsteps thundered down the aisle, and every head turned to see who the malicious intruder could be. Many of them had instantly recognised the voice, of course, and so had the bride's sister.

'Ling!'

Fanny's wail was pathetic as she turned not to Sam but to Ling, her thin arms instinctively stretching out to find the comfort and strength that had protected her all her life. Ling's heart was breaking out of her chest and she pushed past Barney, thrusting Laura into his arms as she did so, ready to face the enemy with venom on her tongue. Fanny stumbled into her embrace and Ling murmured some soothing endearment, but her narrowed eyes were scorching dangerously into the approaching figure. Harry Spence met her gaze and visibly faltered, glancing about him as if he expected someone to come to his assistance. No one did. But not only was his injured pride festering because Fanny had chosen that milksop Sam Tippet over him, but with the Warringtons involved, he had sniffed money again. Money that he could profit from and if he had to fight for it, then he bloody well would!

'How dare you!'

Ling's hissed words attacked him before he even reached the horrified group by the altar steps, and his defence was to direct a deprecating sneer at her as he attempted to brush her aside. He failed. Ling stretched up to her full height, turning Fanny towards Sam who had stepped forward, white-faced and trembling, to comfort his bride. Anger, outrage, burned into Ling's gullet, and she fought the desire to fly at Harry's face with nails outstretched like claws. Instead she glowered at him, her eyes almost on a level with his and glinting with ice.

'Perhaps we could discuss this in the vestry?' the vicar's voice, toneless with shock, suggested from behind her, since it was the first time in his forty years of service that he had ever heard an objection.

'No, I bloody well won't! Everyone yere knows I be the father and—'

'This is a House of God! And I would thank you to—'

Ling had glanced over her shoulder, but Barney was saying nothing though his eyes were darting darkly between

Harry and Sam and the vicar who was quite rightly defending his church and the God he served. But Ling could see that no one was about to say anything to deal with Harry Spence.

'No one knows anything of the sort, you blackguard!' she cried. 'If you think you can come barging in here, making false accusations—'

'*I* be the father. So you can go to hell—'

'No. *I* am.'

Sam had stepped forward, his face like paper. Ling looked at him and her heart bled. Dear Sam. He was willing to bring shame on himself in order to protect his beloved Fanny. But everyone knew he couldn't possibly be Laura's father with his blue eyes and fair hair almost matching Fanny's, when Laura was as dark as the feather-spitting devil who ranted before them now. Not even Harry had expected Sam to make the claim, and for a moment, it took the wind out of his sails and gave everyone a chance to think.

'I have to tell you that it doesn't matter who the child's father is,' the vicar took the opportunity to announce. 'Miss Southcott is free to marry whoever she pleases.'

'And she'd want to marry *me* if 'tweren't for that bloody sister of hers!'

Ling saw Harry raise his clenched fist, saliva spitting from his snarling lips. The years fell away, and they were children again, scrapping over his cruel mockery of Fanny's shortcomings. Well, Harry might not have matured, but she had. Let him hit her, with all these people as witnesses. He'd be locked up for months.

She shut her eyes, waiting for the blow to fall. It didn't. She was aware of movement before her and when she dared to look, she saw that, with his military training instilled deep within him despite the years that had passed, Seth Warrington was holding Harry in an arm-lock about his neck, while the fist that had been poised to smash into Ling's face was now wrenched excruciatingly up Harry's own back. Without uttering a word, Seth frogmarched him back down the aisle and literally threw him outside. The doors were bolted against him, and as Seth reservedly resumed his seat, a cheer went up from the congregation, bringing an embarrassed colour to the good man's cheeks.

'Please, ladies and gentlemen!' The vicar held up his hands. 'I would ask you to forget that most offensive intrusion! We are here today to celebrate before God the marriage of Samuel and Fanny, a most joyous occasion for us all. Now, where were we?'

Ling had returned to her seat, beaming at Fanny as if nothing had happened. But inside she was seething. The ceremony was continuing, the vicar smiling benevolently as he joined the young couple in matrimony, and Ling knew that in their drab, hardworking lives, the quarrymen and their families would soon forget the ugly incident as they enjoyed the sumptuous food and lively celebrations that Seth and Rose were providing. But though she would outwardly shrug off the matter for Fanny's sake, Ling would never forget how Harry had so very nearly ruined her sister's special day.

Outside, Harry Spence picked himself up from the ground, wincing at the agony in his shoulder. Bloody hell, that Seth Warrington had maimed him for life! Well, he'd get back at him somehow! Lie in wait for him — once he had recovered, of course. But then, despite being twenty years his senior, Harry had felt the man's strength and the bastard was ex-army. And he had wealth and influence, so why should Harry put himself at risk? He could see the money he had sought drifting away from him, and it was all Ling Mayhew's fault. She was the one to blame. Always had been. Well, he'd teach her a lesson she'd never forget. Hit her where it would hurt most. He would bide his time. And surely the ideal opportunity would arise.

* * *

'There you are, Spence.' William Duke slammed the handful of coins on the desk. 'It's more than you deserve, I'm sure, but I don't want to see you ever again. I can't have men in my quarry drinking on the job. And don't try to deny it!' he snapped as Harry Spence went to open his mouth in protest. 'I've smelt it on your breath more than once. And as for the missing money, well, I can't prove it, but it's strange that you're the only one who hasn't had anything stolen from your pockets. So, be on your way, and don't show your face here again.'

Harry Spence stared at the elderly proprietor of the quarry at Merrivale, his eyes bulging with anger. This was all because of Ling Mayhew! *She* had driven him to this! Driven him to the carelessness, the *stupidity*, he must admit, of pick-pocketing a few pennies here and there from everyone around him. He hadn't bargained for each man noticing, since unlike himself, they all had families to feed and every last farthing counted. And of course it didn't come anywhere near the fortune he had hoped to get his hands on through Fanny's association with the Warringtons. Fanny and Sam were living in one of the simple one up, one down cottages at Foggintor with the little brat — *his* daughter! But he was convinced there must be secret handouts from the generous couple from Fencott Place. Handouts that should have been finding their way into *his* pocket! And now, because of Ling, he had lost his job as well!

He stormed out of the office, slamming the door behind him. He was fuming, his mean mouth mangling into an even meaner knot and his wild gaze furiously scanning the horizon as he punched the air in his rage. From here, he could look straight across to Foggintor where the bitch lived. He wouldn't get taken back on there or at any other local quarry now, and he was unlikely to find any other work in Princetown. He could hardly apply to be a prison warder when his references would merely reveal that he had been suspected of thieving on more than one occasion! No. He would doubtless end up scraping a living in Tavistock, probably sweeping the streets.

Bloody hell, he would *kill* Ling Mayhew if he thought he could get away with it!

CHAPTER THIRTY

School was over for the day. Ling closed the cottage door with a shiver and went to attend to the range. It was late March and a raw, penetrating fog had sat on top of Dartmoor in a damp, icy blanket. Barney would be frozen by the time work was over for the day, his clothes soaking up the mantle of enshrouding vapour for hours on end. Ling stoked up the range to have it radiating with heat and then sat down to enjoy a hot cup of tea.

This was the time she missed Fanny most and the silence weighed on her like an oppressive cloud. But that seemed to be her life nowadays. Pointless. Her hope had tired. Died. She tried to be a good wife to Barney, reminding herself over and over again of his worth and the affection she still felt for him. But inside she was empty, the cruel chains of sterility firmly locked about her.

She sighed, not even knowing that she had. She hardly ever thought about Elliott now, her mind wanting to bury the reason for her despair. And now her eyes scanned the humble dwelling, seeking some diversion from her depression.

Oh, what was that? She had come in so hastily to escape the bitter weather that she hadn't noticed the envelope on the mat. The postman must have been this afternoon, picking his way carefully through the veil of mist on his trusty steed. Who could the letter be from? Her curiosity aroused, Ling picked it up and inspected the postmark. London. Her heart jolted. Could it be that Elliott had returned to the capital and had dared to write to her? She didn't recognise the handwriting, but then she wouldn't as she had never seen anything Elliott had written. She felt herself break out in a sweat, her hands shaking as she tore open the envelope.

"My dearest Ling,

It is positively ages since I have seen you. Training college and gaining my experience at sea keeps me so busy that I rarely have the chance to see my family except on the very odd occasion my father sails with me. I usually sail with Uncle Misha as Father is mostly kept occupied directing his business from the London offices, or from Herefordshire. You can understand that he and Mother like to spend most of their time together, but Father still loves the sea. I know it is difficult for the wife of a seafaring man, but once I have my master's ticket, Chantal and I will set up home in Plymouth as Uncle Misha and Aunt Sarah did, so that I shall be able to come home to her regularly.

And my darling Chantal is, of course, the reason for this letter. As you know, we are to be married at the end of April, and I should be honoured if you and your husband would come to the wedding. Uncle Richard will be sending you an official invitation soon, but I wanted to write to you first. Well, Richard and Beth are not my real uncle and aunt, just long-standing friends of my parents, as you know. And now they are to be my parents-in-law and they have told me to address them without the 'aunt' and 'uncle', but it seems really strange!

The wedding will be at St Peter's in Peter Tavy, and the breakfast will be at the farmhouse, that is, Rosebank Hall. I have written to Aunt Rose to ask if you can travel in the carriage with them. I really hope you will come as I value your friendship greatly. Please, do say you will come! You can write to me at my parents' address at the top of this letter and they will pass it on.

I await your reply with great anticipation.

Your good friend

Toby Bradley."

A contented smile had gradually crept onto Ling's mouth as she read the letter. Oh, this was just what she needed to cheer her up! Another wedding! And one that would not be marred by some rude interruption! Oh, she could have murdered Harry Spence, although the incident had soon been forgotten since everyone knew what a blackguard he was. Toby's marriage to Chantal Pencarrow would be a much grander affair, of course, although Ling gathered that the Pencarrows were not nearly as well-off as Rose and Seth. Ling had never met them as they did not visit Fencott Place, Richard Pencarrow having livestock to attend daily. But Rose and Seth had always spoken of them with the deepest respect and affection, and Ling would look forward to meeting them.

The more she thought about it, the more excited she became. She realised now her spirits had been so low that she had shunned visiting Fencott Place, unable to find the energy for the long walk. It had been a mistake, digging her own trough of despair deeper and deeper. And now suddenly she couldn't wait for Saturday when she could visit Rose and Seth.

Would Barney accept the invitation to the wedding? She hoped so. Perhaps a day in more stimulating company would inspire Barney to greater thoughts and strengthen their relationship in the way their long-dashed hopes of a child had failed to do. But if Barney would not attend the marriage of Toby Bradley to Chantal Pencarrow, Ling was determined to go alone.

* * *

In the event, Barney was happy to accept the invitation. It would be an entertaining day with free food and drink, and Barney obviously felt well able to conduct himself in the company of, it had to be said, a class above their own. Ling was proud of him as he donned his Sunday best suit, rarely worn now and somewhat tight around the girth, but neatly pressed and with a new shirt Ling had made especially for the occasion.

Ling herself was dressed in a gown of peacock blue borrowed from Rose and hastily let down at the hem. It was the most sophisticated attire she had ever worn and it made her feel special. Even Barney grinned at her and offered her his arm in the manner of a gentleman.

'You looks like proper gentry, m'lady,' he teased, his shining eyes lifting Ling's heart. Perhaps there was hope for them yet. But what a ridiculous thought! Their marriage was stronger than many. She had never told Barney how she felt. Not that her heart lay elsewhere, of course, for that was a secret she was trying to hide even from herself. But that she felt stifled and perhaps they could make use of the Sunday train service for summer outings. Nature might have denied them a child, but there was no reason why they should not enrich their lives in other ways. She would broach the subject tomorrow, she decided as they walked arm in arm to the main Princetown to Tavistock road where the Warringtons' carriage was to meet them. She was sure Barney would agree to her plans for a weekly summer outing, but just in case he objected, she didn't want to spoil the day by starting off on the wrong foot.

The weather had dawned bright and fine, though it still being April, the air was chilly and ribbons of white mist were strung out below them in the Tavy valley. The sun, though, soon burned off the mist, promising a beautiful spring day. The journey was a chaotic one, with Rose chatting merrily while attempting to keep her three small children clean — at least until they reached the church! And Seth, who could converse easily with anyone, talking quietly with Barney about the trade in granite which was being considerably curtailed by the extensive use of concrete. Ling flashed a smile across at her husband and he answered with that old jaunty grin she rarely saw nowadays. A candle of anticipation burned in her breast as the carriage jostled and bumped through the village of Peter Tavy. Today was going to be so special, and not just for the bride and groom. It would be a new start for her and Barney, Ling had decided determinedly. She would lock her secret past with Elliott in a strong-box and throw away the key. Unless she wanted to ruin the rest of her life, she would have to!

The large grassy square in front of the church was a disordered jumble of horse-drawn vehicles and milling crowds. Seth opened the carriage door and jumped down to lift out his son and two little daughters and to assist Rose in a most gentlemanly manner. Ling wasn't the only one to notice Seth's courteous gesture. Barney smartly climbed down ahead of her and then turned back to take her hand, his eyes twinkling. Ling accepted his help with a pert smile, the noisy babble of the amassed happy voices in the square humming in her ears as she emerged from the carriage.

'Ling! And you must be Barney! How very pleased to meet you!'

'Toby! Oh, congratulations!'

The bridegroom, flushed with excitement, had sought Ling out in the muddled embroilment of people and horses, carriages and traps, making her feel special and wanted. He kissed her on the cheek and then shook Barney's hand heartily as if he had known him for years.

'It's good to see you both!' Toby was exclaiming. 'Thank you so much for coming. I've heard so much about you, Barney. But please excuse me -'

They moved on, and Ling took a satisfied breath, her face split in a wide, merry grin as Barney lifted his eyebrows in surprise.

'They all seems very friendly like,' he nodded appreciatively. 'I have to say I doesn't feel out of things at all.'

'I told you you wouldn't. And look at all these people! I should think half the village must be here!'

Indeed, the square was seething with people dressed in working-class clothes weaving easily among the clearly wealthier guests, but Rose had often mentioned that the Pencarrows were well respected within the village and surrounding area, and that Beth Pencarrow was a skilled herbalist with many a local family under her care.

'Ling! How good to see you again! And Mr Mayhew, I assume. How nice to meet you, sir.'

It was Toby's father, Adam Bradley, who had spoken as he briefly shook Barney's hand. The captain was as tall, distinguished and immaculate as ever, his smile just as warm. Ling considered wistfully that, unlike her own father when she had announced that she and Barney were to wed, Adam was delighted with Toby's choice of spouse.

The church was packed, and Ling was relieved that a pew had been reserved for them to share with the Warringtons. At the front sat Toby with his half-brother, James, who at only sixteen was acting as best man. Ling smiled to herself as she remembered the first time she had seen James in the early days when she'd been living at Fencott Place. A young boy, then, he had doggedly followed in the wake of his boisterous elder sister. Ah. Ling clenched her teeth. Today she was putting all the regrets behind her. Today she was beginning a new life, at last accepting her place beside her husband.

She glanced down at Hal Warrington at her other side. At seven years old and in a smart sailor suit, he was gravely tutting his younger sisters who were whispering conspiratorially, dark heads pressed together. Amusement touched Ling's lips and she let her gaze wander about the old church. On the bride's side, every pew was taken, mostly by villagers. At the front sat a petite woman who would be Beth Pencarrow with her sons of about ten and twelve years old beside her, and Ling recalled that Chantal's half-sisters were to be bridesmaids together with Toby's sister, Charlotte. Ling could only see Beth Pencarrow from behind, but she was amazingly slender for someone who had brought four children into the world. But then a farmer's wife would lead a busy, active life, and there would be no time to sit around growing fat!

The gentle medley from the organ flowed into the bellowing introductory chords of the wedding march and the congregation rose to its feet, all whispered conversation ceased. Ling was on the opposite end of the pew from the aisle, but being tall, she managed to catch a glimpse of the bride as she floated on her father's arm past the rows of well-wishers and guests. Chantal Pencarrow was beautiful with a halo of jet black, bouncing curls. It was no wonder that Toby was so deeply in love with her. She was captivating.

Her father was just as striking. Tall, broad-shouldered but slender of waist, he had the kind of face that would have smouldered with brooding good looks in earlier years, but he was still an incredibly handsome man, his shock of dark, wavy hair barely threaded with silver at the temples. He held himself tall and proud, and as they reached the pew behind the Warringtons', Ling saw him dip his head to whisper something in his daughter's ear before moving on.

But there Ling's gaze remained as her heart came to a standstill. For there, across on the bride's side of the church, was Elliott. Sharing a pew with the elderly Dr William Greenwood who had examined her the previous year, a considerably older-looking gentleman and another man of about fifty, all wearing the frockcoats and stiff, winged collars of the professional classes.

Elliott didn't appear to have seen her and she swiftly turned back, her neck rigid as she locked her eyes blindly on the altar. She scarcely heard the minister's initial address as the tones of the organ faded away, and was saved from her buckling legs as he invited the congregation to be seated.

Elliott! What was he doing here when she had so agonisingly driven him from her heart! For several minutes she simply could not think straight as her entire being fragmented into tortured splinters and she had to fight to piece them together again. Elliott was seated on the bride's side of the church. But why? Seeing him again had instantly reignited her passionate love for him like a flash of lightning. Without him, it was as if she had lost her true self, and though she had striven to live without him, she knew she was merely floundering in the mud.

But, dear Lord, what if Barney recognised him during the reception? What if anything was said that connected her and Elliott? She had deliberately never told Barney that

Elliott was the physician on the train who had delivered Laura, and to her knowledge, Fanny had never mentioned it either. Or at least, Barney had never made any comment. But if it came out now, wouldn't it look suspicious?

She hardly heard a word of the service. She sat, stood, sang the hymns, knelt, moving mechanically. But while the rest of the congregation prayed for the newlyweds, Ling prayed for her own deliverance. After the service, there was the hubbub of merry voices and laughter of so many acquaintances, and eventually the bride and groom climbed into the hired open coach and were cheered as the gleaming horses spirited them away to the reception at the Pencarrow family home.

Rosebank Hall stood on the rising edge of the moor. Ling scarcely noticed the carriage jostling her this way and that as it bumped along the rutted track to the farmhouse. She took in the unexpectedly elegant building at a glance. All she could think about was Elliott, and she was grateful for Rose's ebullient enthusiasm as she chatted about the beautiful service and attempted to keep her children in order.

'Oh, thank goodness for that!' Rose declared as they alighted from the carriage and her offspring scampered off to the house and garden they knew so well. 'They can let off steam now!'

'They was so good as gold, I thought!' Barney chimed in with a smile.

'Yes, but it wouldn't have lasted much longer!' Seth chuckled.

Ling responded with a faint smile as she walked on Barney's arm across the tended lawn in front of the house. Guests were milling on the grass, sherry glasses in one hand while they greeted each other yet again with the other. Ling and Barney were introduced to the beautiful bride who spoke to them with the merest hint of a French accent. Ling hoped her replies appeared respectful and coherent, for her heart was racing as she tried to hide herself from Elliott who she could see on the far side of the garden.

He evidently didn't spot her until they were all ushered into the dining-room which was laid for the formal wedding breakfast. Ling knew she could avoid Elliott no longer, and braced herself.

They were seated almost opposite each other. She saw Elliott start the instant he clapped eyes on her, and the shock and then the hurt registered on his drawn face. He looked tired. Had he been pining as she had been, burying himself in his work? Except that Ling had clawed her way out of the pit. Or at least, she had thought she had. Until today.

Their eyes met, locked, their souls intertwining across the width of the table that separated them. An uncomfortable sweat broke out down Ling's back, the fear of discovery trapping the breath in her throat, while at the same time she became oblivious to everything but her need for this man. She saw the colour slowly return to his cheeks and he swallowed before he addressed her.

'My goodness, it's Ling, isn't it?' His voice was calm, professional, instantly recovered. 'Do you remember me?'

Ling thought her heart must have stopped beating. Elliott had chosen his words well, leaving the conversation open for both her and anyone listening to interpret as they wished. Ling knew she must reply, but her mind had turned to a complete blank as she fought to remain in control.

Unwittingly, it was Barney who came to her rescue. 'Yes, I remembers you.' His words were slow, deliberate, and distinctly contemptuous, and when Ling glanced sideways at him, she saw that his face was stiff. After all this time, Barney still held a grudge against the stranger who had surpassed his own frozen courage and saved her from the crushing wheels of the steam engine. God alone knew what Barney would have done if he had known what had gone on between them throughout the previous summer.

'Elliott Franfield, yes, of course!' The exclamation tumbled out of Ling's mouth, desperate to throw Barney off the scent. 'How nice to see you,' she went on politely. 'And this is my husband, Barney.'

'Barney.' Elliott smiled and held out his hand. Barney glanced at it across the table, hard lines about his mouth, but he obviously felt obliged to shake it briefly. Ling inwardly cringed. The hands of her husband and her lover.

'Wasn't it a lovely service?' Ling found herself saying as she searched for a way out of this appalling situation. 'And may I ask how you come to be here?'

'Oh, I've come to know the Pencarrows well over the past few months,' Elliott explained with a casual lift of his eyebrows. 'Dr Greenwood has worked with Beth Pencarrow for years. You know she's a herbalist and the local midwife? Well, now that Dr Greenwood is partly retired, I've taken over all the outlying villages he covers, so here I am! And how about you?'

'I know the Bradleys from when I worked for their friends, Mr and Mrs Warrington,' Ling nodded. 'Through them, Toby and I became good friends. So, who are the other gentlemen who were with you in the church?' she asked, endeavouring to keep the conversation away from themselves.

'Dr Greenwood, Dr Ratcliffe, and the elderly gent is John Seaton. Eighty next year, he'd be proud to tell you himself, and still going strong. Another retired physician, I'm afraid,' Elliott laughed softly. 'Used to tend the Bradleys.'

Ling smiled back, swamped with relief that the potential conflict had been diffused. She could see the sour expression on Barney's face soften as the wedding guest on his other side engaged him in conversation. The dread that something might arouse his suspicions was, for the time being, over, but Ling yearned desperately for the day to pass. All she wanted was to be with Elliott, a suffocating, strangling need. But she couldn't. She mustn't. And while the celebrations erupted all around her, even Barney's rancour dissolved by the excellent food and free-flowing alcohol, Ling felt that, inside, she was slowly dying.

Once the meal was over, she didn't speak to Elliott again. The spacious drawing room had been cleared for those who wished to dance to the strains of fiddle and accordion while other guests wandered across the lawn, chatting, laughing, exchanging reminiscences. The sun began to dip over the Cornish hills to the west, the April air turning cool. The bride and groom departed in the handsome coach for Tavistock and the Bedford Hotel, and the party began to disperse. Ling watched Elliott climb up into the carriage with the other physicians. He paused with his foot on the folding step, and his eyes searched the remaining guests. For three glorious, terrible moments, Ling stared back at him, the pain, the intense harmony of their lost love spearing into her heart.

And then he was gone, and the wound bled.

CHAPTER THIRTY-ONE

Ling was sure the world was standing still as the door opened. She should not have come. And there was Elliott, turned into a block of stone as he stared at her. Seconds passed, seconds in which Ling's wasted life flashed in front of her. Finally, without uttering a word, Elliott stood back and Ling dragged herself inside.

Elliott quietly shut the door behind him, gazing at her in silence, motionless, until she thought her heart must burst out of her chest. Had she made a mistake? Had Elliott found someone else to fill the gaping void in his life? Perhaps his soul had not been mangled by the chance meeting as hers had been, the reopened wound festering until it ran with despair. She looked into the clear depths of his eyes, saw the spasm of pain that twitched at his face. And then he crushed her to him, his jaw pressed against her cheek.

'Oh, my darling,' he choked into her ear. 'You've come back. Oh, thank God.'

She felt his tense body relax as if the agony was emptying out of him and when she looked up, the taut muscles in his face had slackened with relief.

'I-I just couldn't live without you,' she faltered, joy bubbling up inside her like a rising tide, ready to drown out the sands of her conscience. 'I know it's wrong, but I don't care anymore. I've been so miserable without you.'

'And I without you.'

His tight hold on her had eased, but now he squeezed her against him once more and she allowed the magic of him, his lean masculinity, his compassion, his intellect, to wash over her. It was as if she could not get close enough to him, breathing in the zestful scent of the lemon soap he used, drawing him into herself. She lifted her mouth to his and their lips met, delicately at first, ricocheting the desire down her spine, and then with mounting, overwhelming passion. Her body melted, on fire, every fibre sensitive to the slightest touch. They both knew what the other wanted. Needed.

Elliott took her hand and they ran up the stairs, laughing as Ling tripped on the hem of her skirt. Up in the bedroom, Elliott tore at his own clothes while she took off her outer garments. He turned her to him then, the afternoon light falling on his naked body, accentuating the curved muscles of his shoulders and chest, his flat stomach, the sinews in his strong arms. He lifted the chemise over her head, flinging it away, and her full breasts fell into his hands. He caressed them tenderly, reverently, while the breath fluttered at her throat and her hair escaped from its pins and fell down her back in a flaming mane. They moved as one towards the bed, Ling lying down so that Elliott could slide off her drawers and reveal the full glory of her flesh to him. Fingertip met fingertip, the electrifying sensation crackling through their limbs as they stroked each other lovingly and in total rapture. The yearning shot down to Ling's belly as Elliott led her onwards, and she moaned deliciously as he brought her towards the exquisite point that had to be satisfied.

He stopped for a brief moment then and she waited impatiently on the crest of desire. She knew what he was doing and when she heard him mutter a mild oath under his breath, she caught his hand.

'It doesn't matter,' she whispered.

Elliott met her eyes with a frown, but this force, this craving, was too strong for either of them. Then Elliott was inside her, and she clung onto him as their bodies moved in unison, slowly then with growing urgency as they reached the dizzy heights of euphoria together. They stayed, locked in tight embrace as the tension eased and their satiated bodies rolled apart, full and content and marvelling at how they were so meant to be together.

Elliott's lungs expanded as he propped himself on one elbow and smiled down at her somewhat sheepishly. 'I'm sorry. I didn't mean that to happen. It's just that I haven't been able to get you out of my mind. God, I *love* you, Ling. And when I saw you at the wedding, with Barney—'

'Oh, I've tried so hard to be a good wife.' Ling's eyebrows knitted painfully as her eyes bore into Elliott's. 'I really tried to make it work between us. Bring us closer together again. But Barney just can't change. He's happy with his work and his pint of beer. After the wedding, I managed to persuade him to go to Plymouth for the day. We had a lovely time. At least, *I* thought we did. But Barney wouldn't go again. And so . . .' She bowed her head as the colour flushed into her cheeks. 'I had to come back to you, Elliott. To know if you still felt the same.'

'You know I do, Ling. And not just for this.' He paused, waving his hand over the bed. 'I just want to be with you always. Have you at my side whatever I'm doing. If only you were *my* wife and not Barney's.'

His face was savage with emotion, and Ling squeezed his hand. 'I know. But I'll come as often as I can. But I must get back now. I told Barney I was going to visit Mistress Rose after school. I only came to find out if—'

'Well, I think you've had your answer.'

Ling nodded with a rueful smile. 'Yes. But until school finishes for the summer, it's going to be difficult. And that's another two months.'

'Tell you what. There's a new doctor setting up in town, junior to me, someone who'd heard that William retires fully next month. If I can persuade him to hold a surgery on Saturdays, then I can be free then instead of Thursdays!'

Ling's eyes shone. 'Yes! Then I can come here while Barney's at work, and maybe visit Agnes as well!'

'There you are, then.'

'Oh, Elliott!' She kissed him fleetingly on the cheek as she gathered up her clothes. 'Oh, Elliott, I love you so much!' And when he smiled back at her, his eyes soft and tender, her heart soared.

* * *

It somehow didn't seem to matter anymore, deceiving Barney each week. It was as if she had come alive again. And if remorse ever did creep into her thoughts, she only had to remember that Barney had betrayed *her* all those years ago. She was sure of it now. His instant recollection of Elliott at the wedding and his evident bitter resentment was proof enough.

Yes. In Ling's mind, Barney only had himself to blame for her infidelity. His jealousy all those years before had stopped her being with the man she truly loved, for she had never felt for Barney what she felt for Elliott. Fondness, yes. And she still was fond of him. But it wasn't that all-consuming passion that drove all else from her head. But perhaps that was how Barney had felt when he had destroyed that slip of paper.

'We could still go away together. Start a new life somewhere abroad,' Elliott had suggested with zeal. 'Fanny has Sam now. She'd be all right without you.'

Ling was lying on her front in the bed and Elliott ran his hand lightly down the long curve of her naked back. She was propped on her elbows and turned her head to look at him through the tangled riot of her dishevelled hair.

'You really would give up everything you have for me, wouldn't you?'

'Of course. Oh, Ling, I beg you. We could be as husband and wife and no one would ever know.'

'I promise I'll think about it,' she faltered, feeling ashamed of her own hesitation. 'But not now. Just now I want to enjoy being with you.' And she curled herself about him once more.

They didn't always make love. What they felt for each other went far beyond carnal desire. They discussed every subject under the sun, read books together, planted up the flowerbeds and tended the vegetables in the steeply terraced back garden. As the weeks passed, they felt more confident, even risked a walk in the meadows alongside the canal. The summer sun grew stronger as they strolled along each week, arm in arm, everything falling into a glorious routine, even down to the drunken tramp who occupied the same bench by the canal path, huddled in his torn and filthy rags, battered cap rammed down over his eyes and a moth-eaten scarf swaddled about his neck so that his face was entirely hidden.

'Always got a bottle of gin by his side,' Elliott sighed. 'Poor soul, to be brought to that. I've seen him being taken away by the constable several times. But he's soon back again. Mind you, the colder weather when autumn comes will soon see him off.'

They walked on, silently contemplating how lucky they were to have each other, even for those few brief, stolen hours each week. Ling lived for each Saturday when she would be with Elliott again. Once a patient stopped them in the street, but Elliott had smiled genially, introducing Ling as his cousin, and the moment passed without incident.

And so the summer passed with no hint of suspicion on Barney's part. Sometimes Ling would visit Agnes as well, perhaps go swimming or do some shopping, but always seeing Elliott. It all became so perfectly normal, an accepted and legitimate weekly outing.

It was towards the end of August that she began to realise. The seed of uncertainty germinated in her chest and she became more convinced with each day that passed without event. She had been so totally swept up in the joyous elation of being with Elliott again, she had not really noticed. But looking back, there had been nothing since a few weeks after the wedding, shortly before she had gone back to Elliott. And there were other signs, too. She ought to know. Four times she had been pregnant before, and each one had ended in tragedy. Would this one . . . ? She felt drained, empty, not daring to think, but yearning for the long days to pass so that she could be with Elliott again.

'What's the matter, Ling?' he asked anxiously soon after she arrived at the house in Chapel Street the following Saturday. 'You seem, I don't know, distant. And you don't look terribly well.'

Ling blinked at him, and the lump rose in her gullet. She had been with Elliott a matter of ten minutes. She had been with Barney all week and he had noticed nothing. She bowed her head.

'I think I'm pregnant,' she murmured, keeping her eyes lowered, not wanting to see his reaction.

Silence. Interminable. Or so it seemed to Ling. In fact, it lasted but a few seconds while Elliott recovered from the shock.

'Are you sure?'

His voice was low but steady, the lover tempered by the physician. Ling's heart was thrumming, and she looked up at him, her pale skin drawn across her cheekbones.

'Three months,' she whispered back. 'Or at least . . . I'm always so irregular. But I feel sick all the time and so tired.'

He took her hands that she was unconsciously wringing in her lap.

'You'd better come through to the consulting room.'

He stood back, politely opening the door, and helped her to climb onto the examination couch. His hands were so gentle as he examined her swollen, tender breasts and then moved down over her stomach, his eyes trained on the wall as he concentrated on what he was feeling. The same hands, Ling thought, that had caressed and loved every inch of her.

'Congratulations,' he said with a professional smile. But she could tell his voice was flat. 'We must make sure you hold on to this one. Plenty of rest and—'

'I don't know that I want to hold on to it.'

The words were blurted out, astounding her since she had not thought them previously. But perhaps being with Elliott had released what had been tamped down at the back of her mind ever since realisation had dawned.

She heard Elliott draw in a breath. 'But I thought this was what you've wanted for years.'

'It was. Until I met you again. I'd hoped it would bring Barney and me back together. But it's too late for that now.' Her voice trailed off in a wisp of sadness before she slid onto her feet and stared into Elliott's taut face. 'I love *you*, Elliott. If I have this child, I won't be able to see you again. I won't be able to get away. And I can't face that. B-but, on the other hand, what if it's yours?'

'Mine?' Elliott's eyebrows shot up to his hairline. 'It's pretty unlikely. I've always been so careful—'

'Not that first time after the wedding.' She took his arm, shook it earnestly. 'Don't you remember?'

She saw his mouth drop open and then close again, the lips pursed. 'Yes. I suppose so,' he muttered. 'But I doubt it. We'd be very unlucky—'

'So you see I don't know what to think! One minute I want this child desperately, and the next I hate it! It'll ruin what we have, whether it's yours or Barney's. If it's yours, then . . . But if it's Barney's . . .'

She gazed at him in an agony of frustration, wanting to creep away and hide from this nightmare, close her mind to the appalling dilemma. If only Elliott had the answer, but he didn't.

'And what does Barney say?' he asked quietly.

Ling lowered her eyes. 'I haven't told him.'

'Ah. And he won't have guessed?'

'Oh, no,' Ling snorted. 'He won't have noticed. As long as he can have his pleasure whenever—'

'You should stop that for a while. Three months is a dangerous period—'

'Then perhaps it would be a good thing—'

'Ling, you mustn't say that. Life is a precious gift. No matter how we are to blame, what we are to suffer, the child must come first.'

Ling's eyes opened wide, while at the same time Elliott's words tore at her heart. Yes. He was right. Good, kind, upright Elliott. It wasn't what her confused, whirling brain wanted to hear, but he was right.

'Of course,' he said hesitantly, 'we could do what I've wanted all along. Run away together. If Barney doesn't know that you could be carrying his child, it maybe wouldn't be so bad for him. And I don't care whose child it is. It would be *ours*. Only you need to think about it soon, Ling. Don't leave the decision too long.'

* * *

It was the second Saturday in September, and Elliott had invited her to walk with him, enjoying the last of the summer sunshine. They strolled along beside the canal, warm and peaceful. Everything as it always was. Even the tramp in his usual place.

'Ling, you've got to decide,' Elliott said suddenly. 'You can't keep denying it. Pretending the problem doesn't exist. If you wait much longer, it'll start to show and you won't be up to travelling. And I can't just slip away overnight and leave my colleagues in the lurch. I'll need to find a replacement. That'll take a couple of weeks. And I'll need to organise my finances, put the house up for sale. I've got enough money to pay for our passage to New York or Boston or wherever we decide. Not first class, but comfortable enough. There are ships leaving Plymouth quite regularly. I can imagine my parents would want to see me off, so you'll have to get to Plymouth on your own. We couldn't actually meet up until we were safely on board. But you can manage that, can't you?'

Ling shuddered with dread as she walked beside him, her feet dragging and placing themselves in front of each other mechanically. Elliott's words were marching through her head, crushing her, and she reared away from them. But Elliott was right. She must find the courage to face up to facts. Somehow she must untangle the twisted thread of her life, but she had no idea how. She wanted to weep, but there was no point in crying. Tears would solve nothing.

'I'll give you my answer next week,' she croaked. 'I promise. No matter what.'

Elliott dipped his head at her, frowning fiercely. 'I'll hold you to that. You know what I want. But, if you decide otherwise,' he faltered, 'I'll understand. You have far more to sacrifice than I do. And maybe we'll be able to see each other once in a while. As friends,' he added wryly. And smiled, his hurt eyes deep with compassion.

She couldn't smile back, her vision misting with tears. Elliott dropped a kiss on her forehead and putting his arm protectively about her, led her towards his home.

They didn't notice the tramp open his narrowed eyes, check no one was watching, and follow them to Chapel Street.

CHAPTER THIRTY-TWO

'I've seen them, I tells you. And not just once. And t'other day, he kisses her. Bold as brass.'

Barney twisted his head away. He couldn't believe it. This was just Harry Spence being characteristically vicious and malevolent. He would hardly have recognised him, filthy, dressed like a pauper, his face so lined and craggy he looked more like fifty-six than twenty-six. But glinting from the blotchy, red-veined face were the same artful, devious eyes. Oh, yes. This was Harry Spence all right. Harry Spence who had been the bane of all their lives, and Ling's in particular, and who would be capable of any wicked lie to cause trouble between them.

'Evil varmint,' Barney hissed back, for the tramp had accosted him as he had crossed from the quarry to the manager's house. It was a working day and though no one was likely to recognise Harry if *he* hadn't, Barney didn't want to be seen conversing with such a vile-looking vagrant. 'Get out of my sight, you lying bugger.'

He spun on his heel and went to stride away, but Harry caught him by the arm. 'I tells you, 'tis true,' he insisted, his voice low and crackling. 'Always on a Saturday. And you'll be so surprised as I were to know who 'tis. But then again, maybies you won't. I followed them back to his house. And there 'twas. A bloody brass plate screwed on the wall. *Dr Elliott Franfield*. You remembers 'en, I be certain.'

The malice in his words was almost palpable and at any other news, Barney might have landed him a blow to the jaw and left him on the ground where he fell. But . . . Elliott Franfield. Barney froze as the blood drained from his head. He staggered slightly, and glowered at Harry until his head stopped spinning.

'You'm certain 'twas him?' he croaked, not wanting to believe this disgusting apparition.

'I thought as I recognised 'en,' Harry chortled, his face creasing with triumph. 'I knows 'twere back along, but her's not changed much. I sees them going into the house more than once, but 'twere only t'other day I read the plate. I doesn't read all that well, but I can read *that*.'

Barney lowered his eyes to watch himself grind the toe of his boot into the hard earth. Could it possibly be true? If Harry Spence had given him any other name, but Elliott Franfield! The shuddering resentment raged inside him and exploded in a flash of red anger. The bastard had been at the wedding, hadn't he? And had Ling been so infatuated by him, just as she had all those years ago, that she had taken up with him on the side? *Lying* to him, her *husband*, every time she had gone into Tavistock? It was mighty queer that she had taken up the habit of going into town again just afterwards, when she hadn't been there, not even to visit her friend, Agnes Penrith, all winter! Dear God, what Harry was telling him, vindictive as it may be, was true!

He gazed at Harry again, his brow drawn low over his eyes. 'And you'm certain?'

Harry's lips curled in a satisfied smirk. 'Would I have walked all this way from Tavistock if 'tweren't? We cas'n all afford that there train, you knows. Not like your wife. Taking the train every week to make a cuckold out o' you.'

Cuckold. The word sliced at Barney's heart. His pride. The overwhelming love and trust he had always held for his beloved Ling. And all this time, she had been deceiving him. His brain became enshrouded in swirling, blinding fury and Harry's voice reached him as if from the depths of hell.

'I could do summat 'bout it for you,' he whispered in Barney's ear. 'Warn 'en off, like.' And then his mouth twisted into a sneer as he added under his breath, 'For a small fee.'

Barney's senses reeled away and his fists grabbed at the air. Ling. His darling Ling. It couldn't be her fault. The bastard had seduced her with his highfalutin talk. Lured her into his bed. Oh, yes, he could forgive Ling, but she must come back to him. And the only way to make sure she did was to teach that bloody Elliott Franfield a lesson he'd never forget.

'What d'you mean, warn 'en off?'

'Just knock 'en 'bout a bit. A warning, like. Tell 'en if her don't stays away from Ling, there'll be worse to come.'

Barney sucked in his cheeks to consider. He must be quick in his decision before anyone saw him talking with the beggar. 'All right,' he murmured. 'But just a warning. Nort more.'

'You won't regret it,' Harry answered, his sly eyes gleaming dangerously. 'But money up front. I doesn't want to come all the way up yere again.'

'Wait here.'

Barney's heart was thudding as he hurried the few yards to the cottage. He knew where Ling had hidden what little remained of their wedding nest-egg from the Warringtons. You never knew when it might be needed, Ling had always told him thriftily. Well, it was needed now. Two pounds he would take. He might be able to persuade Ling she had miscounted if he took no more, and besides, it was a great deal more than Harry had seen in a long time, he was sure.

He passed the two notes reluctantly into Harry's greedy hand.

'Be that all? I thought—'

'Then you thought wrong. 'Tis all I have. You just make sure he don't come near Ling again. And if you gets caught, I know nort about it.'

Harry gave a livid sneer and doffed his cap mockingly before turning and walking jauntily away. Barney watched him, revulsion bringing bile into his throat. He felt sickened, so stunned he couldn't remember why he had been going to fetch Mr Warren from the manager's house. Ling. Unfaithful. He still couldn't believe it. Didn't *want* to believe it. But when he thought about the woman he had always loved so deeply, she had changed over the years. She was no longer the happy, carefree spirit who had been in her element working for the Warringtons. The death of her parents had broken her, and the loss of the children she had never been able to carry to term. And yet all through the summer, until just a few weeks ago, she had seemed to come alive again. And now he knew why.

Barney sat down abruptly on a boulder and felt it vibrate beneath him. Ah, yes, the train was passing at the end of the track, lumbering uphill to the prison settlement. Were there convicts on board? He felt as trapped as they were. And that damned, bloody train was the cause of it all. Without it, Elliott Franfield would never have come into their lives.

Barney sprang up as another thought struck him between the eyes. The train marooned in the blizzard. He almost ran to Sam's cottage and had to pause to calm himself before knocking brusquely and opening the door before Fanny had a chance to answer it.

She looked up, putting a finger to her lips. 'Ssh! Laura's having her nap. So what can I do for you, Barney? Shouldn't you be at work?'

'Oh, I cas'n find Sam,' he lied. 'I just wondered if he wasn't yere. S-so Laura's asleep,' he faltered, searching for the right words. 'Lovely cheel. You must be so proud. And to think you might've lost her, it being such a difficult birth. Must've been an excellent doctor what delivered her.'

Fanny smiled at him in wide-eyed innocence. 'Oh, yes. Dr Franfield were wonderful. 'Twas so lucky he were on the train.'

Barney felt as if he had been shot by a bullet. It was crystal clear now. Ling didn't love him. She loved Elliott Franfield.

He dragged himself back to the manager's house and gave Mr Warren the garbled message. He returned to his work in the quarry but his vision was blurred with the image of Ling and Elliott Franfield together, holding hands. In bed. Just as it probably would have been all along if he hadn't destroyed the letter the handsome stranger had entrusted to him all those years ago. He had been living under a delusion ever since, and he only had himself to blame. Ling was far above him. He had always denied it, but hadn't he always struggled to draw himself up to her level? Never reaching it, if he was honest with himself, and riddled with jealousy when she seemed so fulfilled when living at Fencott Place among people whose intellect she was on a par with? She could have had a far better life if he hadn't interfered.

He had to summon the courage to open the cottage door at the end of the day. Ling was sitting at the table and she smiled at him, her hair loose and falling about her face in a profusion of chestnut curls. She looked so beautiful and he felt his heart lurch.

'Barney, I've got something to tell you,' she said softly. 'I'm pregnant again. And I'm past the three-month danger period. I somehow think I'm going to keep this one.'

Her eyes were glistening, great pools of past hurt and present hope. A child. What they had both longed for over so many years.

'Oh, my darling,' Barney couldn't help but mutter as he took her in his arms. 'You really must look after this one.'

'Yes, I intend to. I shall go into Tavistock on Saturday. But it'll be for the very last time. I promise.'

Barney understood what she meant though he would never let on, and he felt the balm soothe his wounded soul. The child might be his, or it might be Elliott Franfield's. He didn't care. Ling was coming back to him. She was shaking against him, and he knew why. She was giving up her true love to return to her proper place. His heart danced with elation. There was no need for Harry Spence's evil interference.

Oh, Jesus Christ, what had he done? Harry had left hours ago and would be back in Tavistock by now, planning his move. Perhaps he would carry it out that very night! Barney's blood ran cold. He had to stop him!

He let go of Ling, astounding her as he bolted out of the door. He ran, flying past those who watched him in amazement, faster, faster, must go faster! He must catch the train, the last train, find Harry before it was too late, though where or how, he had no idea. And then the green engine was rumbling towards him, a wisp of grey smoke puffing rhythmically from the chimney. Barney waved his arms frantically, praying it would make an unscheduled stop along the line. But the giant monster trundled past him, leaving him to sink on his knees in despair.

* * *

Elliott gently closed behind him the door of the Fitzford Cottage alongside the canal. Another healthy little human being delivered safely into the world. The new addition was an obvious delight to the happy family, and was rubbing salt into the already raw wound.

Was Ling's child his? It was certainly possible, although it was far more likely to be Barney's. Either way, he had lost Ling, he knew it. Her place was by Barney's side, not his. Much as she loved him, her loyalty was quite rightly to her husband. Elliott had entreated her so often to come away with him, but her high morals, the very same that he loved and admired her for, had prevented it. And now they had taken her, and what was possibly his child, away from him for ever.

He paused for a moment, staring up at the clear night sky. It was almost dark and stars were beginning to twinkle up there, somewhere miles beyond human experience. The air held that familiar autumn tang of dampness, especially here beside the canal. Elliott wondered how many years he would witness the dying season pass him by. Without Ling, it would all seem so pointless. Would he ever love again? He doubted it. She had been, *was*, so special to him, his one and only love. It hadn't been a lie when he said he had thought about her during all those years studying in London. And now she had been whipped away from him by what should have been the most joyous event life could offer.

He walked on, unable to blank out the grief. Five minutes would see him home. To the empty house that had once rung with Ling's voice. The fire in the range would long have gone out with no one there to see to it. There would be no hot meal, not even a hot beverage. How different things might have been if Ling had been free to marry him.

He shivered. It promised to be the first chilly night since the spring and he felt cold inside. As if there was ice in his veins.

It was as he reached the remains of Fitzford Gate that he heard the hurried footfall of someone running along the path at the far side of the canal. He turned round as the figure of a man, no more than a black outline in the near darkness, charged across the bridge, waving frenetically at him.

'The bag,' the stranger wheezed, jabbing his head towards Elliott's medical bag. 'You a doctor?'

Elliott straightened his shoulders. 'Yes. Dr Franfield,' he nodded.

'Oh, thank God,' the man spluttered. 'My mate's fallen down the aqueduct. Broked his leg, I reckons.'

'Right, well, we'd better raise some help. We'll need some assistance if we're to carry him all that way.'

'Oh, no. I'd best take you to 'en first. In proper agony, he be. Maybies you can give 'en summat for the pain. Only you'd never find 'en in the dark on your own. I'll have fer show you. *Then* I'll fetch help.'

'All right. But we must take care not to fall ourselves in the dark. And *you* need to catch your breath.'

'Yes, you'm right,' the fellow panted. And keeping his head low, he hurried back across the bridge.

Elliott followed him and they set out at a brisk pace along the old towpath of the disused canal. Faint lights glimmered from the windows in the Fitzford Cottages on the opposite side, but once they had passed the end of the little dwellings, they were plunged into deep shadow. Moonlight shimmered on the silver ribbon of water, but even that became lost as they entered the trees that had grown up beside the once busy canal.

Elliott concentrated on what was thankfully a relatively even surface. He reckoned it was a good mile to where the canal was carried over the steep Lumburn Valley on a vast embankment possibly a hundred feet high. If someone had fallen down the precipitous bank, he would be lucky to have broken his leg rather than his neck! Elliott hoped he himself could get down to the chap safely to administer some pain relief while his companion summoned the manpower that would surely be needed to carry out the rescue.

'Hurry!' the man called urgently, almost dancing in front of him.

Elliott took a breath in through his teeth. The fellow was understandably agitated, but Elliott wondered what on earth these two individuals had been doing out here as dusk had gathered into nightfall. Though he had not glimpsed the face of the man who had summoned him, he had caught the distinct odour of alcohol on his breath, but it wasn't his role to ask questions. And so he hurried along in the wake of the burly silhouette, for the first time in his life wishing vehemently he was not a doctor whose duty it was to help people at any hour of the day or night. All he wanted was to be home, to be warm, to satisfy his empty stomach and to sink into the bliss of sleep where, if he was lucky, he might be able to escape from the torment that Ling was lost to him for ever.

They had been scurrying along for ten minutes or so, half running and breathing in the chill, damp air, when the stranger turned round so unexpectedly that Elliott had to pull himself up short to avoid colliding with the fellow. In that instant, he saw the whites of the man's eyes glint in the darkness, and for a split second, recognition flashed across the deepest recess of his mind. He had seen those cunning, shifty eyes somewhere before. But the warning came too late.

Harry Spence drove his iron fist upwards underneath Elliott's ribcage. The blow was so powerful it completely knocked the wind out of him. He couldn't move, began to choke, struggling for the breath that wouldn't come. He stood, transfixed, air gurgling and trapped in his throat. He had no strength, every muscle rigid, and the heavy bag slipped from his fingers, landing on the ground with a dull thud. He must . . . breathe. And with a massive effort of will, he forced his chest to expand.

The pain of it seemed to scream through his body as he stared at the snarling face before him. He must defend himself. But even as he gathered his stunned wits about him, a second blow smashed across his jaw and he staggered backwards. The blackguard was standing there, arms akimbo, gloating at his handiwork, waiting to strike again. But Elliott wouldn't give in so easily. He wasn't afraid, just furious at allowing himself to be tricked. Agony tore through his ribs as he launched himself forward, but he had never fought in his life, not even a schoolyard scrap. What did this devil want? The drugs in his bag? The morphine? Then why didn't he take the bag and run? It was obvious Elliott was in no fit state to give chase.

He wasn't quite sure where he was aiming, but his knuckles met with solid muscle that racked his own fist. He heard the evil laugh as the wretch grabbed him by the collar, half choking him, and swung him round to receive the full force of the next punch which landed deep in his stomach. A sickening fire ripped through his entire body and he collapsed onto his knees as Harry's next blow slammed into his face. Panic rather than agony seared into his head as he saw stars and then blackness, and then Harry's fists were raining down on him until he rolled helplessly onto his side.

A deep, hollow stillness. Thank God it was over. But then torture as his hair was being torn from his scalp as his head was wrenched upwards by it.

'Look at me, you varmint!'

Elliott tried, but only one eye would open and that only a slit. He could see blackness, and a veil of red. Nothing more.

'You keep away from Barney Mayhew's wife, d'you hear? You goes near her again, and next time I'll kill you. D'you understand? I'll kill you.'

Harry released his hold with a jerk so that Elliott's face fell heavily against the ground. Yes, he would kill him and enjoy it. But why wait until next time? Barney had paid him a paltry two pounds, so why shouldn't he reap the full pleasure of the attack to make up for it? Barney might be suspected and be arrested for murder. Serve him right. There was nothing to connect Harry Spence with Elliott bloody Franfield. A vicious grin snarled across his face. Ling Southcott. Stuck-up cow. She was the one who had stopped him getting back with Fanny and from getting his hands on some of the money he was sure had come their way from the Warringtons. It was because of her that he had ended up in the gutters of Tavistock, a beggar, frequently locked up by the town's constables. Or, if he was sober enough, spending the night on the vagrants' ward of the workhouse after the gruelling task of breaking a yard of stones. His only solace was the bottle of gin he would buy with pickpocketed money — or methylated spirit when pickings were poor. Damn the bitch to hell. And what sweet vengeance to bludgeon her lover to a bloody pulp!

He sneered down at the body writhing at his feet. It was beyond temptation. His boot found its mark. Again. And again. In a frenzied, unstoppable dance until Harry's breath failed him. The body was motionless now. And as Harry studied the lifeless form, cowardly dread began to creep into his gutless heart. Elliott Franfield was dead. And he could be hanged for murder.

Harry Spence fled back along the way they had come. If he kept going, he would reach Plymouth by morning. Enlist on a ship. To America. Better still, Australia. Give a false name. And no one would associate him with the tramp who used to slump on the bench by the canal.

CHAPTER THIRTY-THREE

Ling stared sightlessly out of the carriage window. She was going to see Elliott for the last time. At least, she imagined it would be. She had made her decision. To allow fate to decide.

It seemed the fairest choice. She would break off with Elliott now, and remain faithful to Barney until the child was born. And if it had Barney's dark eyes and swarthy skin, that was how matters would stay. But if the infant was fair and resembled Elliott, when the time was right, she would agree to his plan of starting a new life somewhere far away from England's shores. She just prayed the baby would not be a tiny replica of herself and bear a similarity to neither of its possible fathers. And, God forbid, if she lost the precious life as she had its four siblings, then . . . She prayed to God she didn't, for she simply wouldn't know what to do. She loved Elliott with a passion that confounded her own understanding, but her duty was to Barney.

He had treated her with such care ever since she had told him she was pregnant. Not that he was ever anything but considerate, but he had stayed indoors every one of the four nights since, instead of spending the evening with his friends. She didn't know how long it would last, and she wasn't sure she wanted it to. Barney seemed on edge, fluttering about her as if trying to prove his love. And the next minute, he was distant, and he seemed to have no appetite. He must be worried sick that her pregnancy would end in a miscarriage as all the other had done. Yes. That was the only explanation.

'Take care on yersel,' he had frowned anxiously as she had set out that morning. 'No running for that there train. And I reckon your friend'll be so pleased as I am at the news. But you'm to tell her you cas'n visit her again. 'Tis too risky for the babby with your past.'

'Oh, I'm sure she'll understand,' Ling had smiled back. Though the smile was forced.

And Agnes *was* pleased. Delighted. Ling had gone there first to tell her, putting off the dreadful moment when she was to give Elliott her decision.

'Now you really must have a physician take care of you all the way. No, I insist,' Agnes said as she saw Ling go to protest. 'I shall pay for one to go out and visit you regularly. Dr Greenwood has retired now, so it will have to be Dr Ratcliffe. It can't be that lovely young Dr Franfield, poor soul, not for a while anyway. Not after what happened to him the other day.'

The blood instantly drained from Ling's head, but she knew she must resist the instinct to react to whatever dreadful news Agnes had to impart.

'Happened?' she repeated, struggling to sound casual.

'It was in yesterday's *Gazette*. Didn't you see it?'

'No. I haven't bought one yet,' her lips articulated.

'Poor chap was attacked.' Agnes shook her head in horror. 'Badly beaten and left for dead, it seems. Happened along the old canal towpath near Crowndale. Luckily he'd just attended a delivery at one of the Fitzford Cottages and the husband saw him going along the path with a stranger. Shortly afterwards, the new mother had a funny turn and the husband ran after the doctor to fetch him back. Ran straight into the attacker and then found Dr Franfield further along the path. Thank God he did, or he wouldn't have survived the night, the article says. Oh, my dear!' Agnes leaned forward and took Ling's cold hand in hers. 'I'm sorry. I didn't mean to upset you. I shouldn't have mentioned it with you in your condition. One can become so sensitive—'

'But . . . he's alive?' Ling murmured, clawing her way back to reality.

'He was when the article was written. Oh, Ling, dear, you look so pale. Let me order some hot, sweet tea.'

Hot, sweet tea. Oh, how very English. It was what . . . Oh, Elliott. Dear God Almighty . . .

Somehow, she managed to spend another half hour in Agnes's company, stifling her desperate, crucifying desire to get to Elliott's side. The instant she felt she could leave without suspicion, she ran down into the town and bought a copy of the paper, searching dementedly for the article. The letters leapt up and down, jigging on the page. Just one sentence jumped out at her. Dr Franfield was recovering at Dr Greenwood's house.

She broke into a run once more, stumbling, not caring about the life inside her. It wasn't far to the Parkwood area. She remembered quite clearly which was Dr Greenwood's house.

The elderly man opened the door himself, and his kind eyes stretched with surprise at her agitated knocking.

'Why, Mrs Mayhew, isn't it?'

'Elliott. Where is he? Is he all right?'

William Greenwood blinked at the breathless, hysterical woman before him, and all became clear. He hadn't spent a lifetime dealing with people in dire distress not to recognise its effects at once. Oh, dear. What had young Elliott been up to? Was there a flaw in his perfect ways after all? They were all only human, and he was a handsome, amiable fellow and this girl was so very striking.

William cleared his throat. 'You'd better come in.'

She was agitated beyond measure, he could see, scarcely able to perch on the edge of the chair he offered her as if it were red hot. William pursed his lips and fixed his eyes on her over the rim of his spectacles.

'I take it you read what happened in the paper?' he asked solemnly. 'And I take it you and Elliott are friends?'

'Yes,' she choked, her brow puckered excruciatingly.

More than friends if William wasn't mistaken. He had thought he had seen a look pass between them at Chantal Pencarrow's wedding. They had disguised it well, but even then he had wondered. Putting it out of his mind. Surely Elliott wouldn't have been so stupid as to become involved with a married woman? But if he had, it would have been from the heart. And now, possibly, the poor lad was paying for it.

'I'm afraid he's in a bad way,' he said gravely. 'He had severe abdominal pain and I had to open him up. There was severe bruising under his left ribs, from being kicked several times, I'd say. I found what I suspected. A ruptured spleen, so I had to remove it. Don't look so alarmed. We can live quite happily without a spleen. But it was tricky. Touch and go. I've never performed a splenectomy before. Few surgeons ever have. It was major surgery and he lost a lot of blood. He was also hit several times in the head and face. You may imagine he's still very groggy, and he's bruised and lacerated all over.'

He stopped as the girl's face contorted. Oh, yes. This lovely young woman loved Elliott with a deep, sincere passion. And William's heart ached for them.

'Would you like to see him?'

She nodded, tears trembling on her lashes, and William wetted his lips. 'It's not a pretty sight, I must warn you. And he may not know you're there. I'm keeping him on laudanum, although the last dose will be wearing off by now. So, are you sure?'

Ling rose to her feet, almost fainting. But she had to let Elliott know she was there for him.

A whimper lodged in her throat. He was barely recognisable as human, let alone the handsome young man she loved. One eye was a dark, oozing slit in its swollen, discoloured socket. Blood was still matted in his hair near a row of neat stitches closing an ugly wound on his forehead, the catgut standing out like a tramline, and the left side of his jaw was stained the colour of ripe mulberries. Where it wasn't livid with bruising, the rest of his face was like putty. His leanly muscled arms lay outside the covers and she could see a large purple blotch on his chest disappearing beneath the snowy sheets. He lay so still, hardly breathing.

Ling swayed, and felt the supportive arm of William Greenwood about her. She had hardly noticed Mrs Greenwood sitting vigilantly by the bedside, and Ling took her place in the chair, her eyes riveted on Elliott's mutilated face and her horrified mind scarcely able to think about the broken body hidden beneath the bedclothes. Mrs Greenwood crept from the room, and Ling was aware of the doctor standing back from the bed. It seemed that Elliott was not for one moment to be left unattended by someone with medical experience, but Ling was beyond caring whatever Dr Greenwood might see.

She brushed away her silent tears and leaned forward, hesitating as she went to take Elliott's hand. His long, middle fingers were strapped together and she glanced up as William appeared at her shoulder.

'He obviously tried to fight back,' he whispered. 'Broke his finger in the process. The man who found him said he saw the attacker lure him away. Reckons poor Elliott thought he was being called to an emergency. The devil probably turned on him so suddenly that he didn't stand a chance. The police have a full description. He wasn't as tall as Elliott but was built like a bull apparently. You can hold his hand if you want to. Just be gentle.'

Slowly, with the deftest touch, she took Elliott's hand and carefully lifted it to her lips. Laid it against her cheek, her tears dripping onto the bandaging.

'Ling.' A barely audible sound scraped itself from Elliott's parched mouth and his good eye opened just a fraction.

A cruel pain stabbed at Ling's throat as she turned her gaze back to his battered face and forced a smile. 'Yes, I'm here, Elliott,' she croaked, and then as the appalled horror swamped her again, she groaned, 'Who on earth did this to you, Elliott? And . . . and why?'

'I . . . don't . . . know,' he grated, wincing as if the very words had caused him grave distress.

'Time for some more laudanum,' William said from behind. 'But first try and get to him to drink some water if you can. He's severely dehydrated.'

Ling drew in her lips. *Oh, sweet Jesus, don't die, Elliott.* She slipped her left arm under his neck to lift his head and taking the feeding jug William passed her, placed the spout between Elliott's lips.

'Drink, my love, for me.'

He did. Sipping. Finding it difficult to swallow. Water sometimes dribbling down his chin. Ling's patience was unending and she crooned and cajoled until the cup was nearly empty and William added a dose of laudanum to the last drops of the life-giving liquid. And within another five minutes, Elliott was asleep.

'Will he . . . will he survive?' Ling dared to ask when they were out in the hall and Mrs Greenwood had taken over the vigil again.

William's eyebrows swooped. 'I'd be a liar if I said a definite yes. He's far from out of the woods yet. But then I didn't think he'd survive the anaesthetic the state he's in, but he did. But, Mrs Mayhew, he *is* still very poorly.'

Ling rolled her head, but there was no escape. 'Who could do such a thing, Dr Greenwood?'

'Are you sure you can't tell me yourself?' William's voice was low. 'The attack was unprovoked and nothing, no drugs, were taken from his medical bag. He still had all his money in his pockets. And yet it seemed planned. Now, I know it's really not my business, but you and Elliott are more than just friends. Don't deny it, Mrs Mayhew. So . . . you don't think it could have been your husband?'

Ling gasped aloud and shook her head in disbelief. 'Barney? Oh, good Lord, no! The idea's preposterous!

Barney's not capable of such a thing. He's a good man.' Her face fell and she lowered her eyes. 'That makes me sound like a proper scarlet woman, doesn't it? But . . . I just married the wrong man. But I'm certain Barney doesn't know about Elliott and me. And besides, it was Tuesday night, wasn't it? Barney was with me. At home. Up at Foggintor.'

William took a deep breath and released it through flared nostrils. 'Well, the police have issued a description. And by God, I'd like to get my hands on the scoundrel when they catch him. But in the meantime,' he sighed wearily, 'your secret is safe with me. And let's pray to God that Elliott survives.'

* * *

'So, had a good day, have you, my love?'

Barney turned from the range, his voice deliberately light and carefree. But his smile faded and turned instead to a frown as his heart began to pound. Ling's shoulders were drooping and her skin was pale as death.

'Ling? Ling, be summat wrong?' But he knew at once that there was, and his blood ran cold. 'The babby . . . ?'

'Is fine. But . . .' Her face crumpled and tears spilled down her grief-ravaged cheeks as she threw the newspaper purposefully onto the table which Barney had already set for their meal. 'You remember Elliott Franfield?' she gulped wretchedly.

'Of course.' Barney's voice was flat, he hoped expressionless. Jesus Christ, he mustn't let her see. See the terror that gripped his heart. Oh, good God Almighty, what had Harry Spence done? What had *he* done?

'It's in the paper.' Ling forced the words from between gritted teeth. 'He was attacked last Tuesday night. Brutally beaten and for no apparent reason.'

Barney swallowed hard, his knees turning weak. Oh, dear God! 'Poor chap,' he managed to mumble.

'Oh, Barney, I went to see him,' Ling wailed, and Barney raised his eyes. 'I bumped into him a couple of times in the summer. I don't suppose I told you. It didn't seem worth mentioning. Anyway, I thought . . . Oh, Barney, he's in a terrible way. They're not even sure if he'll live. How could anyone do such a thing?'

Her tears were flowing freely now, and Barney held her against him. Could she feel him, too, shaking like a leaf? But she mustn't, *mustn't* know!

'Do they knows who did it?' the question strangled in his throat.

'No,' she wept brokenly. And Barney knew for sure that his wife loved another man.

* * *

'I'm sorry, Barney. I know I said last week would be the last time, but I must go and see Dr Franfield again. Find out . . . if he's still alive. You do understand?'

Oh, yes. He understood all right! Ling loved Elliott Franfield. Perhaps even the child she carried was his. Barney's blood seethed, but he mustn't let on that he realised. If he did, it might arouse suspicion. At least Elliott's attacker had disappeared into thin air, thank God. And good riddance. If Harry was never caught, he could never implicate Barney. And so Barney must play the sympathetic fool and comfort his faithless wife over the plight of her lover.

Did he wish Elliott dead? No, of course not. That wasn't the plan. Never had been from his point of view. It would break Ling's heart, her spirit. He wouldn't want that. He just wanted her back. His own heart ached with his love for her. He could forgive her.

But, if she ever discovered what he had done, could *she* forgive *him*?

* * *

'How was he?' Barney asked, his voice trembling not with concern but with abject fear. 'Have they caught the bastard yet?'

'No. But Dr Franfield *is* a little better.' Ling pushed the back of her hand against her nose to suppress her welling tears of relief. 'It'll take months for him to recover, mind, but he's beginning to see out of his damaged eye again and he is in less pain. He can talk a little now, too.'

Talk! Terror ripped into Barney's belly like a knife. 'He hasn't said who did it, then, or why?'

'No. He says he's no idea. He didn't recognise his assailant at all, but it *was* dark.'

Barney nodded in what he hoped appeared a thoughtful manner. The blood had been trundling in his veins all week. The local constabulary had been searching for an *attempted* murderer, but would it have made any difference if it had turned into a hunt for a killer? It was still *his* fault Elliott Franfield had nearly died. And if his part in it were ever discovered, wouldn't he be hanged for it? Guilt churned in his stomach, closing its choking fetters about his neck. Ling must never, *ever* know. If she did, she would be out of that door and into Franfield's arms for ever. He wouldn't be able to stop her, for if he tried, she might reveal what she knew to the police. He would deserve it.

Barney had loved her, worshipped her, since they were children growing up in the small, isolated community. Fate had thrown them together and Ling had believed she loved him. But she had always been above him, and he had always known it. And her heart, the true passion that had been the very essence of her spirit, belonged to a man who was far more deserving of it than he was. To a man who was lying, injured and suffering, because of his love for her; to the man to whom she would long ago have been married if Barney had not betrayed them years before on the day he had jealously destroyed Elliott Franfield's letter.

He tossed and turned all night, sometimes studying in the moonlight the beloved face on the pillow beside him, tranquil now that she knew her lover's life was out of danger. She smiled in her sleep, murmured Elliott's name. Barney turned over, his clenched fist against his forehead. What hope was there for their future now? He had expected to draw Ling back to him. All he had succeeded in doing was to drive her further away.

It was the same night after night, the shadows deepening beneath his eyes as the vicious remorse gnawed into him like a cancer. While Ling's appetite was returning, a peaceful glow blushing her cheeks as Saturday approached once more, food stuck in Barney's gullet, every mouthful he swallowed making him gag. He felt dizzy, light-headed, an emptiness scorching in the pit of his belly.

'What's with you today, Barney?' Sam enquired with a light chuckle. 'Dreaming about that babby again? Well, I think it might have another cousin soon arter 'tis born!' His eyes twinkled merrily. 'Don't tell Fanny I told you, mind. She wanted to tell Ling first. Right, well, I'll go over and tell them to swing the crane over. I reckon we'm ready to move that there stone now.'

Sam shinned down the ladder leaving Barney alone on the ledge near the head of the quarry. Babby. Was it his, or Elliott Franfield's? What did it matter? He could never find happiness again, knowing Ling's heart would always lie elsewhere, while he would take his guilt to the grave.

He wasn't paying attention, lost in his own misery, as the massive crane swivelled round, the heavy chain hanging freely in mid-air. He should have caught the giant hook swaying on the end. But he wasn't looking, and though he caught Sam's horrified shout from down below, it was too late. The chain crashed into him, knocking him off balance so that his foot slipped over the edge.

He tried to right himself but felt his body going, his fingers clawing at the flat surface of the ledge. His scraping hands found a hold, a ridge no more than an inch high. His shoulders jarred as they took the full weight of his body as it dangled over the sheer rock face. Sweat poured from his skin as he realised there was no way even his powerful muscles had the strength to pull himself back up. Already his arms were screaming at him as his tense fingers cramped with the effort of retaining their grip, and his feet flailed wildly as they searched for a hold.

'Barney!' Sam shrieked at him from somewhere fifty feet below. 'Hang on! Us'll be there in a moment!'

He tried. Sweet Jesus Christ, he tried. His sweating palms became slippery, terrified breath quivering in his lungs. Every muscle was on fire. Hold on. Hold on. His life flashed before him, his darling Ling an image of life and love, and his heart felt calmed. She was his reason for being, and yet he had betrayed her. Not just once, but twice. She had never truly been his. She had belonged to Elliott Franfield ever since the day the steam railway had arrived in Princetown. Barney had always known, but it was only now that he could accept it. He had never made Ling truly happy. Because of him, their life was a lie. There was only one way to atone. He must set her free, and this way she would never know of his shame. His love for her went beyond the stars, and perhaps he could look down from the open Dartmoor skies onto her future happiness, and that would suffice.

They were racing up the ladders, would be with him in a trice, hauling him to safety. The time had come. God bless you, my darling. He shut his eyes and let his fingers slip.

It was strange. He couldn't feel any pain. He could hear hushed, indistinct voices all about him. And then the shattered tone of an angel.

'Oh, Barney,' she breathed, too shocked to weep. 'Please . . .'

He opened his eyes, and there she was. Blurred and wavering. Her beautiful face taut and stricken. Perhaps she loved him just a little. And he felt the peace enter his soul.

'Let me go, Ling,' he mouthed, and closed his eyes.

Floating. Hearing her howl of sorrow. His heart slowed and joyfully he felt the life . . . slowly . . . pulse away . . .

EPILOGUE

'With Captain Bradley's compliments, Mrs Franfield, Doctor,' the first mate smiled as he handed a glass of rich, ruby wine each to the couple standing in the bow of the fine old sailing ship. 'A lovely evening, is it not? Calm as a mill pond. But it'll slow our passage to Bordeaux. A fine choice for a honeymoon, if you don't mind my saying so. Oh, and dinner will be ready in half an hour, if that lad of yours doesn't distract the cook too much,' he added with a good-natured grin. 'Taken a right shine to each other, they have.'

'Thank you, Mr Starke.'

The doctor nodded with a smile that reached his kind, green-blue eyes. He seemed a quiet but happy man, but who wouldn't be, just married to that lovely young woman? There had been a wistfulness about Mrs Franfield when they had boarded the *Emily* that morning. Captain Adam Bradley had come to master his favourite ship especially in their honour, and he had explained in a compassionate voice that the poor woman had been tragically widowed three years before. So Mr Starke understood that she must feel strange married to another man, no matter how much she loved him. But Mr Starke had noted with satisfaction that the fresh sea air had already put some colour in her cheeks. Nothing like sea air to rejuvenate the heart and give one strength to begin a new life.

She had been leaning back against her new husband and he had held his arms wrapped about her as if he were pumping his own life force into her. Mind you, he was a little on the thin side was Dr Franfield in Mr Starke's opinion, and he looked as if he'd been in the wars in the past. There was a nasty scar across his forehead and one of his eyes dragged very slightly at the outer corner. But he was a tall, attractive man for all that, in his early thirties, Mr Starke fancied, and matched his handsome bride.

Mr Starke touched his cap as he turned away. He would tell the cook that the couple both needed fattening up.

Elliott and Heather Franfield gazed at each other over the rim of their wine glasses. It had been a long, hard, sad road, the complex tangle of fate trapping them in a web of grief and despair. But now it was over. Time, the great master, had healed. The intense harmony of their love had conquered, and at last they were free. To begin the journey of the rest of their lives together.

'Mama! Mama!'

They turned in unison as the little boy appeared on the deck with the flustered cook hot on his heels.

'I'm sorry, Mrs Franfield! Doctor Franfield!' he called. 'Couldn't stop him! Real live one he is!'

'Don't worry!' Elliott waved back. He took the wine glass Ling thrust towards him as she crouched down and the child scampered into her outstretched arms. Just then, the ship crested a wave and losing their balance, mother and son rolled onto the deck, laughing deliriously. The boy righted himself first, jumping up and down as he held his arms up to the man who held a full glass in each hand.

'Papa! Papa!'

Elliott placed the glasses where he hoped they would be safe, and swung the child into his arms. He shifted him onto one hip, then helped his bride to her feet with his free hand.

They stood together then, the boy between them, staring out as the setting sun spread its scarlet fingers over the flat sea.

'Artie,' Heather smiled lovingly into her son's brooding mahogany eyes, and the man he already looked upon as his father ruffled his ebony hair.

THE END

ALSO BY TANIA CROSSE

THE DEVONSHIRE SERIES
THE GUNPOWDER GIRL
THE RAILWAY GIRL
THE QUARRY GIRL
THE WHEELWRIGHT GIRL
THE AMBULANCE GIRL

Don't miss the latest Tania Crosse release,
join our mailing list:
www.joffebooks.com

FREE KINDLE BOOKS

Please join our mailing list for free Kindle books and new releases, including crime thrillers, mysteries, romance and more, as well as news on the next book by Tania Crosse!

www.joffebooks.com

Follow us on Facebook, Twitter and Instagram
@joffebooks

Thank you for reading this book. If you enjoyed it please leave feedback on Amazon, and if there is anything we missed or you have a question about then please get in touch. The author and publishing team appreciate your feedback and time reading this book.

www.joffebooks.com/contact

We hate typos too but sometimes they slip through.
Please send any errors you find to
corrections@joffebooks.com.
We'll get them fixed ASAP. We're very grateful to eagle-eyed readers who take the time to contact us.

Printed in Great Britain
by Amazon

65729154R00173